CW01653299

2006

ULTIMATE GAY EROTICA

2006
ULTIMATE GAY EROTICA

edited by JESSE GRANT

alyson books
NEW YORK

Celebrating Twenty-Five Years

Manufactured in the United States of America.

This trade paperback original is published by Alyson Books,
P.O. Box 1253, Old Chelsea Station, New York, New York 10113-1251.
Distribution in the United Kingdom by Turnaround Publisher Services Ltd.,
Unit 3, Olympia Trading Estate, Coburg Road, Wood Green,
London N22 6TZ England.

First edition: December 2005

05 06 07 08 09 a 10 9 8 7 6 5 4 3 2 1

ISBN 1-55583-922-3
ISBN-13 978-1-55583-922-2

Library of Congress Cataloging-in-Publication Data
2006 ultimate gay erotica / edited by Jesse Grant. —1st ed.
p. cm
ISBN 1-55583-922-3
1. Gay men—Fiction. 2. Erotic stories, American. I. Grant, Jesse.
PS648.H57A15.2005
813'.010835380'88664—dc22

2005053054

Credits
Cover photography by Thomas Schmidt/Stone/Getty Images.
Cover design by Matt Sams.

CONTENTS

INTRODUCTION

Unbelievable! I have managed to do it again! Chafe myself while working you ask. Well, yes, but I also put together another fine collection of erotic reading for your pleasure. In this volume, you'll find the best yet! And I know I have said that before, but I always mean it. The stuff I get to edit keeps getting hotter, and with it my hard-ons get bigger and bigger.

I've managed to get a little bit in here for everyone. Whether you like them college age and hairless or you're into the beefy, hairy trucker type, you'll find yourself unable to put this book down (with the one free hand you'll have while reading it). Make sure that you're ready for the constant erection you'll have while in possession of this book.

And what hot stories do I have to share with you this time around? A sexy salesman gets more than he bargains for when he's going office to office trying to sell greeting cards. A former farm boy comes back home to find his old farmhand still has the hots for him. A battered husband finds relief from a cute stranger and the Laundromat. Still want more? How about everyone's fantasy of joining the mile-high club with a stranger you never thought you could have? Hell, live out all your fantasies right here in my new book from Alyson. They're swell folks, aren't they?

Enjoy yourself (over and over again) with my latest and greatest collection (I know I did). Just remember that you need to be responsible about your reading and continue to go about your everyday activities. Work, workout, sleep—go on as usual albeit with a hot piece of meat that won't go back down between your legs.

I know you'll enjoy yourself as much, if not more, than my past Ultimate Gay Erotica books.

–Jesse Grant

HIGHWAY HIGH

Dan Budge

I'm not gonna deny it, the life of a trucker can be lonely. Sometimes I drive for days and all I see is dust balls and roadkill. I'm sure you can imagine how horny I get, sitting in my cab, dreaming about cock while riding the rough roads. Sometimes I'm just ready to burst, so I stop along the highway, pull out my tool, and take care of business. One rainy night I was in the front seat, checking out the back pages of a porn mag when I came across an ad. It read something like: Horny and on the road? Get a subscription to *Gay Trucker Monthly* and meet other horny drivers looking for hot, sweaty action.

At first I laughed, cheesy stuff for sure. I tossed the mag in the back, almost forgot about it until I was cleaning my truck one day, and came across it, all rolled up under my seat. I read the ad again, but this time it had quite an effect on me. Don't know what it was. It was like the words went right to my crotch; guess I must've been horny! Just reading it gave me a hard-on, so I decided to bite the bullet and called the 1-800 number, getting myself a subscription. It took a few weeks, but it was worth it.

Gay Trucker Monthly was printed on black and white, smudgy newsprint, but page after page, other truckers across the country were hunting for hot men. They too were riding the lonely highways, seeking release. So I began to scan the ads, learning when and where trucker boys met and got it on. Sometimes they met in bathrooms, other times they stayed by the side of the road, waiting like spiders to catch their juicy bait. "Look for me," one trucker had written, "I'm in the big red rig, Cole's Big One written in silver letters on each side of my baby, off Exit 5 on Interstate 20, every Wednesday of July. Got a thick, eight-inch meat and would love to meet a horny younger man with an oral fetish." Guy had a picture; wasn't quite my type, but I kept reading.

My eyes settled on the hottest hunk. I read his profile in the Hot Leather Men section: Greek god type looking for man-on-man trucker action. I've never been much into the leather and S/M scene, but the pic showed his barrel chest, rippled with a fine dusting of black hair, and his thick protruding nipples, rising like proud mountaintops above a forest; they were just begging to be sucked. He wore a leather hat and bore a wide, manly smile. His jaw was thick and strong, his lips full and perfect; it said his name was Tom. Another glance at his pic set my heart pounding. The write-up below the picture did even more for me; judge for yourself: Six foot leather, muscle man seeking submissive, bottom trucker guys for hot bathroom action. Thick nine-inch tool that's always ready to fill eager holes." After reading it, I was so hard that I shot my load.

In addition to his description, the short write-up listed Tom's routes, when and where he was most likely to make an appearance, but nothing specific. I knew my chances of wrapping my hook around his meat were slim. I rarely if ever went through his part of the country; I had to face it, our paths weren't likely ever to cross. I sighed and tried putting him in the back of my mind. It worked for about a week or two, but he kept haunting me when I least expected. My fantasies were filled with thoughts of him, what he might do to me if he ever came across me along the highways. I had to do something.

Determined and ready to chart new territory, I made several unscheduled detours. For the first few days, I saw no sign of Tom. Sure, I ran into my fair share of hot guys, but I kept longing to meet my Greek god. As the hot dry season waned, so did my hopes of seeing him. I gave up my search late in August.

After a while, I even forgot about Tom. I met a couple of cool truckers, even a nice fellow from down South who had a big hard-on for me. We began dating. We'd met up at a rest stop midway between Chicago and New York and given each other the greasy eye; after a quick intro and a firm handshake, we'd gotten better acquainted in his rig. But the sparks quickly fizzled, and then he stood me up one too many times. It was when I'd sworn off men for a while that I walked into the bathroom at a small rest stop near Nowheresville, U.S.A.

I stood at a urinal when the thickest pair of chiseled biceps caught my eye. I shot a quick look in the newcomer's direction, caught sight of his Superman tattoo, and even then it didn't register. The guy walked over next to me while slowly unzipping his tight jeans; judging by his bulge, he was packing a monster. He reached in deep and pulled out his flaccid snake, flapping it around before letting it settle. Then he began to unleash his flood; he'd been holding it in for a while. He groaned and glanced at me.

"Was 'bout ready to burst," he said with a slight curve of his lips. "Couldn't find a rest stop for miles."

"Yeah," I replied, pulling myself from the sight below his waist. "Not much round here."

His left arm twitched when I noticed the thick, leather armband riding its girth. He also wore black Dr. Martens boots, and I thought this guy looked like a god. Then the realization hit me. My jaw dropped and my lips began to quiver. The stud moved away, washed his hands, and gave me another look-over.

I pulled myself together. "Your name Tom?"

His brow shot up. "Yeah. How'd you know?"

I hesitated, long enough that it dawned on him how I might know him. He began to grin, and his jaw tightened. Then he licked his lips and adjusted his package; maybe it was my imagination, but it looked even bigger.

Tom slid to the urinal next to mine again. I kept my eyes on him, hearing the familiar sound of the gate in his jeans opening; I looked down when the echo of his parting zipper died. Reaching in with his thick, grease-stained hand, he pulled out his heavy weight. At the base of his shaft was a tight black leather cock ring. He slapped his fat weapon around a little while, letting it grow; and I was already stiff like a pole. Possessed, my eyes were fixed on his tool; I'd never been so cock-hungry, and my lips began to tremble again.

Tom smiled and it eased my nerves. "You can have it," he said in a low rumble. "If you want it."

With a weak hand, I reached over and touched his piece. It stirred in response, awakening to a fatter, stiffer tube. Tom certainly hadn't lied about his cock. I wondered if he hadn't sold it a little short—his dick was huge.

"N-nice cock," I stuttered. I'm sure he'd heard it a million times before.

"Thanks." He smiled again. He cast his eyes at the door, and then back at me. "You as horny as me?"

In the late August heat, who wouldn't be? I nodded and he stuffed his thick sausage in his pants, moving toward the farthest stall. He left the door open and I walked in after him. Immediately I dropped to my knees, ready to worship him. Tom pulled out his big meat and slapped my face with it.

"You any good at throatin' big, fat cocks?"

I was out of practice for sure, but I was going to give it my best shot. Eager and determined to prove myself, I parted my lips and nodded.

Taking a handful of hair, Tom pushed my head in his balls. "Lick 'em," he ordered.

Obeying his command like a slave, I licked his droopy, heavy balls, drenching them in spit. I took both in my hands, caressing them, sucking on each gently. We might've been in a public bathroom, but Tom didn't give a damn, freely sharing what he felt. He groaned and threw his head down, shutting his eyes for a second before taking a breath.

"That's it," he said as I devoured his balls. "That's good."

After he'd had enough, Tom yanked my head back by my hair. He held onto me like I was his plaything, and I liked it; in fact, I was harder than I'd been in months. I'd forgotten it was possible to get so turned on.

"Suck it," he said, tugging on my hair. He held his tempting member, slapping it against my cheeks.

As soon as I opened my mouth, Tom assaulted me with his weapon. He stuffed his fat shaft in my mouth, pushing it past my gag threshold. He rammed it in until it met the back of my throat. I gagged and pulled away, wiping sweat from my face. I held the base of his shaft, squeezing hard but my fingers couldn't connect. It had been a long time since I'd sucked anything remotely so big, but I gave it a second shot.

Sensing I'd reached a limit, Tom progressed gently. He smeared his wet meat in my face, waiting for my lips to part—and they did. He reintroduced his coil, inch by inch as I opened eagerly.

"Relax," he whispered softly, and the hair on the back of my neck responded. "Open wider."

I felt my throat loosen. Sensing an opportunity, he pushed his prick farther than what I thought was possible. When he got all but an inch of it inside, he began fucking my face. My head bobbed back and forward. My instinct was to hold half his shaft in my hand, to prevent his huge manhood from choking me, but he forced my hand to my side. As Tom fucked my throat, my head thudded against the stall's wall. I grabbed his thick, muscular thighs and clung to them for support. His eyes closed again and he groaned, this time louder. He clung to a thick thatch of my hair as he rode my face.

"Fuck, your throat is tight!" he blurted, glancing down at me with a grin.

As I struggled with his full-sized cock, Tom put his second hand against the back of my head. He continued to pound away as I beat myself to within an inch of squirting.

Then he gave me a break, plunging only his puffy head inside my dripping mouth. I stroked my cock, stealing a glance at Tom's wide, handsome face. Thrilling in my moist hole, he barely knew I existed. Tom fucked my face relentlessly, pushing his full size inside me again; this time I was ready, and the intensity of his pounding drove me nuts. I couldn't hold back the pool of spit in my mouth, and droplets made their way to my chin, only to fall on his boots.

Sucking on Tom's cock wasn't easy, but it was worth it. Just keeping my mouth stretched enough sapped my concentration. My jaw ached from being pried open, but I delighted in the discomfort; in fact, I craved it. I wondered, is this what the S/M scene is all about? My cock was about to burst.

Tom let go of my hair and slapped my chest. Grasping my nipples, he squeezed tightly until I was sore. He pulled hard, yanking to stretch them. Despite the pain, I was in heaven. Instinctively, my hand crawled up his furry chest, finding his firm, tweaked nipples.

"You want more?" Tom asked.

I groaned my consent.

Suddenly, the ripped trucker pushed my head forward, forcing me to swallow his full cock, until it virtually disappeared in my throat. I forced my lips to part wider, but I couldn't fit his whole bulging member.

Tom wasn't satisfied; He shoved my head in his crotch. He pushed so forcefully that I felt his fat head intrude deep in my throat. It stayed lodged there. The fit was tight but sweet for us both.

"I'm gonna come!" he yelled out.

He tried pulling away, but I held him in me until he began coming—now I was in control. I held my breath as Tom's cream dripped down my throat. He kept coming and coming until my mouth was too full. I tried to contain his flood, but droplets fell on his boots.

Tom kept his dick in my throat, discharging his musky juice. I swallowed, trying not to choke, but the excitement was too much. My face felt flaming hot, and I began to shoot on his boots, drenching them in man-spit. I shook uncontrollably, quivering like a helpless animal. Just as I finished, Tom released my hair. I took a deep breath and slid to the corner. My heart pounded as my lungs filled with air again. I'd barely recovered, but Tom grabbed my hair again.

"Wanna shine my boots?" He grinned widely.

"Y-Yeah," I replied, still shaking.

My lips tasted of Tom's cream, but I wanted more. Slowly, I opened my mouth and licked the tip of his boots, swallowing his and my bitter come. After finishing one boot, I moved to the other and licked the tip clean. I think I must've surprised him, 'cause he grinned and his brow shot up.

I licked the leather in strips until reaching the very top of his boots. Tom provided support by pulling his jeans. With his full boots exposed, I continued my work. The tart hide shone with spit. While looking down, Tom kept himself hard, jerking frantically.

Tom reached for my head, pulling on my hair again. Thinking he would ask me to suck him a second time, I knelt in front of his worship-worthy manhood. Just as I reached for it, Tom pushed my hand away.

"No. Come with me."

Tom put his cock away, trying to find room in his jeans for his huge protrusion. I did the same and followed Tom out of the stall. Just as we were leaving the bathroom, a man entered cautiously. Maybe he'd heard us, but Tom didn't give a damn. Though Tom had freed me, I was still visibly shaken. As for him, there was no hiding his huge bulge, and what had happened in there.

I followed Tom into the woods surrounding the rest stop. We walked for a while, until the small hut that was the bathroom disappeared behind bushes and trees. Soon after, Tom stopped and turned on his heels, waiting for me to catch up. Just as I did, he reached out for me, tugging my arm.

"Show me your ass," he demanded.

By then he knew I couldn't resist him. I stripped quickly. Inspecting my goods, Tom pulled down my underwear, running his rough hand against my smooth, shaved ass; and a hot, high butt it is, taut and starved, I'd been told the perfect fit for a hard prick.

Tom began slapping my ass until it was sore. Using both hands, he massaged my cheeks, inching closer. I thrust my ass in his face, stretching while grabbing the thin tree in front of me. Then Tom began spitting. In one motion, he shoved his wet finger up my well. I held the tree tightly as he pulled it in and out, loosening me.

Tom inserted a second, drenched finger up my crack. He didn't wait for me to get used to him; maybe he sensed I was a pro at this. He shoved both fingers and I swallowed them eagerly, only because I knew the real treat that waited.

I looked back and watched Tom wrap his bulging cock in a Trojan Magnum; he needed the extra girth that the condom provided. After stroking his tool, he pushed it against me. I reached back and pulled my cheeks apart, providing him extra space. With a slow, forceful thrust he was inside me. I yelled out and squeezed the tree, sweat dripping into my eyes.

As soon as he shoved his cock, Tom pulled it out. Then he shoved it back inside in one powerful thrust; slowly, his massive piece was widening me to a new breadth. I groaned loudly and wondered if anyone could hear me. At that point, I didn't care. I was more concerned with Tom, wanting to swallow him whole.

Tom pulled his cock in and out as he fucked me. The pain was ecstasy; how I'd needed that hard fuck! He drilled my ass, feeding me his wrist-thick prick because he knew I could take it. I recoiled temporarily when it got too much, but he held me still, thrusting in and out until the tingling grew, creeping into my cock. I began to stiffen again, and Tom noticed. That was all the evidence he needed.

Tom force-fed me his nine-incher. Still clutching me, he began to slap my ass and ram his cock. He kept pushing deeper, as if I could also take his balls. The fuck was deep and hard, so hard my knees felt like twigs. He pounded my hole, slapping his thick thighs into me. Releasing the tree, I held onto my knees, stretching further and moaning.

My ass completely dilated, Tom grunted, enjoying the ride for all it was worth; I'm sure he hadn't taken an ass like mine in a long time.

I felt him stiffen inside me, and I thought he would shoot, but he pulled out his meat. He too couldn't get enough of me.

"Lie down," he demanded.

I dropped on the dry, cracked earth. Tom stroked his weapon, moving menacingly. Clasping my ankles, he pushed my legs against my chest, until I was bunched up like a ball. My ass met the sky, and the warm, dusty breeze caressed it. Tom mounted me, getting ahold of my shoulders and planting a wet kiss on my lips. His tongue met mine and my cock throbbed its reaction. I wondered if I'd snap like a twig. My spine bent fully, I must've looked like a contortionist.

Tom didn't doubt my capacity to take all of him; it's strange, but for that I was proud. Soon after I felt his serpent's head against my crack, Tom pushed down and force-fed my hungry hole. Since I'd been stretched to my limits already, Tom's heavy manhood slid into me with little effort. As soon as I felt his thighs against my ass, Tom pulled out his throbbing tool, taking time to make himself stiff as a rod; it was hard work, considering his size. When he was as hard as me, he rammed my ass, taking me for the expert bottom I'd quickly become again. He fucked me more savagely than before, but also more tenderly, as he too yearned to find my lips. After the kiss, he nibbled on my lower lip, making my mouth as raw as my ass. His pounding was relentless, and my head was a mess of dirt and leaves.

Tom slapped my cheeks as he grunted. I matched his groans with moans, equally loud. So what if anyone could hear? Tom was fucking the hell out of me, and every minute was better than any past roadside fantasy. My ass was wide open, stretched anew with each powerful thrust.

My body felt numb, overdosed on sweet pain. I beat my hard shaft, taking it to an inch of its limit. My juices began to swell inside me, and I thought that I would shoot a boiling spray. Tom's jabs were now faster, and he was a mess of sweat.

I beat my meat faster still, until my hand grew weak. Tom watched me, matching thrust for thrust. I breathed loudly, clenching my teeth. He did similarly; we were both on the verge of the sweetest explosion. I let go of my cock, squirting so far that I covered my face. Tom dismounted me suddenly, standing over me. He whipped off his condom. Then he fell to his knees and wept. His come began dripping at first, but a thick spray followed. He crawled closer, making his come also reach my lips. I opened my mouth and swallowed his nectar. Tom's legs shook as he discharged his last drops. Then he slapped the head of his snake on my lips, smearing the last of his cream across my face. He groaned a final time and collapsed on top of me. He recovered only so that he could kiss me; it was bliss.

I don't know how long we stayed there, Tom covering me, his ass exposed. Eventually he pulled away. I stared, still hypnotized by his beauty. Tom stuffed his cock in his pants; even flaccid it was impressive. I got up, putting my member away. With my back turned to him, he slapped my ass and chuckled.

"You're one hot fuck."

What could I say? I grinned and probably blushed.

"You drive by here often?"

"Practically all the time," I answered, clearing my throat. The taste of him was still strong.

"Guess I'll be making this my part of the country too." He winked and walked away slowly, one eye on me. I lagged behind, watching him climb in his truck. For the first time since Tom had fucked me, I sat down. I realized then how sore I really was. I'd been in a daze. Tom had mastered me, and if I was a lucky trucker, he'd do so again soon.

MUSCLE IN

Bearmuffin

Jim Manning sat in his black leather furnished office. His beefy thighs were splayed wide apart and resting on the sides of his black leather chair. One hand was wildly fisting his spasming cock. The other hand pressed buttons on the remote control as he played back a college wrestling tournament video on the wide-screen TV.

Stop. Freeze frame. Augment. Yeah, there it was. You could see cocks clearly outlined inside the sweaty wetness of jockstraps.

This was not only a pleasure, it was business too.

Once the meanest, hottest pro wrestler in the United States, today Jim was Pro Wrestling's hottest manager.

He was hard at work searching for the hottest and most muscular of collegiate wrestlers to add to his roster of Pro Wrestling stars.

Yeah, it was just like the old days when he was always jacking off to wrestling videotapes. Fuckin' A right! Those humpy, beefy wrestlers got him good and fucking hot!

Wrestlers with monster muscled bodies, tree trunk thighs, and thick bull necks. Wrestlers with ultradefined washboard abs and perfectly shaped bubble butts all packed in indecently tight singlets so transparent you could see the grimy, sweaty jockstraps underneath.

College wrestling sensation Shawn Garrett suddenly appeared on the screen.

"A-a-aw f-u-u-uck!" Jim moaned loudly.

Jim's massive cock thickened with burning lust as hot bolts of ecstasy shot through his muscles and sent a sputtering, heavy load arcing high into the air and splattering against the wide screen. Long, thick come dribbles dripped over the exciting image of Shawn.

Shawn was an exciting vision of powerful, manly muscularity. Tall and muscular, Shawn's intense good looks were thrilling. Jim was beside himself with lust. What a fuckin' hot wrestler!

"*Yeah*!" Jim grunted hoarsely. "I'm gonna fuck your ass, stud!" His deep-set black eyes widened with excitement. Lusty waves of desire coursed through the slabs of glorious muscle rippling underneath his sleek, sun-bronzed skin.

"Gonna fuck ya, stud!" Jim panted wildly. "Fuck ya good! Real good!" He gripped his pulsing vein-etched prick by the root, gritted his pearly whites and clenched his eyes shut as his sweating body jerked spasmodically in the chair.

"A-a-aw f-u-u-uck!"

Another hard shudder of lust bolted through Jim's hot muscles as he leaned back and sent hot steaming loads of man come splashing against the screen.

When Jim came to his senses, he lit up a thick cigar, blew a heavy cloud of stinking stogie smoke between his hot, cocksucker's lips, and rewound the tape for a playback.

Yeah! Shawn would be his number 1 client. The stud was a diamond in the rough. Jim liked that exciting brand of rough, tough ambition that was boldly etched on Shawn's classic all-American features.

Jim's hot, muscled body shook with wild, maniacal laughter. He was drunk with the power to make and break young wrestlers.

He scooped up a handful of lube and lathered his hot, pulsating prick. The greasy gobs crackled and sputtered noisily like coals in a fire as they melted over his lust-swollen cock.

"*Fuck! Fuck! Fuck!*" Jim grunted lustfully as he whacked of his precome drooling cock. His sweating, hairy nuts were swimming in a raging sea of pent-up man jizz.

Uncontrollable spasms of lust had him on the brink of shooting another wild load. He recalled a Monday morning just a week ago in Lincoln, Neb.

The banquet room at the Marks Hotel was filled to the rafters with eager wrestling scouts, agents, head coaches, and managers. Twenty-five young college studs had reported for the annual "Meat Market." It was the most revealing part of the college wrestling process.

The hulking, towering studs, not one of them weighing in at less than 210 pounds of rock-solid, beefy brawn, were standing in their underwear or sweat-stained, ass-exposing jockstraps, waiting for their turn to be examined, weighed in, measured, and videotaped.

Hope and determination glimmered in their young, anxious eyes. Their future in wrestling depended on the men in that room. And it depended all the more on one man, Jim Manning, the hottest agent in pro wrestling today. It was their one and only chance at pro wrestling stardom.

One by one, the jocks had stepped onto the platform to be inspected, pawed over, and ogled like prize bulls at the state fair. There were some hot, mouthwatering studs, but nothing special. That is, until the last one of them strutted onstage.

Holy fuck! Jim almost spilled his drink. "Shawn Garrett," the head coach announced. The room echoed with loud gasps of amazement and admiration as they zeroed in on the prize stud's magnificently sculpted body.

A scout popped in a fresh tape in the video cam and zoomed the lens in on the Midwestern stud's awesome, lust provoking body.

Shawn's brown hair was cut in a sharp crew cut just an inch above the scalp of his bullet-shaped head. Thick bushy brows joined together over the bridge of his broad nose and shaded a set of piercing baby blues flashing with grit and ambition.

Shawn's angular cheekbones matched his defiant square jaw. Just the barest hint of a silky mustache sprouted over full, sensuous lips.

His thick bull neck was connected to incredible barreled shoulders. Arms sporting the most awesome of biceps splayed away from his super upper torso. His back flared like the hood of a cobra and tapered dramatically down to his narrow waist. His heart-stopping abs were deeply furrowed and silky smooth to the touch. His spectacular V-shaped torso was firmly planted on a set of thick, mammoth tree-trunk thighs.

Jim ached to fall to his knees and worship him.

Shawn stood on the platform proudly shining in all of his manly glory. The stud was naked except for a grimy, threadbare jockstrap that hugged his stupendous basket. The frayed jockstrap was tangled, the tattered elastic obscenely exposing his thick, 12-inch prick. Two inches of foreskin sheathed the blunt knob of his mighty battering ram.

The stud's low-hangers were impressively huge, resembling two baseballs inside his peach-fuzzed scrotum. They were sweaty, obscenely swaying between a pair of tree trunks dusted with fine brown hairs.

"Turn around, Shawn," the coach said. As Shawn moved, his jockstrap fell apart, slid down his mammoth legs, and landed at his feet.

A loud, collective gasp of astonishment went out from among the crowd of jock-loving men. Exposed to everyone's lustful gaze were two sun-kissed globes. His bubble butt reminded Jim of lush cantaloupe halves tanned to a glimmering tan of gold.

"Sorry 'bout that," Shawn said. The stud sounded so surprised and sincere that Jim just about shot a thick load in his jeans.

"Don't worry about it, stud!" the coach replied laughingly. "You can turn around now."

But if Shawn's golden tanned bubble butt had created a sensation, his thick, veiny cock almost started a riot.

Jim's cock bolted upright, seething and throbbing in his BVDs. His wide, fat piss hole seeped juicy strands of precome when he got a load of Shawn's unbelievably huge jock.

Huge blue veins crisscrossed and throbbed all over Shawn's downward-curving 12 inches. His pubes were full and lush.

Everybody was in complete and utter shock, dazed by the size and beauty of what plainly was the most awesome piece of meat ever seen on a college wrestler.

Jim did a double take when he saw a single, thick drop of transparent, glistening liquid slowly ooze from the wide, gaping piss slit of Shawn's veiny cock. Jim longed to lap up that precious come drop.

His heart skipped a beat as he glared at Shawn's blunt knob. He imagined the bittersweet taste of that drop that hung precariously for a single second and then dripped to the floor between Shawn's thick jock toes.

Jim was still in a daze as an assistant coach weighed Shawn in and measured his height. "Six feet 4 and 215 pounds," he proudly announced to the crowd. The men scribbled down the vital statistics.

A hot, thick prick and golden tanned muscled buttocks were all it took to get on Jim's A-list. And no doubt about it. Shawn would shoot to the top of that list.

It was about 5 in the afternoon when the wrestling draft had finished. The men drifted out of the banquet hall.

Jim followed Shawn to the makeshift dressing room behind the kitchen where he found the young stud slipping on an obscenely formfitting T-shirt and butt-hugging faded jeans.

"I've searched for years for a client like you."

Jim laid it on extra thick. He shot a meaningful glare into the jock's baby blues.

"Ours could be a special relationship."

Shawn's eyes widened with interest and understanding. His full lips barely parted so that Jim could see the tip of the jock's tongue trembling excitedly over his lower lip. Jim slipped him a business card. Before he left, Jim took one long look at Shawn's outrageously bulging crotch.

"Call me anytime, stud. You're gonna be a star!"

Wild maniacal laughter bounced off the walls of Jim's office. Jim had awakened from his lust-dazed reverie and watched the screen again as Shawn Garrett's image flashed once again on the TV.

Jim fisted his pulsing prick, rasping huskily with each rapid tug on his lust-bloated cock as wild macho excitement burned through every inch of his body. He was just on the brink of shooting another potent load when there was a knock at the door.

Jim leapt out of his chair and opened the door.

Holy fuck! It was Shawn Garrett!

There he was like a blond god descended from Olympus, standing before Jim in the tightest of sweat shorts. The stud wore gym socks and a red two-sizes-too-small T-shirt, the bottom of which fluttered wildly over his hot, muscled abs.

Shawn winked as he yanked down his shorts and exposed his jockstrap. Jim's eyes grew as large as saucers as he stared at Shawn's magnificent, bulging basket. His cock was clearly outlined inside the pouch. The balls hung low and heavy.

Jim licked his lips and grabbed his cock, giving it a good squeeze in lustful anticipation of Shawn's next move.

Shawn yanked down his jock and his giant cock flew up and smacked the deep furrowed rows of his powerhouse abs. Then it jutted out again at a sharp 45-degree angle. Jim's mouth gaped open with amazement. Shawn's cock was just an inch away from his lips.

"Yeah, fuck, yeah!" Shawn groaned.

He began masturbating.

The heavy slapping sound of a hot fist working over 12 thick inches of fat prick echoed off the walls of the agent's office.

Shawn's muscles went into spasm.

"*Ungh! Ungh,*" he panted hoarsely. He suddenly arched his back, tossed his head, and cried out, "Gr-a-a-ah! F-u-u-uck!"

Hot steaming bolts of jizz exploded from the knob of Shawn's mighty prick and hit Jim right smack in the face, drenching him with hot streams of potent come.

In a flash, Jim found himself on his knees. His hands were feverishly running up and down over Shawn's sweaty muscles. His palms landed right upon Shawn's spectacularly curved pecs, which were topped by thick, juicy nipples.

Jim's nimble fingers twisted and pulled on Shawn's thick, eraser-like nubs as he bobbed his head up and down over the young jock's wildly spasming cock.

"*Uh-huh! A-a-aw, f-u-u-uck!*" Shawn moaned.

A tremor of lust shook the stud's mighty muscles. His mouth yawned open and he heaved a heavy, lusty groan.

"Gonna shoot! *Gonna fuckin' shoot!*"

Jim cupped his hands around Shawn's hard bubble butt and forced the young stud's groin against his face, sending all 12 inches of spasming cock all the way down his cocksucking throat.

Shawn shouted, "*A-a-argh! F-u-u-uck!*" His thick, bloated prick swelled up and then exploded with thick jets of sperm that blasted from his sweaty nuts down Jim's spasming, gagging throat.

"*G-a-a-arh!*"

Jim was choking on the hot, gushing torrent of scalding stud semen as it flowed down the corners of his mouth and chin.

Rivers of hot stinking sweat had broken out all over Shawn's muscle-rippling body. Jim feverishly licked his way from Shawn's awesomely huge nuts dripping with freshly shot come. His tongue moved over the spectacular washboard abs and finally reached those superb, mountainous pecs. Yeah. Shawn's nipples just begged for a super tit workout.

Jim siphoned in those huge, rivet-hard nipples between his thirsty lips as Shawn moaned his burning macho excitement.

When Jim caught one large, sweating nipple between the edges of his teeth and seesawed them back and forth, Shawn bucked and squirmed wildly. He whipped his head back and forth, rasping huskily his supreme macho pleasure.

"*A-a-aw, f-u-u-uck! A-a-aw, gonna come!*"

The intense macho lust was overwhelming, and Shawn was going out of his fucking mind as he grabbed Jim's head and mashed his face over his sweating, saliva-soaked tits.

"*F-u-u-uck!*" He bellowed at the top of his lungs. Both of them fell with a loud crash to the floor as Shawn tightly gripped Jim in a powerful, bone-crushing bear hug.

Shawn lay upon his broad back with his beefy thighs tightly wrapped around Jim's waist. The jock's hot, pulsing pecker stiffened at once and rose full mast rubbing against Jim's well-defined abs. Jim responded with a hearty macho grunt and plunged a horny finger up Shawn's twitching butt hole.

"*A-a-aw, fuck yeah!*" the stud howled. His hot, muscled body thrashed and bucked. He squirmed and flopped like a 250-pound marlin hooked on a fisherman's line.

Jim grinned wolfishly as he rammed two, then three fingers up Shawn's slick hole.

"*U-u-ungh, un-huh! Yo, dude! Up my asshole!*"

Jim jammed his fingers knuckle-deep into Shawn's asshole. Jim stirred Shawn's fudge for a while, as Shawn's tight hole clenched around Jim's probing fingers. Suddenly, Jim popped his fingers out and brushed them against Shawn's full, pouty lips.

Shawn's feverish tongue eagerly popped out of his panting mouth. He slid his quivering tongue anxiously over the funk-drenched finger.

"*Mmm!* Fuck, yeah! My ass tastes fuckin' good don't it?"

Shawn groaned and smiled with macho pleasure as he licked off his own butt juices from Jim's slimy fingers, licking them as clean as a whistle.

Jim glowered at Shawn, his eyes burning with lust.

Shawn hissed, "Yeah, fuck me, stud! *Do me!*"

"U-u-ungh!" Shawn choked a hot grunt as he felt Jim slip his hard, pulsing prick between his sweaty cheeks. The tip of Jim's cock felt rock hard against his hot puckers.

"A-a-aw, fuck! Up my ass, stud! Up my fuckin' hole!" Shawn howled.

Jim plunged his fat, pulsing pecker through Shawn's tightly muscled anus ring.

"A-a-aw, fuck! N-o-o-o! F-u-u-uck!" Shawn screamed loudly. His loud, lusty cries bounced off the walls. Shawn gritted his teeth and clenched his eyes as he thrashed wildly, digging his burly fingers into Jim's broad, muscled back. Jim felt Shawn's slick, slimy butt hole open wider and wider and then quickly suck around his plunging prick.

Their mouths were glued together in hot macho passion. Jim sucked wildly on Shawn's quivering hot tongue. Shawn wrapped his thick thighs firmly around Jim's waist and held him fast in a bone-crushing bear hug. Jim plunged with hurricane-like force up Shawn's spasming butt hole.

Shawn whipped his head back and forth. Hot sweat flew off his hair.

Jim's body shuddered as he felt the heat knotting up within his balls while he clapped a steady rhythm against Shawn's sweaty butt.

The two men were hurtling over the very brink of super macho ecstasy. Hot bolts shot through their sweating bodies. They were ready to unleash the raging pent-up come burning deep within their bloated balls.

"F-u-u-uck, ye-a-a-ah!" Jim howled. "Take my load, stud! Take my fuckin' load!" Jim trembled violently as he ripped right through Shawn's burning hole and pumped thick, scalding jets of stud sperm up his dilated asshole.

"A-a-aw, f-u-u-uck!"

Shawn howled as wild macho pleasure blasted through his quaking muscles making him shoot a powerful geyser of semen that blasted between their bodies. The come just spurted up high into the air and rained down upon them until they were drenched with sizzling man come.

Minutes later, after the last drop of come had seeped from their balls, Jim and Shawn were still in each other's arms.

Shawn looked into Jim's eyes and said, "About that special relationship?"

Jim kissed Shawn.

He grinned.

Pro wrestling superstardom was but a blow job away.

THE MAINTENANCE MAN

Wade Wright

Sammy answered his front door to see one of the hottest looking maintenance men that he had ever seen. He was tall, built with broad shoulders, a small waist, and showing a very pronounced, and exciting, crotch. Sammy quickly looked the hunk over and made a mental decision that the new maintenance man was one hell of a hot-looking man, was probably about 27 or 28, but—damn it—was wearing a wedding ring.

Sammy was 30 and stood only to about the shoulder height of this adorable hunk of a man, and although he did have a good firm built, it certainly was nothing compared to the muscle man who was now standing directly in front of him at the front door. He knew that he had always admired good-looking men in uniform pants, regardless of which type of a uniform, but he quickly decided that this particular pair of pants, with the bulge that was showing, was probably the hottest looking pair that he had ever been up real close to. He quickly noticed that this specific bulge was a little more than just a bulge—part of what was hidden inside was actually extending down the left leg. This sure made Sammy wonder very quickly if this hunk of a man knew just how much he was showing, did he care, and of course, with that much in his basket area, why didn't he wear briefs, so that he could fold it under and kind of hide it?

Sammy had some major concerns regarding whether he had noticed and admired the crotch area a little too long, and had perhaps been seen looking down at it.

"Hi, I'm Jack Jensen, the maintenance man. This is apartment

Number 117, isn't it? Are you Sam Wilson? I understand you have a light problem somewhere here in your apartment?"

"Yeah, huh yeah." Sammy managed to answer. "The ceiling light in the bathroom went out, and even though I put a new bulb in it, it still won't work. Come on in."

Sammy swung the door open as he invited the maintenance man in, and then totally checked his backside out, as Jack entered and went past Sammy. "You are new here aren't you?" Sammy asked.

"Yeah, just started this week. Fact is, I'm still trying to remember which apartments are where. The numbering system for this complex is kinda messed up to me. It doesn't make too much sense."

"Yeah, I've always thought that too." Sammy replied, as he eyeballed the tall, black, muscular, broad-shouldered statue of a man. He fought to keep his eyes from trailing down to the enormous basket area. He did think, *Damn, those pants sure are nice and tight! Damn, I'd love to feel them! Shit, that looks hot!*

"The bathroom is back here," Sammy told Jack.

Jack followed Sammy down the hall toward the bedroom area and into the bathroom.

"So do you live here by yourself?" Jack inquired.

"No, I've got a roommate, but he's not here right now."

"Oh, OK," Jack replied. "What's his name?"

"Jim. Jim Nelson." Sammy answered.

"Oh, OK," Jack replied as he looked around to see what the apartment was like.

"You guys have a nice place here. I've only been in a few of the units so far, but you guys sure have this one fixed up nicer than the other ones I've been in."

"Well, thanks!" Sammy acknowledged. "We try! We both like nice stuff."

Yeah, nice stuff like you, Mr. Jack Jensen, Sammy thought to himself as he watched Jack bend over and put his toolbox on the floor. His thought process continued, *Damn, one hot maintenance man!*

What an ass! I hope like hell he stays around for a while and not the normal two or three weeks, and then off to a better job. Of course with the other ones, who cared, but shit, man, this one is way too hot to let go. Oh, man! Just freeze yourself there all bent over with your ass and those damn tight pants shining right at my face. Damn, man! One hell of a hot ass! Damn, that is good man stuff! Shit, that's hot!

Attempting to recompose himself and not act like his mind was off in the woods someplace, Sammy asked, as the man of his dreams stood back up, "Do you prefer being called Jack, or do you prefer Mr. Jensen?"

"Oh, definitely Jack! I always say Mr. Jensen is my dad! Hey, Sam, do you happen to have a step stool that I could borrow? I did not know this was a ceiling light problem, and I did not bring a stool. Have you got one I could borrow?"

"Yeah, sure do, Jack. Let me get it for you. It's in the kitchen. I'll be right back."

Sammy headed for the kitchen, retrieved the stool, and returned to the bathroom to find that Jack had removed his shirt and was now bare-chested.

"Oh, hope you don't mind," Jack said as he saw Sammy return to the bathroom. "I wouldn't do this if I was in some woman's apartment, but these damn uniform shirts are so damn tight they are hard to move in, so if it's OK with you, since it's just you and me, I'd like to just do without it until I get finished. OK?"

"Oh, yeah! Yeah—of course it's OK." Sammy replied. Then to himself he continued, *Hell yes, you can, and you can take the damned pants off too if you want. Shit, man, look at those pecs! Look at those biceps! Look at those tinny little nipples! Look at that skin! Shit, man, what a hunk! Shit, he is hot! Damn, he is hot! I've never chased after black guys before, but shit, man, this one is getting me all turned on!*

Jack opened the stool and after stepping up on it, he proceeded to work on the lamp fixture. Sammy stood there, with his mouth hanging open, and watched Jack reach up and extend his arms above his head. Sammy sighed. Jack heard the sigh and looked toward Sammy.

"You OK?" Jack inquired.

"Oh, yea, I'm OK." Sammy replied. "Yeah, I'm OK."

Turning, Sammy left the hall bathroom and went into the bathroom in the main bedroom and rinsed his face with cold water. He felt that he actually needed to cool himself back down. Jack's naked and exposed upper half had actually gotten him way too flushed. He grabbed a towel, wiped his face, stood there for a minute or two, and took three deep breaths.

As he returned down the hall to the main part of the apartment, he passed the door to the bathroom where Jack was working. Once again he simply had to stop and gaze at the hunk of a man that was in his apartment. Actually, in his bathroom, half undressed, and while he was in there too! He looked up toward Jack's upper body, and he then looked down toward Jack's waist, and, after loosing self-control, down toward his crotch. Jack saw Sammy looking at this crotch.

Jack smiled, and Sammy immediately turned and left the bathroom area.

Sammy forced himself to stay in the living room and kitchen area, and Jack continued his work on the light fixture.

"There!" Sammy shortly heard Jack exclaim from the bathroom. "It works! Hey, Sam, come look. It's working!"

Sammy headed toward the bathroom and as he turned the corner, he saw Jack standing there admiring his handy work, and at the same time rubbing his crotch. Sammy did not know what to look at—the light, or the hand on the crotch. The crotch certainly did hold a greater amount of interest. Right then, Jack's crotch certainly was shinning much more brightly than the light fixture was.

"Hey great!" Sammy said as he came into the bathroom. Jack realized that once again Sammy was eye-balling his crotch. And he was giving Sammy a good reason to watch.

"Hey, the light, man, the light!" Jack said in a rather joking manner. "The light's not your main interest is it?" Jack asked as he strongly grabbed his crotch, rubbed on it, and then pulled it up after putting his hand down under, and alongside the hang of meat that was going down his left leg.

"What, uh, what?" Sammy asked.

"Sam, I'm not real ignorant. I think you want to see what I have in my pants, don't you?"

"What? What?" Sammy exclaimed. "Why are you saying that?"

"Sam, I know you are a gay guy. I already knew that you had a partner. I already knew his name was Jim. Sam, the only reason I took this job was because I knew this apartment complex has a lot of gay guys in it, and before I go to any apartment, I find out as much about who is there as I can. Why do you think I'd run around without any underwear on? Shit, man, I need it to keep everything in there under control. Why do you think I took my shirt off? Hell that shirt ain't that damn tight! I wanted to flex these pecs in front of you and see if I could get you all hot and bothered, and I think I did! I like to mix work and fun together whenever I can, and that's why I like to work in complexes that have a lot of gay guys. I get my rocks off by letting them admire my hours in the gym. Now, want to see what I have hidden down here?" Jack asked as he started to unbutton his uniform pants.

"Uh, yeah!" Sammy managed to answer. "Yeah, Jack, if you want to show me."

Sammy actually wanted to yell, "Hell yes, man! Hell yes, I want to see it! Hell yes! Hell yes—I want to grab it!" But, he was trying to maintain some dignity and not act as if he was horny as hell, which he was quickly becoming, with the idea in mind that Jack wanted him to see his dick.

Jack unbuttoned the top button of his uniform pants, then told Sammy to finish unbuttoning them and to pull them down. Of course he had no briefs on, which had been very obvious to Sammy ever since he stood at the front door.

"Yeah right, man! Yeah, pull them down and put them down on the floor right on top of my shoes."

Sammy did as he was instructed and found that when he let loose of the pants, he was now face-to-dick with one of the darkest, longest, thickest, and one of the sweetest looking dicks that he had ever seen, either in person or in any mag. The skin looked like velvet!

"Oh, shit! Oh, shit, man!" Sammy exclaimed as he backed his face away so that he would be looking at the entire dick and not just the part attached to Jack's body. "Damn, man! God, Jack, you have got the dick of death! Jack, I've never played with a black man's dick before. I've never seen one like this! God, Jack—this thing is enormous!"

"Want to lick it, Sam? I've got some time before I'm expected to check back at the office, and I sure do want to make good friends with the people that I will be taking care of around here. Why don't you kind of lick that pole so that I know you and I can be some good, tight friends? If I take care of you and your apartment, then I want to know you can take care of me too! See, I've got some tools in my toolbox, and I've got this special tool here in my pants! I really want to use this special tool."

Sammy took about three deep breaths and slowly reached up and took ahold of Jack's bag of balls in his left hand. He took ahold of Jack's cock with his right hand, and then looked up at Jack.

"You aren't even hard yet and this damn thing is almost too damn fat for me to get my hand around. Jack, how damn big does this get when it gets hard?"

"Sam, my young man, you are the one down there with it in your hand. I'm sure if you kind of maybe lick on it and jerk it just a little, it will start getting hard for you, so that you can see for yourself! Come on, man! Get me hard! I'm feeling kind of horny here, and I need a good-looking guy like you to give me some service. I want to watch it disappear right down that hungry mouth of yours. I need to feel your warm, wet, hungry mouth all over it. Eat my dick, man! Use that tool!"

Sam was shocked that this was happening. He remembered how just a few minutes ago when he first opened the front door to let Jack in, he was so overtaken by this man's structure and his outstanding form that at that time he really did want to just throw

Jack to the floor and rape him. But now that Jack was telling him to actually do it, Sam was wondering if what was happening was really supposed to be going on. This guy worked for the apartment company, and Sammy was a tenant here. He had never had one of the maintenance men come on to him like this. He was not mentally prepared for this to be happening right then. This was way too unexpected! Hot, but way too unexpected!

Sam looked back down at the black stick of meat and slowly started to move his hand along the shaft. He slightly pulled on the bag of golf balls that were in his left hand. He took a deep breath! He pulled on the bag a little rougher and grabbed his hand around the shaft as far as he could manage. He pushed back on the dick and felt the skin move along the inner muscle. Then he pulled forward on it and again felt the skin slide. He felt more strength come into the pole. He continued to stroke. He shook his head in amazement as Jack's black "hot rod" got bigger and bigger!

"Oh, my God, Jack! Jack, I never knew a guy could have a dick this damn big! God, Jack! Shit, man! This damn thing is bigger than any dick I've even seen pictured. Shit, Jack, how damn big is this thing?"

"When it's good and hard, like after a good hungry mouth has been on it for a while, it usually measures about 11 inches long and about 61/2 or 7 inches around."

"Jack! You said after a hungry mouth has been on it! You mean you have had guys suck on this damn thing? You have had guys that can actually get that in their mouth?"

"Yeah, man! Yeah, a lot of guys can! And I don't know why, but it's usually the smaller guys that can take it down their throats, and also, those are usually the guys that beg for me to try and ram it up their asses. The bigger, muscle kind of guys usually can't take it in either end. Now, Sam, you look like one of the guys that can really take it and enjoy it! Come on, man! Let's see if I've started working at the right apartment complex or not. I mean, man, if I can't find me enough guys around here to take care of that thing for me, then I will just have to find me another job at another complex where the boys are hungrier and more anxious to make Mr. Jack and his big, black, long dick happy! I know from past experience, I need to be serviced by a guy at least once a day, so I've got to get my men lined up. Sam, I want you to be one of them!"

Sam let loose of the bag of balls and placed both hands on Jack's dick. He started stroking it with both hands clasped together as far as possible. His face was directly in front of the dick and he was stroking back and forth, aiming directly at his own face.

"Yeah, that's the way, man!" Jack said. "Yeah, that's starting to feel real good, Sam. Grab it tight and stroke it hard! Let me know you have ahold of it! Let me feel it! I want to get it as big for you as I can, so you need to start getting a little rougher on it. Stroke me man! There is a lot of meat down there to get all excited. Come on, man—beat me off some. Get it all excited! Get me good and hard!"

Sammy caressed Jack's dick and rubbed his face up against the side of it as he stroked it back and forth. Slowly but firmly it stretched out and started to reach its maximum size. To Sammy, it actually felt like a steel baseball bat in his hand. He moved his mouth to the tip of it. He opened his mouth as wide as possible. He slowly and with hesitation moved his mouth onto the end of Jack's oversized rod. Sammy knew it would be a total challenge to get part of, if not most of, Jack's meat into his mouth.

Grabbing ahold of Jack's hips, Sammy forced his face forward and pulled on Jack's body in an attempt to swallow as much of the big meat sausage as possible.

Jack placed his hands on the back of Sammy's head and slowly and deliberately pulled his head toward himself. Sammy gulped and gagged as he allowed Jack to force his head onto the big meat stick. He had to pull his head back to allow himself to get some air, and while he was off of the dick, he said, "Oh, shit, man! Oh, shit this damn thing is way too big!"

As soon as he had made his statement qualifying the dick as too big, Sammy immediately threw his face forward and once again forced as much of the black cock back into his mouth and as far down his throat as possible. Sammy had now had enough of this—

attempting to take it—and had now turned very anxious to get all of it, if at all possible. He had been hesitant when he started, but he was now hot and ready to force himself to take it even if it was uncomfortable. He realized that for some unknown reason, he trusted Jack enough that even though he knew he would not be able to breathe, Jack would not let him suffocate. He forced his mouth open, and he forced the dick inside as far as possible. The dick head was way more than anything he had ever attempted to put in his mouth. He rammed his face forward. Jack pulled Sammy's head onto his dick. Sammy's throat was completely filled. It was being spread open.

Sammy sucked and licked the enormous piece of meat. Jack used Sammy's head as a jerk-off device. With his hands firmly placed on each side of Sammy's head, he forced Sammy's mouth on and off of his dick until he finally said, "Hey, man! I'm getting real ready! Sam, I'm getting real, real close! Man, I'm about to shoot! I'm getting real close to comin'! Hey guy, I'm going to shoot! Sam, Sam, you want it in your mouth?"

Suddenly Jack's whole body went rigid! He thrust his crotch toward Sammy. He pulled on Sammy's head! Every muscle tightened up! He stood there without saying anything and went as rigid as a marble statue.

Sammy knew that when Jack's dick shot, it was going to be a very big load. He decided that a dick that big couldn't do anything but shoot big loads, and with his actions on that dick, he had gotten himself so excited about getting the chance to play with a dick that big that he was now getting really anxious and excited about taking the full load down his throat. He tried to utter, "OK, OK," but with his mouth so full and spread so far open, he had trouble getting the words out. He was not about to take the dick out of his mouth to say anything. He did not want to find his face or chest getting the shotgun load that he was now wanting to feel hit the back of his mouth.

Jack shot! Jack shot big! Jack shot strong! Sammy pushed his face onto Jack's dick as far as he could go. Sammy moaned and groaned as he tried to swallow the man-milk as fast as he could. Jack stood there completely rigid and continued to shoot. Shot after shot! Sammy continued to swallow.

Finally Jack's dick quit shooting, and he slowly allowed his body to relax. Sammy swallowed the remaining come that he still had in his mouth. He pulled his mouth back from the forced position that he had assumed, the position that he had used so that he made sure he got all of this handsome man's juices. He felt like he had drank the city water well dry. He had never had a dick that big in his mouth before, he had never taken that much come before, and he had never had a black man fuck his face before. He thought, *Now I know why they say, 'Once you go black, you never go back!'*

Sammy pulled off of Jack's dick. He wiped his mouth with the back of his right hand. He looked up at Jack and exhaustingly said, "Shit, oh, man! Oh, shit! God, Jack, you loaded me fucking full! God, Jack! You must have shot a quart of juice into my mouth. Man, I had trouble swallowing it fast enough! God, man, you have got one hot dick!"

"Well, Sammy, my man!" Jack replied, after regaining some composure and strength. "I certainly have found myself a guy that knows how to take it, use it, and eat it! You had fun on my cock, didn't you, boy?"

Sitting back on his heels, grabbing the sides of Jack's tree-trunk legs, he looked up at Jack and said, "Oh, hell yes, I did, Jack. Jack, I've never had that much cock in my mouth all at once before. Oh, shit, man! Oh, when you started coming I had to swallow as fast as I could. Oh, shit, man! Oh, man, you loaded me full! Yeah, Jack, yeah I do have to admit that I had fun. I'm fucking exhausted, but shit yes, I had fun! Jack, I need to catch my breath!"

"So I guess maybe that might mean that when I need to get my nuts off, I can stop by here and let you take care of it for me? Right? Can I count on you as one of my main men on sucking me off when I need it?"

"Well, Jack, I guess so, but I do have a partner, remember? We don't usually fuck around without the other guy being here, so I'm not so sure about just any ol' time. I really didn't expect anything like this to happen today. I've never had some maintenance man strip himself down and then offer his dick to me before. God Jack, especially one like that! Jack, the way you look and the way you are built, I'm sure you can do that to just about any guy and he'll go for it, but I did not intend to make hay with somebody without Jim being here. I'm not so sure I should be doing this again. I'm not so sure that would be fair to Jim. God Jack! I'm getting real confused here. Jack you are so hot! God having sex with you is way too much to believe. Jack, you said you need a guy to do you at least once a day? My God Jack! I can see why you need multiple guys! I don't think one guy could do this everyday! Jack, I want to, but—Oh, I don't know!"

"So how about we set it up so that I can meet your Jim, and see if maybe we can do a three-way or something. Hey, Jim might be more agreeable to letting you suck me off when I need it if he and I know each other. Is Jim a good sucker? Maybe he'd like to suck me off too! Maybe I can line both of you guys up for me!"

"Oh Jack. This is getting so confusing! Yeah, I'd really like a three-way with you and Jim, and yeah, I know I'd like to have more sex with you later, but man! But—Jack—I don't know if all you like is just getting sucked off or if you like other stuff too. I mean, to have a three-way and have one of the guys just wanting to get himself sucked off—well that doesn't usually work too well. What else are you into? Anything else, or just getting sucked off?"

"Hey I already mentioned the guys that love to get fucked by this rod, didn't I?"

STORMY WEATHER

CB Potts

Thank God I filled the wood box before this storm hit, I thought, throwing another log into the fire. There's no way I'd want to walk out in the 60-mile-an-hour winds, face the pelting ice and snow, or brave the frigid temperatures.

Yes sirree, I could sit back, snuggle under a warm blanket on the couch, watch the blizzard rage outside, and engage in my favorite activity. My sweatpants easily slipped down around my ankles, and I slowly began to stroke my man meat to life. No Viagra needed here! Nope, if I wanted an erection, all I had to do was think about Nathan.

Just the sound of his name had my cock throbbing. There was something about that stocky neighbor boy that turned me on so much I couldn't stand it—maybe it was the way he kept the back of his neck shaved close, or his fresh-from-the-football-squad physique. That deep pair of brown eyes didn't hurt. And we won't even talk about the way the boy next door filled out his jeans.

It wasn't all just physical, either. Nathan had spent his years away at college developing a wickedly funny sense of humor, raising sarcasm to an art form. He was well-read and deeply committed to restoring the planet's ecological balance. I guess that's why he chose to live out here in the mountains, like me.

We'd had some good times—hunting turkey, building my garage, even spending the rare couch potato Sunday watching college ball on TV. I'd never played football myself, but I can appreciate a bunch of babes in tight pants as well as the next guy. OK, maybe better.

Despite all we had in common, I never tried to get intimate with Nathan. *It's not that I didn't want to,* I thought smiling. The house was pretty toasty now, and I sat unabashedly basking naked in the glow of the fireplace. It's just that you have to be sensible. We are pretty isolated up here, and if I've read Nathan wrong, if somehow he turns out to be one of those crazy bastards who are violent toward gays, well, they'd never find my body.

Comfortable with my paranoia, I'd turned Nathan into my favorite fantasy. Imagine if all those times at the swimming hole had been sans cutoff jeans? What would it be like to kneel on a soft bed of pine needles while savoring every inch (and I just knew there had to be a lot!) of Nathan's cock? Faster and faster I tugged at myself, letting this wonderful scenario play out to its inevitable conclusion.

It was just about to end, soft towel at the ready, when a strange gleam of light pierced through the darkness outside. It wasn't steady, like a flashlight. Instead, the light danced and wavered in the blizzard, and I knew it had to be Nathan, that neo-Luddite, with his lantern.

Awkwardly, I yanked my sweats up over my rock-hard cock. It's not like you can just will these things away, you know, and there was no way I could finish up the way I intended with company about to arrive.

I pulled the door open at the first knock, bringing in Nathan and a companion snowdrift. His dark eyebrows were frosted white, and icicles hung from the rim of his hat.

"What in God's name are you doing out on a night like this?" I asked. The lantern sent weird shadows around my kitchen, leaving only Nathan and I in a puddle of warm light.

"You know that son-of-a-bitching white birch?" Nathan asked. I nodded. The tree was so huge I couldn't wrap my arms around it. "Well, she came down, took out most of my roof."

My neighbor shed his coat and hat in a snowy pile. "Figured you wouldn't mind some company." A particular shadow caught Nathan's attention, and with a funny grin he continued. "From how you're looking right now, it looks like you either really want company, or you really want to be alone." His brown eyes locked with mine. "So which one is it?"

"I'd really like the company," I managed to croak, made half-incoherent with desire.

Nathan nodded. "So let's go get me warmed up."

"The first thing we've got to do," I said, having finally regained the power of speech, "is get you out of these wet clothes."

Nathan smiled and opened his arms. "Have at it, champ."

As many times as I'd pictured this very event, I never envisioned unbuttoning half-frozen flannel shirts, or the miniature snowdrifts that formed around my bare feet. The threat of frostbite didn't faze me in the least, though, not as I was finally getting close to Nathan's skin.

I'd seen my neighbor shirtless a million times—mowing his lawn, tarring the roof—but never had my fingers had a chance to run across that silken skin. Nathan's pecs were firm under my palms, nipples standing firmly erect with more than a chill to inspire them.

I worked from there to his belt, slowly teasing the stiff leather through the buckle. As his baggy jeans fell to the floor, I knelt. I wanted a bird's-eye view while peeling those long johns down.

My curiosity was soon rewarded, as Nathan's cock swung free. Framed by a thick patch of curly black hair, his sausage was short but as thick around as my wrist. Despite all my fantasizing, I hadn't pictured a stubby monster shaped like a beer can. My mouth began to water just thinking about the challenge of swallowing that girth.

"This is great," Nathan interrupted, gently running his hand over my hair, "but maybe we could adjourn to somewhere a little warmer? With the draft coming through that door," he laughed, "I won't be able to stay like this for long."

"That's fine," I replied. "My condoms are in the other room anyway. I keep them in the tackle box."

Nathan laughed. "That's a strange place. I mean, who do you go fishing with besides me?" The light slowly dawned, and he grinned sheepishly. "Oh."

Once he was dressed properly, I got to work. My first licks were tentative and slow, as if I could hardly believe my good luck. Nathan's throaty grins were very encouraging, and I let the plum-shaped head slip between my lips. Bobbing my head back and forth a few times, I managed to relax my jaw enough to encircle the entire circumference of Nathan's cock. Even if the rest of him was cold, these six inches were red-hot. No danger of hypothermia here.

My lips slid along the fiery surface, exploring the raised network of veins that surrounded Nathan's rod. He was so thick around that I could feel his shaft rubbing against the inside of my cheeks. Once the velvety crown of his cock hit the back of my throat, I knew my mouth had never been so completely fucked.

Nathan wanted more, though. "God damn it, lick my balls," he ordered, pulling my head away. "Tongue me."

Reluctantly, I abandoned my cock sucking to devote my oral attentions to Nathan's sac. My tongue snaked through fine black hair to dance over the puckered surface—but once it did, there was an immediate response.

Nathan's moans were loud enough to wake the neighbors—if we'd had any. As it was, I'm sure a few bears had their hibernation disturbed. He hitched his hips forward desperately, trying to force more and more of his scrotum into my willing mouth. The motion sent his cock bumping all over my face, so that his cock head tangled in my own blond hair. This must definitely be what turns my neighbor boy on.

If I needed any convincing of that, Nathan's next move erased any doubt. In one smooth motion, he disengaged from my mouth and rolled onto his stomach.

"You've got to fuck me now," he said, his tone more than half pleading.

In a split second, I'd pulled another rubber from the tackle box. My own cock, so recently teased and tantalized, was raring to go. I was so hard that I was sure that my load would burst from me at the first brush with Nathan's perfect ass.

I hadn't counted on the coolness of the lube, but thankfully, that slowed my fire somewhat. Good thing too, because worming my way into Nathan's glory hole was the most erotic thing I'd ever experienced.

You could tell right away he was no virgin—his sphincter accepted me with the ease only long practice can bring—but, my God! The muscles lining his Hershey chute were the most talented I'd encountered in all my long years of queerdom. They squeezed and teased, pulling me farther and farther inside.

"Keep going," Nathan grunted. Sweat was pouring down his back as he thrust his hips toward me. "You're almost there."

"Almost where?" I asked, but the minute I brushed against Nathan's prostate, I knew what he was talking about. My neighbor began to shudder all over, the walls of his ass convulsing all along the length of my cock.

Inspired by this reaction, I decided to see how much pleasure Nathan could stand. I soaked my palm with hot saliva and then reached forward and cupped his sensitive balls. Rubbing and pressing, I tried to tease what I knew must be a tremendous orgasm out of Nathan.

"No, no," he protested, shaking his head. His brown eyes locked with mine as he looked over his shoulder at me. "I want you to shoot first."

"There's plenty of time for that later," I replied, sliding my cock head back and forth across his sensitive prostate. "Besides, you're the guest, remember?" With that, I squeezed his balls.

"Oh, my God," Nathan moaned. He shook from head to toe, a veritable earthquake of come. Beneath my insistent hand, I could feel his balls tense and shoot—and tense and shoot again—and again.

Of course it was too much for my overstimulated shaft, and my cock loosed the explosion it had been holding back for all the years Nathan lived next door. I could feel my toes curling against the pine floor as every ounce of desire drained from my manhood. The condom managed to contain nearly every drop, although I felt some hot, sticky overflow coursing down my thighs.

We collapsed together, sweaty in the cherry-red glow of the wood stove. For a few minutes, neither of us could talk, and we merely grinned, content in that postcoital bliss only tremendous fucking can bring. I'd always thought Nathan was attractive, but right now, naked on my living room floor, covered from head to toe in fresh sweat and spunk, he was easily the sexiest man I'd ever seen. I knew this was true, because despite the tremendous workout it had just had, my cock was ready to spring to life again.

Nathan noticed, and laughed. "Holy shit, man!" He looked over my naked form quizzically. "Where do you put in the batteries?"

I laughed too. "Just call me Ever-Ready."

Nathan smiled. "Too bad I didn't know about you earlier. Think of all the time we've wasted."

Too blissed-out to care, I just shook my head. "Doesn't really matter, does it? Think of all the time we've got ahead of us."

"That's true," my neighbor agreed. "And with my roof caved in, I'm gonna need a place to stay for a little while."

"Like you said," I replied, "it doesn't seem like I mind having company."

Nathan grinned and ran his fingers over my sticky cock. True to form, it sprang to attention, hungry for any bit of attention from my favorite neighbor. A few teasing strokes and I was panting. My desire was more than obvious—it was time for me to feel that beer-can cock inside my ass.

Nathan suited up—hopefully this storm would let up before my condom stash ran out—and pressed the swollen head of his cock against my starving sphincter.

"No," he said, pressing his way in with a smile. "It doesn't seem like you mind company at all."

My legs sprawled wide as I struggled to accommodate Nathan's girth. My new roommate gave it to me slowly, allowing my ass to become accustomed to the thickness.

• • • • • • • • • • •

"Is it too much?" Nathan asked. He leaned forward, letting more of his weight rest against my back. "Can you take all of me inside you?"

I grunted. "I'll sure the hell try." Sweat dripped from my forehead as I eased my hips backward, the perspiration owing nothing to the blazing wood fire. Halfway down his shaft, I doubted I'd ever be totally impaled on Nathan—there was just too much cock to work around.

"Man, you're working too hard." Nathan chuckled. "You have to let nature take its course." His arm was a steel belt around my waist, bulging with muscles earned with a splitting maul. "Or in this case, gravity."

With a speed that belied his bulk, Nathan pivoted so that he was lying flat on the knotty pine floor. I found myself astride him, my bowels suddenly, gloriously, full. The sheer force of my weight had overcome any resistance my ass muscles were offering. I could feel Nathan's sensitive balls pressing against my own.

Nathan could definitely feel it too. The occasional pleasurable grunts gave way to louder moans, timed to match the ever-increasing pace of his hips. Each stubby stroke pushed hard against my prostate, causing my cock to twitch like a freshly hooked trout.

Of course I grabbed my meat, feeling the pounding beat of Nathan's cock coursing through my own. Two tugs and my load was bubbling for release.

"I'm gonna shoot, man," I panted, turning to face Nathan. His eyes were closed, skin flushed fire red. "Can you come with me?"

"I'll try," he replied. Hands that had spent hours at hard labor gripped my hips, and Nathan slid me up and down his shaft as if I weighed no more than an armload of kindling. "Just let me stay in this sweet ass for a little while longer."

If I had my way, I'd keep Nathan happily ensconced in my glory hole for all time—but as he had said, sometimes you've got to let nature take its course. The inevitable conclusion to all this ass banging was literally at hand, and with a final groan, I lost my load. The air sizzled with the distinctive sound of spunk hitting the woodstove, a burnt protein aroma familiar in my nostrils.

Three more strokes, shuddering into my ass, and it was Nathan's turn. He enjoyed it before, so I figured I might as well press against my neighbor's sensitive balls now that he was again on the verge.

It wasn't just a good idea, it was inspired. Nathan roused the sleeping bears again, moaning as his hot juice filled the condom near to bursting. He held stock-still for a moment, a stricken deer in the headlights, and then held me in his arms for a long, long silent moment.

Feeling him slip at long last from my ass left me feeling emptier than I thought possible. I turned, taking Nathan in my arms. Now that I finally had him, I didn't want to let him go.

"You know what?" I asked.

"What's that?" Nathan replied. His expression was perfect, a balance between bliss and sleep.

"If I had known this was going to happen, I'd have cut down that damn tree a long time ago."

Nathan laughed. "You? I would've done it myself!"

A GRAND OLD TRADITION

Kris Wright

"But, sir, you won," said the earnest young advisor who knew much of image and little of history. "How will it look if the press finds out you're meeting behind closed doors on the eve of the inauguration?"

The politician, so dapper in his trust-inducing navy blue suit and red-and-blue diamond-patterned tie, smiled his famous smile. "It'll look like a gesture of goodwill, son. A simple gesture of goodwill."

With a nod and a wave, he climbed from the back of his limousine. Secret Service agents flanked him as he walked into the swanky hotel just a few blocks from Pennsylvania Avenue.

Fifteen floors up, he stood at the penthouse door. He looked at his sentries and flashed another winning smile and drawled, "You know the drill, boys. No one in, no one out. No one knows nothing. Right?"

The two agents, in matching dark suits with wires snaking up to their ears, nodded in unison. They were not so young as the advisor, they had been around for the previous administration; they knew the rumors of the old traditions, the secret society. They did, in fact, know the drill.

The politician knocked firmly, rapidly and certainly presidentially. The door opened and there he stood, resplendent in a brown cashmere robe and matching lounge pants. The opponent.

"You're late." He opened the door wider and gestured the politician inside. With a nod to the agents, he closed the door and turned the lock.

"I only have an hour," said the politician, loosening his tie.

"Tomorrow is going to be a nightmare. You wouldn't believe the security."

His opponent crossed to the elaborate wet bar, ignoring the fancy bottles and crystal decanters in favor of the simple bourbon. He poured them each a double and passed a glass to the politician.

"You know I quit that," said the politician, with a frown he reserved for foreign policy meetings.

"You know you want it," said his opponent, swirling the amber liquid in the glass.

"What the hell." The politician took the glass and tipped it toward his opponent. "To tomorrow."

As their glasses clinked softly, his opponent said, "To tonight."

They drank silently, their eyes measuring each other over the tops of their glasses.

Finally, when the bourbon was gone, the politician set his empty glass on the bar and took the glass from his opponent. "Kiss me."

His opponent wasn't the best kisser. He had the stereotypical stiff upper lip of a New Englander, but his mouth was warm and tasted of liquor. The kiss lasted for a full minute. The politician had the fleeting thought of a photographer bursting in on them, their lip-lock plastered on the cover of the next morning's paper. It would never—could never—happen, but the thought made him instantly, achingly hard.

They staggered toward the king-sized bed, groping for each other—a slightly sagging buttock, a bare shoulder, the caress of a strong jaw. It wasn't enough. They were still hungry for each other's touch.

The two men tumbled backward on the bed, the opponent falling across the prone body of the politician. The politician grunted and his opponent pulled back, looking stricken.

"Did I hurt you?"

The politician grinned. "Yeah, but I liked it."

"Kinky cowboy."

The politician stroked his opponent's luxuriously thick hair.

"Where's the little missus tonight?"

"Having dinner with a friend. You know Hillary, don't you?"

"Great gal," said the politician. "Lousy taste in men."

"No kidding."

They laughed, rolling around on the bed like two frisky puppies. The opponent stripped the politician naked, tossing aside his power suit. Slowly, he freed the politician's erection from the confines of his silk underwear, stroking him roughly.

"You're going to make me shoot before I'm ready."

The opponent stood and let his robe fall to the floor, then his lounge pants. His heavy erection seemed to defy gravity. "Suck me," he said. "Now."

"I've dreamed about your cock all week." The politician crawled across the bed until he was nuzzling his opponent's crotch. "Whoa. I'd almost think you were from Texas, big boy."

"Suck it," groaned his opponent again, as the politician took him deep into his public-pleasing mouth. "Harder."

The politician whimpered around the thick length of dick in his mouth, reaching around to grab his opponent's ass. He sucked like a starving man, flicking his tongue back and forth across the swollen head, tasting his opponent's unique flavor. He pulled back, trailing his tongue down the shaft, over the opponent's downy soft balls and then back up to the spit-slick head. His opponent moaned softly and thrust his hips forward, searching for that warm, sucking mouth of political power.

The opponent could feel his orgasm rising, his balls tightening. The politician could feel it too. He pulled away, wiping saliva and precome from his fleshy lips. "Not yet, big boy, not quite yet. You know what I want. What I need."

The politician rolled over onto his stomach. He thrust his ass up in the air, bracing himself on forearms and elbows. Ready. Willing. Needy.

His opponent watched the ass that looked so good in jeans, that was his for the taking. He knelt on the bed behind the politician and guided his cock toward the politician's ass.

"Fuck me. You know I want it," teased the politician.

Indeed, his opponent did know. He could hear it in the politician's voice; see it in his bobbing cock. He searched under the pillow for the lube he'd stashed earlier. He liberally greased his cock because he suspected that in this regard, like so many others, the politician would be a real tight ass.

"C'mon," the politician whined. "Fuck me already."

The opponent braced one hand on the politician's hip and aimed his cock at the politician's ass. Like a heat-seeking missile, his cock found its target and breached the puckered asshole of the most powerful man in the world. Just as he'd suspected, the politician did indeed have a very tight ass. If heaven was bipartisan, the opponent decided, this is what it would feel like.

"Oh, fuck," he groaned, burying his cock in the politician's ass.

"Hell, yeah," gasped the politician, taking it like a man.

The opponent fucked the politician hard and deep, loving the sounds of the other man's whimpers and moans, the way he pushed back against him when he withdrew to the tip of his cock. He grasped the politician's hips and drove into him, fucking him with months—years—of pent-up administration frustration. For every snide comment, for every sweaty-palmed handshake, for every free-thinking, tree-hugging liberal everywhere, he fucked him.

They were joined together, cock into ass, opponent into politician, loser into winner. It was a political fucking machine. This was no presidential powwow, no meeting of the minds, no gesture of goodwill. It was fucking. Pure fucking.

"Take that dick," his opponent grunted. "Take it."

The politician collapsed on the bed, rubbing his cock against the high thread-count Egyptian cotton sheets. "Fuck me! Fuck me! Oh, damn, fuck my ass."

His opponent obeyed his commander, bracing his lean body over the politician's, slowing his thrusts to tease them both. "C'mon, come for daddy."

The politician whimpered at his opponent's forceful coaxing.

"Oh, yes, oh, yes. I'm coming, oh, fuck, I'm coming!"

His opponent was laying on top of the politician now, his cock buried in that tight, clenching ass. He had only to thrust one, two, three more times and he was spurting deep inside the politician, contaminating that tight ass with a lot of liberal seed.

They lay there, pressed together, the opponent's cock going soft inside the quivering, clenching ass of the politician. They were breathing hard, panting in opposite rhythms, which seemed entirely fitting. At last, the opponent moved away, withdrawing from the politician's ass with a groan. He rolled over onto his back, eyes closed, cock glistening.

"You may have lost the race," the politician said with a cocky grin, "But you're the best lay in the free world."

His opponent didn't respond. He'd pressed enough flesh for one campaign.

THE END OF AUGUST

Simon Sheppard

The first dick I ever sucked belonged to my brother's best friend.

Tyler actually looked more like my brother Ned than I did. They were both tall and wiry. But Tyler was more handsome than my brother, with a strong jaw and blue eyes that looked right through you.

It was the last few days of a hot, sweaty August. The next month I'd be heading off to my sophomore year in college. Yale wasn't all that far from my family's upstate New York farm, but I had no way of knowing then that I would never return to the place, that soon the barn and the horses and my youth would be gone. In the meantime, I was spending one last summer with the horses I loved.

I'd always needed to ride, ever since I was a young, skinny kid. I'd grown up feeling inferior to powerful, tall Ned. And I always knew I had a guilty secret, even if I wasn't quite sure about what it was. But riding made me feel strong and free. I loved the feeling of all that power beneath me—the surging animal muscles, just barely under my control, that carried me across the deep green countryside. In junior high I discovered a talent for gymnastics, and my body became stronger, well muscled, but nothing compared to the strength of a stallion snorting at my touch.

And nothing compared, either, to the desire I had for Tyler that overheated summer. Every time I saw him, the memories flooded back. Summer softball games when rivulets of sweat ran down Tyler's smooth, lean chest. The smell of Tyler, five years older than me, the smell of a man. The times when Ned let me tag along with him and Tyler, and we'd all go skinny-dipping down at the lake.

Tyler goofing around on the rope swing over the lake, his wet haunches gleaming in sunlight, his big dick flopping between his thighs, as he swung crazily out over the cool water, let go, and landed with a splash. I was always real careful not to let Ned see me staring at his best friend, at his best friend's cock, knowing they'd most likely beat me up if they ever caught on.

Tyler hadn't gone off to college. Not that he was stupid or anything; he just wasn't cut out for higher learning. He worked at the body shop in town, still lived with his parents, was engaged to the daughter of the guy who owned the Village Liquor Shoppe. But once Ned had gone off to state, I hardly ever saw Tyler at all, just ran into him once in a while around town.

And now I was a college boy, come back home for the summer. It was two weeks before Labor Day. My brother had been home since mid July, but he and my parents had gone to New York City for the week. I'd stayed behind. Tending to the horses—to *my* horse, Thunder—was a lot more appealing than some musical comedy with dancers dressed up as cats.

I was in the barn, just breathing in the smells, enjoying the cool semidarkness.

"Hey." Surprised, I looked up. It was Tyler, standing silhouetted in the doorway.

"Hey, Tyler," I said. "Ned's not here. Family's gone to the city."

"I know," he said, walking toward me, and smiled. I felt a familiar, electric thrill go through me, *zap!*

"What's up?" I asked. *Besides my dick*, I thought.

"Dunno. I'm lonely. Annie's out of town, your brother's out of town." Annie was his girlfriend.

"Sure."

"So," Tyler asked, "want to go down to the swimming hole, for old time's sake?" Though Tyler and I had seen each other that summer, talked some, we hadn't had more than a few minutes alone. Whenever Tyler was around, he'd been with Ned. Now there was just the two of us, late on a hot summer afternoon.

"Well?" He stood there, thumbs hooked into his waistband,

weight slightly shifted to one foot, smiling. Waiting for an answer. Waiting for something.

I realized that a few too many seconds had gone by in silence. "Yeah, that'd be great. Want to go for a ride?"

Tyler wasn't a great rider, not nearly as good as me, but as we rode across the countryside, still green and beautiful despite the new suburban housing tracts that had started to creep in, everything felt so right. Thunder and I were old friends, and Tyler, seated astride Caesar, was still entirely beautiful, the creature of memory, of my boyhood dreams.

No one else was at the swimming hole. We dismounted, tied up the horses, and lay down side-by-side in the tall grass, warmed by the 4 o'clock sun.

Tyler began to unbutton his shirt. "So, Yalie," he said with no trace of a smirk, "how's college?"

"OK," I said. "It's a lot of work, but I enjoy it, mostly."

"And those college girls?" It wasn't exactly as if Tyler had never seen big-city girls; plenty of Manhattanites had summer places up here.

"They're...they're great." I couldn't tell Tyler that I hadn't seriously dated, that I wasn't even interested in girls, not that way. That though a young, well-built guy in New Haven would have no trouble getting laid, I hadn't even tried to get what I wanted, which was sex with a guy. Because, I now realized, I hadn't wanted to go out on a limb and ruin my reputation, not for just anybody, not for anybody who wasn't as hot as Tyler. And nobody was.

Tyler was lying there shirtless. He had perfect nipples. You know how some nipples are absolutely perfect, and you can't explain why, but they are? His were. Perfect. His hands were behind his head. I stared at the dark brown hair under his arms, the only hair above his waist. I breathed in deep and could smell Tyler's sweat blending with the other smells of late summer.

I pulled off my T-shirt and looked down at myself. Not bad. Nice definition, a patch of dark hair trailing down into my jeans.

Neither of us said anything for a while. I lay there with my eyes closed. There was a rustle in the grass next to me. Tyler must have been getting restless. "How's Annie?" I said, just for something to say.

"Oh, that's great. As far as it goes."

Startled at his tone, I looked over at him. He'd slipped off his pants. He was lying there beside me, in just underwear and white socks, one hand shoved partway beneath the waistband of his boxers.

"I'm getting hot," Tyler said.

No shit, I thought.

"Want to go for a skinny-dip?" Tyler asked. "For old time's sake?" Without waiting, he peeled off his briefs and sat up to take off his socks. His big half-hard cock lazed along one lean thigh.

I reached down and unbuttoned my jeans, then hesitated. The head of my dick was already sticking up out of the waistband of my briefs. But before I could strip, Tyler was on his feet, running through the warm grass toward the swimming hole. The muscles of his pale, beautiful haunches flexed in sunlight as he galloped toward the water. He grabbed the rope that hung from a tree branch and launched himself recklessly over the cool water. Naked at last, I followed, my stiff dick bobbing as I ran. I knew he could see I was hard, and I didn't give a damn.

Kicking his muscular legs, he widened the arc of his swing, let go, and hurled himself into thin air, hanging there as if weightless for one long second, the naked object of all my desire.

He landed feet-first in the water with a splash, disappeared for a second, and came up sputtering for air. I didn't bother with the rope. I ran to a little rise at the water's edge and dove in. A few underwater strokes brought me over to him. Even the cool water hadn't made his hard dick shrink. I stood beside him, in clear chest-deep water, the sounds of an August day buzzing all around us, excitement roaring in my ears.

"So we're here at last," Tyler said, "me and Ned's little brother." He swung out underwater with one of his legs and knocked me off my feet. While I was foundering around in the water, he reached out with a scissor kick and wrapped his legs around my waist. His thighs were tight around me, his balls against my belly. He smiled broadly as he splashed around. "So you're gonna make me feel real good, aincha, Yalie?"

I couldn't help myself. I reached down, slid my hands along his sinewy thighs, up to his crotch, and grabbed his dick with both hands.

"Oh, yeah," I said. And I held on tight.

Laughing, he twisted around and reached for my cock too, and kind of rubbed it against his wet, slippery butt. We played with each other's hard-ons there in the water for a few long seconds. Then Tyler spoke.

"It ain't real safe out here, Yalie. Never know who'll come on by."

So we got out of the water, used our T-shirts to dry ourselves off, and went back to the horses. Shirtless, we galloped across the fields, back to the farm. It wasn't long before we were in the stables, Tyler leaning up against a wooden wall with his jeans down around his firm white thighs, me kneeling between his feet. Touching his dick hadn't been weird. I knew how a hard-on felt, seeing as how I'd been making myself come for years. But tasting a guy's dick was something else again.

Tyler was uncut, and even with a full erection, his foreskin half-covered his dick head. I kind of peeled it back and watched his shiny dick head emerge. Then I nuzzled my face against him, feeling his hard hot flesh and silky brown crotch hair against my cheek.

"What're you waiting for?" Tyler asked. "You've been wanting to do it for years, right? Now's your chance. Go ahead. Suck it."

His dick was long but, luckily for me, wasn't very thick. I had no trouble opening wide enough to take the tip of his cock into my mouth. The silky flesh felt unfamiliar against my tongue. Unfamiliar, but right. I slid my mouth farther down. I could hear the horses snort and stamp, but all I could see was the flesh of Tyler's flat belly.

"Oh, yeah," he moaned. He grabbed my head in both hands and started sliding in and out of my mouth. Meanwhile, I fumbled between my thighs till I unbuttoned my Levi's and pulled my own cock out.

My jaws were beginning to ache, but I was getting to really enjoy sucking Tyler's long, hard dick. A trickle of precome left a salty-sweet taste on my tongue. I wondered if I'd want to take his whole load in my mouth. I didn't have to wonder long. Tyler pushed my head all the way down, till his cock head rammed deep into my mouth. For a second I gagged real bad, but then he drew back. Glad to be able to breathe again, I kind of wiggled my tongue along the underside of his shaft, and Tyler shouted out "God *damn*!" and pumped a huge load of hot sperm into my mouth. Being new to cock sucking, I didn't really know if I was supposed to swallow or spit it out. But I wanted Tyler all the way inside me, so I gulped down his salty come. It burned my throat a little.

Up to that second, I hadn't realized how hard I'd been jacking my own dick. But suddenly, I was shooting out a big load of jism onto the hay-covered floor. Thunder kind of whinnied. I wanted to whinny too.

Tyler helped me to my feet, an odd smile on his face. I was already thinking about somehow getting to know him, about showing him how much I loved him, changing my life, maybe leaving school so I could be with him.

But Tyler was buttoning up and heading for the door. Maybe he somehow knew that this would be the only time I'd ever suck him off, that by the next time I saw him, he and Annie would be married, and when I'd try to raise the subject, he'd dismiss it as "kid stuff." Maybe he wasn't even thinking about me, now that he'd gotten his rocks off.

In any case, I had so much to say, and I didn't know how to say any of it. But the next thing that Tyler said, the last thing I'd hear him say that final summer of my innocence, surely left me speechless. Something that changed everything, yet changed nothing at all, really, there on that hot late-summer day.

"You were sure good for a beginner, Yalie. Damn near as good as Ned."

SUMMER NIGHT, SUMMER SUCK

Michael Murphy

It was warm that summer night, and I moved from the kitchen out to the back porch to enjoy the clear skies and all the stars. I was watching the fireflies flickering on and off along the lawn when I was startled by a low voice coming out of the darkness.

"Hi, Officer Murphy. Can I come up and talk a while?"

I had the lights out on the porch and I could barely see the tall figure moving up the back stairs. I recognized the voice, though. That soft Arkansas accent belonged to my neighbor's 19-year-old son.

"Sure, Johnny. Nice night, isn't it? What's on your mind?"

"I'm thinking of becoming a cop. I'm starting college next year and I wondered what you think I should take for classes."

Johnny dropped down to the deck chair beside me. He leaned forward in the darkness with his hands folded on his knees and stared at me. I could just make him out in the light from my kitchen, which filtered through curtains at the end of the porch.

As we spoke, Johnny's earnest, sultry voice and his warm proximity sent a steady wave of sexual tremors through my stiffening cock and swollen ball sac. Just turned 19, the high school graduate was both good-looking and damn sweet. I'd kept an interested eye on him as he'd trimmed the hedges along our property border for the past few weeks, naked to the waist. Slim, yet with broad shoulders and a small waist, he had the beginnings of a well-built body. And in ragged cutoffs, his round butt swelled fetchingly out behind while his obvious package in front was hard to miss. Sandy hair, always a little mussed up, and grey eyes lent him an innocent air. His bright smile and genial wave only added to the sexy aura he exuded.

My mind was drifting as he spoke. I was absently thinking of what his sexy can would look like naked—and spread wide—when he dropped his bombshell.

"I know you're gay, Officer Murphy. Do you think I could suck your cock? I've got some condoms, so it would be safe and shit."

I peered through the night at the young boy-next-door. I shouldn't have been so surprised by his blatant come-on. When I'd joined the police force, I had decided to be open about my sexuality. When I moved to this small Arkansas town earlier that summer I'd also been honest about it. The local gossips had spread the word quickly.

"You're so muscular and all, and you're handsome as hell too. I like your red hair and your moustache and I know you've been checking me out. I hope you're not mad for me askin'," he continued earnestly.

That's when Johnny's hand extended out and landed on my lap. Our chairs were close and his knees banged up against mine as he leaned forward. That hand landed in exactly the right spot, directly on my swollen fuck-stick. In a gut reaction, I let out an involuntary gasp and spread my thighs apart.

Johnny's fingers groped my fat shank, throbbing through the light material of my pants. Taking this as his cue, he leaped forward, dropping to his knees between my legs and burying his face in my lap.

"Fuck!" I grunted at the sudden feel of Johnny's wet mouth clamping over my cock. I was wearing a pair of loose shorts with baggy boxers beneath and I could feel those sucking lips and lapping tongue right through the layers of flimsy cloth. "You're old enough to make up your mind—uhhn—about what you want. Get out that condom and suck away, Johnny!" I groaned out.

I could feel his trembling body between my bare thighs. All of the sudden I wanted to fuck that young, tight ass so bad I could taste it. My cock leaped between Johnny's massaging lips. He gurgled some incoherent reply before lifting his face from my lap and grasping the waistband of my shorts and tugging at them. I lifted my butt off the chair cooperatively, and he pulled both my shorts and boxers down to my ankles and off over my bare feet.

I suddenly felt very exposed as my cock bobbed up in the air between us. My eyes had grown accustomed to the darkness a bit, and I could just make out the fat column of beef twitching in Johnny's face. He was quick though, and I heard him tearing at a condom wrapper with his teeth and then felt his fingers shaking as they grasped my cock and rolled the condom over it.

"What a big fucker, Officer Murphy!" Johnny whispered as he stroked my cock.

"I'm only six years older than you and I'm not on duty. You may as well call me Michael, not Officer Murphy. Shit! That's so fucking sweet!" I gasped out as Johnny suddenly swooped down over my cock with his mouth.

Torrid wetness engulfed my hard-on. A swirling tongue bathed the knob as massaging lips made a gurgling descent down the shaft. Johnny sucked noisily as he bobbed up and down in a hungry rhythm. He was a horny little fucker. I leaned back in the chair and opened up my thighs, feeling hot air on my balls and ass crack as Johnny snorted around the base of my dick. He had sucked it all in, although he was gagging a little as the fat knob thrust past his tonsils.

The kid sucked my cock while he played with my balls with one hand and pumped my shaft with the other. I writhed in my chair and thrust up into his face with my hands on his shoulders and my ankles wrapped around the back of his knees. I fucked his face while he sucked and pumped my cock. It was awesome.

But it was too intense. It only lasted about five minutes before I was grunting like a stuck pig and shooting a barrage of hot come between his smacking lips. He sucked harder as my jizz filled the condom wrapping it and I squirmed around in my chair, blowing air in big gasps.

Johnny pulled his mouth from my pulsing boner with a lewd slurp. He looked up at me in the darkness. I couldn't read his expression in the lack of light, but I could see the gleam of his teeth as he grinned up at me.

"That was awesome. Do you think you could fuck my tight ass too? I want you to be the first."

I was still panting as the final spurts of jizz oozed from my cock head, unable to answer. Johnny proved his boldness once again by rising up and quickly shucking his shorts and underwear, then squatting over my lap with his thighs spread on either side of mine, all in less than a minute. Wearing only a T-shirt like me, he sprawled over my lap and writhed there. Reaching behind his back, he gripped my hard cock, rubbing the wrapped shaft all over his own parted crack.

His chest was in my face as he performed his obscene lap dance. I was still in a bit of shock with the sudden turn of events—and weak from my orgasm. But the feel of that naked ass rubbing against my dick galvanized me into action. Reaching around Johnny's waist with both hands I grasped his butt cheeks. The compact globes were silky-warm to the touch and trembling violently. For all his boldness, he was nervous.

I groped his firm butt as he humped up and down in my lap and rubbed my cock over his crack. The squishy ooze of my jizz trapped in the condom only made me hot all over again. I would have no trouble fucking his sexy ass.

"Let's put a condom on your cock," I gasped out.

"Sure, Michael. Then you'll fuck my ass for me?" Johnny whispered.

"You bet I will."

Johnny stood again and for the first time I noticed his dick. It jutted out in an obscene curve from his crotch. I salivated just looking at it. I wanted to suck on that big thing before I fucked him.

"Nice piece of meat. Nice all over, Johnny," I murmured as my hands fondled his naked thighs and ass.

He moved around in front of me again as he found his discarded shorts and produced more condoms. He must have brought a box of the things. I could just make out his hard sickle arching in the air in front of me as he stood between my parted thighs and got out another rubber. He wrapped his dick with shaking fingers as I slid my hands all over his naked hips and ass. His body jerked between my thighs as I pulled him close and squeezed his plump ass cheeks. I could feel his hot breath as he panted above me.

I steered him with my hands on his ass so that his crotch was in my face. "Before you sit on my lap, let me give you a taste of things to come," I murmured.

Before he could answer, I sucked his cock into my mouth. The curved shaft banged against the insides of my cheeks as he shoved forward and gasped. I licked it with my tongue and massaged it with my lips as he shook against me.

I had both hands on his ass by then and I slid them up into his crack. Johnny straddled me, opening up his butt crevice so that my fingers had free access. While I nuzzled around in his crotch with his hard shank in my mouth, I explored his virgin ass. My fingers slid over taut flesh that quivered delightfully until I found his puckered anus deep in the centre of that open crack.

"Oh, man—yeah, that's so awesome," Johnny panted above me.

I tickled his asshole with a pair of fingers as I sucked his cock in and out of my mouth with noisy slurps. He fucked my face and grasped my shoulders with both hands, pushing back into my fingers as he arched his back and wiggled back and forth. His tight little asshole quaked and pouted as I teased it with my fingertips, exposing his eagerness to get fucked. He didn't know which way to move as I slurped over his cock and fingered his butt rim.

I wrapped my lips around the cap of his cock and twirled my tongue over it as I used my fingers to stroke open the center of his twitching slot. He gasped as I began to slowly insert a fingertip beyond his tight ass lips.

"You gotta fuck me! I want it up the ass so bad," Johnny begged as my finger insinuated itself up into his quivering butt tunnel.

That asshole was damn tight. I worked my finger deeper and wiggled it while his ass shook and his hands gripped my shoulders. We needed lube to ease the way for my big bone.

"I got some grease in my shorts. I was hoping we would fuck tonight," Johnny grunted out.

He'd read my mind, or else he was just feeling that finger stretching his asshole and wondering how my cock was going to fit up there. I smiled around the cock in my mouth as I thought of him planning this night of sex. He'd probably been out there trimming hedges with his shirt off just to tease me. I jabbed my finger deep into him and then pulled it out. The lips of his hole gaped outward as my digit exited. I stroked the distended flesh teasingly, his body wracked with shudders.

I let his cock slide from my lips. "Let's lube your asshole," I said.

He was shaking all over as he bent down to search for his shorts. I ran my hands over his back and butt while he moved until he stood back up with a bottle of lubricant in hand. Groping around in the dim light, I took it from him and managed to flip open the cap by feel. I squirted out a stream of the stuff all over my fingers.

"This will do the trick. Spread your legs again."

He didn't utter a word as he straddled my lap. I reached up under his thighs and rubbed the gooey lube in his crack. My fingers slid around the smooth flesh as I searched out his asshole. Crouching over me with his legs spread, his ass button pouted outward as I rubbed lube all over it. Johnny let out a deep sigh, his butt cheeks trembling, as I teased that tender entrance. He grunted loudly when I worked a finger into the quivering hole and began to fuck his asshole with it.

"How's that feel? Are you OK? You like that finger up your tight butt?" I asked in a whisper.

Johnny squirmed around my finger, thrusting his rigid dick into my chest. He didn't answer at first, focussed on the strange feel of a finger digging around in his virgin butt chute. Then I felt that clamping hole yield, and I immediately shoved a second finger up it.

Johnny let out another loud grunt, followed by an obscene whisper in my ear. "Oh, yeah! Yeah! Fuck that tight asshole!"

I almost laughed at his nasty outburst, but I had a pair of fingers deep up his throbbing hole and that was no laughing matter. It was incredible. I held my fingers inside him while he bucked around in my lap and fucked himself over them. A few moments of that and his asshole was primed for cock.

I pulled his butt down on my lap and thrust my cock up into his crack. He felt my hard shaft against his naked skin and he leaned forward into my chest and began to hump it. I kept two fingers up his asshole while I aimed my cock head at the stuffed orifice. The gooey mess of jizz in the condom still wrapping my hard-on only intensified my excitement as it squished around inside and tickled my aching cock head.

We squirmed like that for a few minutes. He fucked himself over my fingers and stabbed his cock at my chest while drooling over my head. I felt his clamping asshole quiver around my fingers as he grew hotter and hotter. Finally I slid the fingers out, then immediately crammed the head of my cock into the lubed, swollen slot they left behind.

"Oh-my-fucking-gawd," he sighed out in four long syllables.

My cock slithered into him like a hot knife into butter. His asshole was plenty tight, but my fingers had warmed it up—and he was hungry for cock, starving for it. I had the head and a good few inches of shaft buried in one easy plunge. I felt his tight anus envelop my condom-wrapped bone, the squish of my own jizz added lubricant that had me panting.

Johnny took over for the next few minutes. With his hands on my shoulders, he slowly fucked himself down over my stiff shank. His butt cheeks quivered in my hands as he rode my cock up and down until he finally settled in my lap with his balls on my belly. He had the whole fucking thing up his ass.

"I'm stuffed with cock. I'm full of hard, hot cock," Johnny mewled in his Southern drawl.

I shivered to hear the little virgin talk like that. His first dick, and he was loving every stiff, steamy inch of it. I held his ass in my hands, amazed at the smoothness of those firm cheeks. I stroked them lovingly as I felt my cock throbbing deep inside his tight asshole. His sphincter pulsed around my dick as he held himself over it. He began to rise and fall again, little gasps and grunts punctuating every thrust of cock as it entered and then exited his aching butt hole.

I ran my hands over his body as he fucked himself on my cock. His slim build was accented by wide shoulders and the hard swell of muscle in his arms and back. His trembling sides narrowed to that very small waist and then curved out to his lush, sweat-soaked ass. His thighs were strong and hairless, draped over mine and tensed as he rode my pole with steadily increasing fervor.

I inhaled his sweaty stink, mixed with the heady scent of a wild rosebush that bloomed along the wall of the porch. Fireflies continued to flicker behind his back in the gloom of the yard, and twinkling stars blinked above his head. His tight asshole grew slacker, yielding to the cock stuffing it as he humped up and down, faster and faster.

I'd already come once, and I knew I could last a while at that point. I leaned back and reveled in the feel of his slender body over mine as he writhed in the act of getting butt-fucked for the first time in his life. His little gasps and whimpers were like sweet music among the constant buzz of night insects in the background. The heat of the evening settled down over us as we both broke out in a soaking sweat.

His naked ass and thighs slid over mine as he bounced up and down in my lap. His cock lurched against my stomach as he fucked me with it while fucking his own ass with my cock. It went on and on, until he was crying out and pounding up and down over my lap. I gripped his sweaty ass cheeks and pulled them wide open as I thrust up into his steamy hole in time to his bouncing rhythm.

"I'm gonna shoot my load," he moaned.

I felt the growing tension in his body. He was rubbing his cock head all over my stomach and eating up my come-surrounded cock with his squirming asshole. I clamped my mouth over his chest and sucked on a nipple right though the sweat-soaked material of his T-shirt. He cried out.

"I'm coming with a big cock up my ass!"

His asshole convulsed over my cock as he slammed down over it. His cock against my stomach jerked and I felt warm come filling the condom over it. He squirmed in my lap moaning as I held him close and whispered in his ear.

"Let it go. Blow your load. You ass is fucked good now."

He shook in my arms for a good five minutes. I held him while he settled, my cock still hard and buried up his quaking asshole. I hadn't come again yet, but I was satisfied. The night was still young.

Those roses will need trimming, I thought idly as I stroked his ass and waist. That would be a job for him later in the summer. Then I could fuck his sweet ass afterward.

That was a nice thought.

GAME DAY

Michael Bracken

We'd come south for the Baylor-UT game, a football game our team had no real hope of winning despite a new coach and the prayers of 14,000 students. Afterward, while University of Texas fans celebrated, we found solace by wrapping our lips around bottles of Budweiser and Dos Equis and Lone Star in the jam-packed bars along Sixth Street.

I'd ridden down with Jerry and Tom, but had lost track of them in one bar or another and before long realized that my green T-shirt emblazoned with the image of Sailor Bear marked me as Waldo in a sea of burnt orange. I finally ducked into a bar that seemed not to cater to the post-game college crowd, found the pay phone in a dimly lit rear hall between the restrooms, and emptied my pockets. I'd lost my cell phone and only a fistful of change remained from the $20 I'd had in my wallet that morning.

After pumping money into the phone, I realized that the handset, though resting comfortably in its cradle, did not actually connect to the rest of the unit. When the phone refused to return my change, I smashed the handset against it. Repeatedly.

"There a problem?"

I turned to face a muscular guy about 10 years my senior. He was handsome in a rough-hewn way, deeply tanned like he worked outside in the hot Texas sun, with thick black hair cut finger-length, and a dark shadow of facial hair. He wore a black T-shirt, tight-fitting jeans, and low-heeled cowboy boots. I felt my balls tighten at the sight of him and swallowed hard.

"No," I said. "No problem at all."

He looked me up and down and must have liked what he saw—a blond, blue-eyed college boy in a T-shirt, cargo khaki shorts, and Reef sandals.

"I'm Colin," he said. "You?"

"Taylor."

He stepped close and grabbed my stiffening cock through the thick material of my shorts. His whiskey-soaked breath felt warm against my ear when he asked, "You down here for the game?"

I knew Colin didn't mean football. The tighter he squeezed my cock, the less I thought about phoning Jerry and Tom. Even though I'd done the elephant walk with my frat brothers and the three of us had been intimate in various combinations ever since, sex with Jerry and Tom had never, ever made the temperature rise.

"Yeah," I whispered hoarsely. A bead of sweat trickled down my chest. "I'm game."

He pushed me backward, into the men's room, and snapped the lock behind us. I glanced around. The walls had been painted black, a sheet of stainless steel served as a mirror, and the single bulb above it didn't produce enough light to read the instructions on the condom machine.

The room was small, barely big enough for me to drop to my knees on the cold concrete floor. Colin unfastened his belt and unzipped his jeans, revealing his fully erect cock. I wrapped one hand around it, marveling at its girth, and then I took his spongy-soft cock head in my mouth and hooked my teeth behind the glans. I washed his cock head with my tongue, circling around and around. At the same time, I began pumping my fist up and down along Colin's cock shaft.

Colin grabbed the back of my head and pushed his cock deeper into my mouth. "You like that, college boy?"

I liked it, but with a mouth full of cock there wasn't much I could say. He drew back, and then pushed forward again. This time nearly three quarters of his cock disappeared into my mouth. The next time he drew back and pushed forward, I accepted the entire length of his shaft.

• • • • • • • • • •

He held the back of my head and fucked my face with a steady, deliberate rhythm. Soon, I heard his breath catch and felt his body stiffen, and then he came, firing a thick wad of hot spunk against the back of my throat.

I swallowed every drop, then stood while Colin shoved his flaccid cock back in his jeans.

"Not much privacy here," Colin said while I rinsed out my mouth. "We can go back to my place."

I'd lost track of my frat brothers, was out of cash, and had nowhere else to go. I said, "Sure."

I followed Colin out of the men's room and we threaded our way through the bar. Outside, the streets still crowded with post-game revelers, we made our way down the block to a Nissan Maxima parked at the curb.

Colin thumbed the keyless entry and I slipped into the passenger side of the car. The inside of Colin's car held a peculiar smell, like meat gone bad.

"Live far?" I asked as Colin slipped in beside me and keyed the ignition. As he eased the Maxima into the flow of traffic, I thumbed through a half-dozen Lyle Lovett and Willie Nelson CDs I'd found on the floorboard, selected one, and slipped it into the CD player.

"A couple of miles," Colin said. He rolled down the windows and fresh night air filled the car. After half a dozen turns, I realized we were headed toward the new airport. Before long, Colin pulled to a halt in the deserted parking lot of a brightly lit convenience store.

When Colin pressed a button, the Maxima's trunk popped open. He slipped out of the driver's seat, leaving the keys in the ignition and the engine running, and walked to the back of the car. He lifted the truck lid and then, a moment later, slammed the trunk closed and walked inside the convenience store.

He'd untucked his T-shirt from his jeans and the tail hung halfway down his tight ass.

I listened to Lyle Lovett and watched through the plate glass windows as Colin stalked the aisles of the convenience store, finally stepping up to the counter with a box of lubricated condoms, a package of raspberry Zingers, and two 20-ounce Dr Peppers. A dark-skinned, middle-aged man bagged Colin's selections, then Colin reached to the small of his back, lifted his T-shirt, and retrieved a revolver. He shoved it in the cashier's face and I watched the dark-skinned man pull money from the register and stuff it into the bag with the condoms, Zingers, and Dr Peppers.

Then Colin backed toward the door. Just as he pushed the door open with his ass, the cashier ducked behind the counter and popped back up with his own handgun. He squeezed off three shots, shattering the plate glass window next to Colin.

Colin returned fire as he ran to the car, not aiming particularly well. His first shot tore through the corn chip display. The second hit the cigarette rack above the cashier's head. It collapsed and dumped dozens of cigarette packs on his head.

And then Colin was in the car. He tossed the bag of loot into my lap, dropped the Maxima into reverse, and burned rubber going backward. He spun the wheel, shoved the car into drive, and then punched the accelerator. My head bounced against the headrest as we hit the street and soon the convenience store was nothing but a bright spot on the road behind us.

I looked over at Colin. "Are you nuts?"

He laughed, and I realized his cock was hard as steel inside his jeans. Hard as steel and I wanted it, wanted it bad. I licked my lips with the tip of my tongue, then remembered the Dr Peppers. I opened a soda and handed it to Colin, then opened one for myself and wrapped my lips around it.

Colin took us off the main road and we zigzagged through side streets until he finally slid the Maxima to a halt behind a nondescript apartment building in a complex of apartment buildings.

Upstairs in his place, Colin dumped his car keys and the bag of loot on his kitchen table. Condoms, greenbacks, and Zingers spilled out of the bag onto the yellow Formica. Still holding the revolver in one hand, Colin grabbed the Zingers, peeled open the cellophane, and broke a raspberry Zinger in half. He handed half to me, then stuffed the other half in his mouth.

As he chewed, Colin peeled off his black T-shirt, revealing well-defined abs and pecs. He'd shaved his chest, but not recently, and it was covered with prickly black hair. Then he sat on one of the kitchen chairs and pulled off his boots and his socks.

"Come on, pretty boy," he said. "You said you had game."

I pulled my green college T-shirt over my head and stood in the harsh glare of his kitchen light.

Colin poked the revolver's barrel into my belly. "A little soft," he said. "I like soft."

He stood, placed one hand on the small of my back, and urged me down the hall to the bedroom. As soon as I started moving, he grabbed the condoms and the other Zinger.

Colin finished the second Zinger while I undressed. Then he dropped his revolver on the nightstand and peeled off his jeans. He pulled me to him and covered my mouth with his. He thrust his tongue between my lips and I tasted garlic and whiskey and raspberry. By the end of the kiss, his cock stood thick and firm and pressed against my thigh. My own cock stood at attention, but he didn't seem to notice.

He peeled open the box of condoms and tossed a square of foil at me. "Put it on," he ordered.

I peeled it open and then eased it onto his thick cock, my fingers sliding on the lubricant. Then I turned and bent over, and he took me, took me hard and fast, his thick hands gripping my hips so tightly that he left 10 fingertip-sized bruises, his cock so thick I thought it would split me wide open.

While Colin fucked my ass, I grabbed my own cock. My fingers were slick with the lubricant from Colin's condom, and I pumped my fist in rhythm to Colin's hip thrusts. Nothing I had ever done with my frat brothers could compare to this and I wondered how I could even explain it to them. I wondered if I even wanted to.

Colin came, filling the condom with his hot spunk, then I came, firing my wad across Colin's bed. Colin held me until his cock stopped spasming, then he pulled free. When he saw what I'd done, he backhanded me and I fell on the bed, my own come sticking to my naked back.

He straddled my chest, pinning my arms with his knees. The sticky condom clung to his flaccid cock and the come-filled reservoir tip lay on my chest. Colin grabbed the revolver from the nightstand and he shoved the barrel into my mouth.

He thumbed back the hammer. "Suck this."

Wide-eyed, I stared up at him, afraid he'd pulled the trigger. And then I felt the condom unstick from my chest and from the corner of my eye I saw his cock rise to attention.

Too scared to resist, too horny to want to resist, I did what Colin instructed. I sucked on the barrel of the revolver, tasting metal and gunpowder, probing the opening with the tip of my tongue.

Colin finally pulled the revolver from my mouth, released the hammer, and tossed the gun onto the nightstand. We fucked three more times before Colin fell asleep, and I had the bruises to prove it. Then, I lay beside him in bed and stared up at the ceiling. I didn't move until he began to snore.

I slipped out of bed and pulled on my shorts and sandals. I took Colin's revolver from the nightstand, then retrieved the cash and his car keys from the kitchen table and my T-shirt from the floor where I'd dropped it.

After easing out of the apartment, I hurried downstairs to the Maxima. I had the engine fired up and had just dropped the car into gear when something smashed the diver's side window and sent safety glass cascading over me. I stomped on the accelerator and was half a block away before I looked in my mirror. Colin stood naked on the street cursing and waving a baseball bat.

I pulled into an empty parking lot a mile from his apartment. My hands were shaking. I hadn't planned on taking his money or his car when I'd met him in the bar, but I hadn't expected him to knock over a convenience store either.

I quickly counted the money: $327. Then I cracked open the revolver. Three shells were spent, but Colin had only fired two shots during the robbery. I didn't stop to think about it. Instead, I shoved everything in the glove box, shook safety glass out of my hair, and then drove until I found a familiar intersection. A few minutes later, I found Interstate 35 and eased onto the highway between NAFTA semis.

I shoved Willie Nelson into the CD player and cranked the music up loud. Wind through the open window chapped my lips and dried my eyes, but there was nothing I could do about it. I passed through north Austin and Round Rock without incident, the highway still overloaded with traffic. On the north side of Georgetown, the inside of the car filled with flashing red and blue light, and I eased the Maxima to the side of the road.

I sat perfectly still, my hands gripping the steering wheel at 10 and 2 o'clock as a Texas State Trooper approached. A big man with broad-shoulders tapering to a trim waist and a tight ass, he stopped beside my car and I found myself staring at the bulge in his crotch until he spoke.

"Must have been a disappointment," he said. His gaze took in the broken safety glass still stuck in the window frame and his nose wrinkled like he'd caught a whiff of an offending odor. He pushed up the brim of his cowboy hat with the tip of his index finger.

"How's that?"

He pointed at my T-shirt. "Baylor losing the way it did," he said. "Must have been a disappointment."

"Yeah," I said. I handed him my driver's license. "It was."

"Still, no reason to be speeding."

"No," I said. "I guess not."

He looked at the driver's license photo, then looked at me. "Insurance?"

"I don't have it," I said. "It's...it's not my car."

"Whose is it then?"

"My uncle's."

"What's his name?"

"Colin."

When I didn't offer any further information, the cop tapped my license on his thumb, then said, "I need to call this in."

I watched him in my rearview mirror. He returned to his vehicle, spoke into his radio, and waited. I looked away.

A moment later I heard his voice over the loudspeaker. "Step out of the car, please."

I hesitated. I sat behind the wheel of a stolen car driven earlier that night in a convenience store robbery—the gun used in that robbery and most of the money taken stuffed into the glove box—and considered my limited options. Finally, I pushed the door open and stepped to the roadside.

The state trooper held his sidearm in two hands. "Hands behind your head, fingers interlocked."

I followed orders, but asked, "What's the problem?"

"This car was reported stolen three days ago," the trooper said.

"That can't be," I insisted. "My uncle loaned it to me."

"Your uncle named Stella Johnson?"

I shook my head. "He said he just bought the car."

"Yeah," the trooper said. He reached up and grabbed one of my wrists. He pulled it down, twisted it behind my back, and snapped on handcuffs. Then he did the same with my other wrist, capturing my arms behind my back. He patted me down, found nothing, then said, "I'm going to take a look inside. You have any objections?"

I swallowed hard.

He took that as permission and began tearing apart the inside of the Maxima. He found a half-empty bottle of Jack Daniel's under the seat and the revolver and money in the glove box. Then he pulled the keys from the ignition and opened the trunk.

Both of us stared at a days-old body, a naked middle-aged man with a hole in his chest, and I knew then why the car smelled like rancid meat and why Colin's revolver held three spent shells.

The trooper turned to me. "You're in a whole heap of trouble, son."

My shoulders sagged. Like our football team had earlier that day, I'd played a game I had no real hope of winning. I may have scored a few times, but the odds just hadn't been in my favor. I would tell the trooper about Colin and the bar and the convenience store and the apartment, but somehow I knew Colin wasn't his name and he wouldn't be at the apartment when the police arrived.

I didn't resist when the trooper took my arm and escorted me to his vehicle.

COMING HOME TO FARM BOY

Jay Starre

It was two years since I'd last been to my uncle's farm up in northern Alberta, Canada. To my surprise, Dave was there to greet me across the barnyard fence. Formerly on the tubby side, the blond farm boy had the same sweet grin I recalled, but he'd slimmed down, and muscled up. One thing was certain, he'd maintained his natural charm. On top of that, he was cute as hell. In fact, he seemed to have no visible blemish, like one of the fine thoroughbred horses my uncle raised.

Under the brilliant summer sun he shook my hand, his grip friendly and firm.

"Jay! Great to see you. Can you come up and meet me for lunch? I'll be working behind the old pig barn in the upper pasture. Remember where that is?" His broad grin oozed innocence. At least that's what I thought at the time.

I agreed readily, then turned to meet my aging aunt and uncle as they came running down from the shaded porch. I glanced back to see Dave lumbering away, his cowboy hat askew and his jeans muddy from some farm chore. Most of his former chubbiness had shifted to one spot on his tall frame, and I stared at it with interest as he disappeared. My eyes zeroed in on a delectably plump butt that was hot, hot, hot!

Lunchtime found me hiking up the trail onto Dave's property. I'd donned my own cowboy hat, old and worn, which I hadn't deigned to bring to the city with me when I abandoned my uncle's farm two years earlier. I recalled with a grin how Dave and I had met behind this same broken-down barn for our first cigarette—and for our first blow jobs when we'd both just had our 18th birthdays. We were as randy as the goats his parents kept.

With a warm rush, I remembered the experiments we'd furtively performed behind that pig barn. We'd thought condoms were raunchy sex toys, and had used packs of them as we sucked each other off—sometimes several times a day that summer. Although we explored each other's taut young bodies with our hands, we never got around to fucking. I remembered though, how we'd stripped totally naked and sixty-nined in the grass. It had been a hot summer. My cock hardened at the thought of the grown-up Dave and how his body had changed since then. I was particularly thinking of the chunky butt I'd spotted earlier in the day as Dave wandered away from my uncle's yard.

I was pleasantly reminiscing and enjoying the quiet of the rural setting when I glanced at my watch and realized I was a good half hour late. I increased my pace up the last hill and was practically running when I rounded the corner of the remote pig barn.

I halted dead in my tracks. My mouth dropped wide open in total astonishment. I'd stumbled onto a raunchy, nasty sight I'm sure I won't ever forget.

By the broken-down fence, in the shade of a huge oak tree, sprawled my young pal Dave. Initially in my surprise, all I saw was a half-naked guy, my eyes focussing in on a bare white butt spread-eagled between two wooden fence rails. I blinked and gawked, openmouthed. Dave was on his back, his legs high in the air, his feet still in cowboy boots and hooked between the top two rails of that fence. He leaned back on a small grassy rise with his eyes closed. I stared, more of the nasty scene registering on my shocked mind. One of Dave's lean arms was down across his torso and between his thighs. His big cowboy paw was rooting around deep in his own pale-white ass crack. The middle finger of Dave's hand was shoved far up his asshole.

He was jerking off a humongous boner with his other hand.

I froze in consternation, but my explosive gasp of surprise alerted the farm boy. Dave's head shot up and his eyes opened. The pumping hand on his cock froze, and his sky-blue eyes met mine. He managed a startled grin, but his face flushed bright red.

"Shit! Caught in the act! I was waiting and waiting, and I got horny, and then I thought I'd just play with myself a little bit, and I was thinking you weren't going to show, " Dave blurted out in a rush.

My eyes dropped to his butt, too big and too bare to miss. The finger up his asshole was two knuckles deep. Tight ass lips clamped over the digit. I noticed with breathless clarity there was a coating of some kind of slick grease all over his hairless crack.

"Were you maybe hoping I'd see you like that? You look fucking hot!" I blurted out.

I stumbled closer as I spoke, incensed by the sight of that bare ass and stuffed hole.

He was dressed in a snug-fitting green T-shirt and rust-brown cowboy boots, but was otherwise buck-naked. My attention was fixated on his ass, as luscious as I'd imagined. What I could not have imagined was that one of his fingers would be crammed deep into his own asshole, both finger and hole glistening with grease.

More surprising, and exciting, that blunt finger began to slide in and out slowly, his hole stretching and puckering with each persistent thrust. Right before my eyes.

"We gotta use what we can out here on the farm, Jay! I got no big stud to work over my hot butt, so this here finger is about the best I could come up with. Got any other ideas?"

I glanced up and saw Dave was grinning, although his face was still beet-red. Then he licked his lips lewdly.

My innocent farm boy neighbor was a horny skank. By then I'd moved closer and was hovering right over him. My legs shook, my eyes riveted to the sight of that greased finger easing its way into the 20-year-old cowboy's hunky ass. Next to him was an open lunch pail and a container of butter without a lid. Obviously Dave had dipped into this for his raunchy finger-fuck. Dave was leaning back on the grassy slope and had both hands free to continue his butt-play, and jerk-off session. Brazenly, with a sweet smile plastered over his pink-flushed face, he began to pump his huge cock again while I watched from above. Both arms were lean and tense across his firm torso. Then, to really shock the hell out of me I supposed, the cheeks of his chunky ass began to writhe up and down, vulgarly humping the finger planted up his own butt hole.

I decided not to waste another moment and began to peel off my own tight jeans with trembling hands. "Goddamn, you look so fucking nasty," I mumbled.

My eyes never strayed from the sight of that hot ass getting fingered as I tore off my boots and jeans. Somehow I managed to put my boots back on without toppling over in my fumbling excitement. I was naked. My stiff rod waved in the breeze above Dave, the eager fuck tool as unashamed as the farm boy's rigid prick.

"You sure got yourself one big whanger now, Jay. I remember sucking on it right here in this very spot a couple years ago. I thought I'd never get enough of it then, and when you shoved mine in your mouth and slurped down, I used to wish we could be together forever. Anyways, you're here now. Do something with that hard dick," Dave chattered on in a breathless ramble.

His languid country drawl was irresistible, and so sexy. I dropped to my knees like a stone in front of him—practically attacking his ass. I reached out with both hands, grabbing handfuls of smooth, chunky butt flesh. The writhing globes were hot and sweaty, and slick with butter. I barked out a semihysterical laugh, as I thought about his ass being all buttered up. Hot buttered buns!

I crouched on my knees in front of him, his muscular legs splayed to either side of me and his large white butt inches from my own waist. My fuck tool twitched lustily, and it was all I could do to resist plowing into him that very second. I noticed his cock was covered in a condom, and there was a package of them beside Dave on the grass. He still loved condoms.

"Put on a wrapper. Then fuck my ass! I want you, buddy. I want your big pecker up my butt hole," Dave urged.

I glanced up into his eyes. They were so intense, I realized how much he wanted it. And so did I. I wondered how long it had been since he'd had any sex, hidden up here in the northern Alberta boondocks. He looked like he was dying for it.

I released his ass, although I was reluctant to let go of those slick mounds of heat, and reached over him between the rails of the fence. My cock nestled up into his ass crack as I groped for the condoms. I shuddered at the touch of my stiff pole against his satin-hot flesh.

I squatted back on my heels and rolled a condom over my purple rod. The big thing jerked eagerly. I returned to the object of my desire. I stuck out my hand and zeroed in on that fluttering, greased hole. Dave's finger was still busy there, but he obligingly pulled it out as my hands slid into his crack. The hole was suddenly empty, a quivering knot of circular flesh that looked like it was begging for something to fill it. Two of my fingers slid along the opening, working around the hole and pressing against the pouting lips.

"Oh, yeah, Jay! I been imagining you coming home to me like this. I been imagining you finding me with my ass in the air. And then, you play with my butt hole—oh, holy fucking yeah!" Dave groaned, his head flung back and his face flushed with renewed excitement.

I smiled broadly, beginning to relax for the first time. He wanted to get fucked, and I would oblige him happily. But I'd take my time. I sat back on my heels, feeling the hard leather of my boots against my own naked butt cheeks. I took in the awesome picture of my cowboy buddy sprawled on the ground, his boots hooked in the top rails of the wooden fence, his milky white ass cheeks spread far apart, coated with butter and that puckered hole drooling the stuff. One of his hands cupped his own greased ass cheek, the other pumped his fat boner. His cowboy hat half-covered his flushed face as he tossed his head back and forth on the ground. His entire body was stiff with tension as my fingers stroked along his ass crack and over his twittering hole.

The silky feel of his buttered crack was awesome. I wanted to tease and tickle and toy with it forever. With one hand I fingered the outside of his hole, while my other hand stroked and kneaded his chunky butt cheeks, prodding the smooth muscles and causing him to buck and jerk. I had two fingers poised directly on the entrance to his snug butt hole opening, and all that moving around served to force them past the clamping sphincter. My fingers slid into his greasy hole.

Dave let out a deep moan, and I matched it with a satisfied sigh as his asshole spasmed around my buried fingers. I held them inside him and looked up into his face. He was staring back at me with a hungry expression on his face while he pumped his cock. The hard shank was almost at eye level, and it was big.

Now that I was inside him, I went to work fingering the steamy depths of his bung hole. I dug into him, twisting and jabbing at every sensitive spot I could find. I forced my way up past my knuckles and frigged in and out rapidly. Dave hissed and gasped, pressing that awesome ass against my knees and fingers. The hole was hot as magma, and the inner flesh was pliant and pulsing. I was nuts over that slot. I started rubbing my boner with my other hand.

"Oh, God! Finger me! Yeah! Remember what it was like when we used to play around, eh? Our cocks hard and our mouths wrapped around each other's meat. Agh! Yeah, deeper—I want it!" he blurted between hissing moans.

His legs remained hooked between the upper rails and his lower body rested on the grass behind him, but he writhed and twisted constantly, humping up and down and squirming against my hand like some barnyard animal in rut.

I took my other hand off my twitching poker and reached up to stick two fingers in his open mouth, which he instantly sucked into that hot cauldron. I continued finger-fucking his ass and watched as he sucked on my hand, his tongue lolling outside his parted lips and licking on my knuckles with total abandon. Even with fingers up his slippery butt and filling his drooling mouth, the magnificence of his body was undeniable. He was like some perfect farm specimen, his body taut and beautiful. And his actions were as uninhibited as an animal's would be. The imagery got me even hotter.

I was possessed, otherwise I don't think I'd have thought to do it. I wasn't a kink freak, but the nasty combination of Dave's total lack of inhibition, his position on the ground with his boots in the air hooked between those fence rails, the feel of that pulsing anal slot slurping away at my fingers, and his big plump lips drooling over my other hand—it was just too fucking much for me.

I pulled my hands out of his wet orifices, to his groaning whine. "What are you gonna do now, buddy? Fuck me hard up the ass with that juicy pecker of yours, eh?"

I snatched at one of his boots, yanking it off his large farm boy foot. The shiny tooled leather felt warm and heavy in my hands. He gawked at me, his ass still writhing around, his asshole dripping butter and snapping hungrily. "What's going on?" Dave whimpered.

I grinned nastily. "You want to get fucked so bad, eh? How about I fuck you with your own cowboy boot?"

His blue eyes went wide, his face flushed and his tongue came out to lick at his moist lips. I crammed that boot in his crack, rubbing the leather up and down it, mashing it against his dangling ball sac to his grunted squeals. I pressed the leather against his cock, rubbing it into the butter he'd spread all over his crotch. I shoved the toe against his asshole and dug into it. I was crazed.

I was laughing, he was moaning and bucking, fucking against his own boot as I used the whole length of it to mash and thrust against his wide-spread, vulnerable ass and crotch. The sight of that big boot in my hands, rubbing all over his naked ass was so hot I almost shot my load right then. With wildly shaking hands, I prodded his swollen asshole with the toe of his boot, pressing and rubbing and digging. Dave grunted and squirmed, his hands coming down to help me, grasping his own boot and pressing the toe into his spread ass crack. God, that was hot!

I decided it was time to fuck him. His asshole was pink and

swollen, already teased by his finger, my fingers, and the toe of his own cowboy boot. It gaped apart, greasy and excited.

I laughed again, still possessed by that bestial devil he'd called up in me. "Lick your own boot while I fuck your ass," I ordered with a nasty smirk

I shoved the boot in his face, and he snatched it from me, immediately snaking out his tongue to lick and tongue it with big wet smacks. His blue eyes bored into mine. I grinned and placed the head of my pulsing meat at the slippery opening to his hole. While he slurped over his own cowboy boot, I slowly inserted the flared crown of my cock into his ass.

The lips of his slot gaped and then clamped in little spasms as my cock head slipped past them. The torrid heat of his ass enveloped my pecker as I forced it deeper and deeper, farther than either of my fingers had yet delved. Dave twisted and moaned against me, his butt muscles contracting and shivering as my pole pierced him to the farthest depths

His swollen cock bounced against his flat belly and I reached for it. Pole-stiff under my fingers, it jerked constantly as I started prodding his guts with my fuck tool. As I jabbed mercilessly, driving hard into him, his pecker leaped and his dangling balls began to churn and swell. He didn't speak; instead he smacked and slurped over his own greased boot while staring up at me from under the rim of his hat. That was nasty! Even though he didn't speak, he did grunt, just like one of the fat pigs in his barn, and that was even nastier.

I began a rhythm, pounding into him and withdrawing, while squeezing and pulling on his cock. His big meat only grew more rigid and flushed and more purple. His thighs and arms had been as creamy white as his ass and belly, but by then were glowing pink with raunchy heat. Dave's body was practically hairless, and he looked a little like a giant, innocent kid—except for that undeniable vision of him sucking on his own cowboy boot, while humping over my horse cock with gleeful lust, and barking out those pig grunts.

With my free hand I yanked up his T-shirt, exposing a muscular chest, as hairless as his stomach and thighs. I'd revealed two pert nipples just begging to be played with. When I did, pinching those nibs between thumb and forefinger, he shouted out and rammed back against my pounding cock with even more enthusiasm than before.

Sweat was running down my own chest beneath my shirt, while my breath was coming in labored pants. I didn't know how long I could hold out and attempted to slow my thrusts so I could enjoy the ride a little longer. But my farm-boy pal would have none of that and rammed his lush butt up over my slippery cock. He fucked himself so furiously, I had a hard time holding onto his cock as I yanked on it. I kept on pinching his swollen nipples though, realizing the act was cranking up his nasty heat to another unbelievable level.

I leaned back and allowed him to do the work, attempting to catch my breath while he rode my cock. The cowboy skank ran his big tongue all over his own boot, smacking his lips and gazing up at me with a decidedly uninnocent look. His ass was spread wide, his feet still hooked between those top rails, immobilizing him as he banged his butt against my crotch and fucked my pecker with wild ferocity. I couldn't hold out against that. Staring down at his pretty lips working over that boot like it was a hot cock, and feeling the intensity of his steamy butt hole working over my tool, I had to blow my load.

Jism drove right up through my nuts and cock. It spurted into the condom in a hot stream deep inside Dave's farm-boy bowels. While I shot, he rode me with his big bare butt like I was his favorite horse.

I screamed out my ecstasy and collapsed against the fence rails between us. Jism streamed out of my cock. I panted wordlessly as I gazed down at Dave's sex-flushed countenance. He dropped his boot to the grass and laughed gleefully.

"I remember you always blew your load first! Are you gonna suck me off or what, eh?" he suggested with a crude grin.

His cute bowed lips were wet with spit. He grinned up at me. I breathed in deeply and leaned back to pull out of his quivering asshole. I grinned back, just before swooping down to suck up his stiff bone.

"Yeah!" he whooped, thrusting up into my mouth.

While I slurped loudly, sucking his cock to the balls, I slid my hand down into his crack, still wide open and wiggling all over the place. I found the distended hole, slick with butter and swollen open. My cock had just been up there. I slowly inserted two fingers back up the pulsing slot. Dave shouted and squirmed beneath me.

My blond sex-slut buddy yelled gleefully while riding my fingers. I sucked up and down his glistening tube. Dave moaned and thrust upward with his belly, sensations from his butt hole now vying with the wet feel of my mouth over his cock. I could feel the sudden tension in his asshole, and the swelling thickness of his cock. He was about to shoot.

Both of his hands grasped the rail beside his legs, biceps straining as he threw back his head and jerked upward. I pulled my mouth off his cock and ripped the condom away. Come spurted high into the air, rocketing onto my T-shirt and his. It was a sight never to be forgotten, his quivering, muscular body spraying load after load of white creamy come all over.

I couldn't help myself and began to laugh so hard I thought I would bust a gut. He joined me and we both laughed, totally out of control. Finally he extricated himself from the wooden fence and we sprawled out on the hillside in the grass together. We actually fell asleep that way.

A month later back at home in my apartment high over the bustling downtown district, I opened a letter from Dave. In his plain printing, he said hello, and invited me up for Thanksgiving to spend the holidays with him. I grinned when I read the last line.

"I'll meet you up behind the pig barn. I've got my boots all clean and polished. Ready for action. How about you?"

Oh, yes, I'd polished my own cowboy boots and left them out by the door ever since I'd returned from the farm and my nasty rendezvous with Dave. Every time I looked at them I sprung wood. I couldn't wait to put them to use again.

BARNHAM

Andrew Ryder

The note was terse. "Be at Barnham station at 2.30 P.M. this Saturday." A couple of weeks before, Keith had asked me if I would be interested in going to a friend's house. He was deliberately mysterious, telling me no more than that the man was into beating and bondage, and making it clear that I would be in for a heavy session. I was nervous, but excited. "Will I need to wear anything special?" I asked. I was thinking of boots, or jockstraps, or any prohibitions on what I could wear. John, who I see regularly, and through whom I met Keith, usually tells me how to dress. I wanted to make sure I got things right on my first visit, but Keith said that clothes wouldn't be important. Still, I decided to wear a pair of heavy, calf-high lace-up boots, jeans, and a leather jacket: not too scene, but not too vanilla either.

It was raining hard, and the day was raw and grey. The train was unheated, the windows jammed open. When I got to the station, Keith was waiting on the platform, and hustled me down the stairs to the back seat of a waiting car. At least the car was warm, and I began to thaw out a bit. "This is Dick," he said, introducing me to the man in the driver's seat, and in a few minutes we pulled up in front of a biggish house surrounded by lawn and trees. When we got inside, I was ordered to go upstairs to the room to the left of the top of the stairs, strip, put my boots back on, and wait facing the wall while Keith and Dick stayed downstairs to plot out the afternoon session. The room didn't tell me much about the owner. It was sparsely furnished, with a kind of wooden trunk or case in one corner, and a bedspring on a spare metal frame, with no mattress along one wall. I admit that I was nervous, but I stripped off and stood in a corner, my hands clasped behind my neck.

Dick was a big man, about six feet tall, and heavyset. He had short, fair-colored hair and a short, full beard. Hustled into the house and up the stairs, I had not really got a good look at him, but figured I would have another chance when the session started.

No such luck. After a while, I heard their footsteps on the stairs and they entered the room. One grabbed my arms, and the next thing I knew a leather hood had been pulled over my head and fastened in place. There were no eyes, and I could see nothing, although some light came through the hole for the nose. Although there was a zipper over the mouth, they zipped it up after the hood was in place, and when I breathed in I could feel the hood get sucked around my face, clinging tightly almost like rubber. I tensed up, but they fastened some leather cuffs around my wrists, and in no time at all I was helpless.

They were experienced at what they were doing, and knew enough to keep shifting my focus of attention to keep me mildly off balance. One of them pinched my tits, and the other squeezed my balls, increasing both my nervousness and excitement. Suddenly, someone greased my asshole, and without warning, a plug was jammed up the hole, right to the hilt. There was no foreplay or gentle teasing, and I had no chance to relax or adjust. To my embarrassment, I screamed at the top of my lungs. It was not like this was the first time I had been fucked or had something shoved up my ass, but it was painful as hell, and it took a while for my sphincter to adjust and relax. Keith took me in his arms and held me tight, whispering reassurances in my ear, which was comforting, if not a little humiliating. The problem is, I enjoyed the pain, and wondered if my scream had given the wrong message.

My memory of how the scene developed is a bit confused. They put restraints on my ankles and locked them together, making me stand in the center of the room. I know that they started by beating me with whips, belts, and straps to get a measure of my capacity, I suppose. I had spent the night at Keith's a week or so before, and he had given me some sharp blows with a crop on my ass, and the red stripes were still there. He noticed that as they were restraining me and remarked that he had not realized he hit me so hard. At some point, they manhandled me over to what felt like a bench, and told me to lean forward. When I did, there was just air, and I realized that it was some kind of sawhorse. They made me raise myself up onto the central bar, which was a bit difficult because my hands were cuffed behind my back, and then they fastened my feet to opposite corners of the horse. My hands were released and pulled over my head and down, and fastened to the bottoms of the legs on the other side. The two men were very quiet, but Dick said to Keith in a low voice, "Hold him," and I suspected that whatever was coming it was going to be heavy.

They were generous and did not keep me in suspense for long, but told me that I was going to be caned. This was my first time. I had read about it, and heard that it was painful, but had no idea what it would feel like. I guess I thought it would be like getting beaten with a riding crop, since they look similar. I was to get six on each cheek. The first one stung badly, and despite myself, I flinched and tried to move away—too late, of course, since the blow had already fallen. They ordered me to count aloud, and I shouted, "One, sir." It was unexpectedly painful, but also very exciting. They took it slow and easy, giving me a brief interval between each stroke—just long enough for the pain to subside a bit before administering the next one. Counting made it easier, I guess, since I was repeating to myself inside my head, *Just three left; just two left; just one left.* After they finished the first cheek, they switched to the other side, and I started counting again at one. As the caning went on I became more and more restive, and I guess Keith found it increasingly difficult to hold me in place. At any rate, they finally stopped one stroke short of 12. Once the beating had ended, the memory of the pain became intensely pleasurable, and no sooner had the sting of the cane eased, than I wanted more! For some reason, even though I had fought to move away to avoid the blows, or to ease the sting, and even though I had found each one intensely painful, after they let me up from the sawhorse and let me get my composure back, I commented that they still owed me one more stroke. Dick laughed, and said something like, "Wait and see."

I was still hooded, but my arms and legs were free, though not for long. Keith owns a leather straightjacket and has put me in it several times before working me over. I have never actually seen it, since each time I have been blindfolded or hooded, but it feels incredibly sexy against my skin. I know that it has two flaps so that the tits can be exposed, and it has straps that go around between the legs to make sure it is nice and tight. In no time at all, the two men had strapped me into the jacket, and although I did not think of it at the time, I suspect they had gone through this routine before. They led me out of the room we were in, and to another room on the same floor, and ordered me to lie down on the floor. The next thing I knew, my legs, still wearing manacles, had been fastened together and attached to something, which began to pull them up. As they attached me to whatever they were using, the two men commented on the boots I was wearing, saying that they were ideal for the job, whatever it was going to be. At least I had done something right!

It took me a while to realize what was going on. Whatever they had fastened me to, they were pulling it up into the air, and my feet were slowly being raised. I wasn't sure how far this would go— Lying on my back, it seemed at first like they might be raising my legs to expose my ass, but soon I was not just lying on my back, but on my shoulders and the position was pretty uncomfortable. One of them steadied me, and I continued to rise. At one point, I was resting on my head and neck, and got a bit nervous, but they soon passed that point, and shortly I was hanging free, unable to touch the ground, swinging back and forth by my ankles. I was terrified—I was hooded, straightjacketed, and completely helpless. I remembered that the hood had a zipper over the mouth, since they had zipped it up after they had first put it on, and I asked gingerly if they could open the zipper. Somehow, even though I could not see, that made it easier to cope, since I had become completely upside down, it felt as if all my snot was running into my sinuses, keeping me from breathing. Of course, that was not the case. I was just shit scared and had tensed up. I think I said something to the effect that I was frightened, and Keith was dismissive, saying that we (meaning he and I) had done something similar before. What Keith said was true—kind of—but I had never been suspended by my feet. I felt like I was on some kind of adventure course, or learning something in physical education, and had just been put in my place by a strict teacher.

Someone reached down and placed clamps on my tits, and then they proceeded to work my ass over. I do not know what they used, but there were several sets of six on each cheek. I guess they must have used a belt, a strap, and some kind of whip, but I was not too sure. The beating reawakened the sting of the cane, which, to be honest, was no bad thing. I was completely helpless, flopping around like a fish on a line, circling around as they beat me, each blow on my ass shifting my center of gravity, and making me move around a little more. I was terrified but also really turned on. My mind kind of goes into a kind of hibernation at times like this, and stores thoughts and sensations for me to regurgitate and think over later. Deep inside, a part of me knew I would be thinking about this for days, and knew my cock would get hard each time I did.

When they were done beating me, they let me down and led me into what turned out to be a bedroom—at least, they made me lie down on a bed and then attached my feet to opposite corners at the bottom. I was still hooded, and wearing the straightjacket and my boots. They left me lying there for a little while, perhaps to catch my breath, but more likely to allow them to catch theirs. I remember lying there, still hooded and straight-jacketed, panting slightly, my head to one side, feeling completely helpless and vulnerable, but rubbing my cock against the bed.

This time, they gave me a kind of taster's menu of different beating implements: a tawse, a belt, a whip, a cat, a strap, a paddle, and so on. They told me the name of each one as they went along, giving me six of each one on each side, and making me count. It was stimulatingly painful—yes, it stung—but for me this was the first time I had been beaten in this way, and there was something exciting about the way they would name the instrument they were about to use, and make me count the strokes and thank them. Moreover, after the cane, I was on my guard, since it was always possible that they could cane me again. Some I liked more than others, but did not tell them that, and some I liked less. I particularly remember the paddle, which was less painful for some reason, but made an incredible noise with each stroke. I know I tried to evade the blows, and Keith found that amusing, since I was so obviously helpless, and I was going to get beaten no matter what I did.

After the beating the men led me into anther room—the first room I was in, as it turned out, and the hood was removed. I was pushed to my knees and made to suck off Keith, who first put a condom on his cock and then fucked my face while standing up, driving his cock deep down my throat, and making me gag on it before pulling it out for another thrust. His crotch had a clean soapy smell, with a musky overlay. The condom had a slightly sticky feeling and a plastic taste, and the little nipple on the tip kept tickling the back of my throat, making me want to cough. Then Keith removed the straightjacket and told me to go into the bathroom and remove the plug from my ass, get dressed, and meet them downstairs. I welcomed the chance to have a few minutes to myself to recover my composure. I had to pee, and since I was a little uncoordinated I slightly overshot the toilet when the piss first came out, but figured Dick would not notice.

When the scene was over, I was kind of glazed. I was shaky on my feet, and uncharacteristically quiet. Strangely, I regretted that the session was over, although a short while earlier I had been silently praying for it to end. I would not say I was intimidated, but I was certainly cautious and was well aware of my place in the pecking order. When I joined them, we ate dinner, which I had smelled cooking in the oven earlier. Although Keith and Dick talked a blue streak, I concentrated on my plate. There was some kind of steak casserole and Keith had brought a rich red Portuguese wine, which he kept going on about. Afterward, Dick drove us back to the station, but before we left, I was ordered into a small room where the sawhorse was set up, and told to bend over to receive another caning—my reward for having claimed earlier that Dick owed me another stroke.

When we left the house, I was stunned. I have been tied up a lot, and knew I was into bondage—heavily into bondage, and even into pain—tit torture, and some ball torture, but I had never had a beating like this. It was the first time I had been caned. Did I like it? I could not say at first. I thought about it on the train trip home. My ass stung, and every time I moved on the seat I could feel the effects of the beating. I felt naked and exposed, as if everyone could see where I had been and what I had just gone through, although the train was practically empty. But, at the same time, I was extremely aware of my semihard cock between my legs, and kept adjusting my position on the seat to allow my cock to expand and get hard. My ass was sore, and sitting down was actually painful for several days. I was black and blue for almost a week. But, after a few days, I was hungry for more. Moreover, I got off on seeing the bruises, and on feeling the lingering sting from whip and cane when I sat down. What can I say? I knew I would go back. It was too good to give up!

THE TORSOS OF ANGELS

Shane Allison

What are you into? Melvin asked, written in blue ink on a sliver of tissue paper as Eli read the two-ply note sitting on his ashy, hairy right thigh. He took a ballpoint pen out of the pocket of his Jansport backpack and started to write. The tip of the pen was too heavy and ate into the tissue.

I like to fuck and get sucked, wrote Eli. *What about you?*

With his pants cinched around his argyled ankles, Eli lazily slid the answer to Melvin's question back beneath his tan partition. Both of their stalls were coated with ink-penned messages: I HAVE A BIG LATINO COCK; IF YOU WANT TO SUCK IT, LEAVE A MESSAGE. FOR A REALLY GOOD TIME, LICK THE URINAL as well as numerous names, e-mail addresses and phone numbers sprawled across the ceramic-tiled walls in a rainbow of blue, black, and green ink. Eli unfurled the ink-drenched paper to read Melvin's response. *Cool man, 'cause I like to get my dick sucked. You wanna suck me?* Melvin wrote.

Eli read his message, crumpled it up, and threw the note between his thighs into the piss-yellow water of his commode. He traced the jagged circle of the glory hole with his finger signaling him to stick his cock through it.

Eli looked through watching Melvin beat his meat. Melvin stood up off his toilet and worked his plump inches of uncut dark meat through the glory hole.

Eli's tongue twirled around the head of Melvin's cock exuding precome. He moved his tender sheath back and up exposing the wet, pink head. Eli caressed the tip of Melvin's dick with his thumb as he reached between his own legs and turned his attentions to his own cock.

"Suck it," Melvin whispered with his stomach pressed against the fiberglass wall of the stall. Eli flicked his tongue across his sensitive inches. Melvin tightly gripped the top edge of the stall as he got wind of Eli's spit-slicked mouth.

"Suck my cock, man," demanded Melvin.

Spit trickled beneath the blood-induced shaft into musty, black crotch hair.

"You like to suck dick, don'tcha? Melvin asked. "You like black dick in ya mouth, man?"

Melvin's dick expanded hard and thick in Eli's pie hole.

"Uh-huh!" Eli moaned, as his lips smacked against delicate dick meat.

As Eli and Melvin were basking in their moment of *mouth on meat* action, they suddenly heard the door of the men's room open. Melvin retracted his cock out of the glory hole and sat startled back on his commode. It was too late. The 20-something twink knew what they were up to. He unzipped his shorts at the urinal unfurling his boner from its cotton white tomb. He jiggled it a little before a stream of urine skirted from it.

Eli caressed the head of his dick to keep it from losing its erection.

He looked down to discover that Melvin was trying to hand him another tissue paper note wrapped around the body of the pen. Eli took the note and read it: *That guy next to you, what's he doin'?* asked Melvin.

Eli spied through the homemade glory hole in his stall. He wrote back to Melvin and slid the paper and pen back beneath his partition.

He's beatin' off, wrote Eli. The twink walked over to Eli's stall with his fat dick hanging out of the zipper of his shorts. Eli could see him through the slit of his door and started to jack off. He leaned back against the pipes of his toilet and spread his cocoa-brown thighs to give the twink a show.

Eli yanked his dark chocolate fuck stick as the twink watched him in dick-famished anticipation.

The boy pulled his shorts from his legs grown with silken, black waves of hair and pulled his T-shirt up past his six-pack. The shirt grazed against the sensitivity of his pink, perky teats. He observed Melvin in his stall fidgeting with his balls. He sat his bare, butterscotch booty on the rim of the sink continuing to beat his flaccid cock.

"Somebody might walk in," Eli mouthed.

The twink peeled off his flannel skivvies and shorts from around his ankles. The twink stood naked in the doorway of Eli's stall. He wrapped his hand around the twink's cock and squeezed. The boy followed suit and cupped Eli's prick in his palm. Their hands entwined in mutual masturbation.

Melvin opened the door and stood stark naked in the entrance of his stall beating his boner. The twink ran his hand up Melvin's supple torso as Eli continued to massage the twink's dick.

"Wanna suck me?" Melvin whispered to the twink.

He slid down until Melvin's dick came to his lips and ran the head across them.

Eli reached behind the twink and sluggishly slid his index finger in the twink's ripe, pink boy pussy.

The twink could smell the glorious aroma of musk from Melvin's thicket of pubic fur.

I love the smell of sweaty pubes, the twink thought to himself. He worked his dick like a Mister Softee cream sickle, consistently licking and sucking, giving special attention to the dick cheese around his delicate cock head.

"You like that?" Eli asked the boy, as he continued exploring the core of his booty.

"You like this black dick in ya mouth?" The twink loosened his mouth from Melvin's meat for a second to answer. "Fuck, yeah!" he whispered hungrily.

Eli slid his hand beneath the twink's legs and squeezed the boy's high, tight balls as he kept at Melvin's engorged cock deep-throating his impressive inches.

"Kiss me," murmured the twink.

Eli bent the twink's head back forcefully and pressed his smacker hard against the boy's thin pink lips. Tongues reached behind teeth as they French-kissed.

Traces of foamy spit formed at the corners of the twink's mouth.

"I want you to come on me!" the twink said as he whacked his own dick.

"I'm gonna come," Melvin whispered. "I'm 'bout to come." Melvin took his dick and jacked off. "Come for me, man!" the twink demanded. "Come for me!"

"Ahh, I'm comin'!" Melvin yelled out softly. Thick spurts of cock porridge suddenly spewed forth on the boy's right thigh.

Eli slid his finger out of the twink's tawdry tush.

He sat his bare ass on the freezing tile floor beneath the cocks of Melvin and Eli.

Eli stood over the boy pumping his cock steady over his chest as the twink jacked himself off. Melvin fondled Eli's nuts as he watched him choke his cock over the twink.

"I'm comin'!" Eli bellowed. "I'm fuckin' comin'!"

Eli wanted to drop his load with Melvin on the boy, but Melvin had already drained his cock on the twink's face.

Melvin groped Eli's balls harder, squeezing them firmly.

"Let me see you shoot that juice," said Melvin. "Come on me," the twink pleaded, as he beat off on the cold, tile floor. "I'm comin', I'm comin'," Eli shouted.

Suddenly a hot, syrupy load of semen squirted from Eli's dick landing between the twink's gelled spikes of hair. The twink sat watching Eli deface his sweaty body. Eli walked back into his stall, unrolled a handful of tissue paper from the Kimberly-Clark dispenser, and wiped the remaining drops of semen from his cock head.

Melvin got dressed, grabbed his things, and walked over to the sink to wash his hands. The boy sat steady bopping his bologna.

"I want to see you fuckin' come," Melvin whispered. "Let me see you shoot it, man."

Eli looked at them both, said thanks, and left.

"I'm gonna fuckin' come!" hollered the twink.

Melvin crouched down taking the twink's warm, throbbing cock into his hand and jerked him off. Sticky webs of spunk shot across the floor between the stained grout of the square tiles, oozing between the grooves of Melvin's fingers. Melvin picked up his Jansport backpack and headed toward the door, leaving the boy in an orgasm aftermath of creamy jism.

BITCHIN' BRIEFS

Mark Wildyr

I blame it all on his shorts...whomever the hell *his* is! Everything came unraveled the day I found a pair of silk, leopard skin-patterned men's briefs atop a pile of our folded laundry. I wear plain white cotton jockeys. Now, I have a functioning brain and realize my marriage wasn't so great before that dire discovery, but strange briefs among our washing didn't help it along any.

Sharon and I married right out of college before either of us knew who the hell we were. We both had careers. She was a nurse; I was a construction foreman. No one could convince us we weren't madly in love...and we probably were...but we'd passed through that exalted state at least two years ago. Not a bad record among my generation; four years of bliss followed by two years of indifference, drifting toward hostility. We were an economic unit, not a marriage, by the time the leopard skin appeared in our lives. I had come in late after a hard day at work and was holding the gaudy thing in my hand, staring at it curiously when she came out of the kitchen and stopped in her tracks.

"Care to explain this?" I asked coldly, prepared to disbelieve whatever outlandish story she came up with. I knew she was unhappy, but I never dreamed she would be unfaithful. I sure as shit hadn't been, even though it took a lot of effort to stay on the straight and narrow. Our sex life was definitely lacking something...a scrap of fake leopard skin, apparently.

Her neutral look frosted into something more hostile. My wife's full lower lip, once her sexiest trait, shot out in exasperation. "Do I need to?"

I gave her my phoniest smile. "If you found a pair of women's panties in the car, wouldn't you expect an explanation?"

She turned nasty right away, at least five or six caustic remarks ahead of schedule. "Not especially. I'd probably figure they were yours!"

Low blow. Dirty fighting. Lack of interest didn't automatically mean lack of ability, even though I'd failed to satisfy her the last three times we'd been intimate. Besides, she struck a nerve. I'd done more masturbating this past year than performing my husbandly duties.

"Funny!" I sneered, trying to deflect the blow. I held out the briefs. "Does this mean you've gone butch and are wearing men's underwear now?"

"Might make a functioning sexual unit if I had," she retorted, looking down the long nose I used to think so cute. "After all, it takes two to tango. For your information, *darling,* I bumped into this man at the Laundromat and we spilled our loads—"

"Define 'loads' for me, will you, *sweetheart*?"

"Cute, coming from the man who has trouble delivering one. Do you want an explanation or not?" she hissed, stamping her foot and spraying brown locks like she was still a kid in the neighborhood. I was reminded of Margaret in the cartoon *Dennis the Menace* although Sharon was much prettier...even while playing the bitch.

"I think I've got it. You're going to claim his stuff got mixed up with yours. Right? Oh, by the way, define 'stuff' too, will you?"

"You argue like a woman, did you know that?" She arched an elegant eyebrow at me. "But my explanation happens to be the truth. Anyway, it's the only enlightenment you're going to get. And by the way, if you fixed the damned washing machine, like the *man* of the house is supposed to, I wouldn't have to go out to clean our clothes. From now on, you do it!"

"Fuck that noise! I don't have time—"

"And I *do*?" she demanded, spinning on her heels and stomping away, leaving a pair of men's silk underwear decorated with faux feral cat roundels dangling from my fingers.

A week later I ran out of clean clothes. I also ran out of marriage. We were still an economic unit sharing expenses, but that was all. The rest of the sham had fallen away, finally exposed for what it was. Sharon didn't speak to me any more than absolutely necessary, and I held my tongue around her. She fixed her own meals; I fixed mine...well, the cafeteria down the block did. She had her bedroom; I had mine. She did her laundry; I, apparently, was to do mine.

It was late spring, and our busiest season at work, so I hadn't had time to look at the washer. Consequently, I loaded the clothes basket with my soiled rags, ignoring her dainty things, and headed out the door, wondering what laundry Sharon used, and too proud...make that *stubborn*...to ask. Albuquerque's Finest Laundromat, or so it was advertised, was half a mile down Montgomery Boulevard from our house, so that's who I granted my patronage. I'm not certain what I had in mind, but I took along that pair of *his* underwear in case somebody wanted to claim it. Maybe I could find the stud who Sharon apparently felt was more of a man than a lifelong construction worker.

The Laundromat was big and airy and damned near empty this early in the evening. Everything was stark white...walls, machines, tables. A couple of ladies sat in chairs lining the east wall, gossiping while washers in front of them chugged and gurgled and groaned, emitting vapors of bleach and detergent and other more earthy odors I did not care to contemplate. The women were probably comparing notes on what wusses their husbands were, I speculated sourly.

A fellow my age or younger was fussing around with a washer on the west side of the building, so I figured that was the men's section. I hadn't been in a Laundromat in 10 years, and the machines bore little resemblance to the ones out of my distant past. I must have looked confused because the young stranger stepped up and showed me how to set the machines. After I deposited an ungodly amount of quarters, the washers, one for whites and one for coloreds like my mama taught me, pissed and glugged and chugged wearily doing the labor of a dozen washerwomen of yore.

"Hey, you forgot this!" the guy said suddenly, snatching the clean leopard skin from the bottom of my basket. I took a good look at him as he did a double take. The good-looking, fair-haired young stud of around 23 or 24 held up the underwear by the elastic band. "Man, I'd like to see the tan lines these left!"

"Beg pardon?" I asked, grabbing for the shorts.

"These are cut high. Wow! You must carry a heavy package. The damned thing bulges from being stretched." The dude handed over the shorts, looking sheepish. "Sorry about that, but those are bitching briefs." A mischievous smile stretched his lips. "I'm not usually so forward, but...well, I don't suppose you'd let me see those tan lines, would you?"

"What tan lines? Are you nuts?"

"Horny, yes. Nuts, no."

"Horny? Men's underwear gets you horny?"

Lively blue eyes examined me frankly for a moment. "Yeah. That and the dude who belongs to it."

"Crap, don't talk like that! Are you queer or something?"

The smile broadened. "I act like a truck driver," he said, his man's voice suddenly gone soft, "but I'm really kinda lacy."

"Be damned," I sputtered.

The guy gave a genuine smile this time and held out his hand. "My name's Hap."

Too astonished to think straight, I accepted his grip; he hung on a beat too long. "Vurl."

"Hello, Vurl. Glad to meet you. Can I take it a hunky he-man like you's not accustomed to being accosted by flaming flits in a Laundromat? Don't know why; you're one serious baby doll. A real golden boy."

I'm sure I blushed. "Nothing golden about me. Black hair, black eyes, black soul." I laughed nervously. "And I'm not accustomed to being confronted by qu...uh, gays."

"Lucky me. I see you're wearing a wedding band, but you're doing the laundry. The wife on a trip?"

My head still reeling, I automatically answered the question. "You might say that. We're having some problems right now."

"I'll bet the problem's not dancing in the sheets. You look like you bang it pretty good. More than just pretty good. Man, I bet you fuck like a construction worker on overtime!"

"I *am* a construction worker!" I blurted without thinking. This guy spoke a whole new language. I didn't understand half of what he said. "Do OK, I guess," I muttered, idiotically, keenly aware Sharon would disagree with me.

Hap laughed. "I do believe you're a real cherry. Have you ever been with a guy?"

"No!" I snapped quickly. Then oddly compelled to confess, I added. "In college, a couple of us got this guy to go down on us once...that's all."

"That's enough to qualify. College must be six or so years behind you. That's long enough to go without a suck job. I'm a B-boy myself, but we can have a basket lunch in the altar room; it has a lock."

"Huh?" I grunted like a yokel fresh off the pumpkin wagon.

The blond grinned. I couldn't help noticing again how good-looking he was.

"I'm a bottom," he explained. Enjoy a good ass fuck...as fuckee, not fucker. But for a good-looking neophyte like you, I'll suck your cock until you make baby paste. We can go in the toilet; it has a lock."

"I don't know, man. I'm not really into that scene."

"How do you know? You haven't tried it lately. Besides, if you're on the outs with the old lady, you're bound to be hot to trot. Come on. It'll be my pleasure."

When I hesitated, he flashed that engaging grin and sauntered slowly toward the men's room. There was nobody else in the joint except those same two women half a block away on the other side of the laundry, so after a few seconds, I followed him inside. Hap turned the lock on the door and sat down on the toilet seat. I backed away when he reached for me. With a soft chuckle, he caught a belt loop and tugged me forward.

"Man, I've been *dying* to read braille ever since you walked in," he stage-whispered.

I had no idea what he was talking about unless he meant groping me through my clothes like he was doing now. My old cock started firming up beneath his warm palm. Before I could think twice about it, he had my belt loose. My trousers hit the floor with a clank of keys. My shorts quickly joined them.

"Wow, Vurl! You've got a fucking accordion," he gulped as the damned prick started growing in his hand. "A real donkey!"

I was about to answer when he leaned forward and slipped his mouth over the crown. Whatever smartass remark was rising, died in my throat. Hap swallowed most of the thing and rode it back out to the end again. His hands pushed my T-shirt up around my chest and fingered my torso. He came off my cock, leaving it beating in the air.

"Damn, you're something, Vurl! Featherless, tight body, washboard belly, heavy pecs. Shit, I believe you *are* a construction worker. Man, I'd like to go around-the-world with you! Australian sex would be a real pleasure."

"Speak English, dude," I complained.

"I'd like to kiss your whole body," he translated. "Every square inch. Then I'd like you to backdoor me on a big bed. Bareback!" He laughed softly. "You don't have body hair...except where you need it. I like that. And your cock's like a beer can, a tall-boy beer can! I *really* like that! Will you fuck me, Vurl?"

"No, thanks. Don't even know why I'm doing this. I'm no queer." I'd reexamine that declaration later.

"Maybe not," the trim young man said, reaching to take me in his mouth again. "But I'll bet you're a bicycle. You can peddle both ways!"

I forgot about answering him as he seriously went to work. I sort of liked the way his hands wandered my ass cheeks while he rode my pole, taking me in and spitting me out. Nobody had ever tickled my butt during sex. Who would have imagined how great it felt?

Pretty soon he put a hand to my balls and massaged them gently as he drew me closer and closer to my own personal dew point. I arrived like a thunderclap. My balls blew in a mighty eruption. I grabbed his head and fucked his mouth until I worked my way through it. Shit, I didn't know I could produce so much come. On the last spasm, I held him down on me while my muscles trembled and my knees turned to water. Finally, I remembered to let the guy breathe. He showed no signs of distress, slowly washing me with his tongue all the way to the end.

"How was it?" he asked, swallowing hard.

"Fucking great!" I said shakily. Man, I hadn't blasted off like that with Sharon since...since the fucking honeymoon!

Hap was casual about things, and that took the sting out of the aftermath. I felt a little remorse, but it died before we got out of the bathroom. As I sat in one of the chairs while my two washers chugged along, it didn't even make me uncomfortable when he plopped his trim butt down beside me. In fact, I asked the question uppermost in my mind.

"How did you know it was OK to...I don't know how to say this...approach me."

"It was the underwear. Those bitchin' briefs. Any guy who'd wear those is a walking sperm delivery system looking for a receptacle. Suckable. Definitely suckable."

"Actually, they're not mine. I...I got them mixed up with my stuff the last time my...uh, I did laundry. That's why I brought it. Thought maybe I'd find out who it belongs to."

He gave me an arched eyebrow, queer for "I don't believe you for a minute," I guess. "You don't know who these foxy shorts belong to?"

"Got left in the drier, probably. Anyway, found them when I got home."

He pursed his lips. "Hmmm. Let's see if we can figure it out.

There's a Chicken-with-a-Basket who comes in now and then."

"Hap, what the hell language are you speaking?"

"Teenage dream with a big basket...and I don't mean a laundry basket. And then there's this dreamy PG-rated guy." He forestalled my protest. "A good-looking straight who's gay for pay. And for a couple of weeks there was this Girl Scout...that's a soldier on leave...a lonely, needy soldier on leave. No, it couldn't be his. When he balled me in the bathroom, he had olive drab boxers...military issue."

"He *fucked* you in there?" I gasped.

"Oh, *did* he, honey! I think he was a het with hot rocks and no gal to ease his pain and just aching for a matinee. He had a parlor peter...you know the average four to six inches, but he sure new how to use it!" Hap half-turned in his seat. "I'll bet you can match him stroke for stroke. And you're *lots* bigger than him. Why don't we try it?"

"Shit, man, I can't imagine fucking a guy's ass!"

"Oh, darlin,' there's more than one way to fuck. There's a leg fuck, a college fuck, Boy Scout sex, a belly fuck, and even the armpit."

"I don't know what you just said."

Hap sighed dramatically. "They're all ways to fuck without penetration. Oh, babe, I'd like to get you and the Girl Scout in a daisy chain. That would be bad!"

"The armpit?" I asked incredulously.

"Left or right?" he asked, flapping his arms. "Left's deeper; right's more experienced."

"No, thanks."

The conversation turned to other things until the clothes were washed and dried. As we folded our laundry, he kept trying to talk me into a date. As I picked up my basket...the one with the clean clothes in it...he stayed me with a hand on my arm.

"Ooh," he cooed, "biceps! I'm going to be gone the next two or three weeks. Hope I see you after that. But if I don't, I just want to say I'm proud to have danced at your debut."

"Uh...thanks. I think."

I walked out of the Laundromat a new man; at least, a man with a new perspective. Who in the hell needed Sharon, anyway? Not me! As I got in the front seat of my Explorer, I fingered the silk leopard skin. Hap was right...sexy. Even lying flat atop my clean laundry, it still had a bit of a bulge where some unknown cock had conformed the material to its own shape.

It might be fun to track down the stud who put the definition in the damned thing. Maybe I'd start with Chicken-with-a-Basket. If he used the Laundromat regularly, he was probably a college kid living on his own...off campus.

I smiled as I ground the starter. I'd start with the easy stuff...the dry humps Hap mentioned. Armpits. For some reason, the very word caused my cock to stir restlessly. Yeah. I'd start with armpits and work my way through the whole set...you know, leg fuck, belly fuck. And eventually, I'd get down to the real thing...a good ass fuck. And old Hap's trim butt just might be the one. I ought to be ready by the time he got back in two or three weeks...if I worked hard at it.

Throwing the gearshift into reverse, I laughed aloud and brushed the bitchin' briefs with my palm. I owed my exciting new prospects to *his* underwear...whoever the hell *he* is.

THE BUYER

Curtis C. Comer

A bottom-feeder. The go-between man. That's how my job makes me feel sometimes. See, I'm the regional sales rep for a number of national greeting card companies. Not Hallmark or anything that schmaltzy, but some really cool lines based mostly off of the East and West coasts. And working for myself is fun; if I want to knock off early, I can. Since I work on a 15% commission, I can just disappear for the weekend if I feel that I've made enough money for the week. Now, I know that you're thinking that I'm contradicting myself; I mean, I started out by calling myself a bottom-feeder and now I'm telling you how great it is to work for myself. Well, both versions are true. Like any job, being a sales rep has its good points and its bad points. What *sucks* about the job is that most retailers don't like to be *bothered* by reps. They would rather go to the large gift shows in New York, or San Francisco, or Dallas, or Atlanta, if only for the reason that they can then brag to their friends that they *went* to New York, or San Francisco, or Dallas, or Atlanta. Fuck supporting the local schmuck who lugs around the large plastic tubs of greeting cards in all kinds of weather. That's how it feels sometimes. I'm basically a nobody, since I'm neither the person who designs the cards nor the person with the trendy little shop who sells them. That's why I called myself the go-between man. Sort of like the modern-day Matchmaker for Capitalism. Maybe one of these days I'll find something else that allows me the same amount of freedom and say goodbye to the buyers who never come to the phone, who never seem to be available once they learn who it is on the other end of the line. For the time being, though, I'm stuck, and the only thing I can do is shut up and deal with it.

I learned about a month ago, though, that repping could pay off in some really unexpected ways. I had been trying for about a year to get an appointment with Hart Wellman, owner of Wellman's Gifts and finally, last month, had been able to do just that. Somehow, probably by accident, he picked up the phone. I went into my usual spiel and asked if he would like to look at some of my lines.

"Who is this again?" he asked, almost rudely, in what sounded like an English, maybe Welsh accent.

I reminded him that my name was James and ticked off a couple of the card lines I rep. And then, presto! It's one of those things that sometimes happen in the profession: He actually made an appointment.

"What does next Monday look like for you?" he asked, sounding pestered.

"Fine," I replied, flipping through my planner.

"What time?" he asked.

"Is 10 o'clock good for you?" I suggested, almost hesitantly.

"Make it 9:30," he replied.

"I look forward to seeing you," I was saying as he hung up.

Needless to say, I knew that I might be in for a hard sell so, the morning of the appointment, I was careful to make sure that I had everything I needed: business cards, catalogs, price lists, and order forms. I chose the two card lines that I thought to be the most appropriate for Wellman's product mix, and went through each of the tubs of cards to make sure I had all of the samples in order before loading the tubs onto my foldable luggage cart.

I had never *met* Hart Wellman, only spoken to him by phone but, based on the fact that he seemed almost unexcited at the prospect of looking at another card line, I decided to put my best foot forward. After assembling my materials, I ironed a shirt and picked out a tie. Hell, I even polished my shoes. I arrived at 9:25, five minutes early.

"May I *help* you?" asked the 20-something blond behind the

counter, eyeing my luggage cart as if I'd just pulled an atomic warhead into the shop.

"I have an appointment with Hart," I replied, trying to ignore the superior expression on her face. "At 9:30."

Looking horribly put out by the effort, she flipped open a leather-bound agenda and scanned it.

"I don't have anything down for today," she said dryly.

This sort of shit happens to reps all the time. Usually, I'll go back home and try to reschedule but, that particular morning, considering how long I'd been trying to get an appointment, I persisted.

"Just a minute," she sighed, picking up the phone and dialing a number. "Mr. Wellman," she said into the phone, casting an accusing glance in my direction, "there's a gentleman downstairs who says that he has an appointment with you today at 9:30."

I could hear the voice on the other end of the line swear and, before the blond could hang up, footsteps thundered on the stairs to the right of the counter. The man who appeared at the door, however, was *not* what I had been expecting Hart Wellman to look like. In the place of the nerdy little retail queen that I had expected, stood a tall, finely attired man somewhere in his early 40s. His dark brown, almost wavy hair, framed a strong, unshaven face, the hint of a scar on his chin; his green eyes seemed to look right through me as he spoke. His rolled up sleeves exposed large, furry forearms, and his tailored slacks advertised what appeared to be a very large cock.

"Sorry," he said, offering me his massive hand. "There's a shipment coming in today and I completely forgot about our appointment."

"That's OK," I offered, wincing at his strong grip. "I promise I won't take much of your time."

"I'll be just a moment," he said, finally releasing my hand and turning to the blond. As he spoke to her, bits of conversation floating my direction, things about invoices, instructions regarding incoming calls and the like, he would occasionally glance over his shoulder in my direction, his big, green eyes causing my cock to stir. He placed a hand on the counter, his back still to me and, after getting past the sight of his large, hairy fingers, I noticed that he wasn't wearing a wedding ring.

"Call me the *minute* the truck arrives," he said to the blond, signaling the end of his instructions. "But only for that."

He turned to me.

"Are you ready?" he asked, extending his hand toward the stairs.

"Yes," I replied, tilting my luggage cart and rolling it around the counter.

"You'll need help with that," he said, referring to the stairs. "You should let me go first; it's a mess up there."

I let him grab the handle of the cart and followed him up the stairs, grasping the lap of the cart while I ogled his strong-looking back and manly ass.

At the top of the stairs, among boxes of inventory, I rested the cart back on its wheels and reclaimed the handle, following Hart into a very bright office, its walls painted white and illuminated by fluorescent lights. The only furniture in the room was a folding table, its surface clean except for a few catalogs and a telephone, and two swiveling office chairs on wheels. He closed the door behind us and settled into a chair, his hands clasped behind his head, his face as serious as a poker player's.

"Let's see what you've got," he said, his eyes fixed on my face.

"This first line," I said, leaning over the plastic tub, "is a really nice card line with a good retail price."

"I'm not talking about the fucking cards," he whispered.

I could feel my face flush as I straightened.

"C'mon," he said, his hands still behind his head, "I know you fancy me." He glanced at my crotch, quickly meeting my gaze again. "Let's see it."

I slowly unzipped my fly and pulled out my stiffening prick.

"Nice," he said, regarding my boner, but remaining motionless. "Touch it for me," he whispered, locking me in his gaze again.

Dutifully, I stroked my cock, staring at him. I could see the growing bulge in the front of his own slacks, and wished that he would pull it out for me to suck.

"Don't look at my cock," he said, following my gaze. "You'll get that when I'm damned *ready*, boy."

I continued stroking my stiff shaft, hoping that I wouldn't come too soon. I rubbed the head of my dick, slick with precome. I shuddered at the sensation.

"Show me your pussy, boy," he drawled, rubbing the front of his slacks. "Now."

I undid the clasp on my slacks and pulled them and my underwear down around my ankles, my throbbing boner pointing to the ceiling.

"Take them off," he ordered, continuing to rub the large bump in the front of his slacks.

I kicked off my loafers and pulled off my balled-up clothing, which I threw into the second chair.

"Turn around," he said, unzipping his fly. "Show me the pussy."

I turned around, wishing that I could see his cock, and rested my hands on the folding table.

"Spread your cheeks for me," he whispered. "Show me the hole."

I bent over the table and spread my ass cheeks for him.

"Nice," he said, his voice breathy. "Stick a finger in."

I wet a forefinger in my mouth and slowly inserted it in my ass.

"You like that?" he asked.

"Yes," I replied, moving my finger in and out of my ass.

"Fuck it harder," he said.

I obliged by quickening the pace of my thrusts, and could feel my nipples harden under my pressed shirt.

"Come here," he ordered.

I turned around to face him and saw that he had pulled his slacks down to below his knees. His cock, long and fat, was uncut and rested on a hairy tummy, revealed by his unbuttoned shirt. I took my tie off and threw it on the floor as I walked toward him.

"Suck my cock," he whispered, his green eyes boring into me

again.

I pulled off my shirt as I lowered myself to a kneeling position, and threw it across the room, missing the chair that I had been aiming for. I didn't care, and greedily took his fatty into my mouth, causing him to groan. I went all the way down, almost gagging as it hit the back of my throat, but lingered there for a moment, enjoying the musky scent of his hairy pubes and tummy. I reached up and, through the thick, dark hair on his chest, found a pink nipple, which I twisted between my forefinger and thumb, causing him to groan again.

"You like it *rough*, boy?" he grunted, placing a big hand on the back of my head and forcing me back down on his fat dick.

I could only cough my answer with his dick in my mouth, but he seemed to understand and forced my head up and down on his dick, his hands on either side of my head.

"Suck that dirty prick," he whispered, thrusting his muscular hips into my face.

I didn't dare to touch my cock for fear of coming, and it bounced up and down as I sucked Hart's cock, slapping me on the leg.

"You want something bigger than a *finger* in your skanky hole, boy?" he asked, still fucking my face.

Once again I coughed an affirmative answer.

"Get on the table," he said, pulling my face away from his slobbery and swollen cock.

I stood up, naked except for my socks. Hart took off his shoes, then his shirt and slacks, which he draped over the back of the office chair.

"Get on the table," he repeated. "On all fours."

I climbed onto the rickety table, the laminate cold on my forearms.

"How often do you do this?" he asked, standing behind me, fingering my asshole.

"This is the first time," I replied, truthfully.

"Liar," he said, accusingly. He pulled the finger from my hole and slapped my ass. "I'll bet you've buggered all sorts of shop owners just to get a fucking sale."

"No," I replied. "This is..."

He cut me off with another slap to my ass.

"You like being a slut, don't you, boy?" he whispered, shoving another finger up my ass. "Like getting sales that much, do you?" he growled. "For a bit of a fuck?"

"Yes," I said, squirming as he shoved a second hairy finger up my ass.

"Slag," he whispered. "You deserve to get fucked without any lube, don't you?"

"Yes," I replied, my heart pounding.

Honestly, as much as I liked to get fucked, I had always been kind of a lightweight when it came to pain. I hoped that he was joking, that he wouldn't hurt me. When I heard his spit into his hand, however, my heart sank. He slapped the gooey wad of phlegm onto my asshole and worked in two, then three fingers.

"Are you ready to get fucked, slag?" he asked, his voice hard.

"Yes," I replied, my dick oozing a steady stream of precome. "Fuck me."

"Roll onto your back," he said. "*Now.*"

Slowly, I lowered onto my side and rolled over, the table cold on my back. His face was serious, and his green eyes made me want to obey him. He lifted my legs, his strong hands grasping my ankles, and spit again into his hand, rubbing the thick goo onto his cock

As he shoved the head of his cock into my asshole, flames shot up my legs.

"You want more, boy?" he asked, clearly enjoying himself.

"Yes," I replied, my voice almost a whimper.

"Yes, what?" he asked.

"Yes, sir," I replied, my ass pulsating.

"Yes, *Mr. Wellman,*" he said, squeezing my ankles, tightly.

"Yes, Mr. Wellman," I repeated.

"There's a good little git," he said, a sneer on his face.

He shoved the remainder of his cock, all nine inches, into my ass, causing the flames to shoot from my asshole to my head. For a moment I thought that I might pass out. I tried to concentrate, focusing on those green eyes.

"You're a tough little bitch, aren't you, boy?" he asked, smiling.

"Yes, Mr. Wellman," I replied as he continued thrusting his cock in and out of my hole.

"Good boy," he said, smiling again, revealing a row of incredibly white teeth. "Ride that cock for me; suck it with your filthy hole."

As he fucked me, my own cock bounced up and down, slapping my stomach, as if it were keeping time with the rhythm of his thrusts. I didn't know how much longer I could take the pounding. The warm sensation that had, at first, engulfed my entire body was now concentrated in my asshole, which throbbed as if it was grabbing onto his cock, not wanting to let it go.

"Be a good boy and turn over," he said, beads of sweat forming on his forehead.

He pulled his cock out of my ass and released his grip on my ankles, and I turned over onto my stomach. He pulled me from the table so that my feet were on the floor, and pushed my torso down onto the table, shoving another finger into my open asshole, as I lay there bent over.

"Are you ready for a stomachful?" he whispered, very close to my ear.

"Yes, Mr. Wellman," I replied, my cock aching from the load I wanted to release.

Without another word, he shoved his cock back into my ass, pounding me with such ferocity that I was sure the blond downstairs in the shop would hear the squeaking of the folding table.

"Ride it boy," he groaned. "Ride that big cock!"

I grasped the sides of the table, my face against the cold surface. Suddenly, without touching myself, I realized that I was coming.

"Shit," I moaned. "You're getting me off!"

"Yeah," he breathed. "Tighten that hole around my prick!"

As I lay there, bent over the table, the feel of my warm load against my stomach, his thrusts increased in tempo. Finally, with one last thrust inward, he exhaled a warm breath on my back.

"Jesus," he moaned, his hands gripping my hips.

The phone on the table rang, almost making me jump.

"Hand me that," he instructed.

I reached up over my head and lifted the receiver, which I passed to him.

"Yeah," he said into the phone, his cock still in my ass. "Right," he said, "I'll be down in a moment." Then, the phone to his chest, looking me in the eye again, "We're done here, then?"

"Yes," I replied, smiling.

"We're finished," he said, the phone back to his ear. "I'll be right down as soon as we finish up."

As we dressed, he looked at me, all business.

"Do either of these card companies do a rack program?"

"They both do," I replied, buttoning my shirt.

"And you will come in to service the rack?" he asked. "I don't want to have to bother with it myself."

"I can check in once a week," I said.

"Right," he said, tucking in his shirt. "Pick the line that you think is best and set me up with a 72-count spinner."

"Alright," I replied, making a mental note.

"And only set me up with their best-selling cards," he continued. "I don't care to take on the crap they can't get rid of."

"Do you prefer to do a first order as COD or prepay?" I asked, trying to be businesslike.

"Prepay," he replied, a smirk on his handsome face. "I think that's only fair."

"Great," I replied. "I'll write this up and fax you a copy."

"Have the girl downstairs give you a credit card number before you leave," he said, his hand on the door.

"Thanks, Mr. Wellman," I said, grabbing my cart. "It was a pleasure."

"Call me Hart," he said, opening the door, smiling again. "I think that you've earned that."

IN-FLIGHT FUCKING

Christopher Pierce

I really should stop staring at his ass, other people in the waiting area might notice.

Or he might notice himself.

But what else is there to do, waiting to board a plane after I've read all my magazines and finished my book already? There's a gorgeous chunk of man meat not 20 feet away from me, standing there with his bag over his shoulder, looking out the windows at the planes coming and going.

He's hot. Dark brown hair, olive skin, nice lips. The muscles of his arms move when he shifts the weight of his bag over his shoulder. His jeans are a tiny bit too tight, just enough to accent and highlight the beautiful butt they cover. His groin area looks full and impressive too. I wonder if the guy has any idea how amazingly erotic he is, just standing there waiting.

Probably not.

My own dick is getting hard just looking at him. I'd like to touch myself, to rub my cock through my shorts, but I know *that* would get noticed. So I just sit here, watching him.

I would so love to see him naked. I would so love to get him naked. Undress him slowly. I wonder what would happen if I just went over to him, took his bag off his shoulder and set it down, slipped my hands into the top of his jeans, grabbed the bottom of his shirt and pulled it up and over his head. I wonder what his chest looks like. Hairy or smooth? Slender of defined? Small nipples, big nipples, erect nipples? Tattooed or unmarked?

Any or all of the above, it all sounds hot to me.

I imagine him looking down at me and smiling with a small nod of his head, and I'd be delighted to see tiny flecks of gold in his brown eyes. With my mouth watering I'd look down at his crotch, the growing shape of his dick under the fabric of his pants intoxicating. My fist would unfasten his belt, then the buttons of his fly. I'd part the separated halves of his pants to reveal his boxer shorts beneath. I'd touch his cock through the boxers, rubbing it gently. Then I'd grip the waistband and pull them out and down, revealing his gorgeous tool. Big, uncut, dark like the rest of his skin are the first thoughts that jump into my mind as I look at it. A tiny pearl of precome would be oozing from his dick, and before I could stop myself I'd be moving forward and licking off that tiny treasure. Then I'd use my fingers to very gently peel back the protective foreskin, and his cock head would be revealed like a ripe fruit. Despite being dark pink it is still lighter in color than the foreskin and the shaft. I'd open my mouth and take his cock head inside, closing my lips and surrounding it with soft warmth.

All I'd want to do is make him feel good. I'd use my tongue to caress the head and massage it gently. "A-a-ah..." I'd hear the man say, and I'd take that as permission to continue. I'd go for it and suck his cock like I'd never sucked before, with a single goal: to give my best blow job ever. The man would put his hands in my hair and hold my head in place, buried in his crotch. I'd try to take more dick-length down my throat then I ever had before, inhaling his tool and breathing through my nose...

Suddenly the hot guy turns away from the window, and my fantasy dissipates like smoke in air. I hope he doesn't notice me staring. Wait a minute, maybe I hope he does notice. I'm pretty good-looking myself! I'd think I was hot if I were him.

What the fuck am I thinking about?

Holy shit, he's walking this way.

Look away, I tell myself, look away! Don't stare at him like a fucking psycho! He's getting closer. I can't help myself—I look at his crotch, and the bulge there makes me want to stick out my tongue like a panting dog.

He stops right in front of where I'm sitting, and his groin is practically right in front of my face.

What's he doing?

Then I remember—I'm sitting right under the fucking video monitor with the arrival and departure times on it! He's reading the screen, not checking me out!

But then he does something unexpected.

He sits down next to me.

Now, there's plenty of empty chairs here in the waiting lounge. He didn't have to sit right next to me. People hardly ever sit down right next to someone they don't know unless there's nowhere else to sit.

And this hunk was choosing to sit next to me. He slings his bag down off his shoulder and settles into his seat. He relaxes his legs and they spread a little, just enough for his right leg to touch mine.

Public male-male touching is usually broken instantly. It's an unspoken rule—guys don't touch other guys in public. The instant his leg touched mine, I had to make a choice. Should I break the contact or let it continue? It takes less than a second to decide, and the choice I make surprises me.

I maintain the contact.

I guess my unconscious mind is braver than my conscious mind. But the hot guy doesn't seem to mind. In fact, it looks like he's made the same decision I have.

I imagine touching his chest with my hands, running them over his pecs, down the hollow between them, to his abs, feeling the muscles through the skin, then unbuttoning his jeans, slipping my hands into his jeans, reaching around his waist to grab his ass, loving the tightness of my hands trapping his butt cheeks, trapped themselves by the fabric of his pants...

He doesn't look at me. He just keeps looking ahead, out the windows, still watching the planes. I look around myself, to see if anyone has noticed our touching. But there's no one close enough to see it.

I let one of my hands, which had been resting on my lap, move a little closer to him. When there is no response I move it more, until I am touching his leg with my fingers. I flex them, doing a tiny stroking pattern against the fabric of his pants. There's so little reaction from him I wonder if he even feels me touching him.

But I get my response a second later, when I innocently look over at him by turning my head a little to my left. My eyes instinctively drop to his crotch, and there I see the shape of his dick in his pants.

It's getting bigger.

Unmistakably bigger!

I grin at no one in particular as I realize this trip isn't going to be so boring after all. The guy next to me leans back in his seat and stretches his arms up casually. When he brings them down he lets his right arm come down behind me. Very gently he grasps my shoulder. My dick is getting hard. I'm just trying to decide what to do next when the voice of an airline employee announces that boarding for my flight is about to begin.

I've been so into the hot guy that I haven't noticed that the plane has pulled up to the gate and is ready for its passengers.

The sexy man and I break our contact instantly and stand up. We don't look at each other as we sling our bags and get in line with the other people waiting. We wait for the first-class people to board and I look at the guy's back, butt, and legs—which are all sexy from that angle.

I follow him into the plane when it's our turn, down the ramp and into the aisle between the seats. Despite the people around us we might as well be alone. He's all I can see, all I can think about. He glances at his ticket, checks the numbers of the luggage compartment to his left, and slides into his seat.

Shit! Reality check—we're not the only people in the world. We're just two of the people boarding this plane, and by no coincidence will we miraculously be seated next to each other!

I check my own ticket and sure enough my seat is nowhere near the hot guy's. Damn it! The people behind me are getting impatient, I have to keep walking down the aisle and stop blocking the line. As I reluctantly keep walking, I glance back. The sexy guy is looking at me!

He winks at me!

I head down the aisle, knowing the grin on my face is as wide as this plane's wingspan. I find my seat, stow my bag, and sit down between the two least sexy people I can imagine—two elderly women. But I don't care—the hot guy looked at me and winked—our attraction is definitely mutual, the arm wasn't a mistake. I don't hear the safety guidelines or the captain's greeting. I don't feel the plane's taxiing or its takeoff.

All I can think of is him, and my cock hardens in my pants again.

I take off my sweatshirt, use it to cover my lap, and slide my hands beneath it. Glancing to my right I see one of the women engrossed in the book she's reading, and on my left the other one is listening to her portable CD player with her eyes closed. So they don't notice me as I feel myself through my pants. I rub my cock through the fabric and it feels good. I wish I could close my eyes and just have a nice jerk-off session thinking about the hot guy, but I have to stay alert and make sure no one catches me. So I just touch myself slowly under my sweatshirt, just enjoying that even though I wish it was him what was touching me.

Then I realize something. I have to piss!

I awkwardly get up and squeeze past the women into the aisle. The restroom is at the rear of the plane. The hot guy is sitting ahead of me, the opposite direction. I look his way hopefully, thinking maybe he'll be looking back and see me. He isn't, of course. I can't even tell which head is his here anyway.

Oh, well, I think, turning back the other way and heading from the restroom. When I get there I wait for the person inside to finish and come out, then go inside and turn the knob marked OCCUPIED.

I unzip my pants, let them drop, and take out my cock so I can piss.

What was that noise? Someone was opening the door!

"Do you mind?" I say irritably, and crane my neck around to see what air-headed flight attendant or pudgy father of four has ignored the OCCUPIED sign.

It's the hot guy from the waiting room.

My mouth drops open.

"Uh..." I say, "I didn't..."

But what could I say?

What is customary to say to a guy you thought you had no chance of making it with who then shows up at your restroom door on a crowded airline flight?

"Well, let me in before someone catches us!" he says, shoving himself into the tiny enclosed space and closing the door behind him.

"But, how did you...?" I ask stupidly. We are mashed up against each other in the tiny space of this restroom. The handsome stranger's breath is hot in my face.

"How did I know you wanted to do me?" he asks.

I nod.

"Because I want to do you just as badly!" he says with a laugh. "Didn't you see me staring at you in the reflection in the window?"

"Reflection?" I repeat. "I thought you were watching the planes!"

"The planes! I don't watch planes when there's a guy as hot as you within 20 feet of me! That's why I came over and sat down beside you—we were cruising each other!"

"Well, we were—but..." I trail off. "What the fuck."

"We don't have much time," he says, "let's make the most of it."

He leans forward and our lips meet. The kiss is exciting, passionate, really hot, and a little scary—what if someone else has to use the restroom? What if a flight attendant catches us? I push my tongue into his mouth and explore, running it over his teeth and feeling his own tongue.

The stranger tastes good, and I know he likes me in there because he makes a noise that is a combination laugh-sigh. He wraps his arms around me and squeezes me tight. The roar of the airplane's engines is all around us, and I almost forget my fear, almost forget the other people on the plane.

It is just us—me and the hot guy—and we are the only ones that matter.

"Do you have any condoms?" I ask.

He pats his pants pocket.

"Always," he says.

"What's your name?"

"Jerry,"

"Well, Jerry, fuck me!" I say, awkwardly turning around in the tiny space so I am facing away from him. His crotch is right up against my butt. I am so horny for him I want to shove my ass backward into him, but I know he needs all the room he can to do what he's gotta do.

I hear him unzip his pants, tear open a condom package and slide the latex sheath over his meat.

"Got any lube in that pocket of yours?" I ask over my shoulder.

"Sure do!" After digging through his pocket again he squeezes some lube into his hard dick and slicks it up.

"You ready, man?" Jerry asks.

"Yeah," I say, itching to feel him inside my body. "Do me!" There's no time for foreplay. Jerry uses his hand to guide his cock to my hungry hole, and when he's in the right position he shoves himself inside me!

Fuck, it hurts but it's fucking awesome—feels so good. Normally I prefer to have a guy rim me and slowly work his way into me, but this was a tight situation in every way and I just want him to fuck me and fuck me fast! I push my ass back against Jerry's cock and we both groan as he goes in even deeper.

He starts fucking me now, thrusting in and pulling out as much as the tiny restroom allows. Although our range of movement is smaller than I'm used to, this is every bit as hot as the times I've fucked with lots of room. Maybe, I realize, it's even hotter!

Jerry is fucking me fast and hard.

I groan with exertion and am glad that the roar of the engines drowns the sound out.

"Oh, yeah, oh, yeah, oh, *yeah*!" he grunts in my ear. This is so hot, so intense, I grab my cock and start fisting it hard. Pleasure courses thought me from front to rear. I feel ready to explode. I'm almost ready to come, Jerry is fucking me so good!

"I'm gonna shoot!" he says.

"Go for it, man!" I say over my shoulder. "You've just about got me there too!"

Jerry grabs my hips hard and shoves himself into me one last time.

"*F-u-u-uck ye-a-a-ah*!" he groans, and I know he is shooting off inside me. My own orgasm can't be delayed and explodes within me. I angle my cock down into the open toilet and watch my pearl-white sperm shoot down into the hole. The pleasure courses through me and I feel like I'm flying.

Which I am, of course.

"Fuck," Jerry says.

"We did it," I say. "We really did it. Who knew this was possible?"

"What do you mean?" he asks me as he pulls out and zips up.

"Who knew I could see a hot guy and wind up getting fucked by him an hour later, on a plane?"

"This flight's just beginning," Jerry says as he turns me around to face him. We kiss. "The sky's the limit."

BEST MAN

Will Knauss

After getting a late start, breaking down on the highway, and having his car towed to the nearest garage, Jack Bainbridge finally pulled into a parking space in front of McKenna's Men's Wear, the only clothing store in his hometown that rented formal wear. Hours behind schedule, Jack's simple trip home from college had turned into the homecoming from hell.

While driving up the coast for his brother's wedding, Jack's car had suffered the automotive equivalent of a seizure, forcing Jack to spend the afternoon, and what was left of his credit limit, getting the problem fixed. He'd found out that despite how they're portrayed in countless porn videos, auto body shops are not hotbeds of gay male sexuality. There were no swarthy grease monkey's and there were certainly no lucky customers on the receiving end of a through "lube job."

Jack was his brother's best man and he had missed the wedding rehearsal. If he hurried and picked up his tux, he might make it to the restaurant in time for the first course of the rehearsal diner. As Jack got out of his car he could see that the storefront of McKenna's was dark. He let out string of curse words. Couldn't anything go right today?

Praying that Mr. McKenna had stayed past closing time, Jack peered inside the store's front window but saw no one. Where in the world was he going to find a tuxedo before tomorrow?

The sudden jangle of keys startled him as someone inside the store unlocked the front door. Standing in the entrance was an unexpectedly familiar face.

"Little Jacky Bainbridge," he said with a playful hint of sarcasm, "I thought that was you."

Jack cringed at the use of his childhood nickname, but his frustration was quickly forgotten since it came from Chris McKenna, the object of Jack's first teenage crush. Chris was once a star athlete who ran the high school relay with Jack's older brother. Jack vividly remembered watching from the stands as Chris would sprint around the track, his lean muscles straining and his dark hair plastered across his sweaty brow, as he'd triumphantly cross the finish line.

Unlike some of the other guys on the team, Chris always treated his best friend's gawky kid brother like one of the guys. Every time Chris won a race, he'd look up in the stands and give Jack a wave. Knowing that Chris's triumphant smile was meant just for him would always make Jack's heart beat a little faster.

Now, Chris was standing right in front of him. He was a few years older, but still looked good. Better than good, he looked hot.

His dark hair was cropped close. The no nonsense hairstyle accentuated Chris's strong features and masculine jawline. Jack could also see that underneath the fabric of his work shirt, the lean strength of a teenage runner had matured into the thickly sculpted muscles of an adult. Remembering how he once intimately touched Chris's heated skin made Jacks throat go dry. He choked back his desire and managed a feeble, "Um...hey, Chris. Good to see you too."

Chris absently ran a hand over the McKenna family business logo on his chest. "My father said you'd be coming by," he explained, "He was worried when you hadn't shown up by closing time. I told him I'd stay and take care of you." Chris smiled and Jack felt a warm familiar tingle. That smile was still the same.

Chris put a welcoming arm around Jack and ushered him through the front door. "It's been a couple of years since I've seen you." Chris said, his hand lingering over the muscles between Jack's shoulder blades, "College must agree with you, you look really good."

Jack felt like an idiot for blushing at the compliment and offered a simple, "Thanks."

The cool air inside the store smelled like crisp linen and was a welcome relief from the heat outside. Chris took him into the store but made no effort to turn on the overhead lighting. The late afternoon sun that filtered through the shop's front windows created soft shadows throughout the room and still offered enough light to comfortably maneuver around the displays and clothing racks.

Jack felt strange around the man he used to idolize. In an effort to keep up his end of the conversation, Jack casually asked how school was going for Chris. His demeanor abruptly changed and he pulled his hand away.

"I'm sort of taking a break," Chris awkwardly explained, "I'm helping dad out with the shop."

Jack wasn't sure what he'd done wrong, but the warmth he'd felt from Chris a moment ago had simply vanished. Chris was now all business as he pulled a garment bag from a rack beside the main counter. "I have your tux right here. Try it on and we'll check the fit." He said pointing toward the fitting room.

Jack took the tux and closed the dressing room curtain. He quickly undressed. For the briefest of moments he thought there might have been some sort of connection with Chris. The way Chris smiled and casually touched him, keeping his hand stationary for a beat longer than was necessary. It was unrealistic of Jack to think that what happened between them two years ago could be rekindled with a simple "Hi, how you doin'?"

The week before Jack started his senior year in high school there was a midnight showing of *Valley of the Dolls* at the local movie house. Jack couldn't convince any of his friends to go and thought he'd have to miss the cult double feature, until Chris said he'd be happy to go with him. During the first movie, with both of them comfortably slouched in their seats, Chris's leg brushed against Jack's. During *Beyond the Valley of the Dolls*, they shared the armrest between them. This innocent touch would've been enough to make Jack the happiest man on the planet, but when Chris gently placed his hand on top of Jack's, the world started to spin. His hand eventually came to rest on Jack's knee and then moved to his thigh. Jack followed Chris's lead until their hands rested on the straining denim of their jeans. Buttons and zippers were slowly undone and in the back row of the movie theater, they steadily stroked and massaged each other to a silent climax. They'd never spoken about what happened and Chris left for college soon after.

That hand job in a darkened theater had been a milestone in Jack's life. The opposite seemed to be true for Chris. Though Jack's body practically thrummed with sexual excitement being around Chris again, the attraction he felt was obviously one-sided. He felt like a fool and just wanted to get this over with.

He took the tuxedo pants from the hanger and slipped them on. When he saw how poorly they fit, he groaned. He looked like the "after" picture in a television weight loss ad, the kind where the formerly obese proudly show off the voluminous pants that they once fit into.

"Chris, there's a little problem with the pants, they really don't fit."

"Come on out and I'll see what I can do."

Jack pushed the curtain aside and took a few steps toward Chris, using both hands to keep the slacks up around his waist. Chris looked him over.

"Well, unless you plan on going to a clown wedding, those just aren't going to work. Let me double-check the measurements," he said taking a tailor's measuring tape out of his pocket, "I'm sure we have something else that will fit you."

Chris leaned in close and wrapped his arms around Jack, settling the tape at Jack's waist. Taking the measurements was awkward and Jack shifted his weight, trying to maneuver the excess waistband out of the way. His grip faltered and the baggy pants slipped out of his hand, falling to the floor down around his ankles. Standing in front of Chris in only his T-shirt and briefs, Jack made a quick attempt to pull the pants back up, but Chris stopped him.

"Why don't you just leave them off," he suggested, "It'll make measuring easier."

Jack wanted to cover up, but he'd do anything to get this over with faster, so he kicked the pants aside.

Chris knelt down in front of Jack and quietly continued. Jack closed his eyes and tried not to think of the gorgeous man only inches from his crotch. The feeling of his strong hands running down the side of Jack's leg made his flesh tingle. To make an embarrassing moment even more humiliating, Jack started to feel the beginnings of an erection.

Oh, God. He had to think of something else. The national deficit, dead puppies, his 70-year-old sociology professor naked. It wasn't working. Jack could feel the unrelenting stiffness pushing against the fabric of his briefs. Jack's hands remained frozen at his sides. He couldn't cover himself. A sudden demure attempt at propriety would only draw more attention to his raging hard-on. Jack's cock twitched as Chris placed the measuring tape along the inside of his thigh and ran his hand down over his calf. Jack had to say something, anything. Maybe he could joke about it. Who was he kidding, there were no words that could diffuse this situation. His throbbing erection was irrefutable proof that Jack desperately wanted Chris.

"You know," Chris said, his voice serious, "I could measure this too if you want."

Still kneeling before him, Jack looked down into Chris's handsome face. The tape measure had been set aside and Chris's dark eyes were filled with need.

Tentatively, Chris ran his fingers along the bulge pressing against the cotton of Jack's underwear. The feathery touch of his hand made Jack sigh. Chris pressed harder, rubbing his hand over Jack's length, making circular strokes over the sensitive tip were the fabric became moist. Jack stifled a moan. It felt incredible.

Jack reached down and ran his fingers through the soft bristles of Chris's short hair, coaxing him closer. As Chris leaned in and brought his lips to the straining fabric, Jack could feel the hot breath and soft pressure of Chris's mouth on his sensitive flesh. Chris ran his tongue over the significant bulge and began to kiss Jack's rigid shaft. Jack ached for release as his cock strained even further against his briefs, which were now damp with Chris's warm spit.

Jack needed to feel those soft lips pressed against his.

He helped Chris to his feet. They stood eye to eye and there was no mistaking the look on Chris's face. He wanted the same thing Jack did.

Their mouths crushed against each other in a first kiss that was hot and passionate. Aware that they were still within view of anyone passing by the store's front windows, they each stumbled back a few steps into the dressing room. Chris closed the curtain, enveloping them in a private world where they could abandon their inhibitions and unleash the frenzied need they had for one another.

Jack reveled in the sensations of Chris's hard body pressed against his. Their hands greedily grasped at each other. Chris stopped his bruising kisses long enough to say, "I want to taste all of you."

His hand worked underneath the waistband of Jack's briefs, grabbing hold of his rigid length. To be freed of his confines, and to feel the touch of his hand, made Jack cry out, "Yes, Chris. Oh, damn yes."

Chris was quickly on his knees with his lips wrapped around Jack's cock. The warm sensation of that mouth working every inch of him had Jack just about ready to burst. To keep his balance, Jack held onto Chris's strong shoulders and massaged the flexing muscles of Chris's neck as his head bobbed up and down over Jack's hard shaft. Jack shoved forward again and again. Chris took each battering thrust down his eager throat. The pleasure of the expert tongue that teased his sensitive flesh was becoming too much to bear.

"Chris, I'm so close. You're going to make me come!" Jack panted as he felt the exquisite sensations building toward their inevitable peak.

Chris's lips remained firmly wrapped around the base of Jack's throbbing cock. With a skill that surprised and delighted Jack, Chris continued to push him to the edge. Jack's legs began to tremble. Every muscle in his body felt weak as all of his energy drained to the heated core that was the focus of Chris's expert attention.

"Oh, God yes!" Jack shouted as he finally experienced the sweet pleasure of release and pumped wave after wave of thick juice down Chris's throat.

Exhausted and panting, Jack slumped against the wall of the fitting room. Chris stood up next to him, placing a soft, sweet kiss on Jack's mouth. They were in their own solitary place, just Jack and Chris; the only sound was their languid breathing. But the comfortable silence of the store was interrupted by the harsh buzzing sound of fluorescent light. They both flinched as the stores stark overhead lights were suddenly turned on.

"You still here, Chris?" came a booming voice from the back of the store.

"Fuck...it's my father." Chris darted to the other side of the curtain and left Jack to quickly dress.

As Jack listened to Chris deal with his father, he pulled his briefs back on and slipped back into his khaki shorts. There's nothing worse than feeling the adolescent panic of being caught red-handed. Since Jack had managed to hook up with his high school crush for a second time, it somehow seemed poetically appropriate that they'd been caught by Chris's father like two horny teenagers.

Jack came out of the dressing room and greeted Mr. McKenna, who, it thankfully seemed, was unaware that Jack had his dick buried down his son's mouth just moments before. The situation still felt awkward, so Jack made his polite goodbyes.

Chris stopped him at the store entrance, "Don't worry, I'll take care of the tux and bring it to the church tomorrow."

Jack looked into his warm brown eyes and knew that there was so much more that Chris wanted to say. There were things that Jack needed to say too, but couldn't since Chris's father was there.

"Thank you," was all Jack could manage. He waved to Chris and Mr. McKenna as he got into his car and drove off.

The wedding ceremony late Sunday afternoon was beautiful. The reception ballroom of the historic Carson House was filled with people congratulating the happy couple. Chris watched from across the room as Jack talked and joked with his family. He couldn't believe that little Jacky, the cute kid he'd liked for so long, could've grown into such a good-looking man.

A man...though there were only a few years between them, Chris had always thought of Jack as a kid. But little Jacky was all grown up. Yesterday afternoon in his father's store had proven that and radically changed Chris's thinking.

Chris was able to catch Jack's eye and Jack excused himself from the rest of the wedding party. As he made his way through the crowd, Chris couldn't help but admire how stylish Jack looked in his newly fitted tuxedo. With his blond hair parted and slicked back, he looked like a classic movie star. Jack was the best-looking man Chris had ever seen, which made what he had to say even more difficult.

Jack greeted him with a warm and knowing smile.

"The suit fits you," Chris said, "You look good."

"Thanks to you."

Chris wanted to get away from the crowd, so he stepped through the French doors and onto the stone portico outside the ballroom. Jack followed him and they stood overlooking the rolling lawn where the setting set sun cast long shadows across the manicured gardens.

"Look, about yesterday," Chris began, "I want to tell you how sorry I am about what happened."

"You're sorry?"

"You're my best friend's kid brother and I took advantage of you."

Jack seemed confused, but Chris went on, "When I'm alone with you I can't seem to control myself. It happened yesterday at the store and that time we were at the movies."

"OK, stop right there. You didn't take advantage of me, so there's nothing to feel bad about." Jack put a reassuring hand on Chris's shoulder. "The truth is that I've liked you for a long time. I'm glad it happened."

It was funny, all this time that Chris had been so mixed up about his feelings for Jack, and Jack had felt the same way. Chris laughed, happy that they could finally be so honest, "I'm glad too."

They strolled across the vast lawn. The grass and the garden smelled sweet in the summer air and as they moved farther away from the main house, and the music and voices from the wedding reception became fainter. They were alone with only the tall trees to overhear their conversation.

"Why aren't you in school anymore?" Jack asked, "Since we're being so truthful and everything."

"I got caught fooling around with some guy."

Jack said that he didn't think that was such a big deal, but Chris explained that when you attend a Christian university and you get caught fucking the dean's son; it's a pretty big deal. "The next day I was politely asked to seek my academic pursuits elsewhere. That's why I'm back here working for my dad."

"I guess I was scared," Chris continued as they walked into a grove of trees, "That's why I went to such a conservative school in the first place. It was easier to hide my feelings and pretend they didn't exist."

"Coming out is scary and confusing for everybody. Trust me, it's always better on the other side of the closet door."

"I'm starting to realize that there are some definite benefits to facing the truth." Underneath the twilight cover of the sweeping branches, he took Jack in his arms and they kissed. The frenzied passion of yesterday was replaced by a slow and tender exploration of one another.

Jack shrugged off his jacket while Chris removed the studs from the buttonholes of his shirt. Chris ran his fingers over Jack's bare chest, stopping at the dark points of his nipples and teasing them with gentle pressure. Jack rolled his head back and sighed deeply as Chris kissed the sensitive part of his neck. Chris softly nibbled his way to Jack's ear and whispered, "I want to taste every part of you."

As Chris attempted to work his way past the zipper that held what he was really after, Jack playfully held him at arm's length. "Hold on a minute. I seem to remember a certain someone tasting an awful lot of things yesterday," he said undoing the buttons of Chris's dress shirt, "I'm greedy too."

Without any argument, Chris let himself be undressed. Soon his clothes lay in a pile with Jack's and in the deep recesses of that darkened grove they stood before one another naked. Jack placed kisses all over Chris—his arms, his chest, his abdomen—until he nuzzled the potent juncture of Chris's thighs. Chris moaned as Jack began to tongue the delicate skin, taking each of his balls into his mouth. "Yes, oh, yes."

Chris squirmed as Jack shifted his attention and playfully nipped at the sensitive skin surrounding the pink tip of his cock. Then, Jack took the entire length of his erection, his tongue swirling around the thick veins at the base of his shaft. Chris urged him on, "Oh, yes, all the way down on it. God, it feels so good."

The oral attention Chris was receiving sent his head spinning, but he still needed the satisfying fullness of Jack filling his throat. He knelt down on the grass and positioned himself next to Jack so they could both taste each other's flesh. The engorged head of Jack's cock tasted sweet as Chris devoured him. They feasted on each other until Jack came up for air.

"Chris, I want you so much. I want you inside me."

He definitely wanted to experience the tight sensation of sliding into Jack. Chris stretched out, his back against the cool earth, and Jack straddled him. As Jack positioned himself, Chris's aching erection brushed against the hot tender spot between Jack's buttocks. Chris moaned even louder.

Jack coated his fingers with saliva and reached around, lubricating the cleft between his cheeks, as Chris placed his hands on Jack's hips to help guide him down. They each gasped as Chris first met Jack's tight ring of muscle with resistance, but slowly, he opened up and Chris slid his swollen piece in. The fit was incredibly tight and Chris worried that it'd hurt Jack. But the look of contentment and a deep sigh of pleasure as he took Chris deep inside proved otherwise. He leaned forward and kissed Chris deeply, "I've dreamed about this. Take me, Chris, fuck me."

Chris began to gently undulate against the weight of Jack's body, thrusting and retreating and then pushing up again into the confines of Jack's willing body. The friction they were creating was intense. Jack began to ride him, timing his movements with Chris's in a deliberate erotic dance. Chris was completely focused on the beat their bodies created together. He began to move faster, wanting the sweet ride to last forever. "Stay with me, Jack," he murmured, "You feel so good."

Chris carefully cradled Jack in his arms as they changed positions. Chris continued to drive even deeper into his partner with Jack on the bottom and his legs spread wide. Every time Chris shoved into him Jack grunted with satisfaction. Chris sensed that their coupling was racing toward climax. He couldn't hold out much longer.

Chris began to work Jack's hard cock as he continued to pound Jack's ass harder and faster. "More, more," Jack begged as the pressure built for the both of them, "Yes, Chris. Come for me, come for me."

Chris suddenly crested the wave and cried out as he shot load after load inside Jack.

"Oh, yes, I'm coming too." Jack cried as Chris's fist pumped his throbbing member. Jack's hot seed shot out in spurts, making sticky pools in the hollows of his abdomen. Chris collapsed on top of Jack and they held each other, breathless and satiated.

A short time later they dressed and left the sanctuary of the trees. They walked quietly back to the reception hand in hand, the dark grounds illuminated by landscape lighting.

"I was thinking," Jack said as they approached the house, "if your dad can spare you at the store for a few days, why don't you drive back down with me tomorrow. I could show you around campus. Summer session starts soon, maybe you could talk to someone about transferring your college credits."

Chris only had to think for a second before he answered, "I'd like that."

The party was in full swing as the throbbing music the DJ played spilled out into the portico where they stood. As the tempo segued into another song, Chris recognized the opening refrain of an old Olivia Newton-John tune.

Jack obviously recognized the song too. "I love this song," he beamed, " I know its kind of cheesy, but will you dance with me?"

"Dance...together?"

Chris liked Jack. He realized now that he might even love him, but he'd managed to keep the real reason he left college a secret from nearly everyone in town. Chris wasn't sure if dancing with another guy at his best friend's wedding was the best way to come out of the closet.

"Don't worry," Jack assured him, "By now my aunt Hildy will have made several trips to the open bar and will be busting her signature moves all over the dance floor. All eyes will be on her. No one will ever notice two queer boys dancing cheek to cheek."

Jack held out his hand.

Chris realized then that life was too short to worry about what other people might think. "I warn you, I'm not exactly light on my feet."

"That's OK," he said, taking Chris's hand, "You've got other moves that I've come to appreciate."

They went inside. Despite Chris's two left feet they danced for the rest of the night.

UP FOR A MATCH

Paul Scott

It was Friday night and after a week on the road I decided to check the e-mail I had been neglecting. Being a corporate lawyer and working for a company with offices around the country guarantees my spending time on the road. I don't mind the travel much because it allows me to pursue my special interest.

It was around 7 P.M. when I sat down at the computer. Amid the flood of junk mail offering steroids, home financing, and penile enlargement I found three interesting e-mails. As usual, a rush of energy hit me when I saw the titles "Wrestling in Dallas," "Up for a match," and "Hit the mats." As I opened each of them they contained a shirtless photo of a well-built man, stats, and request for a wrestling match. Being on the road often and in many large cities had made me quite popular with my online wrestling group.

Since I was a child I spent Saturday mornings in front of the TV watching the likes of "Big Tex" and "The Masked Destroyer." At the time I had no idea why but I was in awe of these hulking bodies tossing each other around and being tossed around themselves. As I grew older I found myself cheering for the villains as they tore the pretty boys and favorites apart each week. As a kid there was no make-believe or staging in these matches. They were real and grown men were willing to step into the ring with nothing more than a pair of boots and Speedo trunks to do battle and determine who the real man was. Now that wrestling has become story lines and drama that makes soap operas look tame I have stopped watching. Yet, I still love those old days when it was just two men squaring off, sizing each other up, and struggling for dominance.

For the past seven years I have been part of an Internet wrestling league. Men into wrestling connect with each other and set up matches in their hometowns and when they travel. I definitely get my fair share of matches given my well-conditioned physique and travel schedule. I meet the guys I wrestle as a member of the Wrestlestud.com Web site and for the past three years I've been the champion. There is no title belt but there is the acknowledgment on the Web site that I'm the champ when you go to the homepage and see my photo. Most of my matches come from guys who want to knock the champ off or just want to get tossed around on the mat by someone who knows what he is doing. Anything sexual comes at the end of the match when the wrestlers settle stakes.

When I opened the e-mail titled "Up for a match" I read that a guy relatively new to the site was challenging me and was only in town for three nights. Unfortunately, his last night was tonight. It read in part, "Hey Stud or maybe it's dud. I'm in town and looking for a match. I've heard through the grapevine you're the man to beat. I like to start at the top so if you get this and are not too afraid of losing your title let me know when you want to meet up. Later, Nick"

I responded to his e-mail and hoped that Nick was online at the time. Within minutes he had e-mailed me back and agreed to come to my place for a match since I have wrestling mats set up in my basement. In his e-mail response he also took every opportunity to let me know he planned on walking away a winner regardless of how many other men I had beaten. This guy was cocky but I liked his attitude and willingness to stand up to someone who just may make a human pretzel out of him.

When my buzzer rang I answered the door and saw that he was everything he had promised. Nick was dressed in jeans and a black T-shirt beneath a leather jacket. He had a gym duffel with him that held his wrestling gear. As he entered my house and walked past me he gave me a half-hearted shove to let me know he was not afraid of me or what was going to happen. I was impressed by him physically and mentally but was not about to show it.

I had to hand it to him. Nick could walk the walk. If he had any hesitation he didn't show it. However, talk and action are two different things. This was not the first time I wrestled an opponent like this. Often guys get off on playing the tough guy role and cannot back it up, resulting with the match ending quickly and my not getting a decent workout. Nick tossed his jacket on the couch and looked around my living room. He made a joke about trying not to break too many items while he tossed me around like a rag doll. I could only smile and shake my head but I was getting sucked in by his cockiness. When I sized him up I saw a guy three inches shorter than I and 20 pounds lighter who was matter-of-factly telling me I was going to be suffering my first loss in three years.

I told Nick to grab his gear and follow me to the basement where no one would hear him crying in pain except me. When I turned on the lights Nick seemed unimpressed by my mat room. I had spent quite a bit of money and time creating this space that held wrestling mats, a shower stall, mirrored wall, and sauna. He looked around and said, "I guess this is as good a place as any to kick your ass."

By now I had had it with this punk so I reminded him of my record and our size differential. I flexed my bicep to remind him that I meant business just as much as he did. I also reminded Nick that as the challenger he had the option of naming the stakes and the gear we would wear. He chose wrestling singlets over our jocks. One of the rules the wrestlers on the Wrestlestud Web site follow is to wear at least jocks for a match. The winner then takes the jockstrap home as a sign of his victory. After all of my wrestling years I have only gone home twice without my jockstrap, the last time was over five years ago. In a closet next to the mat room I have three large bins holding over 200 jockstraps won from my conquered opponents.

When it came to stakes I said, "Remember not to gamble anything you're not willing to lose, little man." By now Nick had taken his shirt off and was displaying a great torso. He had hair on his pecs and in the deep cleft between them. His nipples were dark and made peaks on what looked like, and I would later find out feel like, two granite mountains of muscle. The hair on his chest ran into a trail that disappeared at the top of Nick's jeans. On its way it passed over a flat and tight stomach with small ridges outlining each abdominal muscle. I could tell by the way he took his shirt off that he was used to having guys admire his body. When he noticed my eyes focused on his pecs he made them bounce up and down, saying "Are you ready for this, champ?" He then said nonchalantly, "Stakes are winner takes all, one fall."

I replied "The only guys who choose those stakes with me these days are the power bottoms who roll over the minute I touch them. I'll be happy to oblige you when I rip that asshole of yours apart. Let's find out how long before you give up your ass."

I took my shirt off and stepped out of the workout pants I had been wearing. I went to the closet and chose the black jockstrap I had been wearing for all of my matches for the past six months or so. It had become a habit. It wasn't a good luck charm since I didn't need luck to take these guys down. I also chose a blue Lycra singlet that was cut low in the front to show off my chest, the straps running along the side of my nipples, making them even more prominent. Just being in this gear gets me excited and causes a rise in my crotch but something else was also giving me a rise down there. I could not help but notice Nick's huge cock as he stripped out of his underwear and put on his jockstrap. It was at least seven inches and semierect as it swung between his legs. I could only imagine how big that monster became when it was aroused. Making it appear even bigger were the low-hanging shaved balls at the end of his shaft. Nick knew he had an impressive package and made a show by arranging his cock and balls inside of his jockstrap as if the pouch of the jock had been made too small. He grabbed a red singlet from his bag and pulled it on over his jock. The legs of his singlet were cut high with white trim to show off his shredded quads. These framed his large package, made to stand out like a beacon by the Lycra surrounding it. I could see that he had some power in those legs and made a mental note to avoid them.

We agreed that since there was no referee the winner would be decided by submission. The first man to say "I give" or be forced into submission would have to give his ass to the winner. We then circled each other slowly on the mats, sizing each other up. Our eyes kept each other's gaze, neither wanting to be the first to look away as if the winner would be decided by this act alone.

The tension was broken when he flashed a smirk and said, "Are you ready to lose that title, big boy? You've been holding on to it just a little too long. I'll make you wish you'd lost it long ago." I like trash talk with my opponents so I was impressed this guy had the balls to call me out. In most of my matches, my opponents are more focused on trying to beat me and forego the verbal taunting so that they don't feel more humiliated when they lose. I was known for humiliating the guys I beat.

With that utterance we locked up. We were testing each other's strength and finding out we were evenly matched. The first hold we exchanged had me trapped in a side headlock. The side of my face was pressed tightly against his left pec. The pressure of his muscular bicep and forearm on my jaw rendered me unable to speak. He mockingly asked if I could feel the pressure or if perhaps he should increase it a bit. I try never to underestimate my opponent's ability but was surprised and concerned to feel the power Nick's body held within.

With persistence I was able to counter his hold and apply a few of my own. The match was only in the first five minutes but we were sweating as if we had each trekked across a desert. Several holds found each of us making efforts to wipe the sweat from our eyes as we tried to achieve the hold that would make the other shout "I give."

After several minutes on the mat I had Nick in a full nelson. I gave him a little of his own medicine, saying "A punk should have a little more respect for the champ but I'm used to teaching boys what it's like to wrestle a man." My adrenaline was pumping by knowing I had him in this hold. It is one of my favorites. My upper body and arms are my best asset and I can apply that hold all day. As I tightened my grip I said, "You're going nowhere except down to the mat. Exactly where I want you."

I continued to apply the hold, keeping pressure on the back of his neck with my clasped hands, forcing his chin down into his chest. He wasn't as smug now and was only letting out small grunts as he tried to catch his breath and relax into the hold so that it would do less damage.

To make the hold more punishing I began to lift him off of his feet so that only the tips of his toes were touching the mat. He let out a more audible yell but was not ready to give in. It only fueled my fire to have my pecs rubbing against the muscles in his back, my crotch rubbing against his perfectly rounded ass. As I lifted him I could feel the Lycra of his wrestling singlet creeping into the crack of his ass, making those ass cheeks stand out and allowing my cock to nest comfortably in that tight crack.

To rest my arms and regroup my strength I allowed him back on his feet. He took a deep breath and started to bend at the waist to reduce the pressure I had placed on his neck. I was losing my leverage. Nick continued to bend until his shoulders were lower than his waist. This served him well in that I was lifted off of my feet. Although I still kept the hold it had none of the power left as it had seconds before.

In one quick movement Nick grabbed the back of my head with both of his hands, began a squat and quickly jerked his hips upward, forcing me to tumble forward over his shoulder. I hit the mat hard on the middle of my back, forcing the air out of my lungs.

When I opened my eyes Nick was standing above me. He grabbed me by the back of my head and sat me up into a seated position as I tried to catch my breath. Although he had a handful of my hair, he did not pull roughly but used it to guide me to where he wanted my body positioned. I was focused on filling my lungs with air.

I had no time to react. His movements were well choreographed and came as second nature. Looking back I know now that he had done this to many other opponents and I was just another one of them.

Standing in front of me with his hand still holding the back of my head he tilted my head back enough for me to see that same smirk I had seen at the beginning of the match. In less than a second my head was trapped in those powerful quads as Nick fell back onto the mat.

His holding the back of my head and falling backward had pulled me forward so that I was lying on my stomach with my face pressed into his crotch while he was on his back with legs wrapped around my head, his calves and feet resting on my back. Every breath I took filled my nostrils with the man scent of his crotch. His pouch was full and made my breathing difficult. Several times he eased the pressure of the hold only to grab me by the back of the head and force my face farther into his bulging package.

He was brutal. He varied the pressure of those rock solid quads on the sides of my head and neck so that each time I thought I was getting accustomed to the pain it would intensify again. He did this each time I attempted to free myself from his leg scissors. With each wave of new pain my hands would fly away from their work of trying to pry his legs apart only to slap the mat in pain. I was able to barely hear a peel of laughter coming from Nick each time he forced me to slap the mat. He eased up only long enough to say, "That's music to my ears, champ." before tightening his grip and exerting his dominance.

With my face placed tightly against his Lycra-clad pouch I could feel Nick getting aroused. His cock began to grow in response to the mouth job I was forced to give him through his singlet. Although I was intent on freeing myself and winning the match, the position Nick had me in was turning me on. I could feel my own eight inches begin to grow between my legs.

As I struggled to free myself, little did I know that Nick was ready to end the match and claim his prize. The last thing I remember about the match was Nick easing up on the pressure around my head and sliding his legs down a couple of inches until they were around the sides of my neck. My chin was resting on the huge bulge that was only being contained by his jockstrap and singlet as my eyes were locked with his. He playfully slapped me on the top of my head, tousling my hair, to both humiliate me and get my attention. He had my full attention at this point. My struggle was useless. He knew exactly what he was doing and I was his helpless prey.

He said, "Say good night, Gracie" and smiled before bearing down on my neck with those vicelike quads. An animalistic growl was coming from Nick as he applied excruciating force to the sides of my neck. I was able to breathe, yet I sensed things going dim. My eyes were closing and my slapping of the mat was slowed until it eventually stopped. My chin slid down along the bulge of his manhood until my mouth and nose were resting comfortable in my opponent's sweat-stained crotch.

What awakened me was a pressure I felt against my crotch. I slowly opened my eyes to see Nick standing above me, still in his singlet, with his foot playfully working over my cock. He looked like a Greek god with his sweat-glistened body and square jaw. Although I had been out for less than a minute Nick had taken the liberty of stripping me of my singlet and tossing it aside. Lying on the mat in my jock with my conqueror standing over me my cock was brought to full attention as it fought against the confinement of the fabric.

Nick matter-of-factly explained to me what I already knew. "You fell right into my trap. I scissored your neck and temporarily stopped the blood flow in your arteries on the sides of your neck, making you pass out for a few seconds. There's no damage done to you physically but definitely to your ego. It looks like we have a new champ."

I went to roll away from the foot action I was receiving. It was exciting me and making me feel humiliated at the same time but

Nick stopped me by increasing the pressure his foot was applying and saying "Oh, no you don't. Just relax and take this as it comes to you. I'm calling the shots now that I'm the champ."

I closed my eyes and took a deep breath as I recalled the stakes we had decided on earlier. I remembered my telling Nick, "Don't gamble with anything you're not willing to lose." If only I had taken my own advice. It had been years since I had bottomed for anyone. I've been a top all of my life except for a few times where I'd tried bottoming with a lover, mostly to satisfy him. Frankly, I had never experienced much of a sense of pleasure while bottoming. It had been so long that I had never considered it ever happening again.

The only other matches I had lost, when I was newer to the wrestling scene, did not involve the loser getting fucked, but only blow jobs. Since I had been champ for the past three years the challenger had always chosen the stakes and since I had won all of those matches there was no chance of my bottoming. I knew that Nick was going to see to it that he received the spoils of victory...my ass.

I asked him, sarcastically, why he had not taken my jockstrap off as well. He replied, "I left it on so that the loser could present it to the winner. I want you to remember this night." I already knew I would not be forgetting this night. He removed his foot from my groin and bent down to grab me by the back of my head.

Nick guided me to my knees and directed my head into his waiting pouch. Through his singlet and jock I was directed to work his cock. His jock and the tight Lycra made his manhood stand out and demand attention, surrounded by two mountains of quad muscles. As I used my tongue and mouth to soak his crotch I could taste the saltiness of his sweat coming through.

He grabbed my hand, placing it on his pec and forced it to play with his nipples. When I lightly twisted one he let out a low moan of pleasure as he threw his head back and grabbed the back of my head, forcing it harder into his balls.

My own cock was at full attention and not used to being ignored after a hard match. However, when I attempted to take it out of my jock Nick lightly cuffed me on the side of the head saying, "Remember you're here to serve the winner. We'll take care of you later if you deserve it. Just think about how my cock is going to feel pounding that tight asshole of yours."

As he spoke he slipped out of the straps on his singlet and slowly rolled it down his sweaty torso. My hands wandered from his pecs and caressed his abs, passing over each of his tightly defined knots of muscle.

He grabbed the back of my head again and guided me to my feet. Although I was taller than Nick, his body now towered over me, making me feel like a novice in the presence of greatness. Looking into my eyes with an air of victory he said in a low voice, "Now take that jock of yours off and present it to the winner. Show some respect."

Both mentally and physically he had beaten me. There was no question who was the victor today. As I bent to take off my jock I thought to myself of the list of my past opponents who would give anything just to watch what was going on here tonight, especially as I knelt in front of Nick with my head bowed down in defeat toward the mat, raising both my hands and making an offertory of my black jock. I felt not only physically but psychologically stripped. Before Him I was laying myself as a prize to be used any way the winner saw fit.

He took the jock and lifted it to his nose to smell the musky scent of a man who had lost his pride. He then placed the jock in my face, instructing me to take a deep breath so that beside seeing and feeling what a loss is I would also know the smell of it.

He directed me to get on all fours as he stepped out of his singlet and jockstrap. With a slight laugh as he did so he said, "I bet you had not thought the night was going to end this way, did you, chump?" Kneeling in front of me as I was on all fours he gently slapped my face with his cock that had grown both in length and girth since I saw him putting on his jock not less than 40 minutes ago.

My mouth went instinctively for it, working the huge mushroom head with my tongue and bathing the shaft with all the saliva I had in me. My breathing increased in pace and my body tensed as I felt him reach around to my ass and begin working my hole. He was kind and gentle initially, playing with my hole and making it pucker and grab for his finger as he lightly tickled it. He ended these rounds of teasing with two or three hard smacks to my ass. These brought me out of my reverie and reminded me of rough waters ahead. All the while he maintained his control of my mouth by driving his cock deep into my throat, forcing my nostrils to rest in his pubic hair at its base.

Slowly he began to work his finger into the hole. I gasped and immediately stopped my focus on his cock. Nick reassured me with a soft voice saying, "Just relax. You're going to like this just as much as I will." He knew I had anxiety and had not pictured this scenario being played out.

After eventually working three fingers into my hole and coaching me on my breathing as he slowly opened my hole, Nick removed his fingers and reached for his gym bag. He pulled his cock from my mouth and told me to put my head on the mat and raise my ass as far into the air as I could. I obeyed. I could not see what he was doing but could hear the tearing of the condom wrapper and him working lube onto his shaft.

The next thing I felt was his hand pressing on my lower back and the quick thrust of Nick's hips. I cried out in agony and lost my breath as I felt my insides being ripped apart by his engorged tool driving into me and forcing me down into the mat. Nick, lying on top of me, clamped around my waist with his muscular arms and whispered in my ear, "That's the worst of it, champ. Just relax into it now and you'll enjoy this."

I begged him not to move until I was ready as I felt tears welling in my eyes and willed the pain to subside. He acknowledged my plea and allowed me to take a few breaths before raising himself back onto his knees and repositioning my ass in the air. Again he pushed my head down into the mat and began slowly removing his cock until only the head was left inside of me. I could feel the blood pulsing inside of his cock forcing an echo through each of the muscles of my tightened ass.

He proceeded to slowly insert himself again, all the while reading my body for signs of acceptance of his member. After several strokes I had relaxed a bit and was able to take all of him without gasping with each thrust. Nick, sensing my increased comfort, picked up his pace and began guiding my hips so that my ass was in sync with his thrusts. As I allowed the muscles around my asshole to relax and accommodate his cock I felt a sense of pleasure building inside of my pelvic region. The pain had subsided to be replaced by a sense of warmth.

After several minutes of his riding me and intermittently working my ass cheeks with crisp slaps, my attention was brought to the precome oozing from my own cock. Since Nick had directed me to focus on his desires I had neglected the needs of my own body. I began to pump my cock as Nick continued to pound my ass. Noticing me working my cock he said, "You know you're only doing that because I am allowing you to, don't you?" When I didn't respond he grabbed the back of my head roughly and thrust his shaft as deeply as it would go into my ass, spearing my insides.

I let out a whimper and said, "Yes, sir. I know you're the champ and I'm your prize. Fuck me like a champ. I thought I was going to make an easy night of you but you're a tough fucker." As I continued grunting out to Nick about my false assumptions of beating him his pace quickened with his breathing. As I said, "Fuck me, champ. Fuck me, champ." Nick drove his rod into me and THEN let out a guttural yell as his juice shot all over the condom inside of me.

When I felt his explosion, I could not contain myself any longer. The spasming of his cock was sending electric waves throughout my body. As I felt my asshole open and closing around his prick I shot my load all over the wrestling mat. It was like a dam had burst and there was no turning back. The come sprayed in what seemed like endless gushes all over the mat and my torso.

I fell to the mat, the sweat of my body mixing with come splayed on the mat. Nick was on top of me and still inside of me, our sweat from the match continuing to serve as a lubricant for our bodies. He did not make a move for several minutes. Words weren't exchanged as I could feel both his and my heart rates returning to normal beats. After several minutes he began nibbling my ear and whispered, "I'll be back in town next month. I see you have lots of jocks in that collection you can afford to lose." To date, although I try my best, my collection has been dwindling all to one opponent.

RELEASE

Jordan M. Coffey

Greg Dixon shut down his laptop and slowly turned, swiveling his chair to face the room. With a smoldering, sexy look in his eye, he smiled, taking in the sight of his lover who was beautifully presented, accented by moonlight, kneeling next to a big, black leather couch. A hot, blue gaze was staring back—and as Greg stood, those eyes traveled down his body, hesitating only briefly on the hard cock that bobbed freely in front of him, before finally settling on his laced-up boots.

He approached the kneeling figure with steady, even steps until he was close enough for the other man's tongue to lick leather or skin or maybe the sticky wetness that was leaking from the head of his dick.

They were both ready.

In another part of town, a similar scene played out.

Seth Wolfe was on the couch, in the sexually charged atmosphere of his living room, watching his lover. The nearly naked, muscled form sat in a chair across the room—blindfolded and trembling.

It was time.

Greg and Seth only knew each other by virtue of cyber-communication—instant-message names and free e-mail addresses. The connection originally stemmed from similar academic interests, posts to several Internet mailing lists segueing into an off-list relationship where they discovered other similarities. Such as they were both in love with much older men. Men who exuded power not just through physical attributes, but attitude and accomplishments. Men with gruff exteriors that hid depths of emotion. Men who preferred discretion in their private lives.

Greg's lover, Wayne, was the head of a multimillion dollar corporation. He had built his fortune from nothing through hard work and determination and had high expectations of those around him. Wayne Bartlett didn't take any shit, but gave it in spades.

Seth's lover, Joe, led men into battle. At first, with distinguished service, around the world for the military. Now, on the crime-riddled streets for the police force. The things he'd seen in his lines of work could break lesser men. Joe Williamson was commanding and strong because he knew that lives depended on it.

It was no surprise to either Greg or Seth that men who wielded power so resolutely would sometimes, in some ways, need to give it over, find a release. And though younger and less physically intimidating than their lovers, they were able to provide what was needed. But, what they discovered in one another was their own need for release—how liberating was the opportunity to share their secrets, though without the specifics of identities, with a kindred spirit. Former geeks who had grown into their own, professionally and personally, reveling in the power they possessed and the men they loved.

"Taste it."

A shudder went through Wayne Bartlett's large frame. He was on his knees, wearing only a leather harness. It was a wonderful elaboration of straps and metal rings crisscrossing the broad chest and muscular back and attached to a cock ring (which was doing its duty quite nicely on Wayne's sizable erection), with a thin strap that fit snugly between the firm cheeks of his ass. For Wayne, it was as if he were tied up without being tied down, though his hands were cuffed behind him.

Wayne's body shook again, but otherwise he didn't move. His

eyes didn't rise from where they were fixed on the dull gleam of his lover's leather-encased feet, although his mind was filled with the starkly erotic vision the younger man presented: hard, primed, totally naked—except for the boots and the tight-fitting, black leather gloves.

"Wayne..." The tone held a hint of warning.

Eyes almost black with arousal finally lifted, but only as far as the rigid flesh pointing in their direction—held transfixed by the beauty and power of it.

"I won't say it again."

One broad swipe of a tongue, which lingered for a second as Wayne let the swollen, leaking head rest in his mouth. He resisted the urge to suckle; he'd been waiting in that spot for a long time, and didn't want to risk being left there any longer.

"Good...good."

A gloved hand came up, and with a few quick strokes, released more drops to settle on Wayne's tongue. The taste, combined with the intense rush of leather scent, almost pushed the older man over the edge. His dick strained against its binding, smacking the defined ridges of his abs.

"*Very* nice."

Greg removed his cock from his lover's mouth, letting it rub wetly across the squared jaw. He stepped back, walking slowly around the kneeling man, until he was behind him, appreciating the rear view. Forcing air into his lungs, he took deep breaths, holding his own arousal in check. The sight of Wayne Bartlett's body had been able to make him hard ever since they'd met. It was like a wet dream come true to know that it was now all his.

Quickly, he reached down and released the cuffs. Moving Wayne's arms aside, he trailed his hands over the firm flesh of his lover's back and ass, tugging on the straps, watching the play of rippling muscles. Desire flared up inside him, and he wanted more. He placed two fingers on Wayne's lips, and the older man sucked them in, wetting them with an eagerness fueled by need. Seconds later, those two slick fingers were inside a passage so tight and hot,

Greg could have sworn his gloves were smoking. He slowly withdrew, smiling at the moans of protest.

"Shh...it's not over yet."

Seth stood. The moonlight shining into the room flashed briefly off of the ring through his left nipple and the buckles on his boots. The leather covering the lower half of his body was dark and smooth and form-fitting. He felt hard and tight with lust. Lust for the man across the room.

Big, buff, tough Joe Williamson—whose sight was now cut off by a leather blindfold. There were cuffs, also leather, surrounding both his wrists, and it looked as if he were bound to the chair on which he was sitting, but he wasn't. The hands gripping the edge of the seat weren't locked in place by restraints, just Joe's self-control alone. And, judging by the size of the bulge in the leather pouch of his thong, there was precious little of that left.

There was enough supple, skin-warmed leather in the room to fill the air with its scent and Seth knew that Joe would be getting off on that. Seth was tempted to blow cool puffs of air over every inch of taut, exposed skin to distract the blindfolded man, to engage another sense, but decided to use sound instead.

He went past, walking around the room, watching the response to his movements in the slight twitches of Joe's body. Finally, he stopped at the stairs. Turning to sit on the third one, he spread his legs wide, rubbing his palms along the surface of his leather pants, and called out.

"Joseph. Come to me."

He watched as Joe slowly made his way around to the stairs searching for the voice, faltering only slightly. When Joe was standing before him, he whispered.

"Good. Now, closer."

And Joe was on his knees, gasping as strong hands kept him from falling forward, groaning as insistent fingers led his face to the juncture of his lover's legs. He hesitated, mouth open, but those fingers pressed him closer still, and he wasted little time savoring the scent, moving to work his tongue over the bulging leather. Making it shine in his eagerness, making Seth moan from his attention, whimpering when his face was pulled away.

"Don't worry...we're not done yet."

There was the snap and zip as pants were unfastened, and then, the sharp hissing sound of Joe's anticipation.

Wayne was on the floor, on his back, knees bent, arms stretched above his head, wrists cuffed together. Greg was settled between the solid thickness of his thighs, and the equally solid thickness of his cock was jumping every so often, pleading in vain for the gift of touch. Demanding hands spread his legs wider, and his toes curled tightly in response, gripping the floor beneath.

One sharp pinch to the head of his dick had him arching, back bowed, hips forward, head moving to expose the corded flesh of his neck.

"There, Wayne. Hold it there."

A soft kiss that turned into sharp bites, moving from nipple to nipple, blazing a trail across his chest, had him ready to take flight. Tremors shook him and whispered pleas escaped him despite his best efforts.

"It's OK. Just settle down now." Soothing sweeps of a hot, wet tongue moved lower and lower, dipping into the crease between his thigh and groin. "Now hold on..." And then, his balls were treated to the same hot wetness, followed by fiery nibbles. Alternating tortures in a seemingly endless stream. Wayne swallowed his scream and held on.

Even over the powerful, seductive fragrance of leather, Joe could smell the tantalizing scent of his lover's exposed cock and balls. The heady musk of sweat and skin with traces of seeping semen. He was allowed to nuzzle the steamy patch of surrounding curls, and he filled his nostrils with the aroma.

"Get ready."

He nodded a little, moving his head in his lover's grasp, as the thick hard-on was placed between his lips.

"All of it."

Joe took it in, deep-throating the erection in a long-practiced move. Easing it in and out, working his tongue, and throat, and lips with a heartfelt willingness. His hands itched to touch, but he pressed his fingers into the hard surface of the stairs and concentrated on the sounds of his lover's satisfaction.

Wayne sucked in a breath at the feel of cool gel on the hot skin of his cock, his already tense muscles straining even more with the force of barely leashed arousal. He bit his lip just short of bleeding when a warm hand joined in. The trifold temperature sensation, blending to a sensual simmering, soon had him making a deep, rumbling sound that seemed to start somewhere in the vicinity of his balls.

"So good, and about to get better."

His legs were moved as Greg positioned him, and he felt the scrape of rubber as the heel of a boot brushed against his thigh.

"Wayne. Look at me."

He didn't want to open his eyes. Didn't want to see the scene before him. Didn't want to know how much closer it would push him to the edge. Didn't think he could take it. Of course, he opened them anyway, and fought to maintain the eye contact.

"Stay with me, here. Ready?"

Every nerve in Wayne's body was screaming 'NO!' but he still managed to give a little nod. Right before his cock was swallowed up by Greg's ass. The harsh sound ripped from him sounded like an animal in pain, but it was the sweetest joy Wayne had ever known. To be trapped, balls-deep, inside his lover.

Greg, too, was high on the pleasure, gliding on the currents of sensation, as he rocked on the dick inside him, finding just the right rhythm. His own dick was sliding through the slickness of his lubed fist as he took himself to the brink.

"Wayne...shit, Wayne." Hissed through clenched teeth as he let go, shooting streams over anything that dared to be in the way. He could feel the muscles of Wayne's thighs tighten, and the strong hips lock in an upright position, and immediately rubbed a taut, sweaty flank in warning.

"Not yet Wayne. Not yet." He opened his eyes, and slowly eased off of the still-hard organ, smiling when he saw the creamy splatters on Wayne's face. Reaching out with a hand that was similarly smeared, he rubbed the spunk around the strong nose and sharp blue eyes, marking his territory with his essence.

In two quick thrusts, Seth was all the way in. Joe was still gripping the stairs, but now with his lover behind him, fucking him in long, smooth strokes. Every other beat or so, Seth's leather-covered thighs would stick to the damp sweatiness of Joe's skin—just one more thing to rile his overwrought senses. That and the ever roaming hands. Relentlessly moving over his back, his chest, his neck, his balls—everywhere but the jutting flesh that was desperate for attention.

"Oh, man."

The pace got faster, the thrusts harder, and Joe didn't dare not keep up. Not even when he felt himself being pulled toward the abyss, despite his ignored hard-on.

"Oh, fuck, Joe."

The older man mentally restrained himself from uttering either pleas or protests, determined to ride out the frantic assault, but his throat hurt from the deep growls he was powerless to hold back.

"Joe...don't come."

Seth's voice sounded raw as well, his statement punctuated by each jerk of his hips.

"Don't come. Don't come. Don't. Come. Don't. Come. Don't. Come." Until he was coming with a soft roar, discharging deep inside Joe's ass. He pulled out, sliding one hand along the slippery skin of his lover's back, while the other finally reached around to grasp the stiff shaft still waiting for release.

"Good. Very, very good."

Greg relaxed on the couch, leaning against one of the overstuffed ends, his body cradled in leather. One boot-clad foot was pressed into the seat, with his arm resting on his bent knee, and the other foot was braced on the floor. Between his legs, Wayne was kneeling, facing the plump-cushioned back.

A leather-covered finger ran down Wayne's spine leaving a mass of agitated, quivering muscles in its wake, and the sofa made a protesting sound as Wayne tightened his grip. The straps had been removed from his cock and ass, and he ached with the knowledge of what was to come.

"Almost there, Wayne."

A gloved palm cupped the sacs between Wayne's legs, finding them so hard and full, they seemed to have merged into one ripe ball. Greg moved his hand to the mound of one ass cheek, palming that as well, his fingers dipping into the deep crack, and then, pulling slightly, he slowly parted the meaty flesh, exposing the puckered opening. He raised his other hand, already glistening with lube, and slid three fingers home.

Wayne was very still, absorbing the pleasure, and frozen with anticipation. Wanting to move, needing to move...forbidden to move. He could feel the rhythmic squeezing of Greg's hand on one side of his ass, and he clenched his inner muscles in response.

"Show me how you want to be done."

Finally free to act, Wayne fucked himself on those three fingers, arching, rocking, tilting, so that he could feel the burst of pleasure inside on each backward thrust. Pressure built as his dick slammed into the soft back of the couch, and his lover's other hand kept clutching his ass, or rubbing his thigh, or teasing that sweet, sensitive spot behind his balls.

"Any time now, Wayne."

Any time now. Any minute now. Any second now. It was going to end with an explosive bang. Especially now that Greg was twisting those fingers, pulling back and pushing forward in perfect counter-movements, meeting him so seamlessly, Wayne kept waiting for his lover's whole hand to just slip inside.

“Wayne...next time, I think we should play on that huge mahogany conference table at the office...right before a board meeting.”

“Ye-s-s-s...” Wayne sprayed out the first real word he’d uttered the whole night, and came—hard—semen spilling down the soft leather in front of him to drip onto his lover’s left boot.

“Looking good, Joe.”

Joe’s dick was in Seth’s palm, and Seth was fondling Joe’s balls, and Joe did indeed look damned good: standing tall, hands clasped behind his back, trembling with desire and the effort to contain it.

It wouldn’t be much longer now; Seth had that situation well in hand. He worked Joe’s erection, milking him in a strong grip, teasing the head as it kept up a steady drool. He sank a finger inside the still-slick hole between his lover’s cheeks, not really to give Joe any added stimulation, but just to feel the familiar tightness once more. But it didn’t mean that he *couldn’t* turn up the heat by applying pressure to the gland hidden inside.

Suddenly, he released his grip, leaving Joe’s hard-on angrily suspended...

“Now, Joseph. Right now.”

The erect flesh jerked once, slit gaping slightly, and immediately began issuing forth its load. Seth reached out again, holding on until it was over, leaving creamy drips that spilled down his right leg, and slid past the buckles on his boot.

Separated by miles and circumstances, and connected in ways they didn’t even know, two men simultaneously followed sticky trails with their tongues, licking along smooth, black leather, until each was lapping up stray drops of come from the toe of his lover’s boot...

While two younger men lovingly looked on and thought about the latest story they could now share.

BRUTES FOR L.T.

Simon Sheppard

Not muscle, just bulk. On a good day, Casey weighed in at 270 bulky pounds, and Casey didn't have that many good days. He'd been big since childhood, had endured schoolyard taunts, had made it through college, watching as the jocks he desired had scored with the prettiest girls. It was only after-hours in the locker room, when he'd secretly service at least a quarter of the soccer team, that he'd felt at all sexy, and even then he realized that he—and his prodigious talent for cock sucking—were being rather heartlessly used.

His mother had always told him he had a nice face, and that was undoubtedly true. He was, in a rosy-cheeked way, exceptionally handsome, and over the years a number of women, usually Christian Girls With Good Hearts, had come on to him, but that wasn't what he was aching for. Not at all.

Casey graduated with a degree in social work, went on to get a decent, socially productive job, and began to jack off to professional wrestling. He knew it was foolish, stupid even; that the theatrically overbutch performers who barked into the cameras and slammed folding chairs over each other's heads were, in a very real sense, buffoons. It didn't matter. Pro wrestlers gave Casey roaring hard-ons on a regular basis. After a rough day solving the problems of the world—no thanks to the bastards in power—Casey would head for home, nuke some dinner, pop open a Bud, and settle down in front of the tube. Due to the devoted fandom of hormonally askew teenage boys, there was almost always wrestling on cable.

Casey had started watching matches back in what he now thought of as the Golden Age, the era of Hulk Hogan and Rowdy Roddy Piper. He'd suffer through Mean Gene interviewing André the Giant—about as far from Bill Moyers as you could get—just to grab a glimpse of Piper in his kilt. He'd read somewhere that most kilt-wearers were indeed naked under there, but then, most kilt-wearers were unlikely to get tossed headfirst out of a wrestling ring. Rowdy Roddy might have worn trunks beneath the tartan, but that didn't put the brakes on Casey's fantasies. He'd sit in front of the Sony, one hand in a bag of microwave popcorn, the other on his dick, and watch 'roid-raging men in tights beating, theoretically, the shit out of one another. There were times he'd sit sprawled in his well-worn La-Z-Boy and wonder if he shouldn't be out trolling the bars for chubby chasers, or at least hitting the Internet chat rooms. But then the commercials would be over, the sweaty, oiled bruisers would resume the head butts and the illegal choke holds, and his flagging hard-on would spring back to life.

He'd jack off during the matches, sometimes even during the interviews, and whenever a particularly delectable wrestler got tossed across the ring, landing with a meaty thump, his dick would swell and tingle and he'd nearly shoot his wad. But he mostly saved his sperm for bedtime. There were whole months when every night he'd crawl in bed, a wad of Kleenex waiting on the nightstand, and fantasize about Roddy Piper. He, Casey, would typically be lying on his back in the middle of a wrestling ring, plump, naked, and erect. Rowdy Roddy would stride across the canvas, wearing a kilt and a championship belt, his formidable chest bare and gleaming. Would walk over to Casey and straddle his head, a shining boot at either cheek. Casey would peer upward. Under the kilt, the wrestler was naked, of course, his thickly muscular thighs framing his hanging cock, which in Casey's imagination was big, slightly curved, and uncut. Casey would grab for Piper's enormous calves and the wrestler would let him. More: Piper's cock would start to get hard. Slowly, he'd squat down over Casey's face. What happened next would depend on which way Piper was facing. If he were facing

Casey's head, he'd slip his now-hard cock head between the fat man's soft, eager lips. If, as was often the case, he faced the other way, Casey, scarcely believing his luck, would watch as Piper's hairy crotch descended, his musky asshole just a sniff away. Casey would stick out his tongue, making contact with the wrestler's hole, and, surrounded by the kilt, would lap happily away.

That was it for the fantasy, generally. Sometimes he'd imagine Piper between his thighs, pushing up at Casey's legs, finally sliding his hard maleness inside. In reality, Casey wasn't much for getting fucked. The few times he'd gotten someone to actually do it, it had been more pain than glee. But sometimes, more-than-rarely, fantasy-Roddy would straddle Casey's meaty chest, sliding backward over his big belly till the heat of Piper's moist hole was just barely rubbing Casey's cock head and then...and then Casey couldn't restrain himself. He'd grab over for the Kleenex and shoot off, moaning and thrashing, the match-up at an orgasmic end. Then he'd toss the damp tissues into a pile in the corner, roll over, and fall soundly asleep.

And so went Casey's life, month after month, though with some minor alterations. As time went on, pro wrestling became more and more popular; its stars were even made into "action figures," butch Barbie dolls for prepubescent boys. Hulk Hogan, after an abortive stab at a movie career, became "Hollywood Hogan," a feather-boa-wearing shell of his former self, a parody of what was already shtick. Rowdy Roddy, likewise, mostly vanished from the scene, to be replaced by a new, even more buff crop of grunters: The Rock, Goldberg, and Casey's new favorite, Skye Blue. Sure, his name sounded like a drag queen or a foo-foo vodka drink, but Skye himself was perfection, all chest and attitude and a butt that looked great in spandex.

Blue became the new object of Casey's adoration, a devotion twice as powerfully obsessive as his love for Piper had been. Night and day, Skye was the one. The wrestler not only fueled Casey's bedtime fantasies, he followed him to the job, popping up in Casey's mind at the most inopportune moments. Casey could be sucking up to his boss or counseling a poverty-stricken client on appealing her SSI rejection when Sky Blue sprang to mind with the force of a side of beef, his massive erection pounding its way through azure tights. "I'm gonna fuck you, pussy!" he'd growl, and Casey's cock would respond in kind, awkwardly filling the crotch of his stretch Dockers. If he wasn't already seated behind his desk, he'd find an excuse to return there.

Whether on pay-per-view or free cable, Skye's matches were not to be missed. Every takedown, every suplex, every sweaty, oddly intimate pin made Casey's heart race. And then it happened: The World Wrestling League was coming to Casey's town, staging a show at the MallMart Arena in just six weeks. Casey stood in line to buy a ticket as soon as TicketVulture opened its terminals, but the 12th row wasn't enough, not nearly. Because Casey had an idea.

One of his clients had gotten off junk and gotten a maintenance job at the MallMart Arena, and when Casey phoned him up, it turned out the Arena was hiring. So Casey went down and scored a part-time job, working evenings and weekends. It would be tough to juggle two jobs, but the prospect of Skye Blue would make it all worthwhile.

At last the day of the WWL's appearance came 'round. Casey pulled his dark blue uniform over his bulky body and drove out to the arena. Already, five hours before the event, hordes of pimply boys and their fathers were lining up at the entrances. Didn't those people have a *life*?

The stage crew was putting the finishing touches on the ring and rigging the lights when Casey arrived. He joined the seat crew, setting up row after row of folding chairs on the arena floor. He himself arranged the chairs closest to the ring, the ones that might, in a theatrical moment, make suitable props for head-bashing. After the chairs were all in place, he helped set up the concession stands, including huge booths selling souvenir T-shirts and programs, and then the doors were flung open and the mostly-male crowds filed in.

He'd been told to hang around during the show in case an

emergency arose, but his next serious work would probably not take place until after-show cleanup. So he bought himself a root beer and went to explore backstage. His uniform and laminated badge gave him access to the dressing rooms, concrete cells where pumped men were changing into their wrestling...togs? Uniforms? Costumes? Whatever. And Casey recognized them all: the Kaos Twinz, Osama bin Evil, Sweet Gavin Ghoul, Team Liberty, the Punishator. And then he turned a fateful concrete corner and there he was: Skye Blue, not more than a few amazing feet away. Even in street clothes, the power of his body was evident, biceps bulging from his T-shirt, thick thighs beneath tight jeans. And his face was, if anything, even more handsome than it was on TV; for one thing, he wasn't screwing it up in mock rage as he issued challenges and taunted his opponents.

Casey couldn't believe how fast his dick had gotten hard. He just stood there stupidly, soda cup clutched protectively in front of his crotch, as Blue and his manager—Casey recognized him too—stood talking quietly. A phrase from his childhood crossed Casey's mind: "A cat can look at a king." Must have been from some fairy tale or something. And if Skye Blue was a king—and he *was*—then Casey was a cat, a fat cat, an overweight pussy. His cock throbbed insistently against his fly.

The wrestler clapped his manager on the shoulder and turned to go. Casey held his breath as the wrestler approached and then, suddenly, for one magical, endless second, Skye Blue looked Casey in the eye and smiled. "Hey," he said. "See you after the fight." Just that. Casey was frozen, speechless and hot with desire. Blue walked on, entered a dressing room, and shut the door. Casey exhaled. Finally.

The next couple of hours were a blur of biceps, body slams, and screaming young guys waving hand-lettered signs. Casey stood watching at the foot of a staircase as the Punishator pinned heavily tattooed Chang, the Kaos Twinz tag-team brawled with Team Liberty, and, in a matchup that interested Casey not at all, Elena fought the Temptress. Then it was time for the climactic fight. To the blare of speed metal, Doctor Destructo, dressed all in black, a skull crudely painted on his singlet, strode down the aisle, accompanied by two henchmen carrying big, nasty-looking axes. Destructo entered the ring, pacing around, flexing, grimacing wildly. Casey, feeling like a traitor to his beloved Skye Blue, couldn't help but notice how incredibly well-built the Doctor was, how big his basket seemed to be.

Just as the crowd's boos reached a crescendo, the music changed. Aaron Copland's "Fanfare for the Common Man." Cliché. Cliché. Cliché, but Casey didn't mind. Not when the bright white spotlights picked out Skye Blue, wearing a sequined cerulean cape, walking down the aisle, climbing into the ring, discarding his robe with a flourish. The arena's lights gleamed on his oiled, muscular flesh. Naked from the waist up, amazing biceps, powerful pecs, nipples so prominent Casey didn't even have to look at the GianTron screen to see them. Thighs, ass, basket, calves. Skye Blue paced around the ring, blowing almost-campy kisses to the wildly cheering crowd.

The announcer made his announcement. The ref, looking puny next to the soon-to-be-dueling behemoths, took his place and gestured, and the match began. Casey wasn't stupid, not even when he was hopelessly blinded with lust, not even when he was standing in the shadows of the MallMart Arena with his hands in his pockets, surreptitiously stroking his full-to-bursting hard dick. He knew that pro wrestling was showbiz, no doubt rehearsed, and that anyone who actually endured the punishment the wrestlers seemed to be dishing out would wind up crippled or dead. Still, his heart rose whenever Skye Blue got the upper hand over Doctor Destructo, sank when Destructo got Skye in a hammerlock or claw hold. In one particularly awful moment, Destructo tossed Blue out of the ring, followed him to the floor, grabbed a folding chair, and swung it at his opponent. It was one of the chairs that Casey had set up, and he hated himself, stupidly, for leaving it within Destructo's reach. But then, just seconds after getting mightily whacked, Skye Blue recovered and leapt into the ring again, and everything was, for Casey, precariously all right. A top-rope slingshot clothesline brought Destructo to the mat, and Skye pinned him, one huge, heaving body pressing down upon another. But Destructo was able to kick out before the count. Damn. The thudding of flesh on flesh went on and on, accompanied by the roar of the crowd, as Casey kept his dick on the verge of coming, not even thinking how awkward it would be to have to finish his shift with a big, dark stain on the front of his blue trousers.

He drifted off into one of his sex fantasies, his eyes still on the battle in the ring, his mind elsewhere. He was on his back, his beefy legs raised over his fat belly, as Skye Blue thrust his huge hard-on into him, again and again and again, until his ass ached with soreness and desire. The wrestler's handsome face was contorted in lust, sweat dripping off his curly blond hair, sweat that dripped, salty as come, into Casey's open mouth. Casey raised his head to Skye's sweaty armpit and inhaled the acrid smell as he was filled with hard, masculine...

"Is Skye Blue," the announcer was shouting as the testosterone-drenched mob went wild.

The fans had almost finished filing out, the arena floor a mess of spilled nachos, empty soda cups, and discarded hand-lettered signs. It was time for Casey to get to work, but hell, he didn't care if he lost this job, not at all. Backstage was where he was headed, Skye Blue's words echoing through his brain: *After the fight. After the fight. After the fight.* They meant nothing, of course, a casual phrase casually uttered. Not even a real invitation. But Casey had come so far, so close...

The way backstage was surrounded by a gaggle of young fans, some skinny and geeky, others as fat as Casey himself had been at that age, a few hunky enough to be pro wrestlers themselves someday. Two burly security guards kept the crowd in check, but Casey's badge got him into the warren of backstage tunnels, to the door of the dressing room he'd seen Skye Blue enter. It was now or never. He hesitated a moment, then knocked.

“Come in.” The wrestler’s own familiar voice.

Skye Blue was sprawled in a chair, his wrestling outfit soaked with sweat. He smiled when he saw Casey, but he wasn’t alone. His manager was there, and another man he’d never seen before, young and handsome and as muscular as Skye Blue. Casey’s heart fluttered, then sank.

“Hey,” Skye Blue said, “thanks for coming. Mind waiting outside for a minute?”

Casey shook his head and backed out of the room, hoping no one had noticed his stiffy. He stood in the corridor, feeling even dorkier than usual, as hunky wrestlers and their hangers-on passed him by.

The door opened. “You can go in now,” the manager said. And the young hunk was leaving too.

Casey walked into the dressing room, feeling like he might faint.

“Hey, hot stuff,” said Skye Blue.

A cruel joke. Casey blushed and bolted for the door.

“Hey, wait up. Where you going? You *want* to be here, don’t you?” And Skye Blue reached down for his crotch.

“Yes, Mr. Blue. Yes I do.” Casey squeezed the words out of his desert-dry throat.

“Then lock the door and c’mere. And call me Darryl.” The wrestler stood up from his chair, almost naked and sweaty and just a few feet away. This couldn’t be happening. It couldn’t.

Casey shuffled along the concrete floor, feet through molasses. “I’d rather call you Skye,” he said, stupidly.

“Whatever,” Skye said. He stepped toward Casey, took his head in his hands, and kissed him softly on the lips. “Whatever.” He kissed Casey again, and this time Casey kissed back. As their tongues met, the wrestler put his arms around Casey’s big waist and pressed up against him, crotch against crotch.

Casey’s arms hung limply at his sides. He didn’t dare to touch the wrestler’s firm flesh. He wasn’t worthy. He was nothing more than a mercy fuck. He...

And then Skye was kneeling, unzipping Casey's blue serge pants, fishing out Casey's hard-on, taking it in his mouth, sucking at it, expertly. Hesitantly, Casey put his hand on Skye's blond curls. The wrestler took Casey's dick all the way down his throat, and Casey held him there. Oh, fuck, it was a fairy tale. A fairy tale come true.

At last Casey guided Skye's head away. He wanted to return the favor, to taste Skye Blue's massive cock. He guided the wrestler to his feet, knelt before him, peeled down his tights, removed his protective cup. Casey almost gasped. Skye Blue's cock wasn't big at all. It was considerably smaller than his own, almost tiny, though bright pink and stiff, head still partly dressed in foreskin. And pretty. Not disappointing at all, really. Hot. Hot and hard and it would feel great inside him. He enveloped the dick in his mouth, where it fit neatly, no gagging, no fuss, and sucked away, tasting precome on his tongue.

"Oh, man," said Skye, "that feels great." Casey sucked harder and played with the wrestler's tight, hot ball sac. "You want to fuck me?"

Casey felt faint. "Me? Fuck you?"

"Sure. Why not?"

"Because I'm...I'm...and you're..."

The blond wrestler smiled down at the kneeling fat man. "Jesus, you don't *look* stupid. You think because I've got muscles I don't like to get fucked?"

"But I'm..."

"And because I got muscles I only like guys who look like me? Well, I don't, you know. I'm turned on by guys like you. I mean, why else would you be here?" And he reached down and ran his hand over Casey's broad chest, giving his meaty tit a hard squeeze, then further down, over his round, furry belly, down to Casey's achingly hard, moist cock. "C'mon, big boy. Stick it in me." He pulled off his tights and, naked, walked over to the dressing table and bent over, his ass just perfect. He reached back and pulled at one cheek, revealing his pulsing pink hole.

“Oh, G-o-o-od...” Casey moaned.

“There’s condoms and lube in that bag over there.”

And as Casey stood behind Skye and slid in his cock, pressing fleshy, hairy belly against smooth, muscled butt, as he plunged in, all the way in, and made Skye Blue moan with pleasure, as he fucked and fucked and fucked as he’d never fucked anyone before, he, Casey, fat Casey, was striding down the aisle of the stadium, bathed in white spotlights, surrounded by cheering fans, and when he came, finally came, making Skye Blue shoot too, the roar rose to a crescendo and everything, just everything, was bathed in a cascade of bright white light.

A ROARING SILENCE

Bob Condron

Neptune emerged from the ocean waves like the sea god of legend and strode toward the beach in all his bare-butt naked glory. Armed, not with a trident, but an equally imposing weapon. A huge, pork sword—the pointed tip sheathed in a heavy, protective coverlet of foreskin—hung between his legs. An awesome cock and low-slung balls that slapped his powerful, hairy thighs with each purposeful step he took toward the shore. Those mighty balls swung first this way then that as he lofted his mighty arms for balance and waded through the foaming tides.

Having reached the bleached white sand, he stood still momentarily, waves gently lapping around his toes, not 20 feet away from where I lay on my beach towel. Closing his eyes, he lifted his face to the sun and ran his fingers through his hair. A smile spread across his face. And then he froze in position. It was an image that deserved to be immortalized. Carved in stone. And if I were a sculptor...

I raised myself up onto both elbows and, shielding my eyes from the glare of the sun, I worshiped him at a distance. His body could have indeed been sculpted from marble had it not been for the all-over tan and the thick carpet of bronze fur. A roman nose added strength to his features. Features that were further complimented by his close-cropped hair and beard.

Puffing up his barrel chest, he flicked his muscular body from side to side, like a dog shaking water from his coat. I laughed. He looked over then, catching my eye, and grinned back at me. He threw me a friendly salute before turning to walk slowly away. My eyes remained glued to his big, beefy rump until it all but disappeared toward the perimeter of the gay nude beach. And all the time wishing that he would look back over his shoulder, if only once. Then, when all hope seemed lost, he did just that. Just before he rounded the corner and was out of sight, he turned and, hand held high, he waved farewell.

"And the gay nude beach is a mere *10 minutes walk* away from the hotel..." the brochure had promised. By who's reckoning? Giant Longlegs—the man with the longest stride in the known universe? I had plenty of time to ponder that particular mystery as I beat a path homeward. Some 35 minutes after I packed up my belongings, I arrived back at base. It was some form of consolation to discover that it was happy hour at the poolside bar so I could at least rest my weary butt on a high stool under the shade of a thatched roof and chill out with an ice-cold Caipirinha or two (-for one) as the sun began to dim and thoughts of *Neptune*—the one who got away—resurfaced. Next time around, I promised myself, he wouldn't slip so easily through the net.

"Mind if I join you?"

I looked up from my half-empty glass to be confronted by the friendly face of a stranger who was no stranger. Big ol' Neptune himself.

"Be my guest." I indicated the stool beside me.

Parking his butt, he grinned and asked, "You recognize me with my clothes on?"

I laughed. "Yeah, even with..."

"First day?"

"Yep. And you?"

"Last, I'm afraid."

"Ah..."

Neptune held out a meaty paw. "The name's Theo."

I took hold and made sure to savor his firm, warm grip. "Bob. Good to meet you."

"First time in Mexico?"

"Mexico, no. This part, yes."

He called over to the barman then turned his head toward me. "Can I get you one, buddy?"

"Same again."

He turned back to the bar as I drank him in.

He looked to be in his late 30s, early 40s, I reckoned. But hard to tell, for there was something ageless about him, even up close. His beard was copper-colored, flecked with gold. Bare feet, tanned toes, square, white nails. A blue baseball cap was perched on his head, a pair of sunglasses on the bridge of his nose and a silver chain rested in the bronzed fur above the hooped neck of his red singlet. Pierced nipples were clearly defined. cutoff Levi's, frayed at the edges, completed the ensemble. A minimum of clothing that in no way obscured the magnificence of his physique.

He turned back toward me, held out my glass and raised his own beer.

"Cheers!"

"Cheers!" He took a good, long slug.

"And you?" I asked.

"Me what?"

"You recognized me with my clothes on?"

"Yeah." The corners of his mouth turned up in a smile as he raised the bottle to his lips. "But I just can't shake the image of you out of them!" Another slug. He looked me up and down. "These sunglasses?"

"Yeah?"

"Aren't sunglasses." He peered at me over the tops. His eyes were startling. Blue as the ocean and crystal clear. "Nah, X-ray specs." As he pushed them up the bridge of his nose, his eyes disappeared once again behind the tinted lenses. He smiled.

"And do you like what you see?"

"You bettcha." Another slug. He wiped his mouth with the back of his hand. "I don't normally stop by the bar this early. Usually have a nap before dinner."

"Really?"

"Yeah." He grinned. "But there's still time for a snooze, if you'd care to join me?"

"A snooze?" I grinned. "Can we take the drinks with us?"

Such are the perks of booking into a gay hotel. Theo simply led the way out from under the thatched roof above the bar, past the swimming pool, across the courtyard, and up the exterior wooden staircase to his room on the third floor.

Curtains drawn he threw aside his baseball cap and sunglasses, turned and locked me in a vicelike bear hug. Crushing his mouth against mine—his skillful tongue forced entry as he began to back me toward his king-size bed.

I was thrown back onto the mattress so hard I bounced. He clambered alongside me, yanked the T-shirt over my head, and tossed it halfway across the room. My shorts were just as forcefully disposed of. Then he pressed me down hard to lie flat on my back as he knelt over me.

I cast an eye nervously to the billowing curtains. "Aren't you going to close the sliding doors?"

"Why bother. People want to look in, let 'em look!" He grinned again. "Now lay still. Let me look at you."

Resting one hand on my chest, I let my fingers play with my chest fur. I slung the other hand behind my head, exposing one forested armpit and scenting the air with bear musk. Fully aroused, my cock was straining up toward my chest.

His eyes swept over my prostrate body and he cupped his bulging basket. "Man. Oh, man. Oh, man. Oh, man! You are the stuff of legend!"

"Whatever you say, big guy."

"And Big Guy says he's going to pump you, stud. Going to pump you till the tears roll down your cheeks. Going to pump you so full of his Big Guy dick that the tip will be poking outta that pierced, hairy navel of yours!"

"You talk a big game."

"Don't just talk." So saying, Theo pounced on my pit, clamping his mouth on that ripe, juicy mound of flesh. Sucking and nibbling and munching as my body wriggled and squirmed under the full weight of him. Then he had my second arm pinned above my head as he nuzzled deep into the damp crevice connecting shoulder and arm. He bathed my pit with the full width of his moist tongue. Finally, his mouth met mine. The smell of my pit clung to his beard as I sucked on his chin, licked his moustache, relished my own taste upon him as I helped him out of his singlet and shorts.

His small pink nipples were incredibly sensitive. Both teats were pierced by a single golden bolt that rattled against my teeth as I nibbled and sucked on each in turn. Meanwhile, he wriggled and squirmed like fresh fish in a bucket. My tongue snaked a trail over his heaving belly before finally burying itself deep in his navel. I felt the hardness of his cock twitch against my sternum; longing to receive the attention it so rightfully deserved, dripping in anticipation of the inevitable. Not yet. I'd make him wait.

Shuffling down the bed, I spread his legs, and lowered my mouth onto the tender flesh of his inner thigh. Right on in there, up against the crease. His heavy ball sac brushed up against my cheek, my beard, and his whole furry body quivered.

I went down on him. Way down. All the way to his beautiful, broad feet. But stopped along the way. First to nibble the tender flesh behind his knees, then on to nuzzle his hairy calves.

"Are your feet sensitive?" I asked as I finally held and caressed his right foot with my big, strong hands.

He didn't reply. Instead, he braced his body against the onslaught as my tongue bathed his undersole from heel to toes and back. Wet tongue on tender flesh. And then his toes were in my mouth. His response was electric. He thumped the bed, flailed around. Whimpering and moaning he buried his face in the pillow as I sucked each hairy toe in turn, played them like a panpipe.

"Enough!' he cried out. "Enough!"

But there was to be no intermission—least not until the end of the first act. Even as I dropped his right foot I grabbed the left. Played the same magical tune. Driving him crazy. A sweet refrain, repeated over and over again. Little toe to big toe. All the way up and down the scale until it was time for the big finale.

Without missing a beat, I bent his leg at the knee and shuffled down the bed to kneel before his solid, hairy buttocks. Looking down, I saw the bush of curly hair peep from his spreading cheeks, traced the crack with my fingers, then I took fast hold of his powerful, rock-hard phallus. My fingers barely meeting around the girth, I changed key, drawing back his foreskin like a heavy velvet curtain and revealing his drooling piss slit. Mouth held fast on his big toe, my hand began to pump up the volume down below.

"Oh, ye gods!" he cried. "Merciful heavens!" And Mount Vesuvius erupted. A single, shimmering bolt of lava shot out of his pulsating dick and high in the air, then splattered against his heaving chest like a round of applause. And another round. And still another...

As he lay back, quivering in the aftershock, I spread the goo over his belly and pecs with the flat of my palms, massaged it in as he relaxed and grew still.

Neptune was no longer a dream but a reality. It was I who left him sleeping.

Day 2. And I'm back on the beach. Same spot. Sprawled on my beach towel, eyes closed, remembering each detail of the day before, wishing that I could turn back the hands of time. Then the shadow fell over me and somehow I knew to look up. Theo. He parked his chunky butt on the weather-beaten log beside me. As he looked down, I had to shield my eyes from the blinding light of his glorious smile. He shifted position slightly and the sun formed a golden halo behind his head. I lowered my eyes and they fell upon the funnel of foreskin shielding the bulbous helmet of his thickly veined cock as it lay poking free from the left leg of his cutoffs.

"Last night sure was a revelation. Never came like that before. Wiped me out!" he said.

I smiled. "Yeah, I kinda noticed."

He fixed me with a look of tender reproach. "You should have woken me up."

"You looked so peaceful. Didn't want to wake you."

"But I never had the chance to return the favor..."

"Believe me, Theo. The pleasure was all mine."

"Not all!"

"No." I laughed.

He chuckled. "Slept right through to this morning. Best night's sleep I've had in an age."

"But I thought you had to disappear home this morning?"

"Was meant to..."

"And you never did tell me where you come from?"

"Same place we all come from, Bob..." He looked off toward the sea. Crashing waves reflected in the aquamarine of his eyes. A roaring silence. "But home can wait a day or two," he finally said.

CRAIGSLIST

Rick R. Reed

He didn't know why he posted the ad on Craigslist. Of course, he had browsed the online ads in the "men seeking men" section now and then, hoping to see a titillating post (Looking to get gang banged tonight; daddy seeking son for spanking; college jock wants to get sucked/fucked) or even better, a titillating pic (muscular, dark-skinned men in sweaty, grimy jockstraps were always best).

But the ads (and often, even the pics of headless men in various states of excitement or "openness") quickly grew monotonous and he would move on. After all, his job at ___________ didn't involve browsing the Internet for sex ads. If it did, half the company would have been in for big bonuses for all their hard work.

So why did he post the following? Was it because he was bored? Was it because he simply wanted to see what kind of responses would fill up his in-box? The mere thought of having his in-box filled made him snicker, yet flooded his brain with a kind of queasy nausea at the double entendre. He paused to think that responses to his ad might invite even more titillating reading than the ads themselves did. Respondents could feel a little freer due to having the inconvenience of public scrutiny removed. Or did he want to post the ad because he thought it was possible to make a long-held sexual fantasy come true? He crossed his legs at his desk, squishing his erection upward in his jeans at the thought of the fantasy: its literal darkness and sordidness.

Finally, he wondered if he was posting on account of the fact that his current relationship with _______________ was getting to be as sexually monotonous as poring through Craigslist men-seeking-men ads for an hour? Both bore the same stamp of the familiar. Both were comfortable, yet waning in excitement.

Perhaps this post, which he had already composed in a Microsoft Word document with the headline "Looking to Make a Fantasy Come True," would inject some excitement into a life that had become as comfortable—and as boring—as an old pair of slippers. Perhaps the simple act of posting the ad and seeing what kind of responses he got would be enough to satisfy him.

Perhaps not.

The requirements to bring his fantasy to life stared back at him from the monitor screen, the crisp black characters lined up on the virtual page, punctuated by the blinking cursor at the end of the message. There was something about just looking at the words, keyed in, spell checked, and double-spaced, that made the ethereal real, the wanton electronic, and the possibility of unfettered infidelity and passionate connection all too concrete of a possibility. These Times New Roman characters, used for everything from composing lullabies, to writing suicide notes, to penning ransom notes, had the innocent power to transform fantasy into reality.

This is what he wrote:

LOOKING TO MAKE A FANTASY COME TRUE

37-year-old-male has a hot itch that needs to be scratched. I've never done anything like this before, but want to make it happen. First the particulars: I'm younger-looking than my age and considered very sexy. I'm 5'10" with a muscular 170-lb. frame

(workout 6x/week). My roots are Italian and Welsh, so I have kind of a dark, passionate thing going on. Bubble butt and a fat 7 1/2-inch cock (about six around). Moderately hairy, masculine with piercing green eyes and buzzed black hair.

OK, here's what I'm looking for: It doesn't matter what you look like, as long as you're height/weight proportionate. It does matter that you can get a really hard erection and can keep it hard for a long time. It matters that you can share a hot bottom with other anonymous tops. It matters that you be sexually insatiable (or pretty close). It matters that you know how to fuck: That means respecting a bottom's limits and starting out slow and then, when the bottom lets you know the time is right, letting all hell break loose and being able to throw a merciless, pile-driving fuck that has your bottom bucking and backing up on your cock and begging for more.

It doesn't matter what you look like because I want to do all of this in complete darkness. The deal is that I will be in my bedroom, which has room darkening blinds, plus heavy draperies. I will be on my bed waiting for you, facedown, ass-up: My hole will be greased and ready. My legs will be spread and there will be several condoms between my legs. You won't be able to see, but you should be experienced enough to get undressed in the dark and roll a condom over your hard dick. Then, you slide on top of me. I want to feel your man body stretched out across mine, the heat of it, the club pressed between the cheeks of my ass. And then I want to feel you sink that cock home.

There may be others in the room waiting and listening. You take your turn, you throw your condom on the floor, and you leave. You do not speak: to me or anyone else in the room if there's anyone there.

If you think you can help me make this dream come true, e-mail me back and tell me why you're qualified. I don't need a pic, because that doesn't matter. I do need to know that you're hot and horny to fuck a tight manhole.

He had to laugh at the last line and the use of the word "manhole." That part was so lame. Did he dare put this out on the Internet? Did he have the courage to make this happen? Could he be honest enough with himself to distinguish between which fantasy was truer: the one about just posting this and seeing the responses, or the other, darker one, where he actually went through with it?

He knew that even if he considered going through with it, he wouldn't have the nerve to do a gang bang sort of thing (*At least not the first time,* he thought, and chuckled to himself again, thinking what a naughty, naughty boy he was)...but maybe he could do a one-on-one thing the next time ________________ was out of town. Maybe.

He went to (pointed his browser? Logged on? Visited?) www.craigslist.com and went to the SF Bay room. He clicked on "men seeking men." He clicked on "post." From there he was directed to several options; he chose the link for "sex with no strings attached (nsa)" and finally, this led him to an option where he could link to "post to men seeking men."

At last, the thrill of a blank template was before him. There were spaces for title, age, posting description, and e-mail address.

He paused, staring. His face was flushed and his heart was beating just a little harder. There was a rushing sound—uncomfortable—in his ears. There was still time to click the box at the top of the screen, ending his session on the Internet. He should be working, anyway. He had those reports to get out...

He could also click on one of the sites on his favorites list and be out of Craigslist (and its promises) in only seconds, removing the possibility of putting in motion a process that could be the cause of a lot of heartache and regret.

Right. He could do a lot of those things. But it was easy enough to paste the right components from his Word document into the Craigslist template; in fact, it took less than five seconds, switching back and forth between open computer screens and programs.

He cut. He pasted. He paused once more before hitting the "continue" button; but he pressed the enter key anyway, feeling heedless. He saw the ad as it would appear on the screen and found it hard to swallow. He scrolled down and was presented with yet another chance to back out (had the folks at Craigslist deliberately designed it this way, so weasels like him had plenty of chances to renege?). He had to enter a "verification" word. No lie, the word was "cheat." He shook his head, gave a mirthless laugh, typed in the word and pressed the continue button once more. Finally, a terms of use agreement came up and by then, he had come too far to consider turning back. He hit "accept the terms of use." He was told he would get an e-mail and that he had to respond to that in order to have his message "published and broadcast."

He knew what he would do about the e-mail waiting in his mailbox: He would delete it without even looking at it. Enough of this nonsense!

He went to his mailbox, clicked on the link in the e-mail from Craigslist and published it.

Let the good times roll.

Let all hell break loose.

Both clichés were correct, he supposed. He would soon see what would happen.

It took only about 15 minutes for the responses to start coming in:

"Dude: I can definitely make you happy with my fat eight inches."
"LMAO"
"When are you thinkin' to do this?"
"Do you parTy?"
"Are you a Republican? I can do this, but not if you're a Republican."
"Nine inches of hot chocolate here."
"How about with the lights on and the sound off?"
"Looking for a dirty ass. Is that part of the fantasy?"
"Hung like a sperm whale here."
"Strangers in the night, exchanging fluids...wait! You said condoms; only BB here. Good luck, man."

He could see a pattern emerging: The responses were leaning toward the humorous and even absurd and, while they made him chuckle, they induced little physical response in him farther south. At the very least, he had hoped for a response that would provoke in him the kind of reaction he used to get from some hot man-on-man porn story found in the pages of some astute literary publication, like *Drummer.*

Finally, he got two more responses. One from a self-righteous hysterical type who condemned his fantasy for being the "kind of tripe that gives self-respecting gay men a bad name" and pressed for "a renewed commitment to standards of monogamy and propriety in the gay community." He then wondered if pics were available.

But one response finally gave him what he was looking for.

Caught your post on Craig's List. Boy, you're just what I'm looking for. Already in a relationship, so I need to be very discreet here, and the dark (and the fun to be had there) sound really great. The whole idea of pitch dark is also hot because it'll just ramp up the sense of touch...you know?

I'm a great total top and know how to use my eight inches (it seemed, from the responses, that everyone in the world had at least an eight-inch penis. Where were these guys hiding when he showered at the gym?). You won't be disappointed.

Let me make your fantasy come true. If my guess is right, you need to be as discreet as I am, so I'm thinking you have some kind of partner, too. Let me come by, slip in, drop my jeans and just lovingly stretch myself out on top of you. I'll hold you tight, breathe hot, beer-scented breath on the back of your neck, bite you just below where your hairline ends...so you'll squirm with the pain and pleasure my teeth will deliver. I'll rub my hairy chest against your smooth back as you feel my cock harden and press against your soft ass cheeks. I want you to thrust up against it, telling me with your body how much you want it inside you.

I'll make you beg, but not with words, boy. I'll make you beg with your ass and I'll keep you begging until you're helpless with want. The feel of my precome smearing across your ass, the rock hardness of my dick, will make you do more than squirm. I'll wait until you're panting and moaning, bucking against the sheets before I slide just the tip in.

And then, slowly, I'll give you just a little more, just a little more. Your ass will want to eat my cock, to gobble it up, but my strong hands will hold you down and I'll tease and tease until you go crazy. See, I'm in control here. You just be the good boy I know you can be.

And then I give it you, so hard and rough that even if there are other guys waiting their turn, you'll send 'em away because when I get off you, you'll be so satisfied, you'll be spoiled for a LONG TIME for the touch of another man.

A lot of big promises, he thought, *a lot of big promises went in to writing that response.* It wasn't hard for him to decide that if there was going to be one he would actually try this plan out with, this man would be that one.

______________ was out of town, luckily, in just two days, gone on a business trip to Phoenix for three days.

The timing couldn't have been more perfect.

He wanted to keep things safe, so he created a new Yahoo ID for himself, "DarkDancer," and responded, giving his ambitious would-be lover a date, a time, and his fervent wishes that he could deliver everything he promised.

As he sat in front of his computer just after pressing the enter key to send the e-mail that could mark a significant change in his life (up until this point, a period of three years, he had been faithful to __________________), he wondered if he had done the right thing.

Did it really matter? The guy probably wouldn't even respond.

He both dreaded and prayed that he was wrong.

The two days passed in an agony of slowness, the hours moving like glue. He saw himself nominated for an Oscar for his cheerful, breezy performance with ______________, even sucking him off on the night before he was to leave for his trip. He fell asleep with the taste of ______________'s come in his mouth and dreams of *Colt* men coming to him in the darkness.

The day of the meeting arrived and it was perfect for a funeral. Outside, the sky was pewter, its gray grimness lit only by an occasional flash of lightning. Thunder rumbled. The rain beat a staccato rhythm on the roof of their apartment building, where they lived on the top floor. The wind whipped the trees around.

"It was a dark and stormy day," he whispered to himself and snickered. He was going around the bedroom, preparing the chamber, so to speak. His mouth was dry and his hands were wet; he felt a queasy mixture of shame, guilt, and lust. It made him recall his Catholic upbringing and when he first started masturbating: The out-of-control pull of his body battling with his religion and juvenile terror of sin. It made the orgasms all the more delicious.

He hoped the same would be true again today.

He fitted the bed with an old comforter they had never thrown away. He pulled the blinds tight and drew the heavy velvet draperies across them. He couldn't see anything, even after his eyes had had time to adjust. It was bottom-of-a-well dark.

The bathroom and a hot date with a Fleet enema awaited him.

And that was not all.

He hoped the guy was for real and he would not spend the afternoon lying face down on his bed, with about half a cup of Millennium Platinum lube up his ass, growing more and more despondent as he listened for a tapping, as someone came gently rapping, rapping at his chamber door. A tapping that might never come. You know how these queens could be, he thought disdainfully, popping the seal on the green and white Fleet box with a fingernail.

He felt almost like he was in one of those isolation tanks as he lay across the bed, waiting. In their e-mail correspondence, they had agreed that he would leave the lobby door open (blocking it with an advertising circular—he hoped no vigilant high security type would remove it; the backup plan was to just ring the buzzer, but that would take half the fun out of it) and his door unlocked.

His visitor was then supposed to undress outside the bedroom, give a quick knock, and enter quickly, letting any light into the room for as briefly as possible.

His heart thudded as he waited. What if this was, like, the world's ugliest troll? What if the guy was morbidly obese or smelled like onion soup? What if he was drunk? Or soaring on crystal meth (he didn't think he could take being fucked for eight hours straight)? Worst fear: What if the guy was some sort of psycho, ready to penetrate him not with a cock, but with something that was also eight inches, yet hewn from stainless steel?

Maybe this was a bad idea.

He stood, and as he did, he heard the creak of their front door opening, the whispering swish as the door's bottom glided over the rug they had placed in front of it.

It was too late. Half of him was overjoyed, half disappointed.

He scrambled to reassume his position on the bed.

Biting his lip so hard he tasted blood, he closed his eyes and prayed for the best.

He listened, tense, as footfalls sounded on the hardwood of the hallway leading to the bedroom. What did the guy look like? He supposed it was OK to imagine whatever he wanted: some 1980s porn star with a big moustache, hairy chest, and a nine-inch cock, some Al Parker stud fantasy. His heart was pounding uncomfortably as he heard the slither of clothes dropping to the floor, the rise and fall of the man's breath, just outside his bedroom door.

He felt himself clench so tightly, nerves making his body rigid, that he didn't know if it would be physically possible to make this fantasy come true. He wondered if he would begin to tremble...

The door creaked as it opened, letting a swath of grayish light fall across the bed, but only for an instant. Whoever was back there closed the door so quickly, he didn't even have time to consider lifting his head from the comforter, to turn and grab a quick look at his visitor. He supposed the guy really didn't have a chance to see much of him either: If anything all he saw was a long, nondescript body lying face down, topped with close-cropped dark hair.

He hoped the man wouldn't say anything. That would spoil everything and make this whole adventure seem a little tawdrier. He wasn't sure why.

He sucked in his breath as the man crossed the short distance to his bed, which creaked as he eased onto it.

And then, slowly, a hand caressed him, running from his neck to his toes, a rough, calloused gliding animal that moved smoothly across the broad expanse of his back, causing an electric tingling as it traversed the lift of his ass, and a shiver as it moved slowly over his muscular thighs and calves, caressing the coarse black hair growing there.

The man's breath started coming a little heavier. He shifted and then was lying next to him. He didn't dare turn his head toward him.

There was a whisper of a kiss on the back of his neck. He hadn't expected tenderness. A hand caressed the short bristly nubs of his hair. Another kiss landed on his ear, finishing up with the flick of a tongue. An arm encircled him: warm, strong, taut, making him feel protected and secure. Fingertips tweaked his nipples, hard enough to make him want to cry out; he bit his lip instead.

His breath was coming faster now, but the tension was being replaced by passion: a raw heat that started in his gut and then radiated both north and south on the terrain of his body.

The man climbed atop him; his weight delicious and suffocating all at once. He tensed, then, thinking there was something oddly familiar about this body that had just meshed with his own: something indescribable about the feel, something in the smell of the man (pleasant and clean) yet oddly familiar.

He let these thoughts disperse as he surrendered more and more to the dizzying sensations that almost seemed to attack: setting his nerve endings on fire, making of his dick a solid piece of hardwood, almost ready to explode, so engorged...

The man pressed into him, sighing, his erection a thick, hot weight at the cheeks of his ass. He wanted to reach back, guide him in, but remembered the man's e-mail, remembered how he said he would be in control.

So he waited. The man continued to kiss his neck, his shoulder blades, the pressure and intensity of the kisses rising in correlation with the man's passion.

And then he was off of him and it was like a cold vacuum had replaced the heavy warmth of the body stretched out on top of him. He wasn't, in the end, some sicko who was going to just leave him lying there, desperate and yearning?

And then he listened as the man bit into the condom packet and tore it open, hearing the gentle rustle of the packet falling to the hardwood floor.

There was a short pause and he imagined the latex being rolled over a purple helmet topping a muscular, thick-veined body.

The delicious pressure and weight was atop him once more and this time, he felt the cock he wanted so desperately pressing into him, slowly, so slowly, while the man distracted him by nipping at his neck and growling low in his throat.

It was like being taken by an animal.

He squeezed his eyes tight, trying to hold himself back, to not allow himself to just thrust up against the cock easing into him, to have it greedily all the way inside him, pulsing and tearing him open. It was a pain he would gladly endure.

But the man was in charge...and he would let him set the pace.

By the time the cock was all the way inside, he was sweating, and could feel the man's sweat dripping down on his back (he had raised himself up on his arms). He grunted and buried himself all the way up to the root, the scratch of his pubes chafing against the baby-soft skin of his ass. The grunt gave a hint as to voice and timbre and again, he thought it sounded familiar, but he let it go in the midst of the heat and the fucking he knew was on its way: coarse, rough, and crude.

Just what he wanted.

He knew the rule was no visual, no aural, but he couldn't help but whimper, "Daddy," just as the man began to thrust. The man paused for an instant, panting, and then resumed thrusting harder and harder, until the two of them became one beast, the boy bucking and pushing against the man, who was pounding the boy with a kind of intensity that the darkness only encouraged.

It was blindingly painful and indescribably pleasurable all at once. The fucking went on and on, until both of them were drenched in sweat and the sheets beneath them became moist and sour-smelling.

And then, with a cry, they were both coming at exactly the same time. The pulsing and rhythms seeming to last forever, each urging the other on to new heights of delirium.

Afterward, they both lay panting and spent. It was only when, after several minutes, the weight on top of him became uncomfortable that he turned slightly, to politely force the man off of him.

Absently, the man stroked his flank.

And he began to wonder, now that his cock was deflating and along with it, his passion: Was this someone he knew?

A cold sweat replaced the warm trickle of just moments before.

Was it better not to know?

He had to. He reached across the bed, hands feeling around for the bedside lamp, with its dim bulb and mica shade; the light wouldn't be too intense, but he had to know.

He switched the light on.

"Jesus." The main cried, audibly wincing at the sudden light.

A quick nausea rose up within him. It couldn't be. He knew that voice.

In fact, he had known it all his life. He turned slowly, sure his heart would burst through his chest, praying that what he was thinking could not be true.

But it was. He shut his eyes and tried to hold down the bile. The man stared back at him with horror.

See, it wasn't so strange that, during their hot fuck session, he had called this stranger, "Daddy."

HOLDING THE BALL

Ben Croker

I took two large gulps. The icy cold water sent a shiver down the back of my throat, as a steady stream of darkly uniformed men with television cameras and bright lights perched on their shoulders closed in around our table. Lenses pointed at me like a firing squad aimed at a death-row prisoner. My heart was racing, my head was throbbing, and it felt like everything around me was running in a slow-motion replay.

The crowd erupted with a collective cheer. I was momentarily blinded by the flashes of light. Simultaneously, like some sort of well-choreographed routine, the whole room rose to its feet, clapping. More uniformed camera crews swarmed into position around me as I took a huge deep breath and rose slowly to my feet. As I tucked my shirt in and buttoned up my suit jacket, teammates took turns congratulating me—by thumping me very hard on the back with their fists, like they were trying to dislodge a stray piece of meat stuck in my throat.

"Ladies and gentlemen, it gives me great pleasure to declare the winner of the 2005 Brownlow Medal to be Jason Cook from the Collingwood Football Club."

Again a loud cheer erupted from the masses. I couldn't hear anything specific now; it was all just a blur of sound and noise. I turned to walk toward the stage. Like Moses and the Red Sea, the crowd seemed to magically disperse before me and reveal a clear path to the podium as I slowly made my way toward it.

I didn't really notice the buzz of movement going on all around me, as I edged closer and closer to the stage. My eyes were singly and firmly focused on the prize that awaited me, my own kind of Holy Grail—the Brownlow Medal. Suddenly, all the years of punishing hard work in the gym and on the training field, the painful injuries too numerous to mention, the blood, the sweat, and the tears—all seemed worthwhile. I had always hoped, way deep down, that I would be here one day; standing on the podium accepting the accolades as Australia's fairest and best football player. But I never allowed myself to believe that it would actually happen—the disappointment of failure would have been too great a burden to bear.

Most of what followed for the rest of the night is just a haze—a series of jumbled alcohol-induced, adrenaline-fuelled memories; countless interviews to a baying media frenzy, shaking hands and making small talk with hundreds of anonymous well-wishers and their wide-eyed hangers-on.

I was the guest of honor tonight, and had to be prepared to while away the post-presentation hours listening to various grey-haired former club champions reminisce about their glory days long gone by. I did my best to maintain my 'interested' face, as the crowds eventually began to dwindle. All I wanted to do was escape and join the others in the hotel room—get completely wasted and party the rest of the night away.

Then...he walked past me again—the waiter, come barman. Another tray full of champagne flutes finely balanced in hand. He stopped at the group of suits standing across from me—a mix of offspring of famous media tycoons, and AFL corporate highfliers, discussing the merits and problems associated with scheduling a mid-season bye. This powerful group of football elite quickly cleaned up the tray of full glasses and replaced them with their empty ones. As I looked up from my less-than-stimulating conversation with Veronica, the half-tanked wife of the club president, the waiter's eyes met mine in a lingering stare. And it wasn't the first time—we had been catching each other's eye like this all night.

He was youngish-looking and had a gorgeous boyish charm when he smiled that I found to be totally addictive. At the same time, he was extremely masculine and self-assured. His broad shoulders and solid chest only faintly hidden underneath the unflattering hotel uniform, made me wonder what heavenly pleasures the rest of his body had to offer. The waiter's eyes were the most brilliant blue I had ever seen and pierced through the crowd whenever our eyes met. I looked away briefly, looked back, and once again he was gone. Disappearing as he had done all night. We hadn't even spoken a word—we hadn't needed to.

The effects of too many preshow Valium, mixed with alcohol, had finally taken its toll on Veronica. She lurched forward, letting out a half-muffled yell as she stumbled over her own feet. I managed to catch her in my arms as she fell forward, spilling her glass of red wine over the front of my shirt, and the champion's medal that was hanging around my neck. Geoff, the club president, apologized as he picked up his wife from the floor and ushered her toward the nearest exit. "Better go and clean yourself up," he said, wiping the red-stained medal with his dirty napkin. "It's not a good look for the photographers." I took the napkin from his outstretched hand and headed off toward the gents.

The men's bathroom had been a hive of activity all night—a result of mixing free alcohol, end of season celebrations, and nervous footballers' bladders. But as the late-night crowd had dwindled, so had the long queue waiting for the urinals. As I pushed open the toilet door, there was only one other guy in there. He was trying to take aim at the urinal while leaning his arm and head against the wall, half asleep. As I headed for the wash basin and grabbed a pile of paper towels from the dispenser, he made a few slow flicking and shaking motions, wiped his dripping hand on his trouser leg, turned around bleary-eyed, mumbled "fuckin' good job, mate!" toward my direction, and stumbled out the door—his fly wide open.

I smiled to myself as I put the plug in the basin and turned on the tap. I ran my fingers under the water for a while until it started to feel hot. I took a few moments to gather my thoughts and regroup. It all still didn't seem real. I just kept thinking that I was going to wake up any second and find it was all just a great big, fantastic, wet dream. The hot water began to steam up the mirror so I turned off the tap and grabbed for a piece of the paper towel. I reached across the basin and wiped a big clear sweep across the clouded mirror. And there he was again: his two piercing blue eyes staring directly over my shoulder meeting my stunned gaze in the mirror—my mysterious waiter friend. I felt the warmth of his breath on my neck, which sent fuzzy tingling sensations shooting down my spine.

I turned around to face him. His tousled, shoulder-length brown hair was perfectly framing his rounded jaw, his chiselled cheeks, his thick, fleshy lips. Up close, his skin looked smooth and milky soft. His long, dark lashes, outlining those deep pools of aqua blue. Without saying a word, he reached for the pile of paper towel and plunged one into the steaming hot water. Eyes still fixed intently on mine, he lifted the wet, dripping towel up slowly toward my chest and proceeded to lightly dab the red stain on my shirt with the towel.

My heartbeat raced as he touched me for the first time—I felt sure that he could feel it jumping through my skin. He once again dipped the towel in the water and lifted it to my shirt, dabbing. My knees nearly gave way as he reached up with his other hand and gently loosened my tie then undid the top button of my shirt. He slid his finger down my chest and undid the second button, then the third. The cold metal of the medal, still hanging around my neck, dropped now onto the flushed bare skin of my pounding chest.

This time he took the whole piece of towel and plunged it fully into the steamy, hot water. He slowly lifted it up to my neck and squeezed, dripping droplets of boiling hot water down the front of my bare chest—my nerve endings screaming out in an intoxicating mix of burning pain and intense pleasure. Our eyes separated for the first time, as he slowly leaned his head down and brought his full lips in perilously close to my supersensitive skin. His lips parted slightly to allow an anxiously waiting tongue to appear. I closed my eyes as I felt his soft lips and the tip of his eager tongue gently pressed against my lower chest. Then in one, slow, sensuous movement, he licked all the way up to the top of my neck—to that incredibly sensitive spot just below my left ear. With his body pressed firmly against mine, we could feel each other's obvious arousal.

Again eye-to-eye now, our faces only centimeters apart, he slid one hand down the front of my trousers and pulled down my zipper. With his other hand, he reached for the medal hanging across my heaving chest, took hold of it between two fingers and raised the medal up to eye level. It was still sticky, dripping and stained by the red wine. Our eyes diverted briefly to the medal, and back again to each other. As he tilted his head back slightly, he gently licked the corner of his thick, parting lips, and slowly lowered the medal down between them. He closed his mouth tightly, and sucked the medal clean.

Forcefully, I grabbed a handful of long hair and wrenched his head backward. The Brownlow dropped from his mouth as I brought his insolent lips up to meet mine. His tongue reappeared as we began to kiss openly and passionately. It was like a pressure valve had been released after all the stress, anxiety, and nervous energy of the night. We were like wild animals in heat, as I pushed him back hard and pressed him up against the cold, tiled, washroom wall. The thrill of getting caught, made it all the more exciting as, hard with anticipation, we both started ripping at each other's clothes in a frenzied rage of pure, unadulterated lust.

I heard voices coming toward the toilet door. As it swung open, I turned the waiter around and quickly pushed him forward into the nearest cubicle, slamming the door shut behind us and grappling for the ENGAGED sign on the door. Two loud, chattering men entered the toilet as we got down to business.

Still kissing wildly, we fumbled with each other's pants and dicks, tugging at anything that moved. Now freed from the restraint of my old "lucky" red jocks, I swung my eager waiter-boy around and bent him forward over the foul-stained, smelly toilet. I reached forward and grasped my hand firmly over his mouth. I spat onto my other hand, reached down, and wiped it hurriedly over the shaft of my throbbing dick. I then guided and pushed it into his tight, waiting hole. I thrust hard. One fast, single motion, all the way in. He let out a loud, muffled groan. It must have hurt like hell.

"Must have been those prawns!" said one of the men from outside the cubicle door, laughing.

I grasped my hand even tighter now around the waiter's warm, panting mouth, as I slowly withdrew my dick, and then ploughed his slightly loosened man hole again. Another, more muffled groan.

"I told you they tasted off," said the other man as he flushed the urinal, and headed back out through the toilet door. It took all the strength I had not to scream out at the top of my lungs. I bit down hard on my lip. The feelings of pleasure were so intense they were almost too much to bear.

Once we were alone again, I loosened my grip on the waiter's mouth. He gasped deeply for air. I ran my hand from his neck down the seam of his black satin waistcoat and onto the smooth, bare skin of his lower back. Pounding away rhythmically, I traced my fingers around his soft, hairless cheeks, his sharp, jutting hip bone, and then ventured down farther to his moist, sweaty inner thigh. He groaned some more as I reached forward and started playing with his rock-hard dick. It was a good-sized handful of pure man meat, and I began jacking it up and down, as I continued to ram my eager dick into his hungry hole.

We convulsed wildly in unison. An electric impulse jabbed through my body from head to toe, I gasped loudly as I came inside him. The impulse surged from me to him, as he exploded his huge load over the toilet seat and cubicle floor. We lay there entwined in each other against the wall, breathing heavily, enjoying every last tingle and shiver. Eventually I let him go. He turned around and smiled. Those amazing blue eyes were even more luminescent in the flickering fluorescent light of the toilet cubicle.

We slowly dressed each other. He took great care, when doing up the buttons on my shirt, to place the Brownlow medal back neatly in its rightful place. He opened the cubicle door, as our now-parched lips came together for one last, long, lingering kiss. He then walked away toward the toilet door. With one hand on the handle he turned back toward me, those blue eyes beaming—a cheeky, self-satisfied grin came over his face. He winked at me, straightened his bow tie, walked through the door—and was gone.

We hadn't even spoken a word—we hadn't needed to.

RUGBY

Andrew Ryder

He'd first caught my eye at a rugby game, when my eyes were drawn to his massive thighs and the way his rounded ass filled his tight rugby shorts. I saw him a few more times in passing. It was hard to tell his age—anywhere between the early 20s and 30s. He had short blond hair, grey eyes, a suntanned complexion, and overall, a boyish quality about him. His cheeks still had some baby fat, and he had a toothpaste smile—brilliant white teeth and an engaging grin. He was shorter than I am—about 5 feet 10 inches tall, and seemed to have a good set of pecs, although it was hard to tell under the loose-fitting shirts he favored. When he wasn't playing rugby, he dressed conservatively, like a preppie, and I was sure that whatever he was into, it was not my kind of sex. He was a real cornfed specimen, the hero of the football team, or class valedictorian.

We finally, accidentally, met in the steam room at my gym. The steam was so thick that at first I thought the room was empty, but as I walked toward the back, I made out someone sitting in a pair of bathing trunks. As I got close he stood up, and saying, "Do you mind?" stripped off his bathing trunks. At first I thought he was asking permission to strip, which threw me, but then realized he was asking if he could hose himself down with cold water—there is a hose connected to a tap in the corner of the room. "Sure," I replied, "go ahead." I'd never heard him speak, and his voice was surprisingly deep and firm, a baritone. He hosed himself down and then leaned back on the bench. It was the first time I had seen him close up, and he was really hot. He had great pecs, like a swimmer's, and a flat stomach, which bulged slightly with muscle when he sat down. He had broad shoulders, and his torso tapered to a narrow waist before widening slightly at the hips. He was well hung, with a thick, circumcised cock that curved lazily over a set of large round balls. When he was sitting, his thighs seemed even more massive, and I had a sudden wish to feel them around my neck. His cock was above average in size, although not as large as mine, but looked immense on his relatively compact frame. His blond hair was darkened by sweat and water, but I noticed that the hair around his cock was slightly darker than the hair on his head. There was a tan line around his midsection, and the untanned skin was a pale, creamy color. At first glance, he seemed hairless, but I later noticed that he was covered with a very fine, almost invisible down. I was glad I was wearing swimming trunks so that he could not see the stirring of my cock.

To my surprise, he opened the conversation. "It sure is hot in here"—a pick-up line if ever I heard one. He spoke with a slight drawl, suggesting that he had come from the South or Southwest. "Yeah," I replied, adding, "Do you come here often?" It turned out that he had been transferred to the area only a few weeks ago on a short-term assignment, and did not expect to be in town long. He was just using the gym now and then to work out. "I'm Seth," he said, holding out his hand. We shook hands and, after I introduced myself, traded information about our respective lines of work. He was obviously enjoying the conversation, and kept eyeing my crotch, which still encased in damp Lycra swim trunks, bulged substantially. I decided to take the lead, and suggested that after we got dressed we should go somewhere for a beer. "Sure," he said, blushing all over his chest, neck, and face. We had left our things in different parts of the locker room and so agreed to meet out front in 15 minutes.

It was a warm afternoon, and when Seth showed up he was wearing a tight-fitting black T-shirt, which emphasized his pecs and flat stomach, a pair of tight crotch-hugging jeans, and an old pair of white leather running shoes. In some ways, he was the opposite of me. I'm about 6 foot 1, have dark curly hair, very dark brown eyes, and skin that looks slightly tanned. I was dressed in a white T-shirt, which set off my tapered torso, black 501s, and high black Chippewa motorcycle boots. Although I do not have a lot of body hair, I have a band along the base of my pecs, which tapers into a fine line down the center of my stomach to my crotch.

His shirt was slightly faded, and looked like it had been washed several times, but from the way it clung to his body, seemed to be made from some kind of synthetic. The sleeves were a bit shorter than usual and for the first time I noticed his full, developed biceps, the black of the shirt setting off his lightly tanned skin and bleached blond hair. His jeans were also faded and shrunk to fit his every curve, showing a significant and appealing bulge between his legs. I found myself revising my opinion about him, but freshly scrubbed and pink from the shower he still looked like some poster boy from a Midwestern agricultural college. He leaned against the wall, and was incredibly sexy. When was he relaxed, he assumed a kind of slouching position that set off his pecs and his crotch to their best advantage.

Seth lived about a mile away, but had walked to the gym because the weather was nice, so we went to a nearby bar and had a few beers. He was like a puppy, engaging, and even sparkling in his conversation, but any time we came close to the topic of sex, he would blush and become tongue-tied. The more we talked, the more I became convinced that he was no virgin, and really wanted to make it with me. Finally, throwing caution to the wind, I decided to ask him over to my place. It's a few miles away, and I had come by car, but I promised to drive him back home afterward.

By now it was obvious that we were going to have sex, but I wasn't sure how the scene would go. He was quiet in the car, but let me rest my hand on his thigh. I figured we might have a quick grope, and that I might go down on him, and then after an hour or so of talking, I would drive him home. However, when we got inside the house, the first thing he did was drop to his knees and, wrapping his arms around my ass, apply his mouth to the crotch of my jeans. This was totally unexpected, but extremely welcome. I was taken aback by the almost desperate quality of his approach, but encouraged him, gently cupping my hand around the back of his head and pressing him onto my hardening rod. From the first time I saw him, I had wanted to have this guy under my control, to make him suck me and serve me. I mentally readjusted my gears as I assessed the likely scene.

After a few minutes, I gently pulled him to his feet, and suggested that we have another beer. It was warm and a bit stuffy in the house, since I had not left the air-conditioning on, and I thought that would give some time to let the house cool down. I realized that although he was aware of his attractive sexiness, he was still awkward, and even embarrassed by it. Our difference in ages made him naturally deferential and prone to agree with my suggestions, and I played on this.

We continued to talk about insignificant things, when I suddenly told him to take off his clothes, pointing out that I had already seen him naked. He stood up and stripped off instantly. He was a hot, vigorous young stud, well muscled, and well hung, with a compact body. He had been wearing jockey shorts, and his still-moist blond pubic hair clung closely to his crotch. His hairless pecs formed two round mounds, jutting out above his flat stomach, and those sexy thighs tapered into well-developed calf muscles and high arched feet. I was itching to play with his tits, cock, and balls, to get him hard, and to make him moan with pleasure, excitement and pain. He had delicate pink nipples that were slightly hard, perhaps from the relative coolness in the air, or from excitement. At first, he stood there with his head slightly bent, his arms at his sides, slightly breathless, but apparently self-possessed and accepting. I had not seen him too well in the steam room, so I casually walked around him, admiring what I saw. Under my slow scrutiny, his cock became full and tumescent, but still rested at ease on his balls. I stroked his ass gently with the palm of my hand, and heard him gasp and then felt him relax as I ran my palm over his back and shoulders. I was dying to squeeze and knead the cheeks of his ass, to play with his cock and balls, and to squeeze his nipples and pecs.

Given the way he blushed when the conversation veered toward certain kinds of sex, it was evident that I would need to feel my way and go slowly so as not to scare him off. I told him to sit down, and we talked some more while we finished our beers. By now, it was evident that he was repressed about S/M but really wanted to try it. I was dying to get my cock into his tight little ass and fuck the daylights out of him, but it was like breaking in a horse. I needed to make sure of him, and make him relaxed enough to submit to my control. Too often, a bottom's fantasies and desires exceed his stamina and abilities, and the scene becomes a turn off. I did not want that to happen now.

He kept eyeing my boots—a pair of tall, smooth, shiny motorcycle boots, and finally I suggested that he come over and lick them. He blushed furiously again, down to his neck and shoulders, but complied instantly, bounding over and sinking to his knees while he ran his tongue over the smooth black leather. As he licked my boots, his cock swelled up to what seemed like a gargantuan size. Swollen up, it was slightly darker than his skin, a dusky pink color. He was obviously enjoying what he was doing. I was not sure how far he had gone in the past, or how far he wanted to go, but there was nothing to be lost by testing his limits. I pulled him up, not too gently, and suggested that we move into the bedroom. He stood there, his face flushed, breathing heavily, his arms at his sides and his head bent down, the image of the perfect slave, his muscular body in a position of limp submission. He was obviously not into the scene—there was no "yes, sir" or dropping to his knees, or asking for permission, but at the same time, I had obviously tapped a strong desire in him. He was slightly awkward and unsure of himself, uncertain of what to do next or where to go, and waiting for my orders.

I hugged him to me, and groped him, grasping his cock and balls in my hand, cupping and kneading the cheeks of his ass, running my hands down his back, and clasping my arms around his chest and his neck. I could feel the rapid beating of his heart, suggesting that he was nervous, but he made no move to resist me, but rather, melted into my embrace. An electric thrill ran through me, terminating at my cock, as I held him in my arms, his smooth naked flesh rubbing against the rough fabric of my shirt and jeans. I was about three inches taller than him, and when I held him in my arms, I could smell his clean fresh smell, a mixture of shampoo, soap, sun-warmed hair, and a very slight smell of new, salty sweat. His warm skin was soft and silky smooth, but as I ran my hands over his body I could feel his firm muscles underneath, as they alternately tensed and relaxed in response to my touch. I felt like I was holding a wild animal in my arms, which although half tame, could bolt at any moment. His obvious desire for a scene, coupled with his undercurrent of anxiety and even fear was an incredible turn-on. I could feel my cock growing hard, but the close grip of the jeans kept it from reaching its full length. That signalled that it was time for me to strip off too.

When we got into bed, we hugged and embraced some more, kissing each other deeply. He was a great kisser, forcing his tongue deep into my throat, and at the same time, sucking my tongue deep into his mouth. I ended up on top of him, and while we were kissing, I grabbed both of his hands and held them down at his sides, and wrapped my legs around his, capturing him in a tight embrace. He went wild, twisting and turning underneath me, but making no move to free himself from my grasp. I noticed that his cock waved around like a flagpole in a strong wind.

"Maybe I should tie you down," I suggested. Seth said nothing but blushed furiously. I took a pair of cuffs from a drawer in the night table and showed them to him, slowly, cautiously fastening one to one wrist, then turning him on his side, and fastening his two hands together behind his back. Hard as I had thought his cock was, it seemed to get harder after I had locked his hands in place. As I pointed this out to him, now he was truly under my control. Although he remained silent, he made no move to resist or to escape. However, his hard cock said it all. Slowly, I spread his legs, and fastened an ankle to each corner of the bed, using a pair of leather manacles which were already in place, concealed under the mattress.

Once I had him tied down, I took a long leather thong and wrapped it around his cock and balls, first wrapping the base of the shaft, and then wrapping it tightly around the base of the balls. It was evidently a new experience for him, and he responded beautifully, gasping, moaning, and flexing his muscles, but remaining hard. His cock continued to jump around, and a little bead of precome appeared at the tip. I was not doing much better: My cock was rock hard, and every time it brushed against him I felt an electric jolt course through me. Not only was he a fantasy come to life, but the scene was totally unexpected.

I went slowly with him. Each time I tried something out, I stopped and paused to give him time to adjust and to see how he responded. I did not want to overwhelm him and bring the scene to a shuddering halt. However, going slowly increased the sexual intensity of the scene, making me more and more turned on.

I started to play with his tits, biting them, running my hands over them, pinching and squeezing them. He responded by squirming, moaning, opening his mouth, and arcing his body to try to rub against me. It was great to see that hot, muscular body squirm—like a Greek sculpture, muscles in relief, the sheen of sweat on his arms, pecs, and stomach, and know that he was completely under my control. He responded instantly to pressure on his tits and balls, moving up and down on the bed each time I flicked his tits or balls up and down.

I released his hands and fastened them to opposite sides at the top of the bed, using leather manacles, which were already in place. I gave him a few minutes to adjust to his new captivity, pinching and kneading his pecs to make him squirm and realize his helplessness. I took his balls in the palm of my hand and slowly squeezed them together until he gasped, then moaned, and then tried to bend over in pain, but of course, he could not since he was spread-eagled on the bed. His stomach muscles clenched in his useless effort to curl up, and he moaned deeply and loudly as I released his balls. I wanted to work on his tits, perhaps putting clothespins on them, but also wanted him to suck me off, so instead, I placed clothespins on the inside of his thigh and added three to the shaft of his cock. He froze and gasped. His cock seemed to go soft for a moment, but he soon recovered, so I did not remove them, but did not go further.

Despite his momentary softness, he was obviously enjoying the scene. He kept getting hotter and hotter, trying to rub against me. His cock was like a barometer—it never got soft, and the more excited he was, the more it jumped around. Precome continued to leak out. Finally, I sat on his chest, placing my cock in front of his face, and allowed him to lick it and suck on it.

Seth sucked cock like a pro, taking it deep into his throat, using his lips, tongue, and even teeth to stimulate and work on it. He nibbled the tip, forced his tongue into the cock lips, licked the shaft, and swallowed it down deep into his throat, keeping it there while it swelled and grew to fill his mouth. His lips and mouth were warm, moist, and smooth. I cupped his head in my hands, forcing my cock deeper into his face. It slipped in smoothly. I kept it there for a while, enjoying his mouth's warm, sensuous embrace, feeling my cock swell up and choke him. As my cock grew to its full size, he struggled for air, but never gave up. He gagged increasingly frequently, producing massive amounts of phlegm, which acted as a lubricant, but kept on swallowing and sucking on my cock, right down to the root. He licked, nibbled, and kissed it with his lips. I never felt his teeth unless he wanted me too. It was an incredible smooth, hot, warm suction, stimulating every part of my shaft.

Several times, he brought me close to shooting, which I put off each time by withdrawing my cock just beyond the reach of his hot, hungry lips. It drove him wild, and I almost creamed myself just watching him writhe and stretch to try to continue to suck and lick my cock. However, I had decided early on that I wanted to end the scene in an explosive orgasm, releasing all my pent up excitement by fucking his glorious ass. Finally, reluctantly, I pulled away, and detached his legs one at a time, refastening them to hooks above the bed, so that they were pulled up over his head, and his ass was completely exposed. When I did this, I was interested to see that there was a small damp spot around the place where his cock and balls had been, demonstrating the panic and discomfort produced by the clothespins on his cock and thighs. However, he never said a word of protest.

Now that I wasn't using his face, I was free to play with his tits, and started by pinching and kneading them between my thumb and forefingers. I gradually increased the pressure, pinching them more and more tightly, pulling on them harder and harder. At first, he gasped and moaned, his body initially going rigid, and then he tried to twist away. As I increased the pressure, he tried to pull himself up by his arms, but with his feet tied up over his head, could not get the leverage to free himself from my control. He gasped, followed by a sigh, almost a moan, and as I pulled on his tits, his body followed. I began to manipulate him like a puppet, forcing him to move slightly up and down in response to my pressure on his tits, making him moan more and more loudly. Throughout this workout, his cock remained hard, continually jerking suddenly in response to a sudden touch or spasm of excitement. I increased the pressure, pinching more and more until his moan turned into a muffled shriek, at which point I stopped. His cock remained hard, although he was obviously new to tit torture, and I fastened some clothespins to his tits. I used clothespins because they were light enough to avoid causing him serious pain, but heavy enough that he would be constantly aware of them, especially every time he moved. By now, his tits were rock hard, and it was easy to fasten the clothespins to them, although the sheen of sweat made me unsure that they would stay in place.

I proceeded to beat his ass. I started with a belt, but as it became obvious that he was not only able to handle the pain but was enjoying it, shifted to a strap and then a whip. The white flesh showed each stroke beautifully, slowly becoming bright red all over as I continued to work on it. His cock was constantly in plain sight, and the more I gave him, the more he seemed to want. It never went down, but from time to time jumped and waved, despite the clothespins fastened to the shaft.

About halfway through the whipping, he began to moan and twist around although his cock remained hard. Suddenly, without warning, he exploded with come, spurting out big creamy white gobs over his stomach and pecs. He looked glorious, completely helpless, covered in sweat, his flat stomach curved in, emphasizing the curve of his pecs. His face was flushed, and his mouth was open as he relaxed back into his bonds.

I was reluctant to see the scene end, but did not want to force him to go further. I half jokingly said, "Maybe you should be punished for that, boy." To my surprise, he blushed all over and replied, Yes, maybe I should." So, I decided to carry on, saying, "Yes what, boy?"

He hesitated a minute, and then replied, haltingly and in a half whisper, "Yes . . . sir."

I continued to beat his ass, from time to time focussing on his massive thighs. Slowly, I increased the intensity of the beating, switching back and forth between a belt and a whip. In no time at all he was hard again, and as the force of the blows increased, he began to twist and turn to avoid the lash, which had the unintentional effect of raising his ass still higher, making it more accessible. Welts began to show up against his reddened flesh, and soon marked his thighs as well. He quickly became covered with a sheen of sweat again and, as he flexed his muscles, his biceps, thigh muscles, and pecs stood out in sharp relief.

I was still dying to fuck him, but given the size of my cock, thought I would first try a inserting a dildo. I greased up his ass, provoking an attempt to pull away as he felt the cold lubricant and the entry of my greased-up fingers. I inserted the dildo slowly but steadily, pausing from time to time to give him a chance to adjust, but never pulling back until it was completely inserted. He initially tried to pull away, flexing his muscles, especially his thighs, as he vigorously tried to resist or avoid the entry. He cried out initially, and then moaned and groaned, but never went soft. After the initial entry, he continued to moan and squirm, but his cock stayed hard, and the more I pushed it in, the more ardent he became, twisting his head and raising his shoulders to try to look directly into my eyes.

I continued to play with the dildo for a while, softening him up and relaxing him as he became more and more excited. His gasps and moans turned from moans of pain to gasps of excitement. Finally, incredibly excited myself, I slipped on a condom and let the dildo slide out before ramming my cock inside of him, straight down to the base of the shaft. That provoked a deep shuddering moan of pain and excitement, which again, turned to gasps of pleasure as I began to pump my cock in and out, slowly and pleasurably working myself to an extremely satisfying climax. His position on his back allowed me to lean forward between his captive legs and kiss him deeply from time to time. He raised—or tried to raise—his shoulders to meet my lips, opening his mouth wide to take my tongue. After I had come, I waited until my cock softened and slipped out, and then worked him off with my hands, producing another explosion of creamy white jism, which spattered his stomach and pecs.

After the scene had ended, Seth seemed reluctant to leave. I certainly wanted to go further with him, much further. We showered separately, but I could see that he was still hot to play, both from the way he kept eyeing my cock and from his obvious fascination with the few toys I had left lying around. It was getting late, and so I suggested that we send out for a pizza, saying that after we had eaten he was welcome to stay the night. He jumped at the offer, agreeing instantly.

By now, given what had gone on, it was obvious that I had severely misread him. He was no newcomer to sex, but was severely repressed. He told me over the pizza that he had been dying to try S/M for years, but had not known how to get started. He wasn't much of a drinker, and wasn't in to the bar scene. However, he had seen me a few times in the gym and on the street, and noticed my boots. He thought I might be into S/M, but thought I looked like such a hot stud that I would not be into sex with men at all, much less S/M.

After we finished the pizza, I took him back to bed and chained him down, playing with him for a couple of hours before finally coming on his chest, and leaving it there to dry. He was insatiable, and I kept having to pull away to make sure I did not shoot too soon. When we finally went to sleep, I left him chained down, his feet together at the bottom of the bed, and his arms together at the top. However, each time he woke up, he arched his body to try to reach over to me, to kiss me, to rub against me, or to suck, kiss, and fondle my cock with his tongue. In turn, I could not resist playing with his cock each time I woke up, which made him completely wild, and led to repeated sex. By the early morning, he was covered in come, mine and his. Finally, I had to release him because he needed to piss, and the room was not set up for a water scene. Reluctantly I fastened him on the floor at the foot of the bed, since we both needed to get some sleep, but I knew that he was even more excited at the thought of being chained to the foot of the bed, lying naked on the carpet. I cannot speak for him, but my cock was totally drained, and completely sucked out.

I would have liked to keep him longer, but he had to go to a meeting, and I had to get ready for work. However, over breakfast, we had a long talk. He told me that I had given him exactly what he had been looking for. Despite myself, I was concerned for him, and worried that he might land himself in no end of trouble if he was not careful. However, he seemed relatively levelheaded, and appreciated my concern. Blushing furiously, he made it clear that he wanted to go further with me—much further, and we agreed to meet for a longer session. A three-day weekend is coming up soon, and I am hoping I can talk him into staying a fourth day. I plan to play with him in my dungeon, and give him an experience he can really think about!

THE HUNK IN HOT PANTS

Stephen Albrow

It was '70s disco night at my local gay bar and everyone was dressed up in their Scissor Sisters finest. Take the guy that I took home, for example—it was his black leather hot pants that did it for me. They were hugging his cute little butt cheeks so tightly; it was almost as if they were trying to strangle the life out of his behind. He was standing at the bar sipping on a cocktail and when he bent over to pick up the cigarette lighter that he'd dropped, I almost creamed my jeans. Two curvy buttocks came poking up toward me. I could swear that his crack was smiling right at me, as if it was trying to lure me into his clutches.

I watched intently, as he bent over farther, reaching all the way down to the floor for the lighter. The farther that he stretched, the farther that the hot pants disappeared into the crack of his butt. To my delight, it got to the point where I could almost make out the opening of his sphincter.

Even from my position at the other end of the bar, his sweet-tasting hole seemed to be begging for a piece of my cock. Right there and then, I was willing to give to him whatever it was that he was willing to take. A dream was waiting to be fulfilled and I needed his sphincter to make it happen.

It was my sister's vibrator that had first gotten me wise to the joys of a nice firm butt. One night while she was out at cheerleading practice, I'd found the vibe in her underwear drawer, along with a tube of K-Y jelly. It was eight-inches long with a bulbous tip, so I greased it up with plenty of lube and set about showing myself a real good time. Up until that night with my sister's vibe, I'd been a teenager struggling to come to terms with his sexuality, but as soon as that plastic prick head touched me deep inside, I knew just who I was and what I wanted. I was gay and I wanted a man!

Boy, that vibe sure did bring about a change in me! Up until that moment of penetration, my butt hole had just been a thing that I crapped out of, but feeling it responding to the force of the plastic crown did something truly wonderful to me. As soon as I felt it stretching my ring, I found my cock getting hard and stiff. The farther that I shoved that plastic schlong inside of me, the harder and stiffer my cock kept on growing.

That night, even after my sister was home, I kept the vibrator with me in bed. All night long, I sat there propped up against my pillow, unable to conceal my sensual enjoyment, as I fooled around with my brand new toy.

Actually, make that my two brand new toys—as well as the vibe, the other new toy that I found that night was the ultra-responsive cornhole between my teenage buns. It felt totally fantastic shoving the vibe up my crack. It was like no sensation that I had ever known before and when I removed the vibe and smelled it, the scent of my butt was almost enough to blow my mind. It was as if I'd discovered a fun park better than Disney World right there in the back of my pants. My smooth firm cheeks came alive whenever I touched them with the vibrating plastic pole, while, once it was inside me, my tender crack seemed to be filled to the brim with pleasure sensors. Every time that I thrust the cock head into that dirty black hole of mine, a whole new wave of gorgeous sensations went coursing through my veins.

The next morning, I awoke as a totally changed person. Suddenly, I was a sex-crazed homo, totally unable to tear his eyes away from any masculine butt that happened to walk on by. Overnight, I had developed a supersensual fetish for men in Levi's jeans, which quickly led to a phase of hanging around pools and checking out the sexy studs in their swimming shorts. Even today, I often drift off to sleep thinking of a pair of wet shorts clinging to a pair of solid buttocks. The material gets wetter and the outline of the butt grows clearer, as the guy swims the length of the pool to where I'm sitting waiting for a screw.

Sadly, back then, at that point in my life, it was all about looking and never about touching. As an 18-year-old I was kind of shy and the thought of going all the way with a guy left me little short of terrified. It wasn't until I had turned 19 that I finally plucked up the courage to enter a gay bar, and that was the moment when I first laid my eyes upon those perfectly pert buttocks in those black leather hot pants.

The fact that it was '70s disco night made my first venture into a gay bar a whole lot easier. I wore these crazy flared trousers and this Afro wig, which made me almost unrecognizable. It was nice to be able to hide behind a disguise, while I checked out the guy with the most awesome ass in the world. I sipped on a Coca-Cola for a while, just watching him from afar. He was a smallish guy, but very muscular, and the hot pants and his tight T-shirt showed off every single one of his muscles.

It was as he was dancing to some old Donna Summer tracks that I finally decided to make my move. I danced close by him for a time, waiting for a chance to catch his eye. Then the moment that I saw him looking, I flashed him my cutest smile.

Bummer! The guy responded by turning his back to me and for a moment I felt my heart begin to sink. I thought that I was getting the cold shoulder, although my disappointment was tempered by the chance that it gave me to watch his butt wiggling in time to the music. He was bumping and grinding with incredible passion, like a lap dancer working it for a big-tipping client. As his crotch pumped back and forward to the upbeat tempo, I could see his butt cheeks actually quivering along to the beat.

And that's when it hit me—all of a sudden I realized that the guy had turned his back on me, not as a way of rejecting my advances, but more as a way of reeling me in. He was getting me hot by shaking his booty right in front of my eyes. Just as importantly, turning away served as a prelude to the fancy dance spin that would bring him face-to-face with me and allow him to move up real close to my body.

The spin happened right at the start of a Gloria Gaynor dance track. The guy pushed his chest tight up against mine and started to hump his crotch forward toward my cock. I felt the outline of his meaty dick through the leather hot pants, as our crotches collided together. Seconds later, I felt his lips pressing up against mine, as he started to French kiss me with lusty thrusts of his tongue.

The guy wound his arms around my neck, as he drew me closer to him. Suddenly, I couldn't resist the temptation any longer. I slid my hands right the way down his back and then took his butt cheeks in the palms of my hands. The leather material made me feel horny straightaway, but that was only the start of it. When I tightened my fingers and dug them into his fleshy cheeks, I could feel myself achieve an instant boner.

The guy had obviously felt it too. He pushed his cock right up close to mine and gyrated it over my shaft and across my balls. I squashed his tight butt cheeks between my fingers, really getting off on the feel of the hard muscle beneath the cool leather exterior. His tongue kept on leaping in and out of my mouth, as I took the opportunity to explore some more of his ass. I ran my hands farther down his cheeks and then slipped a finger beneath the leather material, so that I could feel his naked butt flesh right up against my skin.

It was everything that I had dreamed it would be. I could only get one finger beneath the tight leather pants, but that was plenty enough to get a real sense of what another man's butt would feel like to really grope at and fuck. His flesh was totally hairless and, thanks to his nonstop dirty dancing, there was a thin layer of sweat upon his well-toned rear. Unable to resist it, I broke off the kiss and asked the guy if he wanted to come home with me. He answered me with a second French kiss, before leading me out into the streets to hail a cab.

We climbed into the back of the cab and I told the driver my address. The engine started and, as we sped off into the night, I felt my new lover draping his thigh across my lap. He was nestling up good and close to me, like he really meant business. I could feel the side of his right buttock pressing against my thigh, which sent a shiver of lust running through my body. Quickly, I began to wonder what it would feel like to poke my cock up his crack and to dirty my helmet in his skintight asshole.

The journey home was short, but I was so eager for a piece of his ass that it seemed to take an eternity to me. Eventually, the cab pulled up outside my apartment and, after paying the driver, we started climbing up the three flights of stairs that led to my door.

Naturally, I let the hunk in hot pants go first. It was like heaven watching his butt wiggling from side to side, as we ascended those three flights. Every time that he climbed a step higher, his hot pants really rode up and dug into his cheeks. I could see red marks forming on his lower buttocks where the leather was cutting into them. I planned to soothe the pain with red-hot kisses the second that we got inside.

I closed the door of my apartment behind me and turned back into the room to find that my lover was already stripping off his clothes. His T-shirt had been thrown onto the couch and his hot pants were slowly being pushed down his legs. His gorgeous butt came into full view, just like a full moon rising. It was all muscle and all man and all that I could ever have wanted.

I told the guy to lie facedown on the couch, which he did without hesitation. My prick was throbbing at the thought of tasting his butt hole, but I decided to tease myself a little before I finally made that happen. I planted a kiss on each of his toes, before slowly kissing my way up his legs. His thighs were as solid as tree trunks and I lingered there for quite a while. There was something really special about the taste of the perspiration at the back of his thighs, while I just couldn't help being really turned on by the smell of his spicy deodorant.

My head was spinning with lust for this guy. That lust became totally overwhelming, as I felt my hair brush against the slight upward curve that signaled the end of his gorgeous thighs and the beginning of his totally awesome butt. I could feel saliva building up in my mouth, as I kissed a little farther up his body. I was inches away from paradise. It was time to move in for the kill.

Drool began to pour all the way down my chin, as I stared straight into my lover's crack. My lips kissed his butt flesh and, even better, my naughty nose got gently pressed into the crevice between his lightly tanned cheeks.

I inhaled deeply. A myriad of different smells filled my senses. There was sweat and deodorant and aftershave and God knows what else coming out of that crack. I dug my nose deeper between his fleshy cheeks and pressed it barely a millimeter away from his butt hole. Part of me thought that I could smell traces of spunk in there, but that might just have been the scent floating up from my crotch. Already a few little dribbles of spunk had dripped out of my crown and wet my boxer shorts.

I couldn't tease myself any longer. What had started with a series of slow tender kisses up his thighs, became a mad frenzy of licking and sucking, once my lips and my tongue reached his beautiful butt. I plunged my teeth deep into his cheeks and licked the mound of ass flesh that I sucked up into my mouth. It tasted of pure man and it was a taste that I liked, which made me long for my dick to taste it too.

"Wouldn't you like to stick your prick in that hole?" said my lover, just then, as if magically reading my thoughts.

My answer was a resounding yes. I ran into the bathroom and sheathed up my prick, then I grabbed a bottle of baby lotion to use as lubrication. Running back out to my lover, I squirted the oil onto my middle finger and then began to finger-fuck his butt hole. It felt awesome to feel his interior muscles gripping around my digit. I pushed it inside him, slowly but surely, gradually oiling up his hole, until I felt it was ready to accommodate my erection.

The guy was letting out little squeals of satisfaction, as my finger dug ever deeper inside of him. I kissed his cheeks, admiring their peach-like shape and smoothness, as I carefully prepared him for penetration. It was kind of weird to think that his butt hole was driving me quite so wild with passion. Although I kept on telling myself that they were only two mounds of flesh with a hole in between them, they somehow seemed so much more than that. I inhaled deeply, again, and felt the smell of his butt and his sweat titillating my senses. My crown began to throb, proving that my point was true—this guy's butt was truly something else.

Soon my finger was fully inside him, confirming to me that his butt hole was ready to take on my cock. I pulled out my finger and knelt down on the floor.

"Come sit in my lap," I said to him.

He got up from the couch and climbed on top of me. His butt hole hovered just above my cock for a moment then I felt him slowly lowering himself down onto my erection. An intense convulsion made my cock tremble, as his sphincter took a bite at my crown. He wiggled his booty to force it inside, then thrust his butt backward and swallowed up my shaft.

I almost ejaculated, just from that single thrust. His muscles convulsed wildly around my erection, as they fought to come to terms with the foreign body that had invaded their territory. Such was the force of the convulsions in his sphincter that the pleasure sensors in my cock immediately switched to overdrive. A series of near-orgasmic pulsations shot through my helmet and made me moan out loud with happiness.

The guy's butt hole responded to the feel of my prick with a wave of contortions that totally blew my mind. Not only were his insides twisting and turning around my tensed-up erection, but I also had the feel of his firm buttocks sitting in my lap to help heighten my enjoyment of the penetration. My balls were sitting snugly between his butt cheeks and, as I started to really open up and fuck him, I could feel my own butt hole coming alive. Sure, I was enjoying repeatedly slamming my prick in and out of his sphincter, but my mind was imagining how my own butt would feel getting forcefully penetrated by a big fat dick. I'd get fucked up the sphincter and then go down on my lover and taste my own butt hole on his spunk-soaked helmet.

"Harder," I heard the hunk in my lap say, and instantly I was awoken from my fevered dreams.

I upped the tempo of the fuck so that soon he was really bouncing up and down in my lap; his bounces growing gradually faster, until eventually I was flat-out fucking his back passage. The stink of sex and naked butt hole became totally electric. I thrilled to the sensations, as his sphincter hungrily gobbled up my shaft, spat it out, then gobbled it straight back up again, spat it out, then ate it straight back up again.

As my prick continued to slide in and out of his butt hole, I hugged my arms around his upper body and kissed the back of his head. His firm cheeks and muscular thighs kept on bouncing around in my lap, as he savored the feel of my cock inside his sphincter. Sensing how turned on he was, I reached round his body and took hold of his helmet in my hand. The bucking motion caused by my dick ramming in and out of his hole was plenty hard and fast enough to make his cock slide through my fingers in a jerk-off motion.

"Make my fucking butt hole explode," my lover screamed, between moans of purest lust. I thought about it, and the way that my cock was slamming in and out of his back passage, it seemed more than likely that I'd already done so.

My balls pressed tight up against his butt cleavage, as his sphincter received a blast of my full nine inches. The tightness of his hole forced my foreskin back down my shaft and that allowed his internal muscles to attack my throbbing crown. It was a truly sensational moment for me and I couldn't hold out any longer. My balls exploded in a blaze of orgasmic lust and the next thing that I knew I was filling his butt with spunk.

It was only come, but it actually felt like my entire being was draining out of my body and disappearing up into his crack. His sphincter quickly lapped up my juices, while spurred on by the thrill of my climax; I fisted his boner with awesome speed. My fingers squeezed his erection close to breaking point, as I rammed his foreskin up and down his shaft. He obviously liked the heightened speed of the jerk off, because almost immediately I felt his cock head start to spasm in my hand.

I watched, as my lover ejaculated; his spunk shooting out of his piss hole and landing on his thighs. Liking the sight of that, I kept on jerking and soon I saw a second burst of spunk hitting his stomach. My cock head continued to throb inside his back passage, as he smeared the spent come all over his flesh. He was breathing hard, as if the force of the fuck had totally overwhelmed him, leaving him badly in need of some shut-eye.

"Thank you," he softly whispered to me, then he took my hand, led me back to the couch, curled up in my arms, and promptly fell asleep.

"My pleasure," I said, cupping my fingers around his ass cheeks. I held his buttocks tight, as I tried, but failed, to join him in the land of dreams.

It was plain to me why I couldn't sleep that night. My dreams had just come true and my head was too filled with lustful thoughts to allow me to drift off. I'd finally had my first taste of butt and every part of me had loved it. My fingers had loved the feel of those smooth cheeks; my nose had loved the vibrant smell of masculinity; and, most of all, my cock had adored getting swallowed up by that big black hole.

My handsome lover's muscular buttocks had worked their spell and suddenly I was an ass junkie. There was absolutely no turning back now. I simply had to have my regular fix. It was time to give my sister her vibe back. It wasn't of use to me anymore. Her plastic sex toy might have taught me the way to pleasure a butt hole, but, by doing that, it had made itself redundant. It had taken a boy and made him into a man. And a real man doesn't need to play with toys—a real man prefers the real thing!

THE MEN IN THE MIRROR

Jay Starre

Tony was originally from Argentina. I'd met him on a trip to California and he'd come home to live with me in Vancouver on the west coast of Canada. We weren't really lovers, more like best fuck buddies. Tony obsessed over my sexy white butt, and loved to spend hours working over my asshole.

Many a time I begged Tony to let me reciprocate. I wanted Tony's hard South American ass. But Tony was a total macho type, and claimed he could never be a bottom. Still, I entertained a sneaking suspicion that if Tony loved my bung hole so much, spent so much time down there teasing, fingering, and licking it, he might enjoy the same attentions. I didn't think he was being completely honest with either of us. It was only his macho mind-set that prevented more sexual delights we'd both enjoy. I decided to test out my theory.

We'd showered together and were standing in front of the bathroom mirror drying off when I happened to glance at our reflections. Tony was bent over, his ass facing the mirror. His hard-as-rock buns, coated with a down of dark hair, were so hot-looking in the mirror, I inhaled sharply. As Tony bent farther to rub the towel over his feet, his snug butt hole winked out at me. An exciting notion flashed through my mind like an explosion.

I went out and purchased the proper equipment that next day, and when Tony came home from his job at a construction site, there I was waiting anxiously for him, a lewd smirk on my face.

"Are you horny, amigo?" I teased, reaching out and fondling Tony's dick beneath his jeans. Of course he would be. He always was.

"Are you gonna let me fuck your sweet ass tonight?" Tony chuckled in his exotic accent, grabbing a handful of my butt.

I laughed back as I dragged my buddy into our bedroom. "Look what I've got here!" I giggled nervously. Now if only Tony would go along with my plan until he was hooked.

"A mirror. That's cool! Are we gonna fuck in front of it?" Tony grinned, a light of kinky desire in his amber eyes.

"Let's get our clothes off. I want to try something," I answered, stripping quickly so Tony would have little choice.

Tony always got excited when he saw me naked, so he eagerly tore off his own clothes and tossed them aside. We embraced and then kissed, our tongues mashing together, our hands roaming all over each other's bodies. I lowered Tony to the floor in front of the mirror. It was a huge mirror, covering half the facing wall, right down to the floor. Before Tony knew what was happening, I rolled around and had him facing the mirror on his back.

"Look at that, amigo," I grinned, propping up my Latino friend and pointing to the mirror.

Facing us was the macho Latino's naked reflection. I had his legs spread wide apart, with his sexy can facing the mirror. Between Tony's beefy thighs, his amber ass with its faint down of black hair reflected beautifully in the mirror.

"My butt," Tony chuckled.

But I noticed he was staring at it with interest, never having looked at it quite like that before. I moved swiftly to take advantage of that flicker of curiosity. I scooted behind Tony and propped him against my stomach, raising and spreading his thighs. Tony's asshole was revealed, winking out at us, its tiny pucker surrounded by a wisp or two of silky black hair.

"Looks hot, doesn't it?" I breathed into Tony's ear.

Tony didn't answer, but the pace of his breathing increased. I didn't wait for him to reply. I reached down with one hand and flicked a fingertip across the small opening. The anal ring fluttered in response. Tony gasped, his eyes glued to the reflection of that hole as my finger ran across it.

"I know you love a sweet asshole. Lie back and relax while you watch this one getting teased," I blurted out boldly. I prayed Tony wouldn't laugh it off and turn back to our usual scene.

Instead, I was pleasantly surprised by the absolute stillness in my buddy's body. Tony stared fixedly at his own asshole in the mirror. He seemed enthralled with the unusual image. I knew enough to take advantage of a good thing and smiled lustfully as I leaped full ahead with my plan. I began to tickle the tight hole.

"Look at that button winking at us," I whispered in Tony's ear, taking a swipe at his slot with my finger. I felt Tony shiver, but his thighs remained splayed apart, and his hands didn't move, his eyes fixed on the image of the asshole in the mirror.

I stared too, just as fascinated as Tony by the sudden strangers in the mirror, one a muscular pale blond and the other a slimmer Latino. I shuddered as I felt the silky warmth of Tony's ass lips under my fingertips, watching the blond in the mirror with his hand down in the Latino's ass crack, touching the macho stud's asshole as both men held still, their breathing shaky. I felt like I was two different men, the one in the mirror, and myself. It made me bolder than usual.

In that mirror fingers traced lightly over the exposed puckered rim, spreading it apart so that a glimpse of the inner flesh appeared, then withdrawing to graze it with soft caresses. Tony's breathing became labored, his hips rose up just perceptibly. He was moving into those fingers. The image in the glass of that hot hole being lightly teased by two and three blunt fingers had him snared in a net of nasty desire. Thank God! I was sure the sensations that wracked his body, emanating directly from his sensitive anal lips, were an unanticipated pleasure for the macho stud.

I continued playing with the rim of the hole, tickling it, flicking my fingers across it and watching as it began to open and expand with a will of its own. Tony gasped and shuddered as the hole in the mirror began to bloom like a flower, the inner flesh expanding and pulsing apart. I was just as fascinated. Someone, the blond stud in the mirror, was playing with the hole I'd longed to touch for months. I watched Tony getting his tight hole fingered by that stranger in the mirror, and it wasn't really me. It was a tall, sandy-blond stud, breathing hard, his eyes flashing out his passion for the asshole he now had at his mercy. I was on top for once!

Tony trembled all over as I teased his asshole. My fingers knew what felt good, from personal experience. I dipped a fingertip into the center of the expanding hole, not pressing inside, but merely rubbing back and forth lightly, delving slightly into the warm opening. Tony's eyes were half-closed in breathless pleasure, yet still gazing raptly at the butt hole in the mirror. That hole opened further as the finger slid into the entrance—the slot gaping apart like a hungry mouth begging to be filled. But that finger didn't slide any deeper, or fill it. Not yet. I teased and caressed and drove Tony to the brink.

The dark stud was practically a quivering mass of jelly by this time. His thighs were spread wide apart, his body shaking like a leaf. His dick was hard as stone, slapping up against his belly and drooling copiously. I could hardly suppress a triumphant laugh. I took one of Tony's hands and placed it on his stiff prick.

"Rub it. Come while you watch your own hole getting teased," I whispered crudely in Tony's ear.

Tony's hand responded, grasping his sabre-like cock and flailing it violently. He was so excited he came in less than a minute. Come spurted in an arc up into the air and landed back on the heaving belly.

The asshole in the mirror gaped open at first, as if it was attempting to suck the teasing finger into it, then it clamped down like a vice as Tony's orgasm exploded. I allowed that excited hole to clasp the blunt tip of my finger as it convulsed in wild spasms while Tony came.

"*Dios mio,*" Tony muttered, reverting to his native language in the haze of his violent orgasm.

That was it for the evening. Tony was drained and slightly embarrassed by the escapade. But I was well-pleased and held my own orgasm back for step 2, which I planned to implement the next evening.

Tony came home hot and horny as usual. Wordlessly, I led him into the bedroom and faced the mirror. Tony shuddered, as if dreading the inevitable, but he was meek as I undressed us both. This time I'd placed a sofa chair in front of the mirror and had Tony recline back into it when he was totally nude.

I gazed at the hot stud in the mirror. Tony was so fucking handsome. His deep amber eyes looked out from under thick brows that could smolder with intensity when he was feeling emotional. The short, glossy curls on his scalp were midnight black. His body was lean, with wide shoulders and a nice chest, fine dark down covering most of it and trailed down to his flat belly, then surrounding his slender, but long cock. His naked thighs, which I'd spread apart to lie on either arm of the small sofa, were full of muscular power. He was a lean dude, but had a lushly sexual aura about him, especially noticeable in the plump fullness of his lips.

His firm can was exposed, the hole between the cheeks once more staring out at us. I actually licked my lips as I thought of what I was about to attempt. At that moment our eyes met in the mirror. I saw myself through Tony's eyes in our reflection. Tall, with a smooth chest and huge muscles. The blond in the mirror was a gym stud, with blue eyes under pale brows and a square, pleasant face. The stranger was horny. The two men were going to do things to each other—raunchy, nasty things.

Tony was silent, although his body was already quivering. We shared the same thoughts. What would those guys do? What would that blond do to my fuck buddy? Things I had always wanted to do but couldn't? What was going to happen to the asshole Tony peered at so avidly, once more transfixed by the image of his own butt? One thing was certain, we could watch it all, like kinky voyeurs at a live fuck show.

I moved. This time I knelt down between Tony's legs, but to the side so I wouldn't block the reflection in the mirror. I started teasing his hole with my fingers.

The moment my fingers grazed his asshole, Tony moaned out loud, arching his back and pressing his crotch into those tantalizing digits. I grinned at our reflection. I hawked on my fingers and rubbed the slippery lubricant across the pulsing anal flesh.

"Oh—oh—yeah—*si*," Tony grunted, shoving his butt forward on the sofa.

Tony's eyes never left the reflection in the mirror. I teased his hole with my spit-wet fingers, swiping them back and forth rapidly, dipping into the gaping mouth of the anal orifice as it opened to meet them. But I didn't enter deeply, merely warming up that sweet slot for something more.

"Put it in, amigo. Put it in," Tony muttered in a barely audible whisper.

I knew it was time for the next phase of my nasty fantasy. Tony, and his puckered hole, were primed. My own hands trembled as I reached under the bed for my next instrument of anal assault. I pulled out a long black dildo. I held it up and lay it between Tony's writhing thighs.

Tony's eyes bulged with a mixture of shock and nasty excitement. The dildo was almost two feet long, half of it a thick handle. A round black ball, smooth and glistening, dangled from one end. The ball tapered abruptly into a thin six-inch stem that terminated in the thick black handle. It was obscene, and it looked bizarrely kinky as I held it up against Tony's spread butt crack. The handsome Latino in the mirror panted as he sprawled helplessly on the sofa, awaiting the inevitable.

"What are you gonna do with that thing, *muchacho*?" Tony grunted out in a slurred accent. His sultry brown orbs were transfixed by the obscene reflection in the mirror. That crude black dildo lay in my hands between his own spread legs, threatening his twitching asshole with who-knew-what.

I merely smiled as I began to rub it up and down over Tony's widespread butt crack. The rounded ball end slipped across Tony's quivering ass button, which elicited a series of grunts and gasps from the sprawled stud. After a few teasing moments of that, I reached for a bottle of lube I'd placed strategically beside the chair earlier. I upended it and squirted a stream of clear goo over Tony's ass crack, then slid the rounded ball of the dildo directly into the pulsing anal rim. Pressing against the quavering flesh of Tony's snug hole, the glossy black ball looked huge, although it was not really very big. Tony's eyes bulged as he watched and waited.

I was fascinated too. I rubbed the round head into the gaping entrance, sliding it around, stretching the hole open wider and wider. The rim of the asshole in the mirror began to expand and stretch, slowly accepting more and more of the ball into it.

Tony was grunting, his thighs pulled as far apart as possible, his entire attention focussed on that expanding hole and the black ball beginning to fill it. The widest part started to slide deeper, the slippery lube easing its entry. With a sudden spasm, Tony's asshole gaped open and swallowed the whole ball.

"*Dios-dios*-oh-oh! What is inside of me?" he choked out, his entire body jerking.

He'd never had his hole filled before. The long, thin stem and the handle in my hand were all that was visible, but we both knew what was hidden inside Tony's puckered hole. It was a big black ball of hard rubber invading his guts. I began to feed the stem into the quivering hole. Grease coated the rim, squishing and drooling, as Tony's asshole opened and closed with nervous spasms around the black stem invading it.

I could only imagine the sensations inside Tony's guts as that big ball penetrated deeper and deeper. I fed four and then five inches of the stem into him. Tony groaned and grunted the whole time, but made no objection. His dick had gone flaccid, then returned to its former turgid firmness. We both stared at the image in the mirror—the obscene black stem and my pale hand as it gripped the handle and shoved in and out of Tony's hole. I let go of the handle and allowed it to dangle down between Tony's parted thighs.

"Relax, pal. Let it go. It won't come out," I encouraged Tony.

Tony obeyed, willing his butt hole to let up. The anal rim

expanded and the stem invading it slid back out, like a dark, slowly slithering snake. We both gasped at the kinky image. Then the stem stopped moving as the rounded ball pressed against Tony's sphincter from inside his lubed hole. It wouldn't escape his snug butt hole so easily.

Tony groaned. The sensation of the big ball pressing on his tight ring from the inside must have been novel and exciting. The image in the mirror was just as awesomely nasty. The long handle of the dildo swayed down between Tony's thighs as he squirmed and wriggled around the ball that couldn't escape. His taut butt cheeks jiggled, and so did the handle as it bounced up and down between his legs. I reached out and teased the stretched rim with my fingers. Tony almost screamed at the added sensation, and as we both watched in amazement, the black ball suddenly shot out of the hole, falling to the floor. Tony's hole spasmed in and out, lube dripping as the just-filled cavity convulsed feverishly.

I snatched up the greasy dildo, only this time I reversed it. The thick handle had a wider rim at the end. I shoved it up against the gooey center of Tony's butt hole. While Tony gazed fixedly in the mirror, his mouth gaping open and drooling at the corners, I rubbed that blunt cap into his slot. With a steady shove, I forced the thick piece of rubber up the snapping hole.

"*Dios mio! Dios mio!* I'm getting fucked," Tony wailed.

The thick handle was buried two inches up his tight sphincter. He shook all over, but his hole took it. We both watched in the mirror as my white hand shoved the black handle in and out of Tony's stretched and now more pliant hole.

Tony went crazy. He grabbed his dick and whipped at it. His prostate was being pounded by the blunt end of that dildo. The sensations, combined with the raunchy image in the mirror were overpowering. But this time he didn't come as quickly as the day before. Obviously the sensations emanating from deep in his guts delayed his ejaculation. This was nastily exciting for us both.

We gawked at the image in the mirror. There was the South American stud with his legs splayed, writhing around the black dildo handle probing his lubed asshole. There was the muscular white jock on his knees cramming the slippery obsidian handle far up that straining asshole.

Then Tony did an amazing thing. He reached between his own thighs and grabbed the dildo from me. As he jacked his own dick, he began to shove that dildo frantically into his own hole. I gasped out loud. Tony was fucking himself willingly! It was too good to be true. The brutal black handle rammed in and out, the quivering ass lips pulled open and then clamped down with every thrust. Tony could see it all in the mirror, and so could I.

I began to shoot without even touching my stiff cock. Tony was right behind.

We spurted cream and both shouted out together. I pulled the handle out of Tony's squishy hole and let it drop to the floor. The hole in the mirror drooled and spasmed as the dicks in the mirror erupted over and over.

I sprawled over Tony's convulsing body and deep-kissed him, rubbing our combined jizz into our bellies. My mind was already plotting the next level of Tony's ass assault.

The next night when Tony came home, he moved into the bedroom in front of the mirror even before I bothered to coerce him. The blond Canadian in the mirror smirked nastily as he stripped the dark-haired South American and once again spread his thighs apart on the couch before the mirror.

This time while Tony stared with anticipation, I squatted naked between his thighs and buried my face in the silky down of that parted ass crevice. Tony groaned at the wet sensations of my lips and tongue caressing his bung hole. The small opening seemed already trained. It parted immediately, welcoming the hot lips that sucked and licked at it.

At the same time I was fully aware of what Tony saw reflected in the mirror. He gawked at the muscular body kneeling down in front of him, the pale face busy eating asshole. My own ample butt cheeks were spread apart, the shaved, hairless mounds shaking subtly as I mouthed up and down the ass crevice Tony offered me.

Tony could watch my asshole in the mirror, and he'd be thinking of eating it out, exactly like I was eating out his ass. Tony loved my ass already, now he was learning to love his own. With those thoughts, I felt Tony's asshole spasm wide as my tongue slithered deep into him.

Tony was again a writhing mass of eager jelly when I came up for air. I squirted lube into the spit-wet crack and shoved my fingers between the palpitating lips. Tony grunted like a stuck pig and heaved his ass up, swallowing two fingers to the knuckles. I had him where I wanted him.

For the next half hour I finger-fucked the writhing South American. I added lube every so often, removing my fingers to tease the now-gaping orifice, then ramming them back in. I succeeded in cramming the two fingers to the hilt, Tony shouting out and squirming all over the couch in a fusion of pleasure and agony.

"*Dios!* Fuck me! Do me, amigo. Finger my slut hole," Tony mumbled constantly.

A stream of Spanish obscenities would follow. I showed no mercy, finger-fucking the macho stud to the hilt. All the while Tony locked his eyes on the image in the mirror. He was witnessing some hot stud's violation and humiliation—and loving it. That it was actually himself getting fingered and loving it was the ultimate turn-on.

Finally, I rolled Tony over, placing him on his hands and knees. My hand ploughed the dark-skinned stud's lean butt from behind with rapid hard thrusts, three big fingers crammed up the slippery hole. Tony looked back, his head craned around to get a view of his own jiggling can. He shot his load like that, spilling jizz all over the front of the couch.

From then on, that mirror was our third sexual partner. Before its reflection, Tony was transformed into a total skank. He'd willingly lift one leg and watch as I shoved a big dildo into his pliant hole, or bend over and spread his cheeks and take my dick with beseeching grunts. We experimented with all kinds of positions, and eventually Tony was raising his own legs, and cramming three of his own fingers up his aching hole.

Tony had mutated into the man in the mirror. His ass assault was welcome and even longed for. Our ultimate fulfillment came when both of us were lying before that mirror and staring at our mutual reflections. The fingers of our hands were buried up each other's hungry holes as we blew our wads onto the shiny surface of our reflected world.

MY MAGAZINE GUY

Charles Long

"Hey, bud, will you spot for me?" I managed to ask with only the slightest quiver in my voice.

"Sure," he responded.

I did it! I finally spoke with the guy I called Foster. Though I didn't know his real name, I made up one from the advertisement on the T-shirt he was wearing the first time I spied him in the gym. And Foster, as I called him, spoke back to me! Now I would need to do a clean set of at least eight reps in order to impress him. I lay back on the bench and focused on the bar. Foster leaned over me and grabbed the bar to give me a liftoff. Down to my chest. No bounce. Back up steadily. Eyes closed, no eyes opened. Foster's bare leg was so close to my face that I wanted to steal a glimpse. I imagined that I could smell his scent. Seven. Eight. Don't go for nine or you might bust a vein.

"Thanks, dude," I said.

"No problem."

It was a brief but memorable interaction. Foster had moved on to the calf machine and clearly had forgotten me, but I watched him with secret abandon.

The first time I spotted him I was working out at an unusual time because I had a day off work. There was no denying the guy's good looks. I caught several straight men checking him out and even heard a group of guys talking about his "killer chest" and "awesome guns." Foster is about six feet and must weigh a good 220. His black hair and blue eyes are a breathtaking combination and most days he has a scruffy face. Most guys have one great muscle group and the rest of their body is so-so, but Foster is built solid from top to bottom. While it is clear to anyone that he works out, his muscle development is not that of a bodybuilder but more like that of an athlete.

The next day I changed my work schedule so that I could be in the gym at the same time as Foster. Never before had anyone captured my imagination so instantaneously and so strongly, and I immediately became a bit obsessed. Sadly, Foster did not work out at a regular time, and so I usually saw him only once or twice a week.

Three weeks after I first saw him in the gym, I heard the attendant call him Tyler. The name seemed to fit him, and so I stopped calling him Foster in my fantasies and started calling him Tyler.

My great disappointment was the fact that Tyler never showered in the gym. Once I caught him with his shirt off, drying his face and chest, and I did a double take that he seemed to notice. I quickly headed to my locker, grabbed my gloves, and headed back to finish working out. In my mind, I feared that he knew I was checking him out and that he would avoid me forever thereafter. His chest was covered with short black hair in an irregular V pattern that pointed to a trail that headed down his belly and into his shorts.

After three months I finally asked him to spot for me. Contact at last, but very little interaction.

One day my hormones were raging and so I made a trip to the magazine rack at a local bookstore called Book-Time. Though it was not a porn shop, they did carry several gay adult magazines. I needed something to heighten my fantasies that night while I was masturbating. Unlike most of my friends, gay and straight, I didn't run to bars to pick up one-night stands. A good stroke session would help disseminate some of my libidinal energy.

The first magazine had a hot Latin guy on the cover. The back showed an interracial couple. It was a definite possibility. The second had an ugly, pasty leather guy, and I knew that wouldn't work. The third had a guy with the most amazing body. His head was turned up and to the side. That profile was hot, but that body was undeniably electric. I decided on the third magazine and headed home.

Insatiable, I tore off the clear plastic wrap and threw it on the bed. I grabbed the lube and a towel and lay down to flip through my purchase. Something about the guy on the cover seemed familiar, and yet I wasn't sure why. I began to flip haphazardly through the pages. When I landed on page 65, I froze looking at a picture of the hot cover man. Clearly the man in the magazine was none other than my fantasy man Tyler!

My heart raced and I lost my erection as I tried to make sense of something that just wouldn't register in my mind. I kept thinking that I was mistaken, but through the entire spread there was no doubt that this man was not a look-alike but was in fact my workout fantasy guy Tyler. Once I came to my senses, my erection returned and I had the most intense stroke session of my life. I nearly strained a muscle when I came.

Then I did the most spontaneous thing. I did not want anyone else looking at my man, so I returned immediately to Book-Time and bought all remaining copies of the magazine. The clerk looked at me questioningly, but I had no desire to explain myself to him, so I grabbed my purchase and returned to my apartment. On the way home I tried to decide whether to say anything to Tyler or not.

The following day I was pleasantly surprised to find Tyler in the gym working through his back routine. I rehearsed a conversation in my head. I moved close to him. At the last minute, I chickened out and veered away from him and toward the drinking fountain. This dance went on for half an hour, and I knew that Tyler would be finishing his workout soon. What could I say? Would he freak out on me? What if I was wrong? Maybe it was a twin.

Then I nearly ran into him as I turned from the fountain.

"Whoa," he called as he moved back.

"Sorry about that," I responded. "I wasn't paying attention."

"No problem, guy."

It was my moment.

"Hey, I was wondering if you've done any modeling." Then I felt embarrassed. He probably thought I was coming on to him. His expression didn't change, and I began to stammer. "I thought I saw your picture in a...um...fitness magazine."

"Not me."

"Sorry about that."

"It ain't no thing."

The next few minutes were a blur. I saw Tyler finish another set and then leave, and I was so distracted that I gave up after 10 more minutes. There was no need to shower because I hadn't even worked up a sweat. I just wanted to get home. I packed my gym bag and sprinted to my car.

"Hey, Doug," someone called.

I looked over and saw Tyler leaning against the car next to mine.

"Tyler?"

"Yeah, umm...look I couldn't say anything in there. I don't know how to talk about this." He was clearly nervous. "I think those pictures were me. Was I...where they in a gay men's magazine?"

"Yeah," was all I could muster.

"Man, I'm so freaked out. I didn't think they'd run the pictures in a magazine that would make it to this town. If anyone finds out, I'll die."

My heart was breaking for him. The misery was dripping from his every pore. Tyler was truly freaked and I felt guilty for inducing this panic in him. More than anything I wanted to make him feel alright.

"Look, it's OK. The pictures look great."

Why the fuck did I say that! I wasn't helping him calm down at all.

"That magazine is only available in one store around here, and

I bought all of the copies. I don't know why I did it, but all the copies in this town are lying in my bedroom." I hung my head.

"You did? That's great! I owe you man. Have you told other guys in the gym?"

"Hell no. I don't even talk to most of them. Anyway, it isn't anyone else's business."

"Any of your friends?"

"No one. I know it's freaking you out, and you don't have to worry. I won't tell about your pictures. I won't bring it up again. Sorry about saying anything in the first place."

"I was so shocked when you asked me about modeling. I was ready to pack up and leave town. I was trying to figure out what to do. Look, I don't know you, but I want to buy you a coffee."

What was going to be coffee turned into a meal.

Tyler told me that he needed money badly and some guy approached him about posing. He didn't know that he'd end up naked and bent over a motorcycle, but he went with it. The entire time he talked, I tried to normalize the experience. In the middle of his confession, I realized that Tyler is a normal guy. Once I reached that conclusion, I was able to relax around him and stop being intimidated. He actually opened up to me and told me all about the photo shoot and the experience. Luckily the tabletop was opaque and he couldn't see when I would get aroused at the thought of him stroking his dick, pulling his ass cheeks apart, or pinching his nipples for the camera.

We exchanged numbers, but I expected him to avoid me from there on out. He had confessed his sins and now would likely eschew the one who carried his dirty little secret. Besides, why would this hunky straight guy hang out with a gay guy who had seen his pornographic photos?

Much to my surprise Tyler called that weekend. We met up for a workout and then went out to eat. I invited him to my place, and he accepted.

"I've got a change of clothes in the car. Can I shower at your place?"

"Of course."

"Are you sure you don't mind? I'll let you scrub my back." And a wink. I laughed to ease my discomfort.

He followed me in his car to my place, and when we arrived I showed him around. He loved my apartment and the modern decor. He even flipped through some of my photography books of men and would occasionally comment on their physical attributes. Without a word, Tyler pulled his shirt off, kicked his shoes off, and pulled off his socks.

"They tried their damnedest to talk me into doing a video out there, but I kept saying no."

"A video? And what did they want you to do?"

"They offered me some enormous amount of money to do a guy-on-guy scene, and they had some famous porn guy talk to me. He introduced me to his girlfriend and then told me about how it is easy money. His porn name is Max Edge, but his real name is Bobby."

"Max Edge! He's one of my favorites!" I blurted much too excitedly. "Sorry for that uncontrollable outburst."

"He is a good-looking guy, and his girlfriend is like Pamela Anderson hot."

"I've read that he's straight in real life, but the man will do everything in his videos. And he's good at it."

"He was cool, and his girlfriend was turned on by the whole thing. She wanted me to do a scene with him. I just didn't want to have sex with a guy for the first time in a movie. Then they begged me to do a solo video, but I refused."

"I bet they were frustrated. You'd sell a lot of videos with that body of yours."

"So you like my body?" He smiled at me and rubbed his hand over his chest and down his belly.

"Are you going to beat me up if I say yes?"

He laughed. "No. It's cool. You're a nice guy, and you have a great body too. I've known you were gay for a while. I saw you checking me out in the gym once or twice."

"I tried not to be obvious. You have to admit that you're hard to miss."

"Like I said, dude, it's all good. Can I take that shower now?"

"Sure."

I led him to the bathroom and showed him where the products were and grabbed a towel for him from the cabinet. While I was getting the towel and telling him about the temperamental water pressure, he dropped his shorts and underwear and turned on the water.

"Thanks," he uttered. "Stay and talk with me."

My head was swimming, my heart was racing and my crotch was stirring. I just saw Tyler's perfect penis in real life! I sat on the edge of the sink and watched him crawl under the shower spray. I cursed my lace shower curtain for blocking my view.

"So when did you know that you were gay?" he asked.

"Since I was the awkward, shy boy in third grade."

"Really. When did you first have sex with a guy?"

"When I was 17. And it wasn't a great time."

"Why?"

"It just didn't go well. He was experienced and didn't care about taking his time. But it has been good ever since."

"I bet it's true that gay guys give the best head."

I watched the outline of him soaping his chest and imagined the soft body hair mixing with the lather. "Makes sense."

"Have you ever been fucked?"

"Um...."

"Was that too personal?" He pulled back the shower curtain and eyed me.

As my eyes traveled toward the floor, I caught a glimpse of water running down his thick penis. Hopefully he didn't see me glancing at his dick.

"No. It just surprised me."

He went back to showering.

"I'm still not used to talking to you," I said. "Until a few days ago you scared me."

"Scared you! I'm a big pussycat. Just because I like to workout doesn't mean I'm a big homophobe. I think gay guys are cool. They're always really nice to me."

"I wonder why," I said under my breath.

"I heard that. So will you tell me about being fucked?" he said as he pulled the curtain back again, exposing his wet penis for the second time.

"I'm embarrassed. You're straight, and you might get grossed out."

"I might get turned on, dude. Come on."

"I don't know."

"I'll tell you something personal, if you agree to answer my question. But you have to promise to keep my secret."

"OK."

"This is the most personal thing I've ever told anyone. I think about what it would be like to have something up my ass."

"Really?" My shock was visible, so it was good that he wasn't looking at me. He couldn't have said anything hotter.

"Yeah. I think about it a lot. I had one chick who liked to lick my hole and it fucking drove me nuts. But then she freaked out when I tried to get her to buy a strap-on. She wouldn't even stick her finger in me."

"That bitch," I joked.

"Are you surprised I think about taking it in the ass?" he asked.

Was I surprised? Fuck yeah, I was surprised.

"Lots of straight guys like to have their asses played with. Most won't admit it. Most straight guys are afraid of their asses. Max Edge sure seems to like it in the ass."

"I started thinking that I might be gay since I was wanting something up my ass. When they took those pictures and I had to bend over and show my hole, I got the biggest woody. I was thinking how many gay guys might see that picture and think about fucking me. Did you think about it when you looked at the pictures?"

He turned off the water and opened the curtain wide.

"Did you?" he asked.

"I don't want to answer that question."

"Why?" he asked nonchalantly.

"You're embarrassing me."

"I'm the one who posed naked. I'm the one who just told you I thought about having something up my ass. Fuck it, dude, just tell me. Did you think about fucking me?"

"Yeah, I thought about how nice your ass looked."

"And?"

"And what it would feel like to be inside you." I looked up at him. "Happy?"

"See, that wasn't so bad. Can you dry my back?" He handed me the towel. "Now answer my question. What's it like."

"Well, I usually do the fucking, so I've only been a bottom twice. It was OK. You have to relax and trust the guy, and then it can feel good."

Like a good little gay boy, I dried his back. I had to let my left hand touch his skin while my right hand rubbed the towel over him. There was no denying that I needed to get my hands near that ass, so I kept rubbing the towel lower until I was drying his cheeks.

"See, that wasn't so bad. Get in between the cheeks, bud," Tyler said as he leaned forward.

There it was. His pink hole surrounded by a light dusting of black hair. There was no denying the bulge growing in my pants.

"Will you do me a favor? Will you let me put one of your dildos in my ass so I can see what it feels like?"

Damn, why didn't I own a dildo?

"I would, but I don't have one."

"Hmm. I thought all gay guys had dildos. It's cool."

He wrapped the towel around his waist and walked to the living room where he proceeded to drop the towel on the floor before sitting down on the couch. What was happening?

"It's OK, dude," he almost purred. "I won't bite."

I moved closer to Tyler and then he looked down at his half-hard dick. I leaned forward slowly and rubbed my hand down his thigh. He nodded and then I knelt between his legs. Without further prodding, I took his dick in my hand and then into my mouth. He groaned lightly and laid his head back. All I heard him say was, "Yeah."

His dick grew harder and I found the width of it to be a challenge at first, but wild horses couldn't drag me from it. Tyler lifted one leg partly and then lowered it and then lifted it again. I realized that his ass fascination was getting to him and I needed to answer his questions, so I lifted his leg high and slid my tongue into his crack. As I flicked my tongue over my target, he began to groan loudly and I knew that I had a winner. Then I dive-bombed my tongue into his ass as I pulled his cheeks apart. I was eating Tyler's ass!

I pushed him down on the cushions and threw one leg over the back of the couch. Then I began to suck his rock-hard dick as I wiggled my finger over his pucker. He was quivering and convulsing so I slid the tip of my finger inside him. Though I barely had any of my finger inside of him, I worked it vigorously in a circle as I continued to suck.

"Oh, yeah. That's it. Play with my hole."

I spit on my finger and started thrusting it further into him and then pulling it out. Tyler was going mad, so I began pistoning my finger into his ass.

"Oh, fuck man! That's it. Finger-fuck my ass. That's fucking hot!"

I turned him over and raised his ass in the air. Damn it was a gorgeous ass! I pulled his cock back between his legs and sucked the head while I freed my own cock from my pants. Then I let his cock slap up against his belly as I licked his ass again. Each time I let his dick go there was a soft whack when it hit his belly.

"Yeah, take you clothes off," he encouraged, so I stood and obeyed while he stayed in the same position, ass in the air and face buried in the cushion. He was waiting to have his ass explored more in-depth, and I was willing to oblige. Within seconds I was buck-naked.

Tyler had the most perfect butt I had ever seen. The light dusting of black hair and the perfect pink pucker was too much for me. He kept winking his hot hole at me and groaning in anticipation. Then he put his hand up through his legs and fingered his hole.

"Damn, I need to get fucked. I can't wait any longer."

"I can't believe you're going to let me fuck you."

"Yeah, push that dick inside me, buddy, and show me what I've been missing. It's all for you."

In my wildest dreams, I couldn't have imagined he would be ass-up on my couch waiting for what was next. I knelt behind him and rubbed my dick up and down his crack. He instantly groaned louder and began moving his hips. I continued to tease his hole by poking my dick head at it. Then I began dry humping him while my dick was laying in his ass crack. I reached underneath and stroked his cock, which was as hard as my own.

"Yeah, rub that ass," he muttered into the cushion. "I'm so fucking turned on. Yeah, give me that dick."

He looked back at me over his shoulder and said, "You gonna show me what it feels like to have something in my ass?"

"Yeah, buddy."

"And you won't tell anyone?"

"No way."

"Then do it, man. You got to fuck me now, dude. Give it to me hard."

I reached over to the drawer and pulled out a condom and lube. Then I splashed some lube on his ass and rubbed it around, sliding one finger in and out and then two fingers in and out.

"Dude, don't tease me. Stick that big dick of yours in my ass now."

I broke record time for opening and putting on a condom. Then I positioned my cock against his hole and leaned forward. My weight forced my cock into his inner sanctum. His groans grew loud and desperate as I entered him fully. He pushed his ass back against my crotch and moaned as he wiggled his butt. Then I began to move my hips. There has been no better sight in my life than the one of my cock sliding into his big, muscular ass. I'd have to try hard to delay my ejaculation or I would spew within seconds.

Without thinking I slapped his ass and he responded with a "Yeah." I began to thrust harder and I watched for his reaction. He raised his head from the cushion and looked back at me. It was clear that he was enjoying himself, and I began to thrust harder, bouncing him off of my crotch.

Soon he was saying things to me: "Fuck me, dude." "I knew this would feel great." "Give it to me, man." "Show me what you've got."

I pulled my dick out, and he looked back in shock. He thought that I was done but I thrust my hard staff back into him.

"Oh, yeah. That's it."

So I pulled it out a few more times and thrust it back in. He was loving the fucking, so I flipped him roughly onto his back, raised his legs and slid my cock inside him. His dick was still rock hard and it jumped as I pounded Tyler mercilessly. With one hand I fondled his pecs and with the other I slid my thumb in his mouth.

"Can you give it to me harder?" he asked.

"Oh, yeah."

I began to fuck him with all the thrusting power in my body, and he was in heaven. I'd never fucked anyone like that, and I was so turned on by his hot muscle ass wrapped around my cock that I could barely keep from shooting.

"Yeah, fuck me. Fuck my ass."

Then I stroked his cock as I began the final wild thrusts. He was bouncing on the couch from the force of my action, and then he let out a moan and I felt his cock convulse in my hand. With each spasm, his hole clamped down on my thrusting cock. I pulled out, yanked off the condom and spewed my own come on his belly. One splat even hit the side of his mouth, and he acted as if he didn't notice.

"Wow, that was great," I said as I collapsed on the couch between his legs.

"Yeah. Now if only I could find a woman who would do that to me, I'd be set. I knew it would feel amazing to have something in my ass. Does that make me gay?"

I shrugged. "Not necessarily."

"Now I know that I could do it with a man, though, if I ever need to make money doing a video. I don't think I'd let any other man fuck me, though. Just you." And he nudged me with his knee.

"I need another shower if that's OK," he said.

"Sure, help yourself."

"Then maybe I could spend the night."

Tyler smiled at me as he swung his leg over my head. As he walked toward the bathroom for his second shower, he slapped his ass. "You going to give it to me again?" he called out without looking back.

"Absolutely," was all I could say.

OFFICER MAX

Wade Wright

The Cup of Java Café wasn't the greatest-looking restaurant along the highway, but for Gary it sure did come up just at the right time. He was just finishing up a good "Blue Plate Special" of some great meat loaf, mashed potatoes, sliced peaches, whole wheat bread, and all the rest of some good home-style cooking when he realized that the stool, two spots away from his, was being occupied.

"Hi, Max," the waitress said as he noticed the new customer come in and sit down. "You going to have something to eat, or just a cup of java?"

Looking over toward Gary, the customer, obviously a highway patrolman in full proper, and very well-fitting officer attire, answered. "No, Jenny. I'm just going to have some coffee. Just really stopped in to see if Mom's gone home yet or not."

"Yeah, Max, she left about an hour or so ago."

"Good! Just give me some coffee then, I don't have too much time, I need to get back out on the road."

As Jenny sat the officer's coffee down, he turned to Gary and asked,"So is that your Mustang with the Illinois plates on it?"

Gary turned toward the officer and replied, "Yeah, yes it is."

"Well, you certainly are a long way from home then, aren't you?" The officer asked. "You traveling alone, all by yourself?"

Once again looking over toward the officer, Gary replied, "Yeah, traveling alone, just me and my radio."

"What you doing all the way out here in California, all by yourself?"

"Decided Illinois was not the place for me any longer, and just decided to see where I end up."

"So I assume you are just kind of headed down the road, and no place in particular then, right?"

As Gary stood up from his stool, he continued to answer the officer's friendly question, with "Yeah, I kind of guess so." He then moved over toward the cash register and paid his bill. The waitress thanked him for stopping in, and the officer turned and suggested that he, "Take care, and be careful!"

Gary turned as he started to pull on the door and replied, "Thanks, will do. Bye!"

Gary pulled out of the parking lot, turned right, and once again got onto I-10 and headed west. Thinking back to his short conversation with the officer, he started to admit to himself that perhaps he could have been a little more friendly and outgoing with him since he did seem to be attempting a friendly conversation. "Confronted with an officer of the law, and one that looks like that, I guess is enough to make any person pretty uptight and timid."

Gary's mental image of the officer was, as he figured any person, man, woman, straight or gay would admit, was damn hot! Seldom did he consciously look at guys since he was a straight guy, but he did admit that person deserved a lot of admiration. He obviously had spent a lot of time in a weight room, and also obviously had been blessed with some very favorable family genes. Remembering back to the sight that sat down beside him, Gary listed the man's attributes: Six foot 1 or 2, probably 230–240 pounds of solid muscle, and a whole lot of those muscles packed into his upper arms. Gary could remember very clearly how the upper-arm sleeves were pulled so tightly just to get the fabric around those biceps. He remembered too, how the chest of that shirt certainly was, and needed to be, much larger than the waistline. He remembered he quickly glanced at the man's legs as he started to sit down, close to him, and wondered how a person like him can wear uniform pants that hug the skin as tightly as his pants do, and still not rip. He had definitely noticed that Max's, as he heard the waitress call him, were probably hugging his thick leg muscles tighter than any pair he had seen before. Suddenly he was wondering if all of the California officers looked that good in their uniforms. As he drove on, mentally recapturing the image of Officer Max, he admitted that he had never before had reasons to look at other men and their bodies, and he certainly had never knowingly admired the appearance of a black man before. But, he decided, maybe it was the total combination of the stretched uniform, the big muscles, the body shape, the big chest, the thick neck, the tiny waist, the thigh-high leg-muscle grabbing boots, the bold and strong face, and the mahogany skin tone that was making Gary think that was really one beautiful person. Never before had he ever thought in those terms of another man, even the ones pictured in muscle magazines, but he did have to admit, this one was "pretty."

It was just about 8:30 when Gary had left the café after having his supper, and his rather abbreviated conversation with the officer, who he now was having some trouble getting out of his mind. He was feeling very ashamed that he had not been friendlier with the officer. He did not think he was giving the State of Illinois very good representation. He did not consider himself as a person who would normally act that way, and he decided that Officer Max was a little intimidating when he was there and close to him. He was now getting pretty pissed at himself for acting so childish.

Cruising along, unhappy with himself and his earlier actions, Gary tried to find a good radio station, as he continued to head west on I-10. He kept an eye open for a cheap motel, that he could stop at for the night. Since he was "free on the road" he did not have any kind of a set time schedule, and his motel demands were minimal.

Suddenly, he realized that he had red and blue strobe lights flashing at him from behind, and he looked down at this speedometer to see if he had forgotten to watch his speed. He immediate started to pull over to the side of the road.

The highway patrol car pulled in behind him, and of course left the overheads on. Gary looked into his side rearview mirror and in shock realized he was being pulled over by Officer Max.

"So, young man! Just where in the hell do you think you are going so damn fast?" Officer Max asked as he approached the side window.

"Sir, I wasn't speeding. I was only going about 65 miles per hour and I saw a sign where the speed limit is 70. Really, I wasn't speeding!"

"Just give me your driver's license, kid. Don't try to tell me what I saw. I'm not new at this, understand?"

Gary in his very shaken state, handed the officer his driver's license, and said, "Yes, sir, yes, sir."

"Oh, so Gary A. Smith!" The officer stated as he looked at the license. "Yeah—Gary Smith! That sure does sound like a fake name! Is this a fake driver's license or something? What does the *A* stand for—ass?"

"No, sir—Arthur. It stands for Arthur!"

"Yeah, I bet! What parent is going to name their kid Gary A. Smith so that his initials spell GAS? What—age 23—right? Well is that right, or is that a fake too?"

"No, sir, that is right! Sir, that is not a fake license!"

"Yeah, right! Right! You kids from back East think you can pull shit on us out here and you're just a little too stupid to know we know what in the hell is happening. Five feet nine? Right?"

Gary replied, "Yeah, yes, sir!"

"So, 193 pounds? There's no way you weigh 193 pounds, kid! That's got to be a lie."

"Yes, sir, yes I do weigh about 200 pounds now. That license is about a year and a half old."

"Oh, come on, kid! You ain't that big. There's no way you weigh 200 pounds."

"Yes I do, sir. Sir, I used to be in wrestling in high school, and my body is kind of solid. Sir, I do weight almost 200 pounds."

"Oh, come on here! Hey, get out of the car and come over to the other side."

Gary did as he was instructed, but he certainly was not pleased with what was happening, especially since he was absolutely certain that he was not going over the speed limit. The officer's mean mannerisms was somewhat of a shock too. At the café he had been such a friendly type, and now he was nothing but scary!

"Come on, kid, come over here. OK, take your shirt off! Let me see this body that you say is so tightly built. Let me see if you have got the body you're trying to make me believe you've got!"

"What, sir, what?" Gary was shocked and surprised that he was being told to take his shirt off, out there beside the highway, so an officer could see his build.

"Do it, kid! Do it! Get that shirt off!"

Gary pulled his T-shirt off and threw it on the trunk of the car. In his mind, this was really weird since his body could pretty well be seen while he still had the shirt on.

"OK, kid. Put your hands on the roof of the car. I need to do a pat down to see what kind of shit you're probably carrying with you."

"Sir, I don't have anything, sir. I don't have anything!"

"Shut the hell up and get your hands up there and spread your legs!"

Gary did as he was told, and all of a sudden he realized that he was getting a little more than just a pat down. Officer Max was not patting, be was definitely rubbing, and definitely rubbing areas where no contraband could possibly be hidden. He was bare chested, and as he stood there with his hands firmly placed on the roof of the car, he could look down and watch as Officer Max firmly and strongly rubbed his pecks and even stopped long enough to pinch each of his nipples with his fingers. The officer's hands slowly slid around so that he was gently massaging and rubbing up and down Gary's lats. After he rubbed Gary's chest, and the muscular lats under his armpits, his hands slid down and softly, yet firmly, caressed Gary's waist. The tips of his fingers actually did slide down into the waistband of Gary's Levi cutoffs. Slowly Gary could feel the top button of his cutoffs being unbuttoned, and then the next, and then the next, and then the next. Suddenly Gary realized that he was now standing out there, beside the highway, with his cutoffs completely unbuttoned, and with Officer Max's hands reaching down inside and not only feeling his cock, but cupping his balls too! Gary was totally speechless! He did not know what to do! He knew he was not in control here, and he certainly did not want to piss off Officer Max any more. But for an officer to be doing this, out beside the highway? Gary thought, *It's at least kind of dark, and not in the middle of the day! What in the hell is happening here?*

After Officer Max suddenly pulled his hands back up and out of Gary's shorts, he grabbed Gary's hands and forced them behind his back. In one fell swoop, Officer Max had Gary's hands cuffed.

"There, kid, there! That will keep you under control some!"

Gary was in a state of shock! He had not done anything to even act like he was "out of control." He simply did not know what was going on!

Officer Max pushed Gary up against the side of the car, and then leaned onto him, positioning himself exactly so that Gary's handcuffed hands, palms of course facing back, would lay directly onto the officer's crotch. Officer Max pushed his crotch onto Gary's palms. He moved his body back and forth, and did gyrations so that Gary's hands would be feeling his hidden dick.

"Hey, kid, how does that feel to you? You like the feel of that rod? Come on, man, grab it! Take hold of it! Feel how big it is! How does that dick feel to you? You gay boys like that, don't you? Feels good, don't it? I know damned well you young white boys like a big black cock! Don't you? Ever had an officer's big, long, black cock before?"

As Officer Max was talking and trying to tell Gary about how "you gay boys like that," and asking him if he'd ever had an officer's big, long, black cock before, he was reaching around to the front and attempting to pull Gary's dick up and out of his unbuttoned Levi's. He had his hands on Gary's dick and under Gary's balls!

"What, man! What?" Officer Max exclaimed! "We're standing here with your hands rubbing my dick, making it hard, I've got your little dick and your balls in my hands and you don't have a hard-on? What in the hell is wrong with you, man? You're feeling up one hot fucking cop, right out here beside the highway, you've damn near got your pants all the way off, and you're not sporting any kind of a woody? You got no feelings, or something? Do you know how many gay guys like you would love to be out here feeling my dick and letting me feel theirs? They'd love to have their hand on my meat, man, they'd love it! They'd be tearing to get in my pants at it!"

"Sir! Sir, I'm not gay! Officer, I'm not gay! I really don't understand just what is happening here, 'cause, sir, I'm not gay!"

"Hey, kid, what you are tonight and what you are tomorrow morning could just be two different things! When I saw you in Mom's restaurant, I knew right then that I was going to get in your ass, and I still intend to. Hey, Gary boy, you are traveling all by yourself, and as part of your travels, you are going to be giving it up for this officer. Now you understand? You're saying you're not gay, but after having me and what I've got to give to you, you just may decide you really don't know for sure what you are!"

Gary stood there leaning up against his car, his pants now almost down to his knees, his hands still firmly being pressed up against what felt like a growing log, and he realized that Officer Max was now on a cell phone making a call to someone.

"Hey Pete, I'm over by River Overpass, headed west, and I need a driver. You and Steve get over here right away. OK, see you then! Hurry!"

Officer Max got off of his cell phone and reached down and pulled Gary's cutoffs back up. He buttoned the top so they would stay up.

"Come on, kid! Let's go to my car. Let's say you are now under house arrest. It's my house though! You are going to be my meat for the night! Pete and Steve, couple of guys that live on my farm, are on the way over here to get your car and bring it over to the farm, so as soon as they get here, we'll take you and your car over there, and then just as soon as I can get checked out, it is going to be some fun time in my bed. OK?"

"Sir, sir, I'm not a gay guy. I've never done anything like this! Seriously, sir, I'm not so sure I can do whatever it is you want to do!"

"I know, man! I know! That is what makes this so much fun! See, Gary, I have your driver's license. I am the officer! All I have to do is write up a ticket that says I finally got you stopped, after you were doing about 85 or 90. See, that's why you did not get stopped right after you left the cafe. I needed to let you get far enough away so that you could have actually been going that fast. Now, it's either you and I—and hey, maybe Pete and Steve too if they want—go have some fun together, and maybe I'll teach you some fun stuff about the male body and what you can do with it, or if you want, I can write a ticket. Then, hell, I have no idea who they have in the slammer tonight. But with a butt like you've got, I'm sure whatever drunk is in there, he sure would like to have a piece of it. Then of course there is the little court session and my statement that I had to follow you for 20 miles before I could get you to pull over, and then of course the probable two- to four-week visit to the ol' slammer again, and once again, well maybe, more like every night, that ass is all up for grabs. Understand the situation here now?"

"Yes, sir, yes I do! But why? Why me? I didn't do anything to get this done to me, did I?"

"Hey, Gary, you are one hot stud! When I saw you in Mom's restaurant, I saw you glance over at my crotch, and I damn near needed to get out of there before you gave me such a hard-on that I couldn't hide it. Gary, I was going to have something to eat when I stopped at Mom's but after seeing you, I decided I just needed to be ready to roll at any time! Just as soon as you left, I made damn sure you were on the road in front of me. I kept rubbing my dick the whole time I was behind you. I got all turned on for you when I came into the restaurant and sat down. I took one look at you and though, *Shit, man, he is hot! I need that ass! I want that ass! I'm going to have that ass!* Hell man, when I saw you, I was damn glad Jenny told me that my mom had already gone home. I would have had to fake an emergency to get out of there so that I could follow you. That's my mom's restaurant where we met. Thank goodness I stopped in there when I did, and thank goodness you were still there! Welcome to California boy! This is your first night in California, and you are gonna be a different guy tomorrow! Hell, man, after we get done, you just might decide you need to go on up to San Fran and live!"

Officer Max placed Gary in the back seat of his cruiser and stood by the open door as he waited for Pete and Steve to show up. Gary was getting his first round of being really played with as he sat there, still cuffed, with his pants down to his knees. Completely at the mercy of Officer Max, he was finding out very quickly what it was like to be the one with no control, the one having body parts pulled and tugged on, and other parts finding fingers placed up in spaces that he had never imagined before. Gary was in the process of getting finger fucked, out along I-10, in the back seat of a highway patrol car, by probably the hottest looking patrolman on the force, and for some unexplainable reason, he was not angry or upset! He did not understand it. As Officer Max removed his hat, he leaned and placed his mouth firmly on Gary's right tit, then bit with force—strong, intentional force. Gary simply pushed his chest forward as if an attempt to help, and for unexplainable reasons, he did not attempt to fight back! The bite hurt and Gary knew he should have screamed or attempted some type of reaction. He did not! He mentally prayed that Officer Max would then lean in farther and bite his left tit just as strongly, if not more so!

Just as Gary was pondering his completely confusing situation wondering why he was not getting raging mad for being bitten so forcefully and painfully as he was, Pete and Steve drove up and parked their pickup behind the patrol car. They walked up to the passenger side of the cruiser where Officer Max was leaning in.

"Fuck, shit, man!" Officer Max strongly stated as he stood up from the car, and turned and looked at Pete and Steve. "Shit, man! Damn, I can't believe this!"

"What? What?" Steve asked. "What?"

"Steve, you got the tool box in the back of the truck?"

"Yeah, yeah it's there. What you want?"

"Get those vice grips out of there! Get both of the big ones. I fucking bit the shit out of this kid's tit and he just pushed his chest forward for me to bite harder. I'm going to put those vice grips on him and see just how much those tits can take! Shit, man, I've never had some guy not try to slug the hell out of me when I bit like that!"

Steve returned with the vice grips and handed them to Max. "You sure about this, man? Ever put one of those on one of your tits? Pinches like hell, man, I know! Did it to myself once and it felt like it damn near tore the tip of my tit off!"

Officer Max took the vice grips, leaned in the car, took hold of Gary's left tit, pulled it forward, and put one of the vice grips on it. He watched Gary's face! Gary watched to see what was happening to his tit! He said nothing. Officer Max then started turning the tightening screw and kept watching Gary's face. As he turned and the grip kept bitting onto his tit tighter and tighter, Gary watched, but did not say anything! Officer Max looked at him and asked, "You OK, boy? You OK?"

"Yeah, I'm OK. That hurts like hell, man, but I'm OK, I think!" Gary was answering but Officer Max could tell from the way he was talking he was in real pain. He quit turning the screw and let the vice grip hang down, clamped onto the tip of Gary's tit! He then took the second vice grip and placed it on Gary's right nipple. He again starting the tightening process and he continued to watch Gary's face. Gary continued to watch the vice grip get tightened and tightened, tighter and tighter on his tit. He gritted his teeth, but he did not ask for the grips to be removed.

Finally, just as he stopped the tightening of the grip, Officer Max suddenly threw his head up, and without warning, gave Gary an enormous, almost suffocating kiss! This shocked not only Gary, but Pete and Steve also. "Boy! Kid! Damn! Shit, man! How in the fucking hell can you take that! Shit, man, I've put them on my tits before and I sure as hell could never tighten 'em that fucking tight!

Oh, man! I have never played with any guy that can take that much tit pain! Oh, fuck man, I love you! I have got to get you home and get started on you! Man, I want to play with you!"

Then turning toward the other two, Max said, "Pete, Steve, his car keys are in the car. Meet you guys at the house. OK?"

Pete said, "Yeah, but, Max, you gonna leave those vice grips hanging on his tits while you drive to the house? Those fuckers are heavy! They're gonna jerk up and down like hell if you hit a bump! That's gotta hurt like hell, man! With those fuckers pinching his tits the way they're screwed on there, he has got to hurt like hell, man! He should be screaming like hell right now anyway!"

Officer Max looked into the car, looked at Gary, watched Gary look down at each of them, take a deep breath, and then heard Gary say, "I'll try! I'll try! How far is it?"

"It's about a seven or eight minute drive from here, but I may need to go slow so they don't jump up and down too much. Those fuckers are just hanging there, man! When this car moves, they're going to really jump up and down. Kid, they are really going to pull your tits like crazy, man! Can you do this? That's got to hurt like hell already!"

"Let me try! I want to see if I can take it! OK?"

"OK! Hey, kid, tell you what! You try! If your tits just can't take it any longer, you let me know and I'll stop and take them off. OK?"

Gary looked down, first at the one hanging from his left tit, then the one hanging from his right tit, wetted his lips, kind of closed his eyes some, and kind of shook an OK.

"Let's go, men! Let's go!" Max said as he got into the driver's seat and waved to the other two to follow.

After more than five hours at the house, after Steve and Pete had finally had their fill of the "new boy toy," after Max admitted that "it" had finally run dry, and after Gary had learned more about gay sex in one night than most guys do in years, Max and Gary were finally settling down and actually having some conversation, instead of raw sex.

"Gary! You have shocked the total hell out of me tonight!

Seriously, man, you have! First, I thought you were such a wimp when I first saw you and decided to go after you and take advantage of you. But shit, man, did you show me up! When I had Steve get those vice grips out and I started tightening them down on you, I thought for sure you'd make a screaming fussing fit, but no, you were more fucking man than any other guy I have ever played with! Then you not only learned how to fuck and get fucked, and not just with my dick, but you let Steve and Pete double fuck you! Shit, man! Most guys go through their entire life and never do that! You had dildos of about four different sizes rammed up in you, you got a load—and one fucking big load if I may say so myself, from your big black officer's big black dick, shot right down in your throat—once you learned how to take about six or seven inches of my dick. And then when I thought for sure you probably wanted to quit, you wanted to get fisted! God, Gary! You are one fucking sex machine! I sure can't believe you've never even fucked some guy before, but hey, I believe now whatever you say. So now what? You gonna keep on heading toward L.A., go up to San Fran, what you gonna do?"

Max, I don't know. My life has changed so much tonight! Really, man, it has! I never, in a million years, thought I was like you showed me tonight! My life was real boring back home, and that's why I hit the road. Tonight is the first night I've really felt like I was living! Max, what would happen if maybe I stayed around here? If I could find a job someplace, are there any apartments available that maybe I could afford? Max, you have made me a different guy tonight, and I want to be able to do this more, a lot more, and with you! Max, I've said earlier, I love you, and I am not kidding, I do! I love you!"

"A job? Uh, Gary, what type of work have you done? What can you do?"

"Well after I got out of high school, I worked as a plumber's helper for a year. I did some retail stuff for awhile, and I was a cook in a restaurant for about two years just before I left home. So anyway, that's what I've done, but I can learn. You think I could find something?"

"A cook? Gary, where in the hell did we meet? We met at Mom's restaurant! Shit, yes you can find a fucking job! Mom is always looking for good help, and let me tell you something, if you don't cook the way she wants, you sure will learn quickly. She will make sure you do! Gary, if you want to stay around here, that's fucking exciting to me! I've never had a sex partner that would let me get as rough and as tough on them as you let me get tonight. If you want more of the same, you sure do have a man that wants to deal it out! Gary, let's assume your road trip just came to an abrupt end tonight! OK? Let's call this place...this house, the—how did you say it earlier?—the where you end up!"

SAME-DAY SERVICE

Scott Whittier

Dust and heat were all that strung one nondescript city to another. That's what his job was—putting up with the bad scenery. As long as Gary was on the job, the fat businessmen in those cities could pretend this boring distance wasn't there. He delivered their files and notes, papers and packages, back and forth in a van, day after day. Same-day service.

The only hint of life for hours was a one-pump garage and a convenience store that didn't look all that convenient stuck halfway along the long road. Gary told himself the owners preyed on people who were stupid enough to set out without filling their gas tanks or their stomachs. He drove by without stopping every day. But today he discovered that people who weren't that stupid—people who were just plain unlucky—fell into the same trap.

The rattle came on all of a sudden from somewhere in the ass of the van. It was more of a clanging, like a rusted tin bell tied around a frightened cow's neck. It wasn't the kind of sound that could be ignored, and Gary didn't know what the hell it was. He'd driven trucks bigger and noisier than this for years, but he made a point of never opening the hood. They paid other guys for that.

Gary liked to drive, one hand on the wheel and the other resting on his crotch. He could drive with the windows down and his shirt open and sing out loud to whatever he wanted. He could jerk off with a handful of spit at 80 miles an hour if he felt like it. But slogging through grease looking for whatever the hell was clanking was not his line of expertise. Neither was sitting on the edge of this endless road in a broken-down van that would turn into an oven long before the next driver came along.

So after a few more miles and enough metallic noise to drown out the radio, Gary pulled into the sun-bleached service station. After his tires crunched to a halt on the pebbled dirt and he killed the clanking along with the ignition, he realized just how quiet it was out here. Dust seemed to hang unmoving in the wake of the van. There was no wind. No traffic. No sound at all. He was beginning to wonder if the two ramshackle buildings were even inhabited.

So Gary thought nothing of leaving the van parked by the garage and heading to the store next to it with his shirt wide open and a dark patch of pubic hair sprouting out over the unfastened button of his jeans. Fortunately, the store was open, they had beer, and the old woman at the counter didn't look away from her outdated tabloid newspaper long enough to notice his state of partial undress.

By the time he got back to the van, Gary had finished half a bottle of brew and the dust seemed to have settled a bit. He noticed something else different as he came around the driver's side. There was a pair of legs sticking out from under the van. And that wasn't all. He could see halfway up this guy's torso, and plenty of it. The blue mechanic's coveralls didn't cover everything. The legs were well protected, but the top of the jumpsuit had been left unzipped practically to the crotch.

An exposed V of dark hair and skin was fully displayed right there at Gary's feet. He could see the shelf of this guy's chest and the thick fur that covered it, leading down the ripped stomach to a mass of pubes where the zipper was barely pulled high enough to conceal the bulge beneath. Suddenly Gary felt almost overdressed. His shirt was wide open, showing his smooth, tan chest and big brown nipples, but that was nothing next to the show this mechanic was putting on. Gary had broad, round shoulders and a solid cleft of defined pecs, but the only hair on his masculine body was peaking out of his pants.

Instinctively, he brought his hand to the open button and hung his thumb there in his pubes. It was half a casual stance of observation, and half an attempt to cover his growing cock with his hand.

"Hey there," the mechanic said, pulling himself from under the van and wiping his hand on his coveralls. Somehow that simple act managed to tug the unzipped opening even wider. "Having some trouble?"

For a split second, Gary thought he was referring to the stiff cock that was creeping down the leg of his jeans. He could swear the guy's blue eyes had darted south for a moment. Those eyes almost seemed to glow, framed by the dark bangs and even darker stubble that clung to his wide jaw.

"Yeah, some rattling noise back there," Gary finally answered. "Didn't want to chance it."

"Smart move. I could hear you coming a mile away."

They both laughed, and the mechanic absently reached into the opening of his suit to scratch his chest. His dirty fingers moved through the hair slowly, back and forth, lingering over the point of his nipple where it poked out of the mat of fur.

"I would have been waiting for you, but I was in the john," he added.

"Not a bad idea," Gary said. "Beer goes right through me. Help yourself," he added and handed the six-pack to the mechanic.

"Thanks." The mechanic took a cold, sweaty bottle from the pack and rolled it across his forehead. Then he rubbed it down his stubbled face and across his chest, wetting the hair there with cool condensation. "It's hot as fuck today."

"Yeah." Gary agreed completely. Then he headed inside to find the bathroom and try to coax piss out of a half-hard dick.

Standing at the urinal, he held his dick in his hand and waited for it to soften enough to take a leak. Despite the pressure in his bladder, Gary couldn't help running his fingers over the swollen veins and the fat head. He could rub his thick cock in all that fur as easy as that guy had passed a beer bottle through it. The thought cost a few more moments standing uselessly at the urinal, but it was worth it. And when he was finally buttoning his jeans back up, he left two undone this time.

Screwed into the wall next to the sink was one of those banged-up white vending machines. Just three choices. For 50 cents you could get aspirin, a condom, or caffeine tablets—in that order. Gary always thought the traditional roadside selection was a hoot. Get rid of your headache, get laid, then get alert for the drive home.

Gary found exactly two quarters in his jeans. He slid them into the hollow machine, and the clank of coins was not unlike a mini-version of his van's ailments. He pulled the lever. His luck was bound to start looking up sooner or later. He shoved the foil wrapper in his pocket in place of the change and hoped the condom turned out to be worth more than a couple quarters.

When he walked back into the garage bay, Gary saw that the mechanic had pulled the van inside and crawled back under the rear end. Again, while the grease monkey's head was hidden beneath the van, his body was exposed for Gary's viewing pleasure. Gary also noticed two empty beer bottles sitting in the pack at the guy's side. Just three more to go, and Gary had some catching up to do. So he leaned over and pulled out a fresh bottle. As he did, he got as close as he'd been to the mechanic's open coveralls, and he stared at the spread of fur across that muscled body.

He could smell grease and dirt, and he swore he caught a whiff of musk, of man and crotch. Even if he was imagining it, the smell fit the view. It seemed that Gary wasn't the only one who'd rearranged his fly while he was gone. Somehow, this guy's zipper had gotten even lower. Within the dark mass of pubes, Gary could see the base of his cock. Now the zipper rested about an inch down the solid piece of meat, and it promised several more inches where that came from.

"How's it looking?" Gary asked innocently. He stroked the patch of pubes at the top of his open jeans. He wondered just how much the mechanic could see from under the van.

"Doesn't look so bad," he answered. "In fact, from here, things are looking pretty good."

Gary sucked on the cold beer. He licked his lips and waited. He rubbed his hardening cock head through his jeans. He rolled the bottle over his own bare chest and let the cool glass tighten his nipple into a hard, wet knot. And the entire time, he never took his eyes off this guy. He watched the rise and fall of his hairy chest. He watched the furry, grease-covered forearms disappear and reappear with wrenches and rags. But mostly, he watched the mechanic's cock as it shifted and swelled.

By the time Gary finished his beer, the mechanic's cock was rock-hard and pointing straight up against his hairy stomach. The zipper could do nothing to contain that thing once it got going, and Gary just stood looking down at the generous hunk of exposed flesh.

"I think it's about time for a break," the mechanic said as he finally emerged from under the van.

He sat there on the concrete floor of the garage with his head resting against the bumper, completely ignoring the fact that his dick was sticking out of the waist of his uniform like a hefty addition to his tool belt. He grabbed another beer and pried the cap off with his wrench.

"You want to share this one?" he asked. "You take the first swallow." Then he stood up right in front of Gary, inches away. Slowly, he started pouring the cold beer onto his chest. The golden liquid dribbled through the fur and slicked it to his skin.

Gary didn't need more than that hot sight to make him the thirstiest man on the planet. He dove in and lapped the sweet foam from the crevice of the mechanic's chest. He buried his face in all that hair and felt each strand as it passed over his eager tongue. He slurped at the beer and added his own spit to the mix, wetting every inch of skin and fur. As Gary attacked a nipple, the mechanic stopped pouring and took a drink himself. Gary didn't even notice. He was completely absorbed with the discovery he'd made. Hidden within the hair was a hard nugget of pleasure. He chewed and sucked at the nipple as the mechanic's groans echoed in the hollow neck of the beer bottle.

Then Gary wrapped his arms inside the mechanic's coveralls and peeled the sleeves from those muscular arms. Twisting wrenches and changing tires had done more than put grease under his fingernails. Every muscle and tendon stood out on those filthy arms, and the fur from his forearms crawled up each pumped bicep. Gary took just a moment to admire the prize before him, the blue uniform around his waist, the muscled hairy torso, the throbbing cock jutting from the coveralls. Then Gary grabbed that cock with one hand and the handle of the van's backdoor with the other.

"Let's step into my office," he said.

He led the mechanic by the dick and shoved him into the back of the van. Inside, the walls were stacked with boxes of envelopes and packages, but there was a narrow aisle inside the van just wide enough for the mechanic's shoulder's where Gary laid him down on his back.

Gary was still holding on to that firm cock, and the temptation to fill his mouth with it was almost unbearable. But Gary figured this was a service station, so he wanted service. Instead, he resisted the hot erection in his hand and crawled into the back of the van, over the muscled mound of the mechanic.

As Gary climbed in, he unfastened the remainder of the button's on his jeans and left his shirt on the garage floor outside. Now he straddled this man, letting him see just what he had gotten himself into. Gary would never be the furry mechanic in the middle of nowhere, but he could more than hold his own. His wide, muscled shoulders tapered to a thin waist wrapped by defined abdominals. His dark nipples accentuated the corners of his chiseled, square pecs. And his thick cock stuck out of his own mat of pubic hair, pointing straight up the furry body beneath him.

Gary followed that arrow and ground his erection against the mechanic's hard cock. He pressed and teased him with the pressure. Then he dragged his own cock slowly through the forest of hair—up the taut stomach and through the valley of chest muscles. By the time he was pressing the head of his dick against the stubbled throat, he had traversed the entire length of that furry torso, from rough pubes to soft down to the sharp whiskers of the Adam's apple. And he saw no reason to stop there.

Without hesitation, Gary grabbed the mechanic by his jaw and forced the fat head of his cock into his wet mouth—not that any real force was necessary. The man under him slurped and sucked hungrily, a man starved and parched in the desert. Gary focused on the warm depths of this man's mouth as he pushed in and out, past the tight ring of lips, over the rub of tongue, and into the throat beyond.

When Gary was about to gag the mechanic with meat, he stopped and pulled free, dripping drool and precome onto the dark shadow of stubble covering the panting face beneath him. He wiped himself dry in chest hair and paused.

But that moment was too long. The mechanic seized the opportunity. He grabbed Gary's tight waist and flipped him over. He rolled onto him, pressing his hairy body against the smooth, tan breadth of Gary's back. He ground his hard cock into that perfect, hairless mound of ass muscle.

When the mechanic was lying fully on top on him, pressing his cock into the crack of his ass and rubbing his stubbled cheek against the back of his neck, Gary could only breathe three shuddering words, "My right pocket."

Even though they both had their pants around their knees, the mechanic seemed to have no problem locating the square of foil and ripping it open with his teeth. With his face pressed against the floor of the van, Gary could hear the whole process. The rip and crinkle. The tight unrolling of latex over hard skin. The splat of spit that the mechanic let ooze into his ass crack.

And then Gary felt the insistent pressure of a full and eager cock head wedging its way through his sweaty furrow closer and closer to his hole. He tried to relax. But all he could think of was that big piece of meat he'd been watching all afternoon. All he could think was that a dollop of spit wouldn't be enough to prepare his ass for that thing. All he was thinking was, *Damn, this is gonna hurt.*

And then he exhaled. He tilted his hips up. And he knew he was going to take it whether it hurt or not—he wanted to. Slowly, he felt the head of the mechanic's tool enter him. He felt those greasy fingers dig into his hips, guiding that dick deeper. Slowly, he opened. He let that shaft slide in, bit by bit. He felt another trickle of spit drip onto his hole and follow the mechanic's cock inside him.

And when the whole thing was in him, the mechanic held it there. He held Gary by the hips, pressing that mass of pubes against Gary's smooth, white ass. Then the mechanic collapsed onto Gary's broad back, pressing his hairy, muscled torso against the bent length of Gary's spine. His stubbled chin dug into his shoulder. His stubbled lips were near his ear.

"I'm going to fuck you so nice, it's going to hurt good," he whispered.

Gary didn't argue. He didn't say a thing. He figured he didn't have much to add to the conversation since this guy's cock was already buried deep inside him. He just gritted his teeth and grabbed his own hard dick and hoped this mechanic could live up to his word.

Thank God the van had good shocks. Because at that moment, things began to get bumpy. The mechanic drove his big dick in and out furiously. He pounded Gary's smooth ass as fast as he could. Aching pleasure slammed into the base of Gary's spine and radiated throughout his body as he pumped his own cock without missing a beat.

Gary felt like he'd been split open, but the splitting was done when he'd taken that big thing inside. Now he was wide and receptive, and he raised his ass each and every time the mechanic thrust back into him.

Greasy hands ran up his back. And sweat dripped into the valley of his backbone. He felt hot, wet fur rubbing against him each time the mechanic came in close for a hard pound.

The deliveryman braced himself against the floor of his van one-handed. He could see his triceps straining to hold him against the rocking thrusts from behind. And his other hand squeezed and worked his own cock. Despite the pounding he was taking, and probably because of it, he was as hard as ever. And with each fucking thrust that filled him with this stranger's cock, he jerked himself one stroke closer to exploding.

"Any more room in that tight ass for me to blow my load?" the mechanic asked sarcastically between ragged pants and deep prods. He bucked his hips harder a couple times to drive the point home.

Gary gasped for breath to answer, to beg for it. He felt the cock head inside him swell and that unbelievable shaft thicken even more as it slipped in and out of his used hole. "Fill me up!"

Gary felt dirty fingers dig into him. He felt the deep, final thrusting like a piston from behind. And then he felt each long, slow pulse travel from the base of the cock inside him to the tip, and the mechanic's balls emptied themselves, pumping hot come into the condom.

The throb deep inside Gary's ass coursed through him. The mechanic's shuddering dick seemed to pour into him and echo through the open space it had created. And that sensation resounded in Gary's own cock. He squeezed the base hard to hold the delicious pressure in his nuts and savor one more breathless moment on the edge. And then he milked the full length of his shaft over and over as his own semen spattered across the floor of the van and stained several manila envelopes stacked there. That's what he called a special delivery.

As they stood outside the van zipping and buttoning, Gary could feel the empty chamber inside him that the mechanic's huge erection left behind. He watched as the tool guy stuffed that subsiding cock back into his stained mechanic's uniform. Gary reached over and helped him ease the zipper up over the bulge. He gave it a farewell pat and brushed his fingers once more through the sweaty tangles of chest hair.

"That was a great lube job," he smirked, "but what about servicing the van?"

"Oh, it was nothing," the mechanic answered. "I was done

before I even brought it inside. Just tightened up a few things under there."

"And loosened up something else," Gary laughed and rubbed his sore ass for emphasis.

"All in a day's work," he said, giving Gary's ass a slap as he climbed into the van and cranked the engine. It didn't rattle a bit.

The deliveries were a little late that day. But the pleasant ache in Gary's ass kept a smile on his face for the whole drive.

THE TICKET

Jourdan Lane

Nothing has gone right for me all day. It's been one of those days that just when you think things might start looking up—something else happens. For starters, sometime during the night the electricity surged, resetting my alarm clock. I'm nearly 40 minutes late for work. I have a meeting with clients scheduled for 9:30, putting me 15 minutes late for the meeting itself. That doesn't look so good when you're trying to lure a client over from a competing agency.

Then, the art department decides to lose my art boards for my presentation. When they finally do find them, they are the old boards—the ones we'd scrapped a month ago as crap. I then hear from the boss who is pissed with me for so many reasons by now, but the main one is because of the art department's fuckup. He then gives me a shitty account that he wants ideas on by the end of the day. I try to work through lunch and order take-out from the restaurant a block away; only to get it, eat half of it, and find mushrooms littering the bottom of the container.

I'm extremely allergic to mushrooms and after the day I've had so far, I don't know why I'm even surprised. My Epi-pen that I leave in my office for emergencies is gone from my desk and I have to make due with an allergy pill, hoping that I haven't actually ingested a mushroom. I wait for my breathing to change and my throat to close up. Luckily it doesn't, but I've taken a pill that makes me so fucking sleepy that I can barely keep my eyes open. Oh, yeah, that should work wonders for my creativity.

I manage to throw together some crappy ideas but I'm not able to get out of the office until 7:30. By this time, all I want to do is find something decent to eat, go home, and have a nice long shower before I collapse into bed. In my rush to get home, I pay no attention to my driving and run a red light. Actually, not just any red light; It's the very light that I seem to cruise right through on a damn-near daily basis.

A few moments later I'm greeted with red and blue flashing lights in my rearview mirror. I curse and grumble, pulling out my license and insurance card, and then I wait. By the time the officer finally saunters his way up to my window, I'm more than aggravated. But the moment I look up to hand him my information, all I can do is stare in appreciation.

My aggravation is now gone because the man standing before me—Officer Ken Jackson, according to his name tag—is the hottest fucking stud I've ever laid eyes on. Ruggedly handsome, he has bright green eyes that would melt fucking Kryptonite. My eyes sweep down his body noticing a chest that, even under the uniform, I could tell was ripped to perfection and his lean hips seem to make a perfect V.

I imagine him naked for a few stark seconds and there's a sudden hitch in my breath. My eyes then catch at the large bulge in his pants. I imagine what his naked cock would look like and I'm completely lost. My cock throbs and aches as it is trapped against my body and I want nothing more than to free it from its prison. I swallow hard and lick my lips, my breathing becoming quicker. I then hear him call me by my name.

"Mr. Roberts?"

I answer by just saying "Sean"—my first name.

He then chuckles. "Yes, I know that, sir. Have you had anything to drink tonight?"

I look up at him; seeing his sandy blond hair, beautiful green eyes and I smile. The only thing that comes to mind is how I would love to have a drink—a long stiff drink. I want to have his cock in my mouth providing loads and loads of come to intoxicate me. He is so fucking gorgeous, with his prominent jaw and perfect lips.

God, I wonder just how his lips would look and feel as they slide down over my own dripping cock.

His voice soon pulls me out of my thoughts yet again. "Mr. Roberts, have you consumed any alcohol this evening?"

My next thought is of consuming every square inch of this stud. But finally realizing that this is a cop standing in front of me, not someone I'm ever going to get to fuck, I try to push my desire for him back—at least till I'm home and can pump my cock to him in my memory.

I look up at him, suddenly regaining some sort of composure. "No, I haven't had anything to drink. I've just had a bad day," I say.

He smiles. "I imagine I'm the last person you wanted to see tonight."

"Oh, I don't know about that." I answer without thinking.

He stops writing on his notepad and regards me for a moment. I just want to disappear; but he only laughs, shaking his head. "Do you know what I've stopped you for, Mr. Roberts?"

I nod my head and shift in my seat, trying to ease the pain of my still painfully hard and aching cock. "Yes, sir," I answer. "I know I ran the light."

He nods and begins writing again and seeing that he is occupied—with what I hope is a warning—I let my eyes wander over his body one last time. My eyes draw inadvertently back to the bulge in the front of his slacks. I wet my lips and am trying to get an image in my mind of just how he would taste, when he taps my shoulder. "Can I get you to sign this for me, Mr. Roberts?"

I take the small clipboard and sign my name on the dotted line, watching out of the corner of my eye as the bulge in his pants shifts when he does. I suppress a groan as I hand the clipboard back to him.

He tears off a copy of what I've just signed and then hands it and my cards back to me. "Please do try to be more careful, Mr. Roberts."

I nod quickly in agreement. "I will."

He smiles at me again and I inwardly groan as he turns and

begins walking back to his patrol car. I adjust my side mirror and watch as his tight round ass teases me while he walks; two round perfect globes of muscle there that I'll never be privilege to. I let out a deep sigh as he gets into his car. I finally look down at the paper as I start to put my cards away and I can't believe what I'm looking at; a ticket, not a warning as I'd hoped. Great—just fucking great!

I pull out onto the street and watch as his patrol car disappears from view. A few miles down the road I pull into the small diner that I frequent. My apartment is only a couple of blocks away but I hate cooking for myself. I go in and sit down, browsing over a menu. Nothing really appeals to me after the day I've had, but I finally make my choice. The waitress takes my order and then leaves to get my tea. I bury my head in my hands for a few moments, trying to let my day's frustration dwindle.

By the time I'm finished eating, I'm feeling much better than I have for the entire day. I hurry, determined to get home for a nice cold beer. As I'm walking along the dimly lit corridor to my apartment, I notice someone standing at my door. No, not standing...leaning against the door frame with arms crossed over his chest and one foot crossed over the other, waiting, as if he didn't have a care in the world.

As I get closer, I see that it's none other than Officer Ken Jackson. My heart is in my throat as he looks up, smiling at me with those bright green eyes.

"Hello, Sean," He says, and his voice sounds like nothing but sex to me.

"Officer," I answer. "Imagine seeing you...here."

"You think I didn't notice the way you were staring at my cock?" He asks, turning so that he's facing me and close enough to kiss me if I were to turn my head just a fraction of an inch. "I thought that if you were man enough to stare, I could at least be man enough to let you have a closer look."

I swallow hard. "Um..."

"How about it, Sean?" He licks at his lips and I watch his

tongue, wondering how it would feel if it were licking at my ass. "You interested?"

I nod quickly, shoving my key into the lock. After a swift turn, I'm opening the door, stepping back enough to let him pass. "Very interested."

Ken steps through the door and reaches over, closing it behind him and turning the lock.

"You want a beer?" I ask.

He shakes his head. "Nope, I came here for one thing and one thing only"

"And what is that?" I ask, trying to stall but not knowing why.

Ken steps forward, walking toward me; I keep stepping back until I come into contact with the wall. "You," He whispers, sliding his big hands across my hips. He presses his lips hard to mine. His kiss is passionate and intent and it steals my breath away. He stops and pulls back, just far enough to break the kiss. "You are so fucking hot, Sean; my cock has been hard since I walked up to your window."

I know I'm fairly good looking; I work out regularly, have good muscle tone, and have just achieved a perfect six-pack. My brown hair and light blue eyes are usually the first things people notice. "You aren't so bad yourself, officer," I say with a smile, literally shaking in anticipation.

As his hands pull my hips roughly against his, I let my hands skim around his waist, but his belt, with all of the tools of his trade, is in the way of actually making any progress. My hands find the buckle for his belt and as I begin to slide it off, he pushes my hands away. He takes his belt off quickly and lets it slide carefully to the floor below. I turn to head for the bedroom but he catches my arm and shoves me face-first into the wall.

His body covers mine as he wraps one arm around my chest, the other around my hip, his hand reaching for my throbbing cock. As he touches me, I feel his dick hard and firm along the crack of my ass. His hot breath is suddenly on my neck and he's nipping my ear. "I want," he begins, his tongue laving a long wet line down my neck and then back up to my ear, "to bury my cock so far up your ass, I want you to taste it when I come."

I nearly come right there. I lay my head back, resting it on his shoulder. We seem to be exactly the same height at 6 foot 1, because every part of our bodies just melds together in all of the right places. I reach behind me, cupping his balls and extremely hard cock through his pants, and give a firm squeeze.

He groans and moves away from me. I turn around slowly, afraid that he's changed his mind, only to see him unbuttoning his shirt. I reach out and grab him by his shirt before he can take it off, and pull him into the bedroom. I turn on the lamp beside the bed, wanting to see my stud's body, my prize for the night. He strips off his shirt and drops it to the floor. I can't tear my eyes away from his ripped upper body. The man's chest has to have been cut and chiseled by the gods themselves and it's covered in a thick mass of tawny-colored fur. The hair thins out as it comes to his tight abs and begins again with a thick treasure trail that disappears into the front of his pants.

I reach out, running my fingers lightly through the hair on his chest before giving it a good hard tug. I step closer and incline my head licking the flat disc of his left nipple. I swirl my tongue around it several times and as it begins to harden, I suck it into my mouth and nip it with my teeth.

"Fuck!" He says softly.

I continue with the assault on his nipple and then move over to his right nipple, repeating the torture over and over again. His hands land on either side of my head and he pulls me up into a blistering kiss. His hands move down and unbutton my shirt as he continues kissing me. I moan into his mouth and suck in his tongue as my hands quickly find the enclosure to his pants.

I quickly release him, pushing his pants down his hips but leave his boxers on. My hand finds the hard bulge that my eyes had found so mind-numbing earlier. But what I feel as I caress him makes me pull away from his kiss and look down as I pull his boxers away from his body. The man is hung like a fucking horse. He has to be at least 10 inches and beer-can thick. I swallow hard and look back up into his eyes.

He smiles and pushes my slacks and boxers down my hips. His tongue wets his lips and he chuckles. "You're not going to back out on me now are you?"

I quickly shake my head, wondering if I'll even be able to take it. But backing out? No fucking way.

He leans in and pulls me against him. "It's OK, I'll be gentle." He then winks at me, "at first. Then I'm going to fuck you until you see stars."

His words go straight to my dick. It throbs and pulses with my heartbeat and I kick my pants clumsily from around my ankles. He lies back onto the bed, pulling me with him. I lay over him, his fur scraping against my mostly smooth chest and teasing my erect nipples.

Shifting my hips, I let my cock slide back and forth over his. I'm so turned on that my slit is oozing precome steadily. It's been so long since I've been with anyone, that as much as I want to enjoy this, I know I won't last long at all. I let my legs fall to the side, straddling him.

He pulls my hips hard against his and smiles. "Sean?"

I raise my eyebrows at his casual use of my name. "What?"

"There's no rush," he says quietly, "I'm off duty for the entire night."

I stare at him a moment before I really understand what he's saying. Instead of answering him with words, I lay back down over him and begin tracing his lips with my tongue. He gasps and flicks his tongue out, meeting mine. Our tongues are soon dancing together and I can't help but suck his tongue into my mouth. I love the taste of him and commit it to memory. I soon move down his chin with small kisses and let my tongue flick along his throat. He shivers beneath me and I can't help but laugh as my stud is reduced to moans and whimpers.

His hands find my head again, but they seem to be just resting there, as if he only wants to touch me. I work both of his nipples again and he is soon arching his back, pressing my face even closer to him. My tongue laves down his stomach, following each cut and defined muscle and I love feeling the exquisite texture of his hair against my tongue. When I come to his navel, my tongue dips inside, teasing him.

His hips arch against me and his cock is soaking my chest with his natural lube. I raise my eyes to look at him and he's watching me intently. I let my tongue trail down, keeping eye contact with him and I begin to tongue his furry balls. The musky scent of sweat and man is almost dizzying. With one hand, I hold his cock away from me. I lick and caress every square inch of his balls and when he spreads his legs even further, giving me access to his puckered hole, I groan. I push his legs back even further and lick up and down his crevice, burying my tongue into his hole on each pass and he begins cursing.

"Fuck, yeah, lick my fucking ass."

I shiver because then I know I'm doing something that he's really getting off on. I spit into his hole that is practically winking at me and tease it with my tongue and index finger. His hips begin to thrust and his ass is trying to get more of my attention. I insert a second finger and he groans loudly. "Fuck!"

I love hearing him groan and I love having this stud of a cop at my mercy. I withdraw my fingers and give him one more, long lick, and then I look up at him, smiling.

He looks down quickly. "Why are you stopping?"

I just shrug. "I can't put all of my attention in one spot." I move toward his monster piece of meat that is actually dripping like a faucet. I begin at the base of that meaty shaft and lick ever-so-slowly up the length of him. His salty-sweet essence is heavenly and by the time I reach the thick mushroom head, I'm practically shaking, wanting to try to take as much of him in as possible. I quickly flick my tongue under his glans and then smile as he whimpers like a lost puppy. "Oh, yeah, you like that, stud?"

He nods quickly. I roll my tongue in a complete circle around his dick head, and then I take him in. Slowly, inch by inch, I can feel him stretching my lips and I want more. His smell, his taste, the groans and cries from his mouth, and the feel of his monstrous cock in my mouth is nearly enough for me to shoot.

"Turn around," he says, but it's so hurried that I don't understand.

I let his cock slip from my mouth and look up at him. He moans and looks up at me. "Turn around and let me suck you."

My heart skips a beat as I turn, laying my body over his and resting my cock and balls right over his face. I silently thank the gods that it's me on top of him; I just know that if he crammed his cock down my throat I'd choke to death. I take his cock back into my mouth slowly as he begins licking and sucking on my balls. His tongue rasps along to my perineum and he begins teasing my hole with his fingers. My hips arch up instantly and in the next second, he's swallowing my cock. I pause just as I'm about to chow down on his meat again and I shudder.

He begins sucking my cock, his tongue swirling all around it as his lips caress my tool. His finger sinks into my ass and I cry out. "You're going to make me fucking come. I don't want to come yet."

"Just suck my cock and let me worry about making you come," He growls.

I whimper and take the head of his dick back into my mouth and caress his heavy sac with one hand, squeezing and pulling as I try to take as much of him in as I can. I begin to suck him with abandon as he fucks my ass with his fingers and sucks on my cock. I feel that familiar tightening and I try to put it off, breaking into a heavy sweat. I try to concentrate on his fat piece of meat in my mouth and giving him all of my attention, but it's useless.

The more attention I pay to his cock, the harder he pumps me. I cry out as he finds my nut and massages it as he swallows me whole. "Fuck! I'm going to fucking come!" I yell.

He growls as I shoot my load, spurting shot after shot of my hot spunk down his throat. He keeps sucking though and my oversensitized cock stays hard. It's never done that before. He smacks me hard on the ass. "Get up and lay on the bed."

My body is still shaking from my orgasm and now with the knowledge that he's about to ram that horse cock up my ass. My cock is pointing up at the ceiling, tiny beads of come still trailing down my shaft. Instead of just lifting my legs and baring my ass though, he lays his body over mine and begins kissing me. My mind is reeling at the sensation of his furry chest pressed to mine.

He takes my hands and raises them above my head, and then moves up, kissing along the underside of one arm until he comes to my pit. He nuzzles his face into the patch of hair there and nips the skin lightly with his teeth. His mouth continues to my chest where he gives my right nipple one good lick and then nips it hard with his teeth. I nearly scream at the pleasure-pain of it.

He laughs and does it again. "Like that, do you?"

"Shit yeah!" I say just as he does it again. "Fuck!"

"Yeah, yeah...we'll get to that," He says as he licks back and forth across my chest.

I lay there writhing as his mouth assaults me so deliciously. He looks up at me after a while. "You do have lube, right?"

I nod my head and reach over into the top drawer, pulling out a roll of condoms and a jar of lube. I'm not as nervous as I was before, perhaps because he's been so gentle in the last few minutes.

He raises his eyebrows at the condoms but tears one off. He opens the package and rolls it down over his fat cock and I wonder how he's managed it to fit. He lifts my legs up over his shoulders and gets a good amount of lube into his hand. He smears it over his shaft and then my hole. He slides a finger into me, testing me and then a few minutes later, he's got me stretched to four fucking fingers. By this time I just want him to impale me.

He shifts on the bed and gets closer to me. His mushroom head is resting at my hole and I try to relax. "Just look at me and relax," He says.

I look into his eyes and he smiles reassuringly, "That's it." I'm shaking and sweating as he stretches me further than I've ever been stretched before. His head is sliding slowly into my hole and I reach up, running my hands through the fur on his chest.

A few moments later, it feels like he's splitting me in two, but I try not to tense up. It hurts and feels as if my ass is on fire. He waits patiently and caresses my ass cheeks and as the pain fades, he gives one hard thrust, sliding all of the way in. The pain is there again, but it's only fleeting.

Ken smiles at me again. "You have the tightest fucking ass."

I can only smile thinking that with a dick like his, everything is pretty tight. He shifts his hips slightly, pulling out just a little and then pushing back in. Suddenly all is right with the world. I shove my ass toward him and tweak his nipples hard. "Come on, fuck me!"

He pulls out again and slams his cock deep into my ass and I gasp for air. It hurts so fucking good. Ken inches up even farther on the bed and releases my legs. They slide down and I wrap them around his waist as he fucks me. He's plowing my ass with long, deep strokes and I can do nothing but pant. My body is covered in sweat, a lot of it Ken's.

He suddenly pulls out of me, rips the condom off and I don't have a chance to object before he's buried balls deep into my ass again. I scream out at the sudden pain of him pulling out and pushing back in so quickly, but I find that I'm enjoying every bit of hurt his cock is putting into my ass.

He reaches down and slides his arms behind my knees, pushes forward, bringing my knees up to my shoulders, opening my ass even wider. He leans forward and nips my ear. "I love the way your ass lips kiss my cock."

I want to reach between us to stroke my fuck tube, but his body is pressed so tightly to mine, I can't. He shakes his head. "No touching. I'm making you come, remember?"

Suddenly he shifts his hips and on the next stroke punches hard right into my button. "Oh, fuck!" I scream.

He slams his hips against me and all I can feel is the electrified massage that his cock is giving my prostate and his balls slapping heavily against my ass cheeks.

"Shit!" He grunts in mid stroke.

I want more. "Harder! Fuck me harder!"

His brow furrows and he is suddenly pounding my ass so hard I know I'll not be able to walk for a week. Sweat drips from his brow and lands on my cheek. I lean up and begin licking across his upper lip. I suck it into my mouth and he kisses me hard. I suck his tongue into my mouth and moan as his strokes become faster and even harder, he's fucking me fiercely now and without abandon. I feel that tightening in my balls again and I'm so fucking close. I haven't even touched my prick and he's about to make me come. I pant and moan and he soon follows.

The sounds coming from my apartment can probably be heard throughout the entire building, but I don't care. I feel him expanding and growing in my ass and with the next stroke my asshole is clenching around him, gripping him greedily as he shoves in and out. I scream and practically howl as I spurt my load between us and he doesn't stop his pounding.

"Fuck! Oh, yeah! I'm gonna...a-a-argh!" In one long howl he empties his load into my ass and keeps on fucking as his come lubes me up even more. It's as if he can't stop and he plunges into me the entire time it takes for him to come. He finally looks down at me as his eyes begin to glaze over. He then lets my legs fall before collapsing over me, his cock still buried in my ass.

He nuzzles into my neck and sighs. "You are incredible, Sean Roberts."

"Why, thank you, Officer Ken Jackson," I chuckle. "You're not so bad yourself."

Ken looks up at me and smiles, his bright green eyes sparkling. "You're not mad, are you?"

"Why would I be?" I ask.

"About the ticket," He says cautiously.

I shake my head. "My day was about as shitty as they come, but the moment you walked up to my window, it changed for the better.

"I waited for you," He whispers. "I knew you'd run that light."

"I never thought my damned boyfriend would be giving me a

ticket though," I say.

"You've got to stop running that light," He laughs. "Next time it won't be your boyfriend stopping you."

"I know," I say quietly, then look up at him with a huge grin. "Do I actually have to pay it?"

Ken rises up to look at me. "Well, if you don't, they'll put a warrant out."

I shift my hips, pulling him farther into me, wanting a second round. "Don't let me forget to pay that fucking ticket, then. I don't have a jailbird fantasy."

THE MAN'S INTENT

Michael Huxley

I adjusted the control on my mother's binoculars to a sharper focus, dropped my baggy fatigue cutoffs, and kicked them away. Unencumbered, my jim-dandy achieved its ultimate stretch within seconds. I *had* to get off, just looking at him, and began masturbating accordingly with my free hand when the view beyond the greenhouse panes changed for the better still.

Backhoe Man placed his mammoth tool in neutral and leapt to terra firma. Standing upright, he proved a consummate physical specimen, a confirmation denuded, redoubled when he skinned his T-shirt up and over his head. He wrung the sopping shirt out and, mopping his face, neck, and pits with it, made his way to the eucalyptus stump where various sundries lay. He tossed the shirt, grabbed his cigarettes, and snagged one with his lips from the pack. When he flicked butane flame into the Marlboro's tip and belted his initial drag, I caught my own breath and held it until...he at last exhaled, with near-obscene relish, a concentrated jet of smoke into the diffusive summer air. He took a second lusty drag, locked the cigarette between his lips, and returned to his position on the backhoe, stripped stunningly to the waist.

Dying for a smoke, I quickened my pace. It wouldn't be long. Not long....

He was my ne plus ultra of cockthrobbery, epitomized everything that, from a magnified distance, jerked my nerve: early 30s, blue-collar, ripped, hirsute, and tattooed. He was blond—not *usually* my preference—his dirty, sun-streaked tangle yanked back in a short ponytail. By contrast, his darker beard accentuated rather than detracted from tanned facial features that could only have resulted from a triumphant experiment in selective breeding. Fitted in perfect jeans, his monster ass and thighs, though far more fundamental considerations, were no less compelling.

The man, whose entire attitude bespoke a self-assured virility as immutable as concrete, displayed not one arbitrary gesture. He knew how to smoke a cigarette the right way; that much was certain—the very observation that was pushing me to the fucking edge as the old familiar sensation in my cock tightened its grip on my mind control.

Now, as sophisticated for my age as I like to think myself, the shameless 20-year-old jackrabbit that I also am never fails to dominate in certain situations. There I stood—legs slightly bent, ass clenched, binoculars in hand, vision augmented—fucking my fist while thinking the most inelegant trash: *How'd you like to ride this big, pierced hard-on, you butch motherfucker? Yeah, let's fuck, 'cause if your insides feel half as good as you look, I'll blast us both into fuckin' orbit. Go for it, stud; take me to the root; it's all yours. And so is this, you humping come-instigator, you alpha male, son-of-a goddamn, yeah....*

So much for the linguistics of lust.

My craving a cigarette once again in check, I dealt with the semen-spattered floor, after which I decided to set up my easel right there in the greenhouse—no huge surprise, I realize, but in my defense the light *was* perfect in there. Shit, if anything could waylay my creative process, it was sex. Always and forever sex!

God, I hate these close-ups. What a mistake to involve Wesley in this project, I thought while flipping through the photos of Wesley's flawless fucking hands and feet I'd taken the previous weekend for a drawing class—"Details of the Human Form"—I was breezing through that semester. Impatient and grumpy, having chosen what I considered the least offensive hand shot, I placed a fresh pad on the easel and launched into a quick sketch in pencil, the backhoe's roar in the distance punctuating my mood in ways I wasn't at all positive I cared for.

Wes had approached me on campus to ask if I'd be interested in donating to the upcoming HRC auction. "Something from your nude series would doubtless fetch a high price, considering *that* crowd," he'd cajoled. "Especially since your work is becoming so well known." That was true, due in part to the publicity I'd received nine months earlier for becoming the youngest-ever Grand Prize recipient at the Botti Competition, despite what certain jury members determined to be the "salacious arrogance," the "premeditated audacity" of my submissions. What a farce! That nonsense behind me, I figured it would be excellent PR to donate, and hey, gay rights were at stake.

Then came the bombshell: "By the way," pried Wes, flashing his bleached, oh-so-bankable smile, "what are you up to this weekend?"

Now, Wesley Johnson was nothing to sneeze at. At 23 he had modeled since childhood and was considered among the best-looking men at UCLA, if you like that type. Whether so or not, no one could deny that Wes, a recently "retired" Abercrombie & Fitch poster boy, did have a killer butt. And so, imagining how it might feel to penetrate the cleft between his rounded glutes with my hard-on and pound his fucking prostate, I gave Wes my telephone number, musing, *I suppose I'll find out this weekend while winding my way to class.*

Once his initial shock upon discovering my Prince Albert had subsided, the date went well. His cock proved altogether blow job–conducive, of course—cut, well-proportioned, blah, blah, blah—and before the evening was over, I'd succeeded not only in penetrating his famous mounds, but slamming three loads into the three condoms I wore while fucking him cross-eyed three separate times. What can I say; it turned out the guy craved getting fucked, and getting fucked hard. No doubt about it, the sperm cells were flying that night!

Much to my dismay, however, the gifts and "I love yous" began rolling in right after our first encounter. He gave me clothes for the most part, designer shit I wouldn't have worn if held at gunpoint.

Except for being homosexual, the one tidy little sunburst tattoo on his left shoulder, and having both ears pierced, Wes and I had zilch in common.

I flipped the completed sketch up and behind the pad. Unenthusiastically, I began another.

It's not that Wes is such a bad guy, my mind raced, *if only he were! Sure he's handsome and built, but his looks are not attached to anything that elicits a deeper response from me. He exudes no mystique whatsoever....*

I sighed aloud.

It's time to face the fact that the breakup is coming and soon. Am I too harsh? Well excuse me, but for the past month I've had to resort to my sexual fantasy Rolodex for every orgasm Wesley's supposed to be inspiring when we're together. Like that tow-truck driver with the "let's fuck" glint in his eye who checked me out last week, yeah.... Or the road worker on La Cienega—yum—speckled with asphalt like some grungy, banished archangel.... Even that homeless fucker with the devastating arms I spotted talking on the pay phone at 7-Eleven yesterday. Hmm, I wonder what's going on out there; I don't hear the backhoe. Where did I lay the goddamned binoculars...?

Scanning the property: the backhoe shut down, the crew settling beneath a tree for their lunch break, my spurtworthy paragon nowhere in sight.... *Shit, just when I have a plan.* Having remembered that, before she left, my mother instructed me to collect some paperwork the foreman was expected to deliver, I'd wasted no time deciding that Backhoe Man was the logical choice for inquiry. I had to get a closer look, hear his voice, shake his hand, pump his flesh.

Just then, as if by invocation, he emerged from inside the garage, larger-than-life through the binocular lenses, jotting notations on a clipboard. My ears and cheeks flushed instantly. I needed to get a grip and get the fuck out there, so shifted gears—something I'm quite good at. Already shirtless, I jammed my ball cap on backward, yanked my cutoffs *way* down in front, and headed out the door as seemingly collected as always, at least to the untrained eye. Walking straight toward him, I called out, "Hey. Excuse me.... You the foreman?"

He glanced up. "I guess you could say that. You're...Jim, right?"

"Yes. Sorry to bother you."

"No, it's all right," he countered. "Your mother said you'd be house-sitting." He extended his hand. "I'm Adam Cabrini."

Jesus, his grip.... Stay cool, James. "I see," I commented with topical emphasis, "Adam from Cabrini Constructors..."

"Bingo," replied he, releasing my hand. "What can I do for you, Jim?"

"Yes, the paperwork my mother said you'd have ready...?"

"Right, the checklist for the historical society—it's down in my truck."

"There's no hurry..." my voice trailed off.

Adam fell silent, turned to survey his morning's effort. Then: "This project's quite an investment for your mother: a curving, 700-foot driveway set in pavers, terraced into a hillside, the retaining wall running the entire length on the incline..."

"No huge setback for her."

"You have to admire a career as successful as hers," he commented.

I shrugged my shoulders. "Acting's her passion..."

"So what's your passion, Jim?"

Glanced by his curve ball, I managed to reply, "I'm...a visual artist doing time at UCLA, if that's what you mean."

"That'll do, I suppose."

It was imperative I say the right thing immediately. "Dude, not to change the subject but...could I bum a cigarette?"

"Yeah, I'm due for a fix myself but they're down with my shit."

"It's no big deal..."

"Relax; we're on break. I'll grab your checklist while I'm down there." He paused. "By the way, how do you know I smoke?"

"I noticed you from the greenhouse, when you were down by the tree stump."

"One of the pleasures of my profession: the nine-hour smoke break."

"You did seem to be enjoying it."

"And...you must have excellent binoculars."

Big-time busted, I deferred: "What can I say; you're very quick. I like that."

"Then observe how quick," he said, taking his leave.

Watching him retreat, I became transfixed upon his backside from ponytail to bootheels. The way his jeans fit those legs, that fucking ass, the naked torso erupting with such amazing breadth from his denim waistband—his lats flaring up and out to support massive, tattooed shoulders—was a breathtaking integration. When all at once he looked back and caught me staring, he simply cocked an eyebrow and resumed his descent.

What are the odds this testosterone overdose might be hot for me? I asked myself, shaken to the core. *One in 10, I presume* (I replied), *so chances are he's straighter than the shortest distance between a sperm and an egg cell, a prick tease whose craving for the ego gratification I'm sure he scores nonstop from homosexual men is bottomless. That last glance back, though...*

I'd already played and replayed his every word in my mind, scrutinized the possible implications behind his every vocal inflection, facial expression, and body signal, when I noticed him heading back, manila envelope in hand.

Don't blow it, James. You've played it well so far.

"Knock yourself out," he said, handing me his cigarettes and lighter. He then placed the envelope on the Jeep with a pat. "The checklist, my friend—don't forget it's here." I thanked him cursorily, clamped a Marlboro between my lips, and lit it without compunction. The kick provided by blasting that first greedy drag into my lungs was fucking eucharistic.

"Better now?"

"Yes," I swooned, exhaling, returning his pack and lighter.

He fired up his own smoke, then ventured, "When did you quit?"

“Six months ago. Is it that obvious?”

“Don’t sweat it. Welcome back.”

Propped against the muddy Jeep, we smoked in silence for a second—a silence Adam broke with an ironic snicker.

“What’s the joke?”

“I was just thinking: ‘Long live the health and fitness-obsessed nicotine junkies.’”

“Shit, don’t remind me,” I said. “I’ll never hear the end of it at the gym after being everyone’s poster boy for exemplary behavior.”

“So where do you lift?”

“Private studio in Venice, no frills, close to my apartment. And you?”

“I have equipment at home.”

Upshift, James.... “Then you’re something else about doing your homework, ’cause, if you don’t mind my saying so, your body’s...fucking brilliant.”

“I didn’t have half your definition when I was your age. You do that excellent body art justice. Let’s see the piece on your upper back.”

“I’ve either designed or transposed it all myself,” I boasted, turning.

“Round your shoulders just a bit. Yeah, this is incredible. Looks almost like Miro, or Kandinsky’s later stuff.”

Utterly blown away, I exclaimed, “No one’s *ever* recognized that before! Kandinsky’s ‘Composition IX’ inspired that section! You know *art*.”

“Yeah, well, not judging by what I call my ‘prison tats.’”

“Give me a break,” I scoffed. “Your work is déclassé *extraordinaire*. Oh, it’s primitive all right, and crudely executed, but it *damn* well realizes your intent.”

“And what would my ‘intent’ be?”

No fear, James. No fear... “To further amplify an already hyperbolic masculinity.”

Time warped. Our sudden eye contact waxed complicit. He said, “We’re a couple of freaks, you realize?”

"No doubt," I agreed.

"My telling you how fucking much I want you isn't going to cost me my front teeth—is it, Jim?"

"No. It's not."

"So...how's that for direct?"

"Not bad, but I can top it."

"Oh, yeah...?"

I took a final drag off my cigarette, dropped the filter to the ground, and crushed it beneath my sandal.

"I gave myself a killer orgasm looking at you through the binoculars earlier."

He replied, "Now there's a visceral compliment," without a second thought.

"Let's step inside the house, Adam."

"I have to take a leak anyway." He followed me to the kitchen entrance, flicked his cigarette butt away. Once inside, he said, "Feel my heart."

My right palm flattened against his mighty left pec. The heaving surface beneath his chest hair, dusted with grit, proved both hard and yielding to the touch. "Jesus Christ," I exclaimed, though my own heart was pounding as frantically.

He leaned into my ear, insinuated his tongue for a split second. He whispered: "You're to blame for that, gorgeous. Now...*where's the frigging bathroom*?"

I suppressed a laugh. "Harsh segue, Cabrini..."

"Maybe so, but I won't be able to piss if I get much harder."

I showed him to the guest bathroom right off the kitchen, then stood in the doorway and watched. He flipped the toilet seat up. Unzipped his jeans. Wasn't wearing any underwear. With some difficulty, he managed to haul an unwieldy, beautifully circumcised handful through the gaping fly. Dispatching his initial dribbles down dead center, he sighed with relief once his urine began to rush in earnest from his stunning semihardness. The splashing torrent went on and on: forceful, livid yellow, and loud. Not at all like Wesley's polite little tinkle, always aimed toward the back rim just above the water line.

"Wow, you had to go something fierce."

"I don't delay getting better acquainted with the likes of you for no good reason," he replied, the deluge beginning to subside.

"This may sound lame, but...I love the way you piss."

"I've won awards," he joked, milking his dick dry and, much to my dismay, packing it back into his jeans and zipping up.

"Oh, my God," I blurted, "don't put it away!"

He ignored me, flushed the toilet and exited the bathroom without washing his hands. Striding past me, he said, "Come here, Jim."

I followed him through the kitchen, panicked to think he was about to leave. But instead, he took me in arm and backed my body against the door with his own. Upholding my face in his proletarian hands, he read my eyes with such searching gravity that I nearly burst into tears.

We began making out with tongue-stoking abandon, an extended exercise in bliss that engorged my cock to frenetic rigidity, a reaction, in turn, that I could feel we shared—his reaction rotating against my own—a fact confirmed visually when I broke away, glanced down, and beheld his glans pounding sanguine and wet, well above his belt line.

He groped me through my shorts, but stopped short. "What have we here?"

"I'm pierced. Pinch it. Hard..."

"This, I gotta see first..." He unzipped but did not unbutton my shorts, reached inside, and, liberating my outrageous carnal stretch, allowed it to jut at a stiff angle up through the opening. Whispering, "Would you look at this..." with the guttural inflection of cock worship, he took my precome-doused, PA-pierced cock head between thumb, index, and middle fingers, and proceeded to pinch me through the roof, all the while taunting, "You *like* that...? Does it feel *good*...?"

"Let's get naked, Adam."

"Not now, babe. We'll save that for later."

"*Later*," I groaned. "I want you *now*."

"Just kick back, Jim; I'm not gonna leave you like this." He fell to his knees before me. "Drop your shorts and lean against the door. Yeah, that's perfect." He nuzzled his bearded face beneath my scrotum and began to explore at his leisure—sniffing and licking, inhaling and lapping—that mysterious place from which my hard-on stemmed. His voice phlegmy with desire, Adam slurred, "Your scent...and the way you taste...knocks me fucking out, man."

"I've never been higher with a man before," I confessed, wholly beside myself.

"Yeah? Well, dig this..."

He slipped his lips over my hoop and took me to the friz in one voracious downstroke with a fine head of saliva. I sucked my breath through clenched teeth and cried out, "*God*, yes," as close to overdosing on ecstasy as I thought possible—until, that is, his second downstroke, and his third, and the next one, and the one after that... Gladly losing count, I was elevated from that point upward to nothing short of absolute erotic transcendence for an all-too-brief infinity. Once the thrilling twinges that always signal my impending orgasms had begun in earnest, with Adam they quite unexpectedly evolved into rhythmic surges of such overwhelming ferocity, that only halfway between first glimmer and ejaculation I found myself unable to imagine them growing any sharper, any more intense, any better, but they did—exponentially more so with his every oral descent. When the searing upheavals converged in a sustained frenzy I gasped, "Holy shit," and unable to endure the pleasure escalating another second, slammed my satiation in white-hot increments from a place far too joyous to pinpoint, fathoms deep into Adam's incomparable fellatio.

My involuntary growls and bellows abated to impregnated silence. A belated come-shiver quaked my body. Had I died? I suppose not, seeing that the moment Adam rose to face me I started right in.

"Here," I barked, fumbling with his strained top button. "We need to get these fucking jeans undone..."

He gently stayed my hand. "It's OK, babe; I'm gonna hold off for now."

I was floored. "You've *got* to be kidding me. Look at you! It's *obvious* you need to come."

"I'm a big boy, Jim; I'll be fine—at least, I think so! But I've gotta get back to my crew. They saw us come in here together. They know me. I'm going to catch hell enough as it is." Noting my mute consternation, he lowered his voice to an intimate level. "What I 'need' is for us to spend some time together. A quickie just ain't gonna do it for me. Not with you."

"But when?" I demanded. "I am dying to get naked with you, Adam, and I'm not ashamed to admit it. I wanna jump you so bad it hurts, OK? I've had it with playing it cool!"

He grabbed my shoulders and held me at arm's length. His voice, firm with resolve, remained subdued. "I'll see you after work. I'm spending the night here. You got it?"

What was he telling me? What? As if of its own volition, the supposition, "You're not involved with anyone," simply fell from my mouth.

"Just you, kiddo."

I stood there, thunderstruck to observe this strange new life form shift into ever-sharper focus. "My God...you're for real...aren't you?"

"You bettcha."

Just like that—yes—I made the conscious decision to trust that he wasn't yet another sheep in wolf's clothing. Suspiring any remaining misgivings, I proclaimed him, "Adam: The Man..." very much aloud to myself, and fell at ease for the first time since being lured to his shore.

"Yes," he emphasized, unhanding me. " 'The Man' seriously out of here." He reached down his jeans and forced his persistence way down one leg. "Damn...you got me so turned on it's almost like I wet my pants. Here, smell this hand."

My olfactory response to the composite of burnt tobacco, his calluses, and Adam au jus was not unexpected; withdrawal from his hand proved difficult. Fucking difficult.

The Man, who knew exactly what he was doing, how to best realize his intent, prepared to leave. He said, "No need for me to drive all the way home if I can toss my clothes in your washer tonight."

"Yeah, like you need to ask."

"I'll send the guys home around 4; we're running ahead of schedule anyway."

"I'm taking off for the gym in a few but I should be back before that. You need anything while I'm out?"

"Do you have condoms here?"

"Plenty. I've got it all. What else?"

"You have enough food?"

"What do you think? I'm a fucking bodybuilder."

"Which reminds me..." He retrieved the cigarettes from his back pocket, tapped one out, and laid it on the island. "Sorry, I'm running low, but this'll at least get you to a store. Buy two packs for me, if you would. I'll pay you later; my wallet's down in the glove compartment."

"No problem. You want to wash up real quick? Rinse your face, or..."

"And not take you back to work with me?" he interrupted, drawing me into his tattooed, Herculean embrace. "No thanks."

After Adam kissed me as sweetly as he did just then, I could not help but say it, "Aren't we in love...?"

"I know I am," he stated without breaking eye contact, "but I really gotta fly."

I dismissed him from my arms. "My best to your crew who knows you so well..."

"Let's see," he retorted. "What can I say; you're very quick. I like that."

I scowled faux suspiciously. "We'll talk later."

He glanced over his shoulder before closing the door behind him.

Dazed with happiness and anticipation, I contemplated the

quiet for several heartbeats then walked straight to the phone, picked it up, and punched in.

"Wesley? Hey, I'm glad I caught you at home... Y'know, that would be cool, but it's 12:45 and I'm just now leaving for the gym. Can you meet me at Arabica afterward? We gotta talk, Wes... No, I have to cancel tonight; that's what I... We can discuss it at Arabica, Wesley... Around 3. And if you get there first, snag an outside table... Please don't stress, Wesley; you've no idea... Whatever, then: Suit yourself... Look, I'm running late. Are we cool for Arabica or what...? All right, then; I'll see you there." I hung up the phone and let it rip.

"God *damn* it to motherfucking hell!"

I gathered my things and was out the door in a whirlwind. At once noticing I'd forgotten it on the hood of my Jeep, I placed the manila envelope on the passenger's seat with my gym bag, lit the cigarette I'd not forgotten, and eased downhill, overland, in first. I bumped over the curb onto the road with caution and, after turning left—after shifting into second, then third, then cleanly into fourth—accelerated toward Venice Beach with this in mind: He did not turn his noble, pagan countenance one way or the other, as Jeep and backhoe approached, and then achieved, their brief perigee.

THE SLUT BOTTOM

Thom Wolf

Looking over his shoulder at the reflection in the mirror, it seemed to Jack that his ass had never looked better. Framed in the straps of a vintage jock, his cheeks were ripe and succulent; the skin was creamy and several shades lighter than his suntanned spine. He ran his palm across the curve of his right mound, caressing the flesh, squeezing. It was the best piece ass on the scene—all the tops had told him so.

He turned away from the mirror to finish dressing. Heavy house music blasted from his stereo and a half drunk glass of Jack Daniel's rested on the bedside table. The clothes he had chosen for that night were laid on the bed; cargo pants, a white vest, socks, and boots. His semiaroused cock and tight balls were securely fastened by a wide leather strap that he had put on straight after showering. His balls and his ass crack were freshly shaved that day and anointed with balm. His asshole was clean, inside and out; set for a heavy session. He hadn't been fucked in four days, nor beat off in two; he'd been saving himself for this evening.

He gave his cock a squeeze as he stepped into the cargo pants, which were deliberately a size too big. The baggy waist hung low on his hips, showing off the range of his taut, golden abdomen, and the lines that dipped from his hip bone to his groin. The pants hung low enough to show the black straps of his jock and a tantalizing hint of the ass crack below.

He finished dressing. He would only wear the vest until he reached the club, where he would take it off and shove it casually down his pants; it would serve as a handy come rag later.

He sat on the bed to finish his drink. His laptop was open and signed on. He double-clicked the link to his web page; scrolling through the message board to gage the reaction of his fans to the new photographs posted in the gallery. The pictures were taken by a friend called Red last weekend; 24 high-definition images of Jack's juicy ass, filled with an assortment of objects—a three-inch butt plug, 10-inch dildo, a can of beer, a cucumber, Red's dick. The shoot had sparked much interest on the board as the fans discussed a wish list of further items they'd like to see in Jack's rectum; snooker balls, a wine bottle, and increasingly large dildos. The most popular request was to see his delicious hole double-fucked by two massive cocks. Jack noted the demand, excited. He would speak to Red later and arrange a photo shoot. He logged out of the site and shut his computer.

Jack wanted something on his stomach before going to The Cock Ring.

The porno house at the end of Westgate Road was showing a vintage '80s movie when he arrived, his favorite era. He breathed in the acrimonious scent of poppers, sweat, and come, savoring it for a moment, before exhaling and taking an aisle seat halfway down the house; he sat beside a beary looking man dressed in leather. On-screen, big-dicked Chad Douglas buried his fat tool in the ass of a young California blond. Jack sat back for a moment to watch the film and in seconds his cock began to throb. He loved these '80s movies—massive-dicked studs ramming their bare dicks in the greediest of holes. Those boys knew how to take a cock. Chad was pounding the hell out that boy's butt, pulling his giant dick all the way out of his hole, and slamming it home roughly without the slightest consideration for how the boy was feeling—pretty damned good, Jack imagined.

The leather bear turned to look at him, scrutinizing Jack's features in the irregular light of the cinema screen; his profile was strong, with a long straight nose and clear jaw. Jack's hair was blond, cut into a short, choppy style. At 27, he was probably a good 20 years younger than the bear. The man leaned nearer.

"You're not my type," he whispered gruffly.

Jack grinned, turning slowly to look at him. He saw a squat forehead and deep eye sockets. The lower half of the face was hidden in hair. "You're not my type, either," he said confidently. "But I still want to suck your cock."

The bear hesitated a moment, giving the suggestion some thought, then he sat back in his seat. He stared at the screen, enjoying the fuck, and he widened his thighs. He unzipped his jeans and said, "Suck it."

Jack leaned across his seat, bowing into darkness. He thrust a hand inside the bear's jeans and found a decent-sized piece of meat. He tugged the sweaty organ out into the open, catching its pungent odor, and began to work it. Using his mouth and his hands, he caressed the shaft, exploring its length and girth, its powerful sinews and gnarled veins. He opened his mouth around the blunt head, teasing it with his tongue, tasting the salty fluid that formed on the tip. He sucked more of the shaft into his mouth, drooling spit down the sides, swallowing it deeper. It was a decent stretch for his jaw to take the full width of the man.

The bear put a rough hand on the back of his head, forcing him lower, while lifting his hips from the dank-smelling seat. *He wants to make me gag,* Jack thought, knowing better. His breath rasped through his nostrils. The bear was quick, holding Jack's head in a rigid grip while he filled his mouth with the bitter taste of spunk. Jack swallowed it all, eventually leaning back and licking his lips. The bear grunted something incomprehensible.

Jack ignored him, staying in the cinema just long enough to watch the end of the scene.

The Cock Ring was full when he arrived, just before midnight. By 1 the place would be packed. The rank odor of sex hit him as he stepped through double doors, 10 times more potent than the stink in the cinema. Almost everything in The Cock Ring was painted black: the floors, the brick walls, the surface of the bar, the tables. The walls were hung with chains, wide mirrors, steel mesh, and danger signs.

There was always a mix in the crowd—leather men, bears, skinheads, army drag, men in chaps, men in jocks, some naked, along with and a smattering of pretty disco bunnies looking out of place in hot pants and cropped tops.

Jack peeled his vest above his head, stuffing it down the waist of his pants. The club was sweltering. He made it to the bar on the first floor and bought himself a beer and a bottle of poppers. Thankfully the beer was cold.

Although it was early, the action had started. Jack stood for a while, at the edge of the dance floor, watching a couple of leather dads spit-roast a skinhead in front of the DJ booth. Those closest to the action had stopped to watch, the rest of the floor continued dancing. The skinhead, looking to be somewhere in his early 20s, was naked except for a red necktie and black boots. Jack looked at his ass, which was white and hairless—as smoothly shaven as his head. His asshole was red, well fucked, gapping slightly each time the top pulled out, hanging open in anticipation, waiting to be filled by that big daddy-dick once again. The leather man fucked him bareback.

After a few minutes Jack moved on. He was here to participate, not observe. He moved around the side of the dance floor and into a long, narrow corridor that ran behind it. This area of the club was even darker, with just four low-watt lightbulbs illuminating the passage. The narrow route was full of bodies, many of them busy. There was five open doorways running off from the corridor, opening out into large chambers; some of these rooms were just empty cells, others were stocked with toys, mattresses, slings, plasma-screen televisions showing nasty, small-studio porn. Music from the neighboring dance floor reverberated through the walls.

As Jack shoved his way down the packed and sweltering corridor, a rough hand pushed down the seat of his pants, dry fingers jabbed at his asshole. He turned to look at the man who had staked a claim on his ass. He was another leather man, in chest harness and chaps. His hair was steely grey, buzzed into a short crop. His eyebrows were thick and dark, shadowing deep-set eyes. The lines across his brow and round his eyes, and the flecks of white in his slate-gray 'stache, put his age somewhere between 45 and 50. He was a big man, muscular, with a gallery of tattoos etched across his shoulders and down both arms.

Even before he set eyes on his long, fat cock, Jack had seen enough of the man to know that he wanted him. He searched the man's eyes for permission to touch. The man nodded, once. Jack wrapped his hand around a log of cock, it was fat, veiny, and wet, all the elements he adored. With his hand still down Jack's pants, his fingers jabbing brusquely at his juicy asshole, the man shoved him into the nearest room.

Unlike some of the others, this room was sparsely furnished, with just three bare mattresses on the floor, already occupied by rutting men. The leather man swung Jack around and pushed him; face-first, against the bare brick wall. "Umph!" Jack groaned on impact, the breath forced from his lungs. The leather man did not waste time. His hands came around Jack's waist, loosening his pants, shoving them to his ankles. Jack wriggled his butt, enjoying the caress of air on his exposed skin, allowing it to cool his sweaty crack. The leather man squatted, tugging Jack's cargo pants over his boots, giving his ass a firm slap as a direction to lift his feet. The pants, along with his vest, were cast into the room behind. Jack didn't care what happened to them.

Leather Man's rough hands were on his ass, prizing his cheeks apart. He spat a gob onto the hole. Jack felt the trickle of saliva down his crack, the rough prickle of the man's 'stache, a moment before his tongue started working on his anus. Jack rested his elbows against the wall, giving his body without condition. It was received gratefully; Leather Man lavished spit and tongue on his juicy hole.

The sounds of sex in the small chamber began to drown out the thunder from the dance floor; the loud slap of skin against skin, the verbal abuse of a noisy fuck somewhere behind Jack, out of view, the rumble in his own chest, signalling satisfaction.

"Look at this hole," he heard Leather Man say.

Jack turned his head. He was talking to another man—younger this one—in his mid 30s. He wore the uniform: chaps and harness. His skin was a dark shade of brown. He had a handsome face, broad and clean shaven. His hair was a short black fuzz.

"Nice," the black man said, squeezing a butt cheek. "Let's open it up a little."

Leather Man grunted. "Stick your ass out."

Jack widened his feet, bending at the knees, giving the two men exactly what they wanted—his ass, high and wide. The black man stuck his face in the open crevice, tasting Jack's hole with long, wet strokes. Leather Man scooped a palm full of thick white lube from an open tub and worked it slowly over his hand, coating his fingers and knuckles, watching while his black partner made a feast of Jack's ass.

The black man withdrew. He stood up and stroked his dick slowly. Jack murmured as Leather Man smeared lube into his crack, working over the pliant ring. Leather Man's thick middle finger met no resistance from his sphincter as it slid into his rectum. Jack's hole took two and then three fingers effortlessly. He squeezed his ring around Leather Man's hand, chewing on the fleshy digits.

Leather Man withdrew. The black man's dick was already prepared. He moved into position behind Jack, guided his thick cock toward the opening. Jack waited patiently for the first cock of the night to enter his ass. His body tingled with confident expectation as the blunt head nudged his hole. The pressure increased, slowly widening him, stretching him wider, wider. He grunted loudly as the black man's cock broke through his sphincter and forced itself deeper into his cavity. He pushed his dick all the way in and let it sit there for a moment, not moving. As soon as the black man sensed that Jack was ready he began to move, getting straight into a rhythm.

Jack began to sweat more profoundly, not just a result of the throbbing cock inside him. The room was heating up; down on the floor, nine bodies writhed and contorted in a mass of sweating flesh, a crowd of spectators began to gather, some wanking at the scene before them, others just quietly observing.

Jack's rectum tingled as every inch of the black man's cock grazed his hole. He withdrew all the way, his big head popping free of Jack's hole, before thrusting inside, very slowly, very deep. He wrapped his arms around Jack's torso, lifting and turning him at the same time, until his face came round to Leather Man's expectantly hard dick. Jack went down in a single motion, swallowing it all. He worked the cock in his mouth enthusiastically but it was the blunt log in his rectum that really concerned him. Each throbbing inch inside his ass, each tiny fraction of movement, was ecstasy. He worked his sphincter, clutching greedily at the black monster. The black man dug his fingers into the flesh around his hips and began to give it to him harder, faster—rabbit-fucking the last dregs of resistance from his hole. Jack was dizzy with the sensations, his head as well fucked as his ass. He slobbered on Leather Man's cock, saliva dribbling down his face as he took both cocks deep inside his body.

The black man's thrusts became increasingly erratic until he gasped, "Oh, yes," and blew his load into Jack's guts. Jack melted with pleasure, white-hot spunk flowing through his ass, filling his anal cavity. The black man withdrew slowly and Jack felt an amalgam of semen and lube ooze out of his loosened hole, spilling down his crack. He tightened his sphincter, preventing more of the precious load escaping.

The black man slapped his ass, once, very hard, and walked away. Jack turned his head, catching sight of his broad shoulders as he retreated from the room. There was no time to regret his departure. Now that his ass was nicely loosened, Leather Man was ready to take his turn. He grabbed hold of Jack and threw him on the floor. Despite falling onto the mattress, Jack landed heavily on his back, legs sprawling. Leather Man pounced, grabbing Jack's booted ankles, hauling them to his shoulders, rolling his hips and raising his ass.

His cock was noticeably thicker than the black man's. Jack

gasped as it tore into his rectum.

"Shut the fuck up!" Leather Man said, spitting a huge wad into Jack's face. Saliva dribbled down his brow, over his nose and cheeks. Jack's tongue slivered out of his mouth and caught all the spit it could reach. Encouraged, Leather Man leaned over him and dribbled a long trail of saliva into Jack's open mouth. Jack caught it all and swallowed.

Leather Man got stuck into his ass, burying his dick deep, stirring up the spunk the black man had deposited. He grunted and thrust his way to a hard come, ejaculating a second potent load into Jack's pliant come hole. Leather Man withdrew, his place taken a few seconds later by a sinewy skinhead. The skinhead put his hand over Jack's mouth, muffling his cries, fucking him hard, dumping another load of spunk into his ass. The forth deposit was provided by a muscular Latino who swore in Spanish as he slammed Jack's ass.

Jack's hole was sloppy and wet. He lay back on the mattress for a moment, putting his fingers to his asshole. The ring was hot and swollen, beginning to tire. He slipped two fingers inside, stirring the come pot. He brought his fingers to his mouth, tasting the juice of his ass and the unique blend of four semen types. He licked his fingers until they were clean.

Four pairs of hands reached down for him. He didn't resist as the men turned him over and hauled him onto his hands and knees. They fucked him hard and fast, their faces did not register with him, all he cared about was their cocks and the spunk they deposited inside him. More men came to use him, fucking him, filling him, Jack stopped counting their numbers. He didn't care anymore. He just wanted them. He wanted them all. Some men protected themselves with condoms, most didn't. As they withdrew their sheathed dicks, Jack pleaded with them to empty the come-filled rubbers over his face. They all obliged.

His ass was so loose, so sloppy, that when two huge bears tried to double penetrate him, it accepted the test quite easily. Two big, chubby cocks filled his hungry hole. Finally, with one man beneath him, another behind, both of them inside, Jack was satisfied. He came in a blissfully slow stream, ejaculating thick gobs of come with the consistency of paste across the belly and chest of the man beneath him.

When it was over, one of the men, bald with a 'stache, helped Jack to stand up. As Jack bent over to retrieve his clothes from the floor, the man inserted a thick butt plug into his hole. Jack gasped, surprised, but there was no resistance left in his anus and the three-inch-wide plug entered him easily.

"It's a present," the man said. "To stop any of that good stuff leaking out."

The reflection of his ass was now very different to the one he viewed seven hours earlier. The tight, puckered hole was loose and inflamed. Translucent come dripped steadily from the orifice, captured in a stainless steel dog bowl. Jack squatted above the bowl in front of the mirror, looking at his ass. He did not move until he was certain that every drop of semen had been evacuated from his hole. It gathered in the bowl, a runny white splooge.

When his ass was empty, Jack lay facedown on the floor and tipped the bowl over his ass, rubbing the come over his butt quickly, massaging it into the skin like an expensive balm before it got cold.

THE STAFF OF LIFE

Jack Whitestone

From my earliest recollection as a child admiring Charles Atlas and Joe Weider muscle-building ads in the backs of comic books, I've been drawn to chests—particularly husky ones bearing a crop of manly hair and showing large, hardened nipples.

When I reached high school, my mother used to starch my shirts until they were as stiff as cardboard. The shirts' rigid cotton would scrape against my nipples like sandpaper, mildly chafing and stinging, yet somehow delighting, my areolas.

By this time, I was drawn to Grant, who attended the same high school as I did. Our after-school activities provided plenty of occasions for us to be together, and we secretly found opportunities to practice our wrestling moves wearing only our jockstraps. Tussling around on the floor or bed would lead to stripping off our jocks and probing every part of each other's naked bodies.

I was intrigued with Grant's big nipples. While mine were taut, erect, flesh-colored cones, his were broad welts, the color of succulent, dark red apples. His nipples were even more pleasing because a carpet of hair was beginning to fill in across his chest, unlike mine, which barely supported a few sprouts.

The pleasures of my sexual awakening combined with the continual provoking of starched shirts against my nipples made me even more fascinated with Grant's bare chest. One time I asked him how he developed such large disks and his secret for growing chest hair.

"Push-ups," Grant confided. "I do lots of push-ups, and that makes my nips big and my chest hair grow."

I did push-ups every morning and evening, well into my early 20s, before I began to doubt the credibility of his advice.

I haven't seen Grant for many years, but I was reminded of him when a man moved in the house down the street. Something seemed strikingly familiar about my new neighbor. It was as if Grant had grown up, become a little more beefy, and changed his name to Luke.

Luke is what you would call a "man with some meat on his bones." Husky and a little over six feet tall, he is handsome and outgoing. I don't know which is more magnetic—his good looks or his engaging personality.

I often take morning walks in the neighborhood around the time that Luke speeds off to work in his pickup. Sometimes, he hollers, "Good morning!" and gives me a thumbs-up gesture as he passes. Other times, he stops, and we chat a bit about some trivial neighborhood news. I like talking with Luke nearly as much as I enjoy looking at him because of his rich, resonant voice. A deep and powerful voice, it's nonetheless engaging and friendly.

When I first noticed Luke's resemblance to my pal Grant, I wondered if Luke also sports large nipples and a hairy chest. It was hard to tell. The city where I live is known for its hot summers, yet Luke wears long pants and a long-sleeved, collared shirt over a white T-shirt no matter how high the temperature. Too bad, I mused, that Luke never wears shorts or a short-sleeved shirt so I could gauge how hairy he actually is.

Yet I found clues. Even freshly shaven on his way to work, Luke's beard area is visibly defined, raising my suspicions that he nourishes a lush crop of body hair. He likely shows 5 o'clock shadow before noon. The backs of his large, weathered hands show a bit of finely textured, dark hair, and I like to imagine this coat of hair travels up his arms, across his chest and belly, and down his legs. I notice too that Luke's T-shirt is puffed out just enough to suggest it is riding on a pleasing wave of hair.

As I'm taking a walk one Sunday morning, Luke slows his truck to a stop and rolls down the window. Although not a workday, he is wearing his usual long pants and long-sleeved shirt over a T-shirt.

"Where are you off to?" I ask, resisting a temptation to reach through the open truck window and slip my hand down under his T-shirt and explore his burly chest.

"Church," Luke answers, shocking me out of my fantasy.

"What church do you go to?" I ask.

"Well, it's really not a traditional church like you think about in a building. It's a men's devotional group in someone's home."

I had heard about an organization that preaches men must assert dominance over their wives and families. "Do you mean—?"

Luke cuts me off with a hearty laugh. "No, it's nothing like that. We're a small group of men who study and practice a simple ritual that keeps us in tune with creation.

"I'd tell you more, buddy, but I have to get going. How about if I come by your place this afternoon and tell you about it?"

"Sounds fine," I reply as he speeds off, giving me the thumbs-up signal as his truck disappears around the curve.

A man of his word, Luke shows up at my front door that afternoon. I'm watching the end of a TV program in the bedroom, and I invite him to finish the show. He sits in the recliner while I take a seat on the edge of the bed.

"So, Luke, what goes on in your men's group?" I ask as the TV show's credits begin to roll.

"It's just a few guys who keep in touch with creation by using the life force that's within us."

"Uh-huh," I say, thinking that this is a lot of New Age hocus-pocus.

Luke senses my unspoken skepticism. "Too often people lose sight of man's connection with each other and with the universe. In our men's group, we take part in a ritual that reenacts creation's gift of life."

I must have looked puzzled. "The prophets teach us that our bodies are temples," he explains. "Once a week, we use our temples for their highest purpose. We share our life force in thanks for the abundant life we are given.

"The key to life is symbolized in a man's semen," he continues. "It's the miracle of creation. Each man's temple is given a staff of life when he is born, and he is entrusted to use his staff to unlock the powers of the universe."

I ask how this is done.

Luke stands, and his eyes seem to penetrate my soul. "It's a ritual that should not to be taken lightly," he says, his voice a coarse whisper. "I'm not sure you're ready for it."

He hesitates and then begins to unbutton his shirt. I had fantasized about this day but never expected it to happen.

I begin to quiver from anticipation. "I'm ready," I say. He silently removes his outer shirt, exposing muscular arms covered with a silky blanket of hair. The snow white T-shirt seems to be fastened to his chest by two protruding lumps on his pecs. My mind runs wild thinking about his nipples beneath the thin layer of cotton.

I don't have to speculate long. Luke pulls off his T-shirt, revealing an abundance of dark hair I always suspected lay hidden under his layers of shirts. The sea of hair on his pecs is anchored by erect, swollen nipples, the color of ripe raspberries. I haven't seen such huge disks since I used to admire the nips on my buddy Grant. Hair sweeps across Luke's chest and cascades down to his belly, where it spreads out like a river delta.

"Come here," Luke says. His voice is low, but his command firm. "The staff of life must be awakened from its hibernation before it can release its life force," he instructs.

"My nipples are the gateway to the staff of life," he continues, placing my hands on his pecs. I don't know if the throbbing I feel is Luke's heart pounding or my own racing pulse.

Pulling off my shirt, he grabs my tits with his large hands. He pulls me toward him until my face is buried in the pelt of man fur on his chest. As he squeezes my nipples, I eagerly suck on one of his huge welts while my hand plays with his other one.

Moving to the bed, he lies down and pulls me on top of him, twisting my nipples as I suckle his. I can feel what he calls his staff of life beginning to stir beneath his trousers. As I continue to suck on his nipples, he unzips his pants and pulls them off. I pause to gasp a few breaths of air and glimpse the bulbous package concealed beneath his jockstrap. His pubic hair is so dense it cannot be contained by the jock and spills over the top and onto his muscular legs. As he returns to working over my nipples, I grow excited knowing that his manhood is separated from me by only a small veil of cloth.

Luke's jock is not large enough to restrain his swelling cock, and a testicle is forced out. "My life force needs the warmth of your mouth," he says.

Keeping a tight grasp on my nips, he guides my face down from his nipples and across the field of hair on his stomach. He allows me to pause long enough in my downward journey to ream out the bit of sweat that has pooled in his navel. When my mouth is at last engulfed over his testicle, I begin gently licking this life-giving ball of manhood, savoring the rich aroma of his manly scent. His second testicle emerges, and, one by one, I caress both of these precious jewels with my mouth.

Luke pulls me up, releasing his grip on my nips. "Get your pants and undershorts off," he orders. I comply, exposing my hard cock. "Looks like your staff of life has awakened too," he says. I nestle my cock against his hairy legs as I kneel in mouth-warming homage to his testicles.

Although I can feel his cock beneath his jock, I can barely contain my anticipation of seeing and touching it. He doesn't make me wait long. Pulling his jock down, Luke reveals a thick, strapping, uncircumcised cock. Although rock hard, a sheath of foreskin covers much of the head. I instinctively want to taste the flavors of manhood I know are captured there. Luke, however, has other ideas. Controlling my movements with his hands on my nips, he pulls me back.

"There's an order to our ritual," he says. "The staff must be approached with patience. Start by working your tongue over the base."

When a drop of precome emerges on the head on his cock, he tells me that it must not be wasted, and I eagerly lap it up. I like savoring his man juice, and I tell him so.

With that, Luke removes a hand from one of my nipples and pulls me upward until the tip of his finger touches my hole. "Turn around and straddle my face," he orders. I dutifully shift positions, so that my mouth is again buried in his crotch and my legs spread across his face.

He places a finger at the opening of my hole. "This is your vessel," Luke tells me, "where my staff will release its life force."

My mind spins in excitement as his rugged, hairy hand toys with my opening. I swallow his immense cock, completely burying my face in his thicket of pubic hair. Up and down my head bobs until it feels as though I'm swallowing his cock down to my Adam's apple.

"I like feeding on your staff," I tell him. I don't know which is more on fire—his cock or my mouth.

Luke has more things in store for me. "Your vessel must be primed to accept my staff." Pressing his face to my crack, he explores the edge of my hole with his tongue. The bristles of his unshaven face rubbing against my cheeks sends waves of passion through me. I tighten and then relax as his tongue pushes its way inside me. As his tongue becomes feverish in its work, his strong hands return to their work on my nipples.

Luke reaches over to his crumpled trousers and pulls out a small vial of oil and, after lubricating a finger, slips the finger inside me. I can picture his hairy hand at the door of my hole, and I spread my legs further to receive him.

"If I'm going to plant my seed in you," Luke says, his fingers probing the inside of my opening, "you must open more."

Between gulps of swallowing his rod, I answer, "Enter me. Have me."

With that, he lifts my head up. "Anoint my staff," he says. I obediently dribble oil across his cock, which feels so hot in my hand that I expect the oil to begin to sizzle.

Using his body, he forces me on my back and, face-to-face, he wraps his strong arms around my shoulders and places his lips over mine. Then he shoves back a bit and uses his powerful hands to pin my thighs, spreading my legs wide so that I am fully open to him. "Are you ready for the staff of life?" he whispers.

"I'm ready. Plow me. Spread your seed." My hands hold tightly to his nipples as I brace myself for his assault. He pauses a moment, teasing my opening with the head of his cock. Then he drives it inside me. A shock ripples through my body, and I instinctively recoil. Yet I'm determined to yield to him.

He forces my legs further apart. His thrusts are at first slow and deliberate but soon become faster—each one driving deeper inside me. Within moments, he is ramming me hard, and my legs can spread no further. Satisfied that I am as open to him as I can be, he leans forward, releasing my legs but pinning my forearms. Feeling his hairy belly against my cock incites him to ride me harder. I'm spread-eagle to him, and his hammering is so forceful that I feel his balls slam against my crotch with every punch.

Knowing that he has penetrated as deep as he can, he moves my legs so they rest over his shoulders and my ankles encase his thick neck. The burly stubble of his beard against my legs makes me tingle. Chest-to-chest and mouth-to-mouth, he pummels me with his ferocious cock.

His pounding is relentless. It isn't long until the friction of his belly against my cock begins to force the come out of me. "I can't hold it any longer," I moan. "I'm going to shoot."

"Let go, buddy," Luke says. With that, my come streams across my stomach and chest in a torrent.

He pauses, sliding his staff out of me. "I won't waste a single drop of your seed," he says, tenderly licking up my spilled juice.

As I lay under Luke in ecstasy, he interrupts my bliss. "Are you ready to complete the ritual?" he says. Without waiting for an answer, he forces my legs wide open and plunges his still-rigid cock deep inside me. It feels different and hurtful now, and I instinctively clench up. "That's good," he breathes, "Make your vessel hold my staff tight."

I know I am participating in the fulfillment of a man-to-man ritual, and I try hard to relax and receive him and to savor every moment of this powerful exchange of our manhood. He is frenzied now, slamming his cock in me. I hold tight to his nipples and place myself fully at his mercy. His body shudders, and I feel him exploding deep inside me.

He lays on top of me, panting and the sweat glistening on his chest hair. His cock no longer feels uncomfortable. It belongs inside me. Locking his arms around me, we drift into a dreamlike state.

When I awaken, which seems to be an eternity later, his cock has slipped out of me, but he is still holding me close. "How do you feel?" he asks.

"Like I have been man-fucked," I murmur. "Hard."

A trace of a smile crosses his face. "We used our temples for their highest purpose," he gently corrects me in his throaty voice.

"I'd like you to come to our men's devotional next Sunday. We'll repeat the ritual. The other men can witness it."

The idea of men watching me give myself to Luke arouses me. I think about what will go on in their minds as they watch Luke licking and fingering my hole. I wonder what they will think as they see his strong arms around me and my legs pinned under his massive shoulders. I can imagine them watching as I'm impaled on his enormous staff. "What will the men be doing?" I ask.

"They'll be admiring my staff and your vessel. As they are moved, they'll anoint us by spilling their seed on us.

"Until then," he continues, "save you seed. Honor your temple. I want you to open your vessel to receive my life force again and again."

I might have looked hesitant. "Don't worry, buddy," Luke reassures me with a smile. His hands grasp my nipples, which are by now sore and tender from the workout he has given them. "My staff of life will guide you."

UNDER THE MOONLIGHT

Michael Murphy

The setting sun was creating a red halo around him when I spotted the hitchhiker ahead on the side of the road. His bare chest caught my eye, wide-shouldered but slim. A pair of lean thighs below cutoff shorts pulled me off the highway to screech to a halt. He ran up to my jeep with a bright grin plastered over his face.

"I'm only going about 50 miles, then I'm camping for the night. But you're welcome to go that far with me."

He leaped into the front seat as he replied. "I'm Jack. I'll take a ride out of this hellhole gladly, even if it's not far."

We laughed together, instantly at ease. He was cute, with red hair I'd mistaken for the glow of the sunset. Smooth-cheeked and bright-eyed he laughed nonstop at whatever I said for the next hour as we drove along in the gathering dusk of the Colorado summer. Either he was just naturally lighthearted or he was a simpleton airhead. I liked him, though.

"I'm heading for California, David. I'm going to be an actor. Maybe I'll be a bartender first," he admitted with a self-deprecating grin.

"If you want, you can camp with me tonight. I'm heading for Salt Lake tomorrow."

It was decided, and not without my cock having a say. It had been hard for the past 50 miles while Jack's naked knee continually grazed mine—as if by accident. He was a sweet 15 years younger than me, only just 18 and fresh out of high school. I was aching for a crack at his hot young body, although I really had no expectations. He was just too naive-looking.

We made camp off the highway in a quiet ravine with a grassy flat spot perfect for a pair of sleeping bags and a small bonfire. We shared a meal of fried beans and hot dogs, not especially gourmet but he didn't complain. I was beat, and rolled into my sleeping bag not longer after that, saying good night while checking out his bare chest in the light of the fire and nursing a hard-on. He smiled innocently and thanked me for the dinner before he crawled into his own sleeping bag.

I awoke with the moon bathing our camp in soft light. A figure hovered across from me on the other side of the remnants of the campfire. It was Jack. My eyes focussed on the most striking detail of the scene—a big hard-on jutting out from his slim hips. Fuck! That cock rose straight up in the air, hard and throbbing. Below it hung a pair of silky nads, their smallish size only emphasizing the hugeness of the column of meat above.

Jack was standing in the moonlight with a stiff cock, naked except for a pair of boots and socks. I realized he was staring at me, and then I realized my unzipped sleeping bag had slid off most of my body. Naked too, my cock and balls were in plain sight. My schlong was already swelling as I came fully awake, and as it did I saw Jack's hand move to encase his own boner and begin to pump it slowly and suggestively.

Was I dreaming? The cute, but naive, young punk was standing only a few feet away from me, mostly naked and pumping his stiff cock. He was staring at me hungrily, his eyes glued to my stiffening dick, and his tongue out to lick at his soft lips.

"Do you want to fuck, David? I'm really horny and I like you a lot."

That was a real surprise. Jack's soft voice was full of emotion. It was obvious it had taken guts to speak his mind and ask for what he wanted. I wondered if he was new to gay sex—at his age it was a likelihood. My rising cock lurched at the awesome sight of his naked body in the moonlight and the thought of his tender innocence. I wanted to fuck him, no question.

"Let's go for it," I smiled reassuringly. As I spoke, I rose to my feet and stepped around the small fire to meet him. Completely naked, there was no hiding my throbbing wood and my excitement. My hands came out toward him as he emitted a small gasp and moved to slide into my arms.

I felt Jack's slim form nestle into my embrace, grasping his waist and feeling the hot flesh there. He trembled against me, his torso warm against mine, our cocks bumping against each other in a shaky lust.

He offered me a weak smile, our faces close. "I'm not cherry or nothing. I've done it before, a couple times. I want to suck your big cock, and then I want you to fuck me hard up the ass. Is that OK?"

I almost laughed at his blunt sincerity, but then couldn't resist and pulled him close to smother his mouth with a passionate kiss. He opened up to me with a wet slurp and my tongue dove between his plump little lips. He pushed against me as he continued pumping his own hard shaft while grabbing at mine with his other hand, both of his hands now mashed between our pressing bellies.

My hands on his waist slipped down to cup the naked cheeks of his ass. I stabbed my tongue into his mouth as I felt the sleek skin of his butt, hairless and trembling. That ass swelled from a slim waist in two round globes of hot muscle. He clenched his butt when my hands first cupped his ass, but then as he gurgled around my exploring tongue, he spread his booted feet apart, opening up that sweet ass to my fingers' investigation. I was shaking nearly as much as Jack when my hands slid into the heated crevice of his ass crack. Sweaty-slick, and smooth as satin, Jack's butt crack opened further as he groaned, then half-squatted and pushed backward toward my fingers. It took only a moment to find and settle on his crinkled butt hole.

A tremor went through both our bodies as my fingers stroked and probed his totally hairless asshole. The slot was tight, but the tender lips actually pushed outward toward my fingers as if seeking their touch. I felt heat flood my head as I massaged that pouting butt hole and realized I would soon be fucking it.

Innocent or not, the kid was hot for it. His body writhed in my arms. The combination of his tender youth, that flawless satin body, and his absolute craving for sex was something I could only have dreamed about. Jack's hand was around my cock, rubbing and squeezing it in time to his other hand on his own shank. Our two bodies slithered together in a close body-fuck as our passion rose to match our smacking kiss and probing hands.

As he played with both our cocks, I rooted around in his sweet ass crack. I was amazed at how sleek and smooth that butt was, and how eager his asshole felt against my tentative jabs. I had no intention of hurting him, and was merely rubbing his ass lips and pressing into the slick center, but he responded by wiggling against my fingers and gasping around my tongue enthusiastically. He was putty in my hands. I sensed I could do anything I wanted with this pliant young piece of tail!

The warm summer night was punctuated by our gasping slurps as we kissed, and the sudden distant howling of coyotes. Those eerie yips sent a sexually charged shudder through our entwined bodies. That twitch served to inexplicably open up Jack's asshole, and my prodding finger all at once jabbed into his tight ass channel. We both jerked.

My finger was knuckle-deep, encased in quivering heat. The inner muscle clamped and vibrated around that finger, a preview of things to come for my cock. Apparently Jack was thinking along the same lines. He abruptly broke our kiss and moaned out loud.

"Your finger's up my ass," he practically sobbed in my face, his eyes on mine. "It feels awesome! Work it around and stretch my asshole before you put your cock up there."

I did that, staring into his eyes in the moonlight. I slid my finger up into his tight asshole, twisting it as I probed deeper. His mouth gaped open in a deep sigh, and his tongue came out to lick at his plump lower lip. His butt mouth opened as well, yawning momentarily as I thrust my finger up into him, then it clamped down over my invading digit before opening again as I worked ever deeper. I stroked his trembling ass cheeks with one hand while stretching open his ass lips with the fingers of the other as I poked even deeper. I twisted and jabbed, watching his reaction. The sexual desire in his eyes and gaping, wet mouth were unmistakable.

"You like my finger up your ass?" I couldn't resist whispering as I jabbed deeper.

"Fuck, yeah! I love it. Go deeper," Jack gasped back. And then he made a very sexual move, something that elicited a few gasps of my own.

Jack was still pumping both our cocks slowly between our bellies, and as he spoke, he dropped his head on my shoulder and leaned into me. He raised one knee up to wrap a foot and calf around the back of my thigh. That opened up his ass. He thrust backward with his hips and sank down over my finger.

My finger slithered all the way up his sweaty hole, buried to the hilt. He moaned and licked at my shoulder as his entire body quivered with that finger crammed home. The yips of coyotes in the distance became a long wail, a bestial sound that jibed perfectly with the sexual heat of the moment. I stared down at Jack's back, slender but muscular, as it narrowed to his tight waist. The swell of his ass widened where my hands cupped it. One hand worked around in his parted crack, the middle finger stroking deep into his crinkled asshole. It was like some nasty dream.

The milky flesh of his buttocks gleamed in the moonlight. His body was lightly tanned, mostly with myriad freckles, but that ass was pristine alabaster. My big hands on the milky globes emphasized the sexual heat that enveloped us both.

I fucked his hole with my finger, in and out and in circles, feeling it out as it began to open and stretch. Jack shuddered and moaned, licking with little lewd smacks at my shoulder. He gripped my cock with fierceness, pumping it in a slow, sensual teasing that had me growing hotter and hotter.

"I'll get condoms!" I blurted out suddenly. I had to fuck him.

Jack lifted his head and grinned at me, the trembling of his lips around his white teeth testifying to his rapt desire. His body trembled against mine, his ass quivering around my probing finger and his cock jabbing rigid and hot against mine. He nodded shakily in answer to my statement, then disengaged, dropping his booted foot and slowly turning around—my finger still planted firmly up his butt hole.

I gawked at his beautiful, trim body. He'd turned completely around and was leaning forward with his hands on his knees, his feet wide apart and his ass spread. My hands were still on that ass, opening the crack as I teased his tender asshole. Jack was more than ready to get fucked.

Shaking with excitement of my own I tore myself away and stumbled naked to the nearby jeep to rummage through one of my packs in the moonlight for the condoms and lube I always carried with me. You never knew when you would stumble on a sweet ass to fuck.

I turned and was racing back to Jack in moments, the goods in my hands. He'd remained bent over, presenting his ass to me. His head was craned around to watch for me, and he grinned as he waved his butt lewdly in the moonlight. The coals of the fire sparked fitfully just behind him, adding a romantic element to the sexual heat of the situation. My cock bobbed in front of me as lewdly as his waving butt cheeks. I noticed his eyes fix on it, and it lurched with eager pride. My cock was big and fat too. Jack would feel it.

"I want to suck that fat thing first, Michael. Can I?" Jack asked. It was said almost politely, and both of us noticed the tone, giggling like two school kids with sudden nervous tension.

"OK. I'll wrap both our cocks first, Jack. Then I'll lube up your asshole while you suck on my cock."

The nasty proposition hovered in the air as we both moved around. Jack turned so that he remained bent over, but was facing me. I handed him a condom, and with his face in my crotch, he wrapped my dick with shaking hands. I took another condom and leaned over him to reach under his belly and roll the latex over his stiff meat. His cock was big too, and very long, jerking like an angry snake in my fingers. A moment later his body shuddered when I squirted lube all over his spread ass from above.

The lewd squirting sound of lubricant pouring over his butt was matched by the raunchy slurp of his lips as he engulfed my cock with his mouth. Hot tongue slathered over my bone. I gasped as I thrust up into his mouth. With his head down in my crotch, I delved into his ass crack with both hands, dropping the lube to the grass. The slick grease I'd poured over his ass made a smooth ride as I located and probed his asshole. This time instead of one, I jabbed a pair of fingers up his slot.

Jack gurgled over my cock, shoving half of it past his tonsils with his hands on the base. His slim body lurched as two fingers probed up into his ass. Impaled from both ends, he quivered between cock and fingers like a strung bow.

If inexpert, Jack's slurping mouth was enthusiastic. He slobbered noisily as he gobbled cock and tugged on my balls. His bobbing face was driving me wild, and the feel of his tight hole clamping and convulsing around my fingers was just too much.

"I gotta fuck you up the ass!"

He practically spit out my cock, and with a low moan twisted around to offer me his white can. My fingers twisted around inside the hot punk's butt inferno, stretching it and teasing it. He planted his boots wide apart and hunkered down for the coming fuck. His back arched and his shoulders tensed as he quaked around my fingers up his butt and waited impatiently for my cock.

"Do it. I want that fat fucker inside me. I can take all you've got to give," Jack claimed.

I stood between his feet with my condom-wrapped boner banging up into his parted crack. A lewd sheen of sweat and lube coated the pale cheeks and smooth crevice. My fingers were still probing in and out with squishy insistence. Jack's greased ass jiggled as he wriggled it fetchingly. My rigid cock rubbed against the gooey flesh as I searched for his hole.

My cock head pinpointed Jack's hole as my fingers slid from it. I planted the blunt helmet on target and began to press forward. Quivering ass lips stretched and spasmed. I'd opened them up with a pair of fingers, but the resilient young slot had immediately clamped back down. It took Jack's willpower to open it back up, and he did just that. With a deep groan, he pushed back to meet my probing cock head. Dank flesh opened and then enveloped the entire crown of my cock. The flared rim of the cap popped into him.

"Oh, gawd! Your-cock-is-so-fucking-fat!" Jack spat out in a series of grunted syllables..

I gnawed at my lip and panted for breath as I felt that snug hole wrap around my cock head. It was awesome. "Are you OK?" I managed to gasp out.

"Fuck yeah! Shove that fat thing up me! I want it all!" Jack groaned bravely.

I stared down at his butt. My cock was stiff and fat as it pointed up into the greased crack. In the washed-out light, the blood-engorged column looked dark and dangerous. Jack's butt was milky white and trembling wildly. I had both hands on his cheeks pulling them open as I held my cock head just inside his clamping sphincter. I began to shove forward, Jack's ass lifting a little as he strained against the pressure. He moaned and I gasped.

The fuck tunnel surrendered as I drove forward. Fat cock head slithered up into him inexorably. I watched as my shaft began to disappear between his milky buns. Deeper, and deeper. The slow, steady thrust was met by heated convulsions, but there was no stopping it until I was nestling my ball sac up against his sweaty, lubed ass.

"I'm all the way in! I'm all the way up your ass," I groaned out.

Jack didn't speak, his grunts answer enough. He was obviously attempting to accustom himself to all that shank up his butt. I held my cock inside him as I reached up, grasping his shoulder with one hand and the top of his head with the other. His mop of short red hair was damp under my palm as I cupped his scalp. I pulled back with a hand on his shoulder and a hand on his head as I began to fuck him. His mouth hung open and his tongue lolled out as he groaned deep in his chest. My cock began to ride in and out of his greased asshole.

The slick slot was steamy and snug as I began to thrust in and out. Friction heated up both his hole and my rod as I fucked, both of us grunting and snorting like pigs in time to the steady penetration. I drove all the way in and stopped, my fat cock buried in his pulsing guts, then I pulled almost all the way out, teasing his ass lips with the blunt crown before thrusting deep again.

I held his head and shoulder as I fucked him, and he punctuated every deep pump with those pig snorts. One of his hands worked frantically on his cock, jerking off as he got fucked. The slap of my hips against his greased ass created lewd smacks. He spread his boots wider apart and writhed under my assault, grunt after grunt meeting every stabbing jab. It was nasty and sweaty and exciting.

The coyotes yipped intermittently as we drove ourselves to a climax. The moonlight bathed us in eerie light as my cock pounded in and out, more and more rapidly. My excitement multiplied with the torrid burning along my cock shaft and the aching roil in my banging nut sac. Jack's tight hole quivered up and down the length of my sliding shank like fingers massaging it or lips sucking it. I was slamming full force into his butt by the time orgasm hit me.

"I'm shooting! I'm shooting a hot wad up your butt!" I cried out in the night.

"Yeah! Fuck me good! Come up my ass!" Jack answered, his hand flailing over his own stiff dick.

I spurted, my body jerking spasmodically. With my waning strength, I pulled out of his ass and yanked the condom off my cock. Jizz splattered over a cheek of his moon-white butt and dribbled down it as I held my hard cock against the trembling flesh.

"I'm blowing too," Jack gasped.

I felt his body lurch. My hand on his head slipped down to his ass, digging into his convulsing asshole to probe and tease while his cock exploded in his hand. He pig-snorted and twitched, while I probed his squishy, fucked asshole with a pair of fingers. I leaned into him with my spurting cock laying down a slimy coat of jizz over greased butt cheek. He unloaded like a burst pipe into the condom over his own blowing rod.

It was fucking awesome!

We took a few minutes to settle down, our bodies twitching and our lungs heaving. Finally Jack stood up and leaned back against me. My fingers lazily explored his stretched asshole as I realized I was more than ready to continue our fuck sooner rather than later.

"That was so cool, Michael. Let's do it some more after we take a rest."

We were thinking alike. I smiled as I leaned down and kissed his neck. What else could we do that night? Ideas tumbled through my head. The naive hitchhiker was ripe for more nasty action. Would I eat his ass, or have him eat mine? I had a few dildos in my pack. Hmm.

AUTHOR BIOS

Stephen Albrow is a purveyor of "filth"—there's really no other word to describe his work. His pervy prose appear in a startling array of top-shelf publications, including *Torso, Mandate, Shemale International, Cherry Boys,* and *Men.* Satisfaction (and a very sticky climax) is always guaranteed!

Shane Allison has been called a fag, a nigger, and a genius. His poems and stories have appeared in numerous anthologies, magazines and online magazines, including *Mind Caviar, Velvet Mafia, Suspect Thoughts, I Do/I Don't: Queers on Marriage, Velvet Heat, Best Black Gay Erotica, Out of Order, Outsider Ink, Oyster Boy Review, New Delta Review, Mississippi Review,* and countless others. He is the author of five chapbooks of poetry; *Black Fag* (Future Tense Books) and *I Want to Fuck a Redneck* (Scintillating Publications) being his most recent. Hot kisses and thank you's go out to Jesse Grant and the cast at Alyson Books. He is a friend of poet Jarret Keene.

A native Californian, **Bearmuffin** lives in San Diego with two leather bears in a stimulating ménage à trois. He has written gay erotica for *Mandate, Honcho, Torso, Manscape, Hot Shots,* and other gay publications.

Derringer Award–winning mystery writer **Michael Bracken** is the author of eleven books including *All White Girls* and *Yesterday in Blood and Bone,* and nearly 1,000 shorter works that have appeared in literary, small press, and commercial publications worldwide.

Bracken is also the editor of eight published or forthcoming crime fiction anthologies.

After a short career as an editor, **Dan Budge** began freelancing in 1999. His writings include *Under the Black Cross,* over 500 erotica short stories, and an article in the February 2003 issue of *Instinct.* His not-so-secret dream is to write the monthly adventures of DC Comics' greatest heroes.

Bob Condron is the author of two gay erotic novels: *Easy Money* (Idol/Virgin) and *Sweating It Out* (Zipper/Millivres). He is the editor of the anthologies *Daddy's Boyz* (Starbooks Press) and *Working Stiff* (Alyson Books).

After 20 years of working with numbers, **Jordan M. Coffey** rediscovered the joy of working with words. Since taking the plunge into professional publishing, Jordan has had several stories accepted to anthologies and is damned excited to still be above water.

Curtis C. Comer grew up in the Midwest and moved to San Francisco in 1987. His stories have been included in the Alyson anthologies *Starf*cker; Best Gay Love Stories, 2005;* and *Ultimate Gay Erotica, 2005.* He relocated to St. Louis in 2003, where he writes and lives with his partner, Tim.

A mild-mannered sales and administration worker in a manufacturing plant by day...a wannabe porn writer by night! Although he recently had some nonfiction articles published in the popular Australian gay magazine *DNA,* this is **Ben Crocker**'s first published piece of fiction...ever! The short piece featured in this book is hoped to be the starting point of his first novel, detailing the life and loves of a gay professional Australian Rules football player. Any story ideas, suggestions, or comments will be willingly accepted at ben1971@hotmail.com.

Author-editor **Michael Huxley** has compiled four anthologies of literotica for Starbooks Press. His most recent work appears in the poetry collection *Van Gogh's Ear; Friction 7; Best Gay Love Stories, 2005; Best Gay Erotica, 2005; My First Time, 4; I Do/I Don't: Queers on Marriage;* and *Walking Higher: Gay Men Write About the Deaths of Their Mothers.*

Will Knauss first caught the writing bug in the third grade when he won a local poetry contest. His prize was an original cast recording of *Annie!*, which now proudly hangs next to his desk in his New York City apartment. He currently writes and edits reviews for www.coolcinematrash.com. His fiction was featured in the *Ultimate Gay Erotica, 2005* anthology.

Jourdan Lane writes full-time, working out of her home in South Texas. *The Ticket* is her second published story and she is currently working on a novel called *On the Edge.* You can learn more about her and her works in progress at www.jourdanlane.com.

A romantic at heart, **Alan Long** writes poetry, short stories, and erotica in his spare time. Recently, writing has taken on a prominent role in his life, and he hopes to publish more in the future. He lives by himself in Dayton, Ohio, and holds a full-time job.

Michael Murphy lives in Vancouver, BC, where he is an actor and personal trainer, dabbling in writing on the side. He loves a man in uniform, and a tight young ass, too. His first erotic gay story was published in *Ultimate Gay Erotica, 2005.*

The erotic fiction of **Christopher Pierce** has been published most recently in *Bound & Gagged, Men, Freshmen, Honcho,* and in the anthologies *Ultimate Gay Erotica, 2005; Men Amplified; Fratsex;* and *Friction 7.* Write to him at chris@christopherpierceerotica.com and visit his world online at www.christopherpierceerotica.com.

CB Potts's story is based on true events. "I've had enough trees come crashing into my house to last a lifetime," CB says. "What I need is more hot neighbors!" CB works as a freelance writer in upstate New York, and ironically enough, specializes in writing for the construction industry...when not churning out endless streams of smut.

Rick R. Reed's fiction embraces the demimonde of Chicago, where serial killers, pedophiles, and those who've bargained with the devil seek life's simple pleasures including torture, pain, sexual degradation, addiction, and murder. Published novels include *A Face Without a Heart*, nominated as Best Novel of 2000 by the Spectrum Awards. He says sex consists of a relatively small "vocabulary" of acts, which can be combined in endless permutations. Each scene brings something new and different. As a result, sex is an adventure: mysterious, sensuous, erotic, and exciting. "Good sex is about discovery, about stretching boundaries, and about fun, and this is what I aim to show in my writing."

Paul Scott is the pen name for a respected mental health practitioner. He happily resides in San Francisco with his partner and their two dogs. He enjoys writing erotic fiction in his free time and knows friends wouldn't believe it was his writing if he told them so.

Simon Sheppard is the author of four books, including *Sex Parties 101, In Deep: Erotic Stories, Kinkorama: Dispatches from the Front Lines of Perversion,* and *Hotter Than Hell,* and he's the coeditor of *Rough Stuff* and *Roughed Up*. His work has appeared in over 125 other books including many editions of *Best Gay Erotica* and *The Best American Erotica* and his columns, "Sex Talk" and "Perv," appear in queer magazines and on the Web. He lives in San Francisco and hangs out at www.simonsheppard.com.

From Vancouver, BC, **Jay Starre** has written for gay men's magazine's, including *Men, Freshmen, Honcho, Torso,* and *American Bear*. Jay has also written for more than 28 gay anthologies, including the Alyson's *Friction* and *Ultimate Gay Erotica* series and *Full Body Contact*. With all these stories under his belt, he admits his imagination has finally begun to match his libido.

Jack Whitestone enjoys weaving tales from his own experiences. When he is not spinning these tales, Jack puts positive spins on news stories as part of his public relations work in Arizona.

Scott Whittier is an advertising copywriter in Boston whose work has appeared internationally and won top honors. Published in many magazines and Alyson collections, Scott is also the coauthor of the *Romentics* gay romance novels with his boyfriend, Scott Pomfret, at www.romentics.com.

Born an Okie, **Mark Wildyr** presently resides in New Mexico, the setting of many of his stories, which explore developing sexual awareness and intercultural relationships. Over 30 of his short stories and novellas have been acquired by Alyson Books, Arsenal Pulp, Companion Press, Southern Tier–Haworth Press, and Starbooks Press.

Thom Wolf has been writing erotic fiction for over a decade. He is author of the novels *Worlds Made Flesh* (Idol, 2000) and *The Chain* (Zipper, 2003). His stories have appeared in numerous anthologies including Alyson's *Friction* series, *Just the Sex*, *Bearotica*, and *Twink*. He recently collaborated with Kevin Killian on "Too Far" for Frozen Tear II, a project cofunded by the Arts Council of England. Thom lives with his boyfriend, Liam, in County Durham, England.

Kris Wright's fiction has appeared in over a dozen anthologies including *Ultimate Lesbian Erotica, 2005* and *The Good Parts: Pure Lesbian Erotica*. She lives with her husband in Virginia and is pursuing a graduate degree in humanities. She can be reached through her Web site at www.kristinawright.com. She is, of course, a liberal Democrat.

This publication is a first for **Wade Wright**, now a senior resident of Arizona. Wade drove away from snowy Ohio at the age of 21, deciding on Arizona, and then graduating from the University of Arizona. He is now the grandpa of two granddaughters and the survivor of two sadly shortened gay partnerships.